"IVAN IS DEAD AHEAD OF US!"

Anger flushed Captain Samuel Fuller's face as he turned to his XO. "Now you know what it's like to trust the Soviets, Mr. Coria. Activate the target-seeking sonar. I want to have a clear shot if I need it."

"Sonar reports Soviets diving, Captain."

"Take us down, Mr. Coria," Fuller responded. "Stern plates maximum angle. Prepare to attain test depth."

The U.S.S. *Copperhead*'s bow dipped in response, but at 1,650 feet the boat had to level out. They could only observe as the Soviet sub spiraled down to a depth twice that level.

Fuller smacked a balled fist into the palm of his hand.

"Until next time, you Red bastard! Then we'll see if you can outrun a Mark 48 torpedo!"

Richard P. Henrick
Beneath the Silent Sea

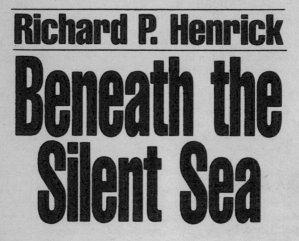

ZEBRA BOOKS
KENSINGTON PUBLISHING CORP.

ZEBRA BOOKS

are published by

Kensington Publishing Corp.
475 Park Avenue South
New York, NY 10016

First printing: August, 1988

Printed in the United States of America

"War is the highest form of struggle for resolving contradictions, when they have developed to a certain stage, between classes, nations, states, or political groups, and it has existed ever since the emergence of private property and classes."

— Mao Tse-tung, *Selected Works,* Vol. I, p. 180.

"Without preparedness superiority is not really superiority and there can be no initiative either. Having grasped this point, a force which is inferior but prepared can often defeat a superior enemy by surprise attack."

— Mao Tse-tung, *Selected Works,* Vol. II, pp. 165-6.

"All warfare is based on deception."

— Sun Tzu, *The Art of War*

CHAPTER ONE

The sea was calm, its fog-shrouded surface only occasionally rippled by the arrival of a gentle swell from the northeast. From the stern of his cramped, wooden fishing trawler, Wu Chao the elder watched the ghostly dawn develop. All was quiet, except for the creaking sounds of the boat beneath him, and the resonant snores of his two nephews, clearly audible from the interior cabin. The boys had worked long into the night, when a huge flock of squealing gulls pointed the way to a school of feeding bonito. Unfortunately, just as they were about to drop their baited hooks, the sound of an approaching vessel made them change course to take cover in a nearby fog bank. No sooner had they disappeared into the thick mist, when the sharp bow of a Chinese patrol boat became visible. Wu Chao was well aware that they were trespassers here, and if caught were subject to instant arrest. Yet the gods were with them, and soon the engines of the PLN patrol craft could be heard fading in the distance.

This left them with the frustrating task of trying to relocate the bonito. For a good two hours they crisscrossed the surrounding seas, yet all to no avail. His nephews were especially disappointed. This was only their third season as fishermen, and they had never before gone an entire two weeks without a major strike.

As a forty-year veteran of the seas, Wu Chao preached patience. He reminded them that the waters would produce their anticipated catch when the fates so willed it. Meanwhile, they could but continue their search to the best of their abilities.

By its very nature, youth was impatient, and his nephews were no different. To ease their frustrations, the elder produced a bottle of plum wine. The spirits soon produced the desired effect, and both youngsters were sound asleep by midnight.

Wu Chao remained at the helm throughout the night. With the aid of a battered compass, he steered the trawler toward the southwest. Even though the fog remained thick, he had no fear of striking any obstacles, for he knew these waters well. They wouldn't be encountering the first shoals for at least another three hours. By that time the sun would be high in the heavens, and the fog would hopefully have long since dissipated. This would put them just north of Dongsha Island. Though these waters were claimed by the People's Republic, Wu Chao had fished here many times before. In each instance, he never failed to fill his hold with fat tuna. With this hope in mind, the wiry white-haired fisherman continued to watch the new dawn develop from his boat's square stern.

The air was brisk, its scent ripe with the rich smell of the surrounding South China Sea. Fourteen days ago, they had left the harbor of Fangshan, located on the southern tip of the island of Taiwan. This had been Wu Chao's home for the last thirty-eight years. His family had originally lived on the mainland, south of Shanghai, and had fled to Taiwan in 1949, along with Chiang Kai-shek and the Nationalist government. His ancestors had made their living from the sea for many generations, and following in his grandfather's footsteps, Wu Chao became a fisherman.

Despite the political turmoil that continued to tear his homeland apart, Wu Chao was able to successfully ply his trade. There were millions of hungry mouths to feed, and the local seas provided a convenient source of fresh fish that merely needed to be plucked from the depths and then brought to market.

For three decades now, if one could remain clear of the PLN patrol boats, a bountiful catch was almost insured. Yet for the last several years, Wu Chao noted that the local waters were almost completely barren, the by-product of overfishing. This meant he was increasingly forced to seek new feeding grounds, far away from Taiwan's protective shores.

Ten years ago, his father never would have dreamed of having to sail as far as Dongsha Island to find the bonito. Not only were they much more likely to encounter a PLN patrol in these waters, but they faced fickle weather and the possibility of a mechanical breakdown as well. With few options available to him, Wu Chao weighed the risks involved and made the difficult choice that sent him on his present course.

A seagull cried overhead, and the elder looked upward in an attempt to catch sight of it. Meeting his weary gaze was a thick wall of roiling mist that veiled

9

the sky in a shroud of gray. Looking back to the sea, he examined the whitish froth that bubbled forth from the tips of the trawler's single propeller. The throttle was set half open, and the engine purred along contentedly. Earlier he had activated the boat's primitive autopilot. This device was actually a series of jury-rigged ropes that held the steering wheel in place. Such a system freed him from having to remain at the helm.

Soon he'd be awakening his nephews. He'd pass control of the trawler to them while he ducked inside for a couple of hours of sleep. By that time, they should be close to the shoals that ringed the northern perimeter of Dongsha Island. Here, if the gods smiled upon him, thick schools of fish awaited them.

Wu Chao stretched his tired limbs and yawned. Turning away from the sea, he peeked inside the boat's single cabin. There, the prone figures of his nephews could be seen. Both were strapping lads, who seemed to be growing in both height and intellectual awareness with each passing day. Since he had no sons of his own, Wu Chao had volunteered to raise the boys when their father was killed during a typhoon, seven years ago. Wu Chao had little time to mourn the death of his only brother, for his widow and two orphaned sons now depended upon him for their survival. Although Wu Chao had a wife and two daughters of his own to support, he took on the added responsibility quite willingly. Gathering them together under one roof, he merged the two families into one.

It was difficult to adjust at first. Beyond the physical demands of having three more mouths to feed, Wu

Chao now found himself with a second wife to care for. Ever cautious not to make his original spouse overly jealous, he somehow learned to share his affections between both women.

Three summers ago, the boys were old enough to join him at sea. The added help was much appreciated, and though the fish were increasingly hard to locate, they managed to eke out a living.

Seeing his nephews stretched out before him, Wu Chao inwardly smiled. Now that they were growing into manhood, their resemblance to their father couldn't be ignored. The elder realized that his brother lived through each one of them. Certain that he was right in adopting them, Wu Chao knew that the sacrifice had been a worthy one. There was no telling what would have happened to them if he hadn't been there to take them in. As fortune would have it, it had been a badly sprained ankle that had kept Wu Chao on land that fated day when the killer typhoon struck. In all, six boats failed to return to their village after the storm finally passed. One of these carried his beloved brother.

Wu Chao had been extremely hard on himself afterwards. He blamed his brother's death on his own absence aboard the doomed fishing boat. His mourning brought him to the depths of depression and, for a time, he had even considered suicide. Just when things looked their blackest, the gods miraculously intervened to see him past this crisis. He remembered each moment of that magical afternoon to this very day.

As was his habit since accepting the fact that his brother was lost at sea, Wu Chao had been drinking heavily the night before. Because of his lame ankle, he had been unable to make his way home from the tavern, and he'd fallen into a drunken sleep deep in the mountains that lay between the central village and his seaside home. He awoke with a splitting headache, and upon opening his eyes, at first had trouble orienting himself. He took in the narrow footpath that he lay beside, and then set his startled glance on an orange-robed stranger sitting cross-legged on the other side of the trail. It took only a single look at this baldheaded elder to know that he was a holy man.

The monk's intense crystal-blue gaze bored into Wu Chao, and the fisherman felt instantly ashamed of himself. He struggled to sit up, and after brushing off his dust-covered garments, implored the stranger to identify himself. The priest silently nodded, and Wu Chao felt a surge of electricity run up and down his spine in response to this simple head movement. No words were needed as the stranger stood up and beckoned the fisherman to join him on an adjoining path. Only when Wu Chao shakily rose and began following this mystery man, did he realize with a start that his sprained ankle no longer hurt!

Astounded by this curious development, he followed the monk up a narrow earthen footpath. The trail gradually steepened, and it took a total effort on Wu Chao's part to keep up with the elder. The sun was high overhead when they finally reached the mountain's summit. Here the trail ended at a simple circular structure, which the fisherman recognized as being identical to the Queen of Heaven temple that graced his own village. Known as Tianfei, this goddess protected all boatmen, and was revered in almost every

12

port in Southern China.

Assuming that the orange-robed stranger was a priest of this sect, Wu Chao followed him into the structure. Here they sat down before a single burning candle. After igniting a fragrant sandalwood joss stick, the priest picked up a handful of slender yarrow stalks. Wu Chao identified these stalks as belonging to the *I Ching*. The fisherman had had his fortune read in this manner on several previous occasions, and although he really didn't take such divinations seriously, he respected the laws that the so-called *Book of Changes* were based upon.

Using his right hand, the priest went on to pass the yarrow stalks through the incense. After removing one of the sticks from the mass, he then divided it into two parts. He repeated this process four more times. Only then did he proceed to count the stalks that remained in his right hand. He took several minutes to study the results, then looked up solemnly into the fisherman's expectant stare.

The events that followed were hazy. Wu Chao remembered hearing the priest clear his throat, and then at long last begin speaking. Strangely, he knew all about the tragedy that had recently befallen the fishermen and his family. As a disciple of Tianfei, his purpose was to console Wu Chao, and to lead him back to the path of life. A series of strange incantations followed, and Wu Chao felt dizzy and eventually slumped to the ground unconscious.

When he awoke he found himself at the spot beside the footpath where he had spent the previous night. The orange-robed monk was nowhere to be seen, and while Wu Chao was wondering if the encounter was

13

nothing but a drunken hallucination, he rose to continue on his way homeward. Only then did he realize that his ankle had indeed been miraculously healed!

The fisherman returned to his family a new man. No longer feeling guilty for his brother's death, he gathered his dependents before him and swore to do everything within his power to take care of them in the future.

A second legacy of his encounter with the orange-robed monk was a new interest in the *I Ching*. He purchased his own set of yarrow stalks and a leather-bound book to properly interpret them. Though he was never to encounter the orange-robed elder again, he dreamed of him often. After such visions, he never failed to consult the *I Ching*. In each instance, the hexagrams he chose somehow proved to be a portent of things to come. In fact, it was the *I Ching* that set the date of their current fishing trip. Conscious of his boat's empty hold, Wu Chao wondered if he had somehow misread the yarrow stalks. If this was indeed the case, their entire voyage could be in vain. To get a better understanding of their current circumstances, he decided to cast the *I Ching* one more time, here on the boat.

Wu Chao took a last fond look at his sleeping nephews and turned toward the trawler's bow. Here, beside the helm, a small satchel containing a few personal items was stored in the chart locker. It didn't take him long to extract the red silk handkerchief that held his yarrow stalks.

He kneeled on the wooden-slat deck and lit a single joss stick. The fragrant scent of rich sandalwood met his nostrils. Mixed with the smell of the surrounding

14

sea, the spicy incense seemed to come from a far-off world. After passing the yarrow stalks through the sandalwood smoke, which acted as a spiritual disinfectant, he turned toward the south and bowed three times. Then, with his right hand, he began the task of swiftly separating the stalks to determine which hexagram currently influenced them. In such a way he was able to tap the wisdom of the ages and the laws of life. For the *I Ching* showed the interaction between heaven—the creative male, yang principle; and earth—the receptive female, yin principle.

The series of hexagrams that soon sat on the handkerchief before Wu Chao were totally unfamiliar to him. To properly interpret them, he needed to use the leather-bound book, which he quickly extracted from his satchel. After determining the proper page, he turned to a pictured representation of the same series of sticks that currently lay in front of him.

He was somewhat surprised to find that the first hexagram he had cast represented yang as a winged dragon. This was a powerful omen, and he carefully looked up the hexagrams that followed. With a bit of effort, he eventually formulated an interpretation.

The casting symbolized two brothers, whose constant bickering arouses the ire of a dragon whom they've awakened. Puzzled by the meaning of this omen, Wu Chao could only guess that it had something to do with his nephews. Yet they were certainly not prone to arguments. The two young men hardly ever disagreed, and when there were differences between them, they always settled these minor misunderstandings quite amicably. While Wu Chao was pondering his relationship with his own deceased brother an excited voice came from behind him.

"Uncle! The bonito, they're all around us!"

Instantly snapped out of his reverie by these words, Wu Chao swiveled around and caught sight of his older nephew, who was pointing toward that portion of the sea which lay at their stern. Once again, the lad shouted, "I've never seen anything like this before, Uncle! They're swarming on the surface like a bunch of frenzied sharks!"

While his other nephew joined his brother at the boat's fantail, Wu Chao hurriedly wrapped up the yarrow stalks and replaced them in the chart cabinet. Anxious to get the first hook in the water, he quickly forgot all about the curious divination. Thoughts of a much more immediate nature guided his steps as he joined his young crew on the trawler's stern.

The fog-shrouded surface of the sea was alive with white froth. Bending over the transom, Wu Chao was able to get a clear view of the source of this disturbance, for the silvery flanks of individual fish passed only a hand's length away. His eyes widened in wonder.

"They're bonito all right," he cried out passionately, "who knows what has brought them to the surface like this, but whatever it is, we owe it an offering of thanks. Now, come on, lads! Let's get those hooks in the water. I guarantee you that our holds won't stay empty for long."

Spurred into action, Wu Chao's nephews sprinted over to their stout bamboo fishing poles. The hooks were baited and the heavy nylon line tossed out into the surging water.

Meanwhile, Wu Chao returned to the helm, where

he shifted the engine into neutral. The boat was at the mercy of the current as he ran over to prepare his own fishing pole. The first two fat bonitos were already flapping on the deck by the time he got his own hook into the water. Barely ten seconds passed before his line tightened. He wasted no time setting the hook. Since the heavy-duty rods were not equipped with reels, he then had to yank the line back and pull the fish into the boat. The squirming bonito which lay at his feet was a good twenty-five pounder, seemingly identical to those which his nephews were busily pulling in.

For a good quarter of an hour, the action continued. Wu Chao gauged the passage of time by the dozens of bonito that now lay on deck, and the familiar soreness that was beginning to course through his upper arms and back. The veteran fisherman had just finished landing a particularly feisty brute, when his older nephew cried out loudly, "They're gone, Uncle! One second they were there on the surface, and the next, completely absent."

"Where could they have disappeared to?" asked his younger brother.

Wu Chao finished unhooking the bonito he had just pulled in, and returned his gaze to the sea. The fog had begun to dissipate and the gray surface of the waters had a ghostly stillness to it. It was apparent that the school had indeed moved on, and he could only shake his head in response.

"We were very fortunate that the bonito stayed in our midst as long as they did. We've taken our fair share. Besides, it's time to get these fish on ice before they start to stink. Let's get on with it, and perhaps then we can think about turning back toward home."

While the boys began stacking the fish in the cooler, Wu Chao took a moment to stretch his strained limbs. With his practiced gaze locked on that portion of the sea immediately behind the trawler's stern, he silently thanked the gods for such a bountiful catch. In the midst of giving thanks, he suddenly remembered his morning's *I Ching* reading. Though its meaning remained unclear, the divination had been followed almost instantaneously by the arrival of the school of bonito. Surely this was a good omen.

Yet, who were the two bickering brothers that the hexagram told of? And in what manner did the sleeping dragon express its anger after being awakened by their arguing?

With his eyes still riveted on the surrounding sea, Wu Chao wondered if he'd ever be able to grasp the significance of such a reading. The hexagram of the dragon was a powerful portent, and had never been uncovered by him before. Since such a thing was beyond his rather limited understanding of the *I Ching,* he supposed he could always seek out the orange-robed monk, who lived high in the mountains above their village. This holy elder would surely be able to explain the hexagram's symbolic meaning.

Merely thinking about the monk caused a strange warmness to suffuse his body. Swaying dizzily, he was sure he could smell the scent of sandalwood burning nearby. Just as he was about to turn and share this peculiar phenomenon with his nephews, a disturbance in the water nearby diverted his attention.

Approximately a dozen meters beyond the boat's transom, a circular pattern of whitish bubbles had formed on the sea's surface. Unlike the disturbance left in the wake of the bonito, this distinctive design reminded him of the trail of escaping air left behind by a sounding whale. Yet they had not seen any other evidence that such a behemoth was nearby, and Wu Chao doubted that a creature of this size could slip by them undetected.

Scratching his chin in confusion, Wu Chao fought the sudden instinct to run to the helm and get away from this spot with all due haste. A heavy, queasy feeling formed in his gut when another circular grouping of bubbles formed on the surface.

The veteran fisherman would take to his grave, long afterwards, the astounding series of sights and sounds that he next witnessed. For before he could cry out in warning, the sea erupted in a mass of seething foam. Quick to penetrate the surface and soar skyward was a massive, white tubular object. Too stunned to move, Wu Chao looked on in amazement as a trail of smoke and fire shot from the object's tail with a deafening roar. Only then did he recognize it as a missile.

Oblivious to the burns that reddened his face and exposed skin, Wu Chao watched as the rocket lifted up toward the heavens. Seconds later, it disappeared in the fog, although the roar of its engine was still clearly audible.

As the throaty blast gradually faded, Wu Chao continued looking up into the sky where the rocket had ascended. Beside him, his two shocked nephews did likewise. A strained silence continued to prevail, broken only by the far off cries of a sea gull.

A gentle breeze, full of the scent of the sea, hit Wu Chao squarely in the face, and he slowly lowered his

19

line of sight to take in the surrounding sea. Having served in the military in his early years, the grizzled fisherman had seen his fair share of modern weaponry. Yet never had he heard of a rocket that could be actually launched from beneath the water's surface!

It was evident that man was continuing to develop one more horrible killing device after another. The object that had just blasted off into the heavens was clearly one of those monstrous devices. Either that, or it was an alien spaceship manned by the gods themselves!

Anxious to share this sighting with his fellow villagers, the elder backed away from the transom and commanded his young crew to get on with their duties. Babbling away excitedly, his nephews reluctantly returned to their task of storing the catch while Wu Chao positioned himself behind the helm. He wasted no time engaging the gears, opening the throttle, and swinging their bow back to the north.

Only when they were well underway did his thoughts return to his early morning divination. Though he really couldn't explain why, somehow he got the distinct impression that what he had just witnessed was the manner in which the flying dragon would express its displeasure after being awakened by the two quarreling brothers. Now he only had to find out who these brothers were. For if they didn't stop their bickering soon, the dragon would fully express its anger, and all of mankind would be forced to pay the ultimate price of their folly.

CHAPTER TWO

The flight from Shanghai took a little less than two hours to complete. Admiral Liu Shao-chi had spent the entire spring and summer in the bustling port city, and was looking forward to this visit to the interior. Even though his stay would be but a brief one, he looked forward to the fresh air and open countryside with eager anticipation.

The Soviet-made Ilyushin airliner landed at the Guilin airport with barely a jolt. While the pilot expertly applied the brakes and reversed the thrust of the engines, Liu anxiously peeked out the window. His face broke into a warm smile at seeing a crystal-blue sky. Even from this limited vantage point, he could make out the dozens of majestic limestone mountains that made this region one of the most visually striking areas of China. He knew that the proper descriptive term for such unique topography was *karst,* indicating an irregular limestone zone dotted with sinkholes, underground streams, and hundreds of caverns. Three hundred million years ago, Guilin and its environs were covered by a surging sea. The mountains of limestone had been formed as they were forced upward by the movement of the earth's crust and then weathered by the water and the wind. The results were the massive, irregular mounds that had inspired painters and poets for centuries.

While the plane began taxiing toward the terminal, Liu realized that it had been over four decades since he had last visited this portion of the People's Republic. Though it seemed only yesterday that these hills were his exclusive home, it took only a single glance at his reflection in the window to gauge the swift passage of time. His full head of thick white hair, lined forehead, and heavy jowls belonged to a man rapidly approaching seventy years of age.

Born in adjoining Hunan Province, Liu was originally drawn to Guilin to hear the stirring words of a certain young political activist whose name was Mao Tse-tung. Liu was then an impressionable fifteen-year-old, and his trip to the Guangxi Autonomous Region was his first excursion away from the village of his birth.

Politics had certainly never been an important part of his life before that time, and he accompanied his father somewhat reluctantly. Yet the new scenery was magnificent, and with his eyes opened to the vast world that surrounded him, Liu only had to hear a brief sampling of Mao's vibrant rhetoric to be caught up in the Communist cause.

Much to his father's dismay, Liu was not at his side when the time came to return home. For on that very same evening that he first heard Mao speak, he enlisted in the People's Army. He had remained a member of this organization ever since.

Shaking his head with the fond memory of that glorious day, Liu Shao-chi, First Admiral of the

People's Liberation Navy, prepared to get on with his current duty. As the jetliner pulled to a stop beside the central terminal, he stretched his cramped limbs and yawned widely to clear his blocked ears. Before exiting the plane, he took a moment to thank the flight crew for a smooth flight and landing. Only then did he duck through the hatch and make the short descent to the tarmac.

Waiting for him at the bottom of the ramp were a pair of young, stern-faced PLA sentries, and a most familiar-looking senior officer. Sporting a balding scalp and a well developed paunch, General Huang Tzu animatedly greeted Liu with a warm smile and a firm hug.

"Welcome to Guilin, old friend. I do hope that your flight was a comfortable one."

Liu turned and briefly examined the exterior of the airplane from which he had just emerged. "That it was, Huang," he responded, "our Soviet comrades put together an excellent piece of equipment. From what I understand, the pilots barely have to fly these newest versions. They merely sit back and let the computers take over."

"Don't forget whose technology was originally responsible for such devices," reminded the general with a wink. "The Americans are clever inventors, but their security and business practices leave much to be desired."

"So I understand," returned Liu. "Fortunately for us, American laxity in these areas has saved us millions in research and development ourselves. I can't tell you how much the People's Navy has benefited from cheaply purchased Western technology trans-

23

fers. Our latest success is certain proof of this."

Noting a sudden sparkle in Liu's eyes, General Huang beamed expectantly. "Then the test results were favorable?" he quizzed hopefully.

Discretion flavored Liu's response. "Patience, Comrade. There will be plenty of time to discuss such things once we are alone."

Eager to know more, the general pointed toward the terminal. "My car is waiting for us. I have secured a guest house for you in the central city, beside Solitary Beauty Peak. Would you like to stop there to freshen up before going on to the site?"

"I don't think that's necessary," Liu replied. "I rested well last night, and can't wait to see that which has called me here. Is it all right with you if we proceed straight to your little discovery?"

"Why, of course," retorted the general. "If the road remains clear, we can be there within the hour."

Satisfied with this response, Liu signaled his host to lead the way. With the two sentries preceding them, they quickly crossed through the terminal. The airport was filled with scurrying travelers, most of whom Liu identified as tourists. They were mainly older, well-dressed individuals, and Liu recognized a variety of languages which included English, German, Dutch, and French. Well aware of the hard currency these travelers were leaving behind, he nodded cordially in response to the curious stares he and his comrades inevitably drew.

Waiting for them outside the terminal's main entrance was a shiny black Red Flag limousine, designed with features copied from both the Mercedes and the Cadillac. At their approach, the vehicle's driver snapped to attention. As the sentries joined the chauffeur in the front seat, Admiral Liu and the general settled themselves in the plush leather seats of the car's rear section. A thick glass partition guaranteed their privacy. After using the intercom to give the driver their destination, General Huang turned his attention back to his esteemed guest.

"Would you care to join me in some tea, Comrade? Or perhaps you'd prefer a drink of a bit more substance. I believe that we're carrying a bottle of excellent cassia wine."

Liu grinned. "Cassia wine, you say? Why, I haven't had a drink of such nectar since I was a lad. Will you join me?"

"Does the sun rise with the dawn? Why, of course I'll drink with you, old friend. Then perhaps you'll share with me the results of your latest weapons test."

A sly smile painted the general's face as he bent forward and opened the elaborately inlaid teakwood cabinet which was set into the glass partition's base. By this time, the car had begun moving, yet this hardly affected him as he picked up a crystal decanter and poured a gold-colored wine into two long-stemmed glasses, one of which he handed to Liu Shao-chi. Raising the other glass, he offered a toast.

"To old friendships! May the great sacrifices of the past not be forsaken."

Lifting his own glass, Liu nodded and took a sip of his wine. The delicate taste of fermented cinnamon bark met his lips, and he expressed his pleasure with a satisfied sigh.

"It's been much too long, Huang. Do you realize that my father used to brew this stuff himself? My

25

mother would always give us a glassful whenever we weren't feeling well."

"It was the same in my family," returned the portly general. "To hell with modern medicine! With a tonic such as this, who cares about feeling ill?"

Nodding agreement, Liu took another sip of the wine, and then diverted his glance to the passing countryside. Even though the windows were heavily tinted, he was afforded an adequate view of the collection of brick and stone structures they were now passing. These habitations became denser as they approached a large bridge. Seconds later, they began crossing a wide river.

"Ah, the Lijiang," observed Liu fondly. "This river is surely the pearl of all of China's streams. Has it been polluted as yet?"

The general followed the direction of his guest's glance and responded, "Actually, the Lijiang is still in pretty good shape. Although it hasn't been an easy task to keep it that way. Only last month, we caught the local tire plant in the process of dumping thousands of kiloliters of raw effluent into one of the river's tributaries. As an example to the locals, we tried the tire plant's manager, and had him publicly executed the very next day."

"Good for you," Liu shot back. "Fools such as that can't be tolerated. Pollution of our natural resources is one of the greatest threats our country faces. Back in Shanghai, portions of the Huangpu River are so full of raw sewage that the health authorities constantly fear for the lives of those who live near its banks. Cholera and typhus often rage in epidemic proportions, and for all practical purposes, the river

26

there is dead. If only we had the resources to track down all the polluters. Yet, because the industrial base of the city has grown to such an enormous size, finding all those responsible would be impossible. No, what we have to do, is to change people's values."

"An execution now and then should help do that," sighed the general. "Fear has a way of causing the guilty ones to think twice about their actions."

Silently nodding in response to this, Liu took another sip of wine and watched the rest of the city pass by. Their driver was an expert at smoothly weaving the limo in and out of the heavy bicycle traffic, and ever so gradually the habitations began to thin out. Taking in the lush green tropical landscape, Liu sat forward excitedly when he spotted a particularly jagged mountain in the distance.

"Isn't Reed Flute Cave located at the base of that mountain?"

As his host nodded that it was, Liu continued, "On the day after I enlisted in the People's Liberation Army, one of the officers led a group of us to that very cavern. How our eyes widened when our tour guide revealed that the large grotto inside the cave was once the temporary home of the infamous Dragon King. *The Journey to the West* was one of my favorite childhood tales, and I could just picture the Dragon King's maidens, his treasure, and the shrimp soldiers as they lived amongst the stalactites and stalagmites."

"These hills are full of such colorful legends," commented the general. "That is one of the reasons the ancient poets were drawn here in such great numbers. Now, tell me, Liu Shao-chi, how did things go aboard the *Red Dragon?* The suspense is killing me!"

Liu took a last fond look at the strangely shaped mountain, then calmly sat back in the plush leather seat. Only after taking another sip of his wine did he answer.

"Well, you can relax now, Comrade. The People's Republic now has the services of a fully operational, submarine-launched ballistic missile system."

"That's music to my ears!" exclaimed the joyous general.

A satisfied grin etched Liu's face as he added, "As originally planned, the test-firing took place in the South China Sea, in the waters north of Dongsha Island. The missile then attained sub-orbital velocity before its six MIRV'd warheads splashed down in the test range south of Hainan. By the way, the CEP was less than fifty meters."

"Why, that's remarkable!" returned the general. "At long last, our enemies' most hardened targets can be eliminated. With such a weapons system operational, I see no reason why our previously discussed plan can't succeed. This will be especially apparent once you see the site we've chosen."

Hastily checking his watch, Huang Tzu continued, "Now, getting back to the missile test, is there a chance that the firing was observed by outsiders?"

Liu Shao-chi answered him firmly, "It's extremely doubtful. The liftoff took place in a heavy fog, which should have veiled the launch from the ever watchful eyes of the surveillance satellites. And besides, the nearest Russian and American intelligence vessels were hundreds of nautical miles distant at the time."

"Wonderful," observed Huang smugly. "It appears that your people have succeeded in accomplishing a most difficult task, Comrade. What's the reaction been from the premier's office?"

Before answering this question, Liu looked his host straight in the eyes. "As expected, Lin Shau-ping greeted the test results in his usual reserved manner. It's obvious that the Premier and his advisers continue to resist the weapon system's continued development and eventual deployment."

Huang Tzu's face reddened. "Our new leader is a spineless pup! Little does he understand the *Red Dragon's* true significance."

"That might be so," interrupted Liu. "But as it appears now, further funding for the project is doubtful. My aides in Beijing paint a somber picture. For the premier continued to insist that a submerged offensive platform, such as the *Red Dragon,* has no place in our fleet. He'd rather spend the money on augmenting our defensive coastal surface capabilities."

With this comment, the general's facial expression soured. "It's our fault for allowing such a youngster to attain supreme power so quickly. The trouble is, the fool is not mature enough to have a sense of history. Speaking of the devil, what's the latest news on the U.S./Soviet summit?"

"The conference will take place at United Nations headquarters in New York City in three weeks' time. Preliminary reports show that both governments are very close to agreeing on a comprehensive ban on all nuclear weapons. The Western press is heralding this event as the summit of the century, and even *Pravda* is getting in the act. Why, just yesterday, they actually printed a front page article extolling what the world will be like once nuclear bombs no longer exist."

"That's easy enough for them to say," observed Huang Tzu solemnly. "For the Soviets have assembled the most powerful collection of conventional forces that this world has ever seen. Without nuclear deterrence, they will be impossible to stop. Don't the Americans realize this?"

Liu returned his gaze to the passing rural countryside. "The Western powers are as naive as our young leader, Comrade. They see only what they want to see. The painful lessons of history are thus ignored, to give their citizens a false sense of security. Yet, you and I know differently. We'll never forget man's true nature. For struggle is an inherent part of human makeup. War will always be with us, regardless of so-called peace treaties and summits. It's the very nature of the beast!"

Liu's comment was emphasized by a blast of the limo's horn. Both men looked out the window as the car dramatically slowed. Several minutes went by before the source of the slowdown became evident.

The wooden cart was a ramshackle affair, pulled by a single black ox. Two skinny, khaki-clad peasants stood on each side of the rickety vehicle, completely oblivious to the urgent blasts of the limo's horn. With their faces covered by their broad-brimmed hats, they appeared to come from another time and place.

Liu couldn't help but smile at this obstacle which represented a portion of the People's Republic too often forgotten in the hectic, cosmopolitan environs of Shanghai. Eight hundred million of his countrymen lived in such a primitive, unhurried manner. As it was in the past, and would be tomorrow, the peasant

30

was the backbone of China. With only a tenth of the nation's land cultivable, the peasants' task was to feed a population of a billion individuals—more than that of America, the Soviet Union, and Western Europe combined—in an area only a little larger than the United States. Unable to forget his own rural roots, Liu silently wished the two peasants good fortune as the Red Flag limo whipped past them on the road's shoulder, leaving a cloud of dust in its wake.

Once again checking his watch, General Huang Tzu commented, "We should be turning off the main road shortly, my friend. From there, it's only a ride of ten minutes or so. I do hope you're agreeable to a brief hike. The roadway to the site is not yet completed, and the only way to get up there is by foot or on horseback."

"That sounds like just what the doctor ordered," returned Liu. "After that plane ride, these old legs are just begging to be properly stretched. Now, why don't you tell me a little more about how you managed to find this place?"

"I'd be glad to, my friend. But first, how about a refill? This local cassia wine is addictive!"

Liu accepted another glass of the tasty spirits and sat back as the general explained.

"The initial discovery occurred exactly ten days ago. Fortunately, it was one of my PLA survey teams that chanced upon the entrance. The report went straight to my desk, and I was thus able to insure that news of the find was not released to the public. So far, only a handful of trusted individuals know of the site's existence. All are sworn to secrecy.

"As you will soon see for yourself, the cavern is one

31

of the largest yet uncovered in this region. The initial investigation indicates that it has not been inhabited for at least four centuries, since the primary archaeological evidence left behind are several exquisitely preserved Ming Dynasty porcelain vases."

"Do you feel that the cavern was heavily visited by man at that time?" interrupted Liu.

"Most certainly," answered the general. "We suspect that up to one thousand individuals could have been living there full time."

"You don't say," marveled Liu.

Conscious that he had his guest's complete attention, Huang continued, "And even that astounding figure is on the conservative side. My unit's chief engineer feels that the site could have easily held up to ten times that number. For not only is the cavern of huge size, there's also plenty of fresh air, and both hot and cold natural springs inside as well."

As Liu absorbed this fascinating fact, the limo abruptly slowed down and executed a hard righthand turn. The going now was far from smooth. In fact, the ride was so rough it took a total effort on the white-haired elder's part not to spill his cherished drink.

Beside him, his host was having an equally difficult time keeping his hand steady. When the vehicle bounced over a particularly jarring pothole, his efforts went for naught, and his wineglass went tumbling to the floor. A pained expression was etched on the veteran army officer's face as he watched his drink soak into the crimson carpet.

"What a horrible waste!" observed Huang disgustedly. "And to think that's the end of a most delightful vintage. Oh well, at least it didn't spill on our uniforms."

The pavement suddenly smoothed out, and Liu took advantage of the temporary lull to hastily finish off his own drink. No sooner did the last drop of cassia wine pass his lips, than an even rougher section of roadway was encountered. As the limo rattled and shook, both passengers grabbed for the hand-straps mounted above each door. Steadied thusly, they attempted to peer out to examine the passing countryside, yet found the view currently veiled by a thick cloud of dust.

"We haven't got far to go now, my friend," offered Huang, his voice trembling with each passing concussion.

"I hope not," returned Liu. "Otherwise, your car will be a total loss."

Grinning at this comment, the general sat forward and took another glance at his pocket watch. Liu was content to sit back in his own seat, and silently absorb the punishing ride. He was in the midst of visualizing the work that currently sat on his desk back at Naval Command in Shanghai, when the car suddenly braked to a stop. Expecting to find that this poor excuse for a road was now blocked by some sort of immovable obstacle which even their masochistic chauffeur would not dare to drive over, Liu looked up when the intercom loudly buzzed. His host promptly picked up the headset. Whatever Huang heard caused a relieved smile to turn up the corners of his mouth. Hanging up the intercom, the general caught his guest's inquisitive stare.

"Have no worry, old friend, for we have at long last

reached our destination. From here on, we travel by foot. Would you care to join me?"

Grateful that the automobile portion of their journey was over, Liu wasted no time in following his host's lead and exiting the limousine. A gust of hot, humid air greeted him. Taking a moment to scan the surrounding landscape, he viewed a collection of tree-covered limestone buttes. No evidence of man's presence was visible here, except for the rock-strewn dirt roadway that had brought them to this desolate spot. Noting that the previously spotless automobile was now completely covered with a thick layer of dust, Liu's gaze drifted to a narrow earthen footpath that led up into a nearby hillside. His host followed his glance.

"That goat-track leads directly to the cavern. The hike is only a couple of kilometers at best, yet most of the way is uphill."

Liu inhaled a deep lungful of air and found it sweet with the fragrant scent of newly blossomed acacias. Catching sight of the vibrant white and yellow clusters which emitted this delicate honeylike fragrance, he responded, "Don't worry, Huang. I can easily handle such a climb. Not only do I still ride a bicycle to work every day, but I swim a full half hour as well."

"Your fitness shows," returned his host. "Though our youth is gone for good, at least we're not confined to our beds as so many of our old comrades are."

Absorbing this grim observation, Liu pointed farther down the valley, where the pitted road which their limo had been following disappeared around a thick stand of acacia trees.

"Where does that lead?" he questioned.

"The road continues traversing this valley, extending another three and a half kilometers," the general promptly answered. "A small commune is situated at the end of it, and nearby is a tributary of the Lijiang. We don't foresee any problems with the locals. Although to appease their curiosity, we've made up a cover story stating that the Army is in the process of excavating a dangerous radioactive mineral from these hills. So far, any peasants we've met up with have given us the widest of berths."

"It sounds as if you've covered all the angles," observed Liu matter-of-factly. "Shall we get on with that hike now? I'm as anxious as ever to finally see what has excited you so these last couple of days."

Beckoning his guest forward with a wide sweep of his hand, Huang led the way to the nearby path. Liu followed, with the two ever-present sentries taking up the rear.

As they began their climb, Liu remembered the last time he had followed his old friend, Huang Tzu, up a similar path. The year was 1934, and both were mere youngsters, who had only recently joined Mao Tsetung's People's Liberation Army. The Chinese Communist Party was in its infancy at the time, and faced opposition from both the ruling Kuomintang Nationalist Party under Chiang Kai-shek, and the invading Japanese forces. Limited to a small region of southeast China, the Communists faced a Nationalist blockade. To escape this effective policy of political and economic containment, Mao ordered the entire Communist community to pack up and move to the southwest, to the farthest frontiers of China. And thus, the Long March began.

Liu's rather limited view of his country's vastness was rapidly expanded as they passed through the backward provinces of Kueichou and Yunnan. Here they easily met the challenge of the antiquated, inadequately armed forces of the local military governors, who were in reality but remote survivors of the warlord era. Next they crossed over the wild gorges of the Yangtze, skirted the edge of Tibet, where their enemies were bitter cold and hunger, and finally descended through Kansu into the northern part of Shensi province. This was a remote backward region, yet it was easily defended and directly adjoined the vast Mongolian steppe. From here they were in an excellent position to resist the impending Japanese invasion.

Altogether, the Long March covered some six thousand miles of wild, mountainous country. Constantly harassed by the ten Nationalist armies sent out to destroy them, they crossed over eighteen major mountain ranges and over twenty-four rivers, fighting at least one brisk military skirmish each and every day.

One engagement was particularly memorable. While crossing Western China, they found themselves having to cross the Tatu River. Only a single bridge spanned the Tatu here, and it had to be utilized, for the river was in the midst of a roaring flood. Well aware of this, the Nationalists had removed most of the wooden floorboards from the three-hundred foot bridge. They had also positioned several machine-gun nests on the opposite bank to make the crossing even more precarious.

Mao himself asked for thirty volunteers to cross the bridge and take out the gun emplacements. Both Liu and Huang Tzu were among the first to offer their services and were instantly accepted. One by one the guerillas began the assault, utilizing the sixteen iron chains from which the bridge was suspended, to swing themselves, hand over hand, to their objective. Several of their comrades were cut down, but because of effective covering fire, and the protection of the splintered remnants of the bridge flooring, they succeeded in advancing. It was Huang Tzu who made a name for himself by climbing up onto the remaining planks and lobbing a grenade into the deadly machine-gun nest. This proved to be the turning point of the battle, and Huang's heroics spurred on the rest of their troops. Soon afterwards, the Tatu River bridge was theirs.

By surviving that fateful day, Liu and Huang's friendship was sealed. Both had persevered, and lived to once again serve Mao after the Revolution's successful conclusion. Though much had happened since those glorious days, they would never forget the lessons they learned during the Long March, when one hundred and thirty thousand of their comrades set out to conquer a nation, with only twenty thousand surviving to eventually see this dream come true.

Stirred by such memories, Liu Shao-chi took in a deep breath of the clean mountain air and glanced up to examine the broad shoulders and back of his old friend. Conspicuous bands of sweat stained the armpits of Huang's green cotton uniform, yet his pace remained a brisk one. In fact, it took a total effort on Liu's part to keep up with his friend. Conscious that the years had been good to both of them, Liu shifted his line of sight to take in the passing countryside, all the while doing his best to increase the length of his stride.

It had been much too long since he had last been in such a desolate wilderness setting. He spent most of his time these days either chained to his desk in Shanghai, or attending meetings in the halls of government in Beijing. Both cities were crowded with millions of inhabitants, and one learned to live with this constant crush of humanity, which allowed little time for solitude.

Having been born and raised in the country, Liu genuinely missed the unpopulated wide-open spaces in which he now found himself. The fresh air was like a tonic, while the magnificent landscape soothed the weary roots of his soul. They were presently passing through a thick grove of blooming acacias, and Liu marveled at the bright yellow blossoms whose sweet fragrance reminded him of his childhood. In his mind he could see his beloved mother entering their simple home, with her arms full of ripe acacia blossoms. She would use them for perfume, and Liu always looked forward to the autumn, when the blooms ripened to their full intensity.

Life seemed so simple in those days. As peasant farmers, their only concern was the land and its crops. Big cities and political intrigues belonged to another world, far removed from that of the farm.

Liu often wondered what his life would have been like if he had returned home with his father, instead of enlisting in Mao's army. Could he have ever been satisfied with such a simple life? Doubting he would have ever known differently, he supposed that he would have made a thrifty, capable farmer. For these values, which he had inherited from his father, guided his life to this very day.

The path continued to steepen, and Liu found himself turning his attention back to his step. Trees no longer hugged the trail here. In their place were shelves of cracked limestone and an occasional thorn bush. A raven cried mournfully from above, and a gust of warm, humid air blew in from the south. He was beginning to feel the effects of the climb in the calves of his legs, and reached up to wipe off a thick band of glistening sweat from his forehead. Just as he was about to halt and give himself a moment to catch his breath, a strange pounding noise rose in the distance. This resounding racket had apparently caught the attention of their leader as well, for Huang Tzu stopped dead in his tracks and lifted his head to listen intently.

"It sounds as if my men are continuing with the excavation up ahead. We're less than a quarter of a kilometer from the cavern's entrance at this point. Shall we halt here for a moment to take a breather?"

Sensing that the general was only making this offer to accommodate his guest, Liu once again wiped his forehead and responded, "Don't stop merely on my behalf, Comrade. I'm quite capable of pushing on to our objective without a rest."

Shrugging his massive shoulders, the general grinned. "If that's the case, my friend, let us continue. For proper refreshments should await us beyond the next series of switchbacks."

Determined to match his host's blistering pace without complaint, Liu fell in behind Huang as he pivoted to resume the climb. Ten long minutes later, they reached the summit of the dusty trail. Here the general halted briefly to point out an area at the bottom of the vast tree-lined valley which now lay before them.

"The entrance to the cavern lies just behind that grove of acacias. We believe this particular opening was created as a result of the severe earthquake that shook this sector last month. That would explain why the site hadn't been previously uncovered by the local peasants."

The sound of the distinctive pounding which had previously caught their attention was clearly audible from this vantage point. Still unable to see the individuals responsible for this racket, Liu was able to just make out a grouping of army tents set up amongst the acacias. As he sighted this bivouac, he involuntarily exhaled a sigh of relief.

The trail leading down to the campsite followed the meandering path of a gurgling brook. The sound of this tumbling stream accompanied them as they entered the valley and approached the rock-strewn grove from the south. Only then did Liu catch sight of the first of the soldiers who were stationed here.

The majority of the troops were but youngsters. Bare chests glistening with sweat, they were wielding sledgehammers to pound away at the limestone which lay at the base of an adjoining solid rock shelf. The work was loud and strenuous, and allowed the four newcomers to advance well into the tree line before being challenged by a startled, rifle-toting sentry. One look at the baldheaded senior officer who led this foursome onward, was enough to cause the young recruit to instantly stiffen at attention. Merely nodding in response to the soldier's crisp salute, General Huang continued on to the limestone ledge where the rest of the soldiers were gathered.

Liu watched as the first of the junior officers caught sight of the distinguished pair of new arrivals. Quickly, he put his whistle to his lips and blew a series of three deafening blasts. This signal was all that was needed to gain the attention of his men, who dropped their sledgehammers and scrambled to form their ranks. Two dozen men were quickly gathered at attention before them, their bare chests heaving from their exertions.

The whistle-toting officer stepped forward and politely issued his greetings. The distinguished visitors had not been expected for another twenty-four hours, and the red-faced lieutenant humbly offered his sincere apologies for not anticipating an earlier arrival.

The general calmly absorbed the junior officer's nervous ramblings. To set him at ease, Huang Tzu praised his squad's progress, and after introducing Admiral Liu, dismissed the rest of the men for the day with a hearty "Job well done!"

After slaking his thirst with a cup of cool spring water, Liu joined his host at the base of the limestone ledge. A narrow tunnel was cut into the rock here. The soldiers had been in the process of widening this aperture, and Liu noted that there was a large wooden crate placed on the ground immediately adjacent to the elongated opening. His host approached the crate and removed a pair of miner's hard hats, one of which he handed to Liu. After switching on the battery-operated lantern set into the helmet's brim, Liu donned the hard hat and followed Huang into the

41

tunnel's mouth.

It was just wide enough to walk single file, and Liu had to duck his head to keep from striking the jagged roof. Yet the tunnel extended for less than a dozen meters, and within a short time he was standing fully upright in one of the largest natural caverns he had ever seen.

The grotto's sheer size left Liu speechless, and he was glad that his portly host allowed him a few minutes of silent contemplation to fully absorb the enormous size of the rock chamber in which they now stood. The air was a good twenty degrees cooler than that outside, and all was still except for the nearby trickle of running water.

Directing the light of his lantern into the room's vast recesses, Liu viewed a virtual forest of thick stalactites hanging like giant icicles from the ceiling. Equally as impressive were the dozens of stalagmites that hugged the cave's floor. The place seemed enchanted, reminiscent of a scene from a fairy tale, and Liu could almost visualize the trolls at work, busily storing away the Dragon King's treasure.

A good portion of the grotto was empty except for a smooth stone floor. Liu estimated that the roof was high enough to accommodate a six-story office building, with room to spare. So wide apart were its walls, his lantern's beam was unable to illuminate the space in its entirety. Liu was just about to express his wonder aloud, when his host's deep voice broke the eerie quiet.

"Well, my friend, what did I tell you? Isn't this place awesome?"

Liu answered excitedly, "It is indeed incredible,

Comrade. If we only had this place back in 1934, we could have hidden the entire People's Army in here, and Chiang Kai-shek would never have been the wiser."

"That's so true," responded Huang Tzu breathlessly. As his words echoed in the distance, he added, "What you see here is only the so-called tip of the iceberg. Tunnels radiate in three other directions, leading to chambers just as large as this one. Our survey teams have yet to fully explore these adjoining grottoes. My lead geologist feels that they could go on for hundreds of kilometers. Just two days ago, we discovered an underground river that could very well empty into the Lijiang. One of our most experienced speleologists is also an expert with the kayak. He has volunteered to use one of these vessels in an attempt to determine the stream's true extent."

Genuinely impressed, Liu shook his head in wonder. For as the general had said in his initial report, here was a place large enough to support an entire underground city, if they so desired. As fate would have it, such a spot had been actually discussed between them over three months ago, long before the cavern's entrance was chanced upon. To actually see such a spot with his very own eyes, renewed Liu's belief in that greatest of mysteries which had guided their country for over four thousand years.

Huang Tzu could sense his guest's awe, and beckoned him to have a seat on a nearby ledge. As Liu did so, the balding general cleared his throat and spoke out forcefully.

"At long last, old friend, the reins of history are in our hands. For too many decades, we have been forced to merely sit back and watch others rule our destiny. Yet, the gods have been amazingly kind to us and our brave plan. That which in the past was but a desperate, frustrated dream, now has an excellent chance of becoming reality.

"You have brought me news of a most significant nature. The *Red Dragon's* successful test of its submarine-launched ballistic missile system signals a turning point in our beloved country's destiny. Our years of painful sacrifice have at long last paid off, and soon we shall take our rightful place as the ultimate superpower, second to none other on this planet!

"In three weeks' time, the leaders of the United States and the Soviet Union will sit down at the so-called summit of peace. As a result of this meeting, nuclear weapons will be outlawed from the planet. Though this indeed sounds like an ideal way to bring peace to the world, we know that it is all just a sham. Both countries have amassed huge conventional armies, and with the nuclear deterrent absent, will utilize these forces to begin a new and dangerous chapter in imperialistic aggression.

"Our Soviet neighbors have already made the first tentative moves, as my intelligence sources show the arrival of an entire new division of troops along the Amur River. The Russians have had their greedy eyes on Manchuria for over a century, and are just looking for an excuse to move their troops across the border, as they did in Afghanistan.

"Equally dangerous are the Western powers led by the United States and its lacky, Japan. As the People's Republic opens its markets to the world, the capitalists flock to our shores. We already face a perilous trade imbalance. Have we already forgotten the lessons of the Opium Wars, when these same powers forced China to become a nation of drug addicts, to pay for the goods being pulled out of our country?

"For too many years, we have been weak and allowed ourselves to become the dupes of these running dogs of imperialism. Our current premier is playing right into their hands. Lin Shau-ping is young and inexperienced. Though his intentions may be good, he has no sense of history, and is leading our country into certain disaster. Doesn't the fool realize that after this summit, China—the world's most populous nation—will be at the complete mercy of its enemies? If only our beloved Chairman were still alive. Mao would most definitely see the whole picture, and demand that the People's Republic have an equal voice at this all important conference. Yet our commander is no more, and now it is up to us to insure that our people's sacrifices have not been made in vain.

"The cavern in which we now stand can be the protective root from which the new China will blossom. The gods have led us to this place. Now it's up to us to make the most of this stroke of good fortune, and take the initiative.

"Three months ago, we talked of a purely theoretical operation, precipitated by our view of the current state of world affairs. Since that time, our worst fears have indeed come to pass. But two new factors now tip the scales in our favor. The first part of the solution came into our possession the moment that army surveyor stumbled across the entrance to this grotto. Now, you have informed me that the People's

Liberation Navy has attained the second factor so vital to the success of our scheme. With respect to purely logistical concerns, could the plan of action that we discussed be applied before the summit seals our doom?"

Liu Shao-chi thoughtfully considered this question and hesitated a moment before answering. "The *Red Dragon* is currently berthed beneath the protective confines of its top-secret sub pen, located on the coast south of Hangchow. As we speak, the vessel is being loaded with a complement of sixteen *Xia*-class missiles. Each rocket is tipped with six fifty-kiloton nuclear warheads, with a range of over 5,000 kilometers. It will take at least ten more days for the loading to be completed and the crew fitted out. All in all, I'd say that, barring any unforeseen technical difficulties, the boat will be ready to sail in two weeks' time."

Huang Tzu's eyes widened at this revelation. "Excellent, Comrade! This will give the vessel just enough time to reach its patrol area before the summit convenes."

"Are you suggesting that we actually go ahead with a launch at that time?" quizzed Liu incredulously.

Huang seemed disappointed with the tone of his guest's response. "Why, that's only obvious, Comrade! Don't tell me that you think we have any other options. The People's Republic is threatened as never before, and the implementation of this plan will guarantee China's survival.

"Come now, my friend, look around you. Can't you see what this cavern truly means? To insure that the Chairman's great dream isn't cast to the wind, we must act, and act now! It is up to us to put aside our selfish fears and dare for greatness.

"A preliminary survey shows that this grotto complex can safely accommodate up to 1,000 individuals. Under the veil of secrecy, we will gather together our most loyal followers. They will be carefully chosen to represent a cross section of our country's population. Young and old alike will be transferred to the sheltering confines of this underground world, to await their call to destiny.

"Meanwhile, the *Red Dragon* will situate itself in the North Pacific, where it will launch a crippling preemptive strike against our barbarian foes. With no idea of the true source of the warheads that will all too soon be descending from the heavens, the paranoid leaders of the United States and the Soviet Union will inevitably blame each other, and swiftly push the button leading to further punishing reprisals. The nuclear genie will then be released in all its spiteful fury, and untold devastation will fall upon the lands of our enemies.

"Snug and safe in this cavern, with our select population's every physical need satisfied, we merely have to wait for the two Goliaths to slay each other. Then, when our instruments say that it's safe, we will emerge victorious! Gathering together the survivors, a new and glorious China will emerge from the radioactive dust of our long, hard-earned past. And the true principles that underscore the theories of our beloved Chairman will be applied to all humanity. For at long last, China will finally become the *Zhong Guo,* the central country, to which the entire planet will turn for guidance."

The general's spirited discourse echoed in the distance, and Liu Shao-chi couldn't help but be inspired by the picture that had formed in his mind's eye. Three months ago, when this daring plan was first discussed, he had participated as a mere tactician. At that time, he never actually thought that such a scheme would be seriously considered.

As a trained naval officer, he had been on the plains of Kunlun and had witnessed firsthand the unbelievably destructive force of a nuclear explosion. At that time there was no doubt in his mind that such devices would be utilized only as a last desperate measure. For surely there could be no real winner in such a conflict.

Yet today, political realities necessitated a re-evaluation of their situation. The threats on their border could not be ignored. And it was obvious that their inexperienced premier was not the man to see them through this crisis. Was China's continued existence as a country thus indeed threatened? For if this was truly the case, Liu knew that he would give his support to any scheme, no matter how desperate it might be, to insure the Republic's integrity.

Returning the vibrant stare of his portly baldheaded comrade, Liu shivered in awareness of their situation. The cavern's temperature seemed to suddenly drop, and the sixty-nine-year-old naval officer shifted his glance to include the assortment of icicle-shaped stalactites and stalagmites visible in the distance. Ever reminiscent of a fairy tale scene, the grotto seemed to pulse with a life of its own.

Was a new civilization indeed destined to germinate inside its rocky bowels? Trembling with this thought, Liu could only pray for the clarity of mind needed to answer this all important question before events in the outside world precipitated an outcome that would lead to the end of all their hard earned dreams and aspirations. For above all, the survival of the People's Republic had to be assured!

CHAPTER THREE

The bar was called The Doll House, and was known for its cold beer and the hottest go-go dancers on the beach. Located off the Kamehameha Highway, it was within walking distance of the U.S. Naval base at Pearl Harbor, and was mostly frequented by those warriors who cruised silently beneath the seas in submarines.

For Petty Officer First Class Reginald Warner, the gaudily decorated bar was practically his second home. A sonar operator by trade, his sensitive ears fully appreciated the establishment's excellent stereo system, which continually blasted out a furious, pounding, "demon" rock and roll.

Born in Philadelphia, Reggie, as he was known among his shipmates, was second generation navy. His father had been a cook aboard the USS *New Jersey*, and Reggie was proud to carry on the family tradition in balmy Hawaii. He was currently passing on his legacy to a younger shipmate, Petty Officer Third Class Marty Stanfield, who was also a Philly native. Both black men were assigned to the same ship, and shared a cramped apartment only a few blocks away.

From their current vantage point beside the bar's central stage, the two sailors lifted their beer mugs in a toast while patiently waiting for the next dancer to appear.

"Here's to straight courses and a steady helm!" shouted Reggie, whose raised voice was necessitated by the deafening music.

Nodding in response, his drinking partner took a long sip of his brew and looked up at the stage expectantly. "Where the hell's the next girl? A guy could die from loneliness around here."

"Easy, bro," returned Reggie. "You certainly are tighter than a whip tonight. Just be cool, and Mother Nature will take care."

No sooner were these words out of his mouth, than the resounding strains of Ted Nugent's "Little Miss Dangerous" broke from the stereo speakers. To a chorus of wailing guitars, a tall, miniskirted Oriental burst through the curtain. Her shapely body immediately began undulating to the wild rhythm, and both sailors looked on with eyes full of wonder.

This was their first visit to the Doll House since returning from a four-week patrol, and Reggie knew that this girl was a newcomer, and a welcome one. He'd always had a soft spot for Orientals, and this one was a real looker.

She couldn't have been much older than twenty-one, with a face that was equally as striking as her superb body. Because of her long shapely legs and big bust, Reggie guessed that she was a Thai. He had had shore leave in Bangkok only last year, and he would take to his grave the memory of the amazing assortment of sexy locals he had sampled while visiting that notorious fleshpot by the sea.

51

Relishing the early hour, which made them the only paying customers in the place, Reggie reached into his wallet and removed a thick wad of bills. He flashed the bills at the dancer, who wasted no time in coming forward to work her meager audience while they were still turned on.

Seductively bumping and grinding her hips, she teased the men for a full minute before reaching for her dress zipper and yanking it downward. This left her completely naked, except for a sequined G-string embroidered with a gold dollar sign.

Reggie was astounded by her solid breasts, which had the largest nipples he had ever seen. He felt himself growing hard, and grinned while his shipmate leaned forward and began stuffing dollar bills into her narrow elastic waistband. Her expression was cool as she accepted the tip and then slowly began working sideways, until she was standing right in front of Reggie.

The worldly twenty-five-year-old from the City of Brotherly Love played it cool himself, his glance never leaving her big dark eyes. Unable to coax the least bit of emotion from her, he thumbed through his wad of bills and pulled out a crisp fifty. He made certain that she saw its denomimation as he folded the bill lengthwise and reached out to deposit it under her G-string. This caused a gradual smile to shape her luscious lips, and Reggie prayed that her interest was not limited merely to his money.

"I think she likes you, Reg!" shouted his drinking companion playfully.

Ignoring this comment, Reggie gave the girl his

sexiest stare and silently willed her forward. Strangely enough, the dancer seemed to take the bait and crouched down at the very edge of the stage. Then, in a broad sweeping motion, she bent over and kissed him briefly on the lips. Her scent filled his nostrils, and Reggie found himself fully erect, his heart pounding away like a schoolboy. Not easily infatuated, he was somewhat shocked by the effect this young woman had on him.

She danced for two more songs, then was replaced by a flat-chested blonde, who was a Doll House veteran. Unable to get the Oriental out of his mind, Reggie wondered what the best way would be to get to know her on more intimate terms. So deep was he in thought, that he didn't even notice it when a tall, miniskirted figure stole up behind him and then tapped him on the shoulder. When he eventually turned to see who was disturbing him, he almost fainted from shock as his eyes took in the face and figure of his Oriental beauty.

"I just wanted to thank you for the tip," she shouted into his ear.

"It's my pleasure," he responded, his heart still fluttering with her surprise appearance. "Can I buy you a drink?"

"I'd enjoy that," she promptly replied.

Hardly believing what he was hearing, Reggie signaled that he'd join her in one of the booths, then quickly turned to address his shipmate. "Bingo, my man! Old Regeroo scores once more. And brother, is this one a heartbreaker! Now, since I scored first, I get the pad. And that means I don't want to see your ugly face until the sun's well over Diamond Head!"

Not leaving until he was certain that his roommate got the message, Reggie sucked in his gut and casually sauntered across the room to join his latest conquest. Two mai-tais later, he learned that his new-found love had a passion for soul music. With a wink, he informed her that one of the best soul collections on the entire island of Oahu lay in his pad, only a few short blocks away. She seemed genuinely excited by this announcement, and after squaring it with the manager, signaled Reggie to lead the way.

The tropical air had never smelled sweeter as he took his date by the arm and led her up Salt Lake Boulevard. It was a glorious, warm afternoon, and they reached his apartment in less than ten minutes' time.

Her name was Kim, and she had a passion for Otis Redding songs and good Scotch, both of which Reggie was able to provide in ample quantities. "Sitting on the Dock of the Bay" proved to be her favorite tune, and when the shapely Thai heard it blare forth from the speakers, she instinctively began dancing. It didn't take much prompting by her host to convince her to continue, and before long she had freed herself from the constraints of her leather miniskirt. This left her naked once again, except for a black lace G-string appliquéd with a large pink heart.

Reggie felt a familiar tightness grip his loins, and drinking in her long, lean legs, narrow waist, and perfectly formed breasts, he decided it was time to join her. Without hesitation, he stripped off his Hawaiian shirt and khaki shorts. Dressed now only in his skivvies, he rose and began dancing beside her.

An all-city halfback in high school, Reggie had an excellent physique himself. Still able to run a mile in under six minutes, and do fifty pushups without stopping, he had muscular thighs and a well-developed chest and biceps. He was also no slouch on the dance floor, and showed his guest how a Philly "soul man" strutted his stuff.

In response, Kim did her best to copy each of his moves. But the Scotch she had consumed was taking its effect, and when she stumbled dizzily, she found herself securely in her dance partner's strong embrace. Their bare skin touched, and her gaze dropped to identify the stiff object that was suddenly poking her hip. She gasped audibly upon spotting the longest, thickest erection she had ever seen.

Noting her new preoccupation, Reggie whispered into her ear, "And it's all for you, my gorgeous Oriental fox."

Not hearing a word of complaint, he guided her over to the couch and pulled her into his lap. She smelled of jasmine, and cooed contentedly when Reggie began expertly working over her melonlike breasts with his lips. As his tongue tweaked her button-sized nipples erect, his hands began their own exploration. Her velvety skin was unbelievably smooth, especially along her inner thighs. His touch left a line of goose bumps in its wake, and just when he was in the process of circling her thick pubic bush, her hands gently pulled his head up to hers. Their lips met, and the urgency of her kisses left no doubt as to her degree of passion.

When his fingers found her love channel hot and primed, Reggie pulled her long legs apart and mounted her. He was extra careful to penetrate her slowly, for his oversized organ could just as easily cause pain as it could pleasure. Yet her kisses and grunts urged him ever forward, and soon she accepted his all.

They made love for the entire afternoon. As he expected, the Thai proved to have an insatiable sexual appetite, and he willingly did his best to satisfy her every need. Constantly whispering in his ear that she had never had so much of a man before, she seemed to like it best when he lay deep inside of her. Reggie was an expert "stickman," and was adept at establishing a steady, grinding rhythm with his hips. This tactic drove the beautiful Oriental crazy and she screamed in orgasm time after time. Reggie joined her in bliss only after he was certain that she was fulfilled. His hot seed mixed with her essence, and only then did he realize that dusk had fallen and the room had grown dark.

Their evening love session was even more ferocious than their initial coupling, and was confined mainly to the bedroom. It wasn't until midnight that Reggie was able to drift off to sleep. With his Thai lover locked tightly in his arms, his dreams were quick in coming.

He was awakened by loud, persistent pounding. His eyes popped open, and it took him a few minutes to orient himself. It was pitch-black inside the bedroom, and peering over his lover's sleeping body, he checked the time on the bedside digital clock. It was 5:37 A.M.

The knocking proved to be coming from the front door, and he rose stiffly to cross into the living room to see who in the hell had the nerve to disturb them at such an early hour. Not bothering to cover himself, he angrily disengaged the lock and yanked the door open.

Marty Stanfield had been expecting a hostile greeting, yet couldn't help but grin as he took in his stern-faced shipmate's naked figure. Struggling to keep a straight face, he cringed when Reggie's voice rose in an angry shout.

"Jesus, Stanfield! What the hell do you think you're doing? It's five thirty in the fucking morning!"

"Sorry about this, bro," Marty responded sheepishly, "but the skipper wants us back at the *Copperhead* on the double. Seems like our R and R has been cut short. Scuttlebutt says we'll be setting sail with the morning tide."

"But that can't be!" Reggie protested. "Why, we only just got back from a patrol!"

Marty Stanfield shook his head. "I hear you, Reg. But try to tell that to Captain Fuller. Now, are you coming along, or will I have to report you as A.W.O.L?"

As this new call to duty registered in Reggie's mind, his tone lightened. "I'll be there in a sec, Stanfield. Just give me some time to jump into some clothes."

Peering around the door frame to see if there was anyone else in the living room, Marty Stanfield's face lit up as he spotted a familiar black leather miniskirt tossed carelessly on the coffee table. Catching his roommate's glance, he winked and asked, "By the way, Reg, how was she?"

A look of pure ecstasy crossed Reginald Warner's face as he turned and disappeared into the bedroom to gather his personal belongings.

* * *

Captain Samuel Fuller had been at his beachside condo on Turtle Bay when he received the call sending him back to Pearl. A twenty-five-year naval veteran, Fuller took this unexpected order from COMSUBPAC in stride. It proved to be a bit more difficult for his wife, Peggy, to accept though, for lately it seemed that she never had much time alone with her husband. Yet, as a good navy spouse, she hid her true emotions with a brave smile, and helped her husband pack his few things. After filling a thermos with hot coffee, she then went out to the garage to warm up their battered Chevy Jimmy, for the drive across Oahu.

The trip went too quickly, and soon she was in the process of dropping her husband off at the entrance to Pearl's Southeast Loch. Other submariners were in the process of kissing their loved ones good-bye here, and Peggy succeeded in holding back her tears until her husband was well out of sight. She was afforded a brief glance of his present command as she turned onto North Road. Lit by a series of powerful spotlights, the USS *Copperhead* sat berthed beside a tender. Its black, cigar-shaped hull lay low in the water, and in the early morning darkness, an American flag could just be seen flapping from its elongated sail. The sub appeared lethal and mean, and Peggy issued a silent prayer as she guided the automobile through the Halawa Gate. Not knowing when she'd see her husband again, she turned onto Kamehameha Highway and prepared herself for the long, lonely drive home.

Meanwhile, Samuel Fuller crisply saluted the current officer of the deck and got a quick update on the status of the boat's complement. Satisfied with what he heard, he turned toward the open access trunk that lay just aft of the sail, and climbed down its tubular steel ladder. This put him on the sub's topmost interior deck. Proceeding forward, he walked down a narrow passageway and passed through a curtained hatchway. Before him was that portion of the vessel reserved for the ship's officers. A single brown-haired figure sat at the wardroom table, calmly sipping a mug of hot coffee. His attention was focused on a detailed bathymetric chart which was spread out before him. So absorbed was he, Fuller had to clear his throat in order to get his attention.

Startled by this unexpected sound, Lieutenant Commander Vincent Coria, the sub's executive officer, looked up and caught sight of the captain. A warm smile etched his handsome face as he greeted Fuller.

"Well, good morning, Skipper. I didn't expect you for at least another half hour."

While an alert orderly relieved the captain of his bag and handed him a mug of steaming black coffee, Fuller responded, "I guess Peg and I are old hats at this sort of thing. With her invaluable help, she had me dressed and packed in no time at all."

"That's a hell of a fine woman you've got there, sir," commented the XO.

"Why, thank you, Vinnie. From what Peg tells me, your own wife and new baby are doing just fine. We were hoping that all of you would join us at our place for dinner one night soon."

The XO grinned. "We'd enjoy that, Skipper. Though it looks like it might be a while before we're back on dry land."

"Speaking of the devil, have our orders arrived yet?" questioned the captain.

"They arrived a little over a quarter of an hour ago. The packet is on your desk."

Peering over the XO's shoulder, Samuel Fuller glanced down at the chart which his second-in-command had been studying. His practiced eye took in a portion of the Pacific located approximately five hundred nautical miles northwest of Honolulu. A distinctive range of rugged underwater mountains gave this sector a familiar appearance.

"So we're headed for the North Hawaiian Seamount Range once again," Fuller mused. "What does Barking Sands have in store for us now?"

Surprised at the captain's intuitiveness, Coria nodded. "You hit it right on the head, Skipper. That experimental underwater SOSUS grid of theirs mysteriously quit transmitting sometime Sunday evening. Since all the gear checks out on their end, the powers that be need us to check out the surrounding waters for the presence of the bad guys."

With his eyes still glued to the chart, Fuller commented, "I seriously doubt that it's the Russians, but I guess we'll be going out there to take a look no matter what I think. That damn SOSUS equipment is getting so sophisticated almost anything could have caused the glitch."

"I agree, Skipper. But that's the Navy. I just wish there was another boat close by that could have done the checking. The crew was looking forward to that two weeks of R and R that was promised them after our last patrol."

"Tell me about it," replied Fuller. "Lord knows what my wife had planned for us, but from that long look that was hung on her face when she drove me over here, it must have been something special. Peg's been bringing up the subject of retirement once again, and I'm beginning to wonder if missions such as this one are even worth a crock."

Surprised by the captain's response, Coria diverted his glance when a chubby blond-haired officer entered the wardroom from the forward hatchway. Lieutenant David Costner was their weapons officer, and had served aboard the *Copperhead* on only two previous cruises. A straight-faced, no-nonsense, twenty-six-year-old, who had a Bachelor of Science degree in physics, Costner stiffened upon viewing the captain. Yet his remarks were addressed solely to the XO.

"Sir, Petty Officer First Class Warner has just reported for duty. This gives us a full complement."

"Excellent," replied Coria, then added, "What kind of shape is Mr. Warner in, Lieutenant?"

"What do you mean, sir?" queried the young officer.

"What Lieutenant Commander Coria wants to know," the captain answered, "is if our esteemed chief sonar operator is sober or not."

Blushing, the weapons officer, who was the current officer of the deck, struggled to reply, "Mr. Warner does appear a bit ragged around the edges, sir."

"I thought as much," returned the captain, whose demeanor remained serious. "Well then, Lieutenant, make sure he hits the showers and then his bunk. I'm going to want him razor-sharp in six hours' time."

"Yes, sir!" shot back the eager lieutenant. "I'll personally see to it."

As he turned to exit through the hatchway, the XO added, "We'll be getting underway shortly, Mr. Costner. But before we move an inch out of this harbor, I want you to make certain that the crew's quarters are buttoned up tight. The last time that I walked through there it looked like a pigsty."

"Aye, aye, sir!" retorted the OOD, who only then fully pivoted and climbed through the aft hatchway.

With his departure, the atmosphere in the wardroom significantly lightened. There was a broad grin on the XO's face as he shook his head in wonder.

"So Warner's at it again," he observed. "I wonder who he was in the sack with this time?"

"Genius certainly has its quirks," returned Samuel Fuller, who was also smiling. "You know it's talented characters like our senior sonar technician who make this job that much more interesting."

"You said it, Skipper. Warner might have his social flaws, but it's always comforting to know that he's on sonar. He's the best that I've ever served with. Not only is his hearing sharp, but he's got the instincts to smell out Ivan long before his instruments pick anything up. I've seen him work and sometimes it's a bit scary."

"At least we've got him on our side," added Samuel Fuller, looking at his watch. "The tide should be running with us now, Mr. Coria. How about joining me topside and getting this patrol started?"

Folding up the bathymetric chart, the XO scooted out of the booth he had been seated in and joined Samuel Fuller in the passageway. A good three inches taller than the captain, Vincent Coria straightened his khakis and followed his commanding officer forward to the sail's access hatch.

The USS *Copperhead* was a *Sturgeon*-class nuclear attack sub. Launched in 1974, the vessel was 292 feet long and had a submerged displacement of 4,640 tons. Though far from the newest class of warship in the fleet, the *Copperhead* was a potent offensive platform, armed with the latest in fire-control systems and weaponry. The ship had also been recently fitted with the BQQ-5 sonar array, the same underwater detection system that had proven so effective in the newest *Los Angeles*-class vessels. Manned by a crew of 107, the *Copperhead* was a proud ship with a spotless service record.

The sun was just breaking the horizon as two khaki-clad figures gathered at the top of the sub's open sail. The shorter of the two individuals sported a distinguished head of pepper-and-salt hair, and could have easily passed for a corporative executive. After surveying the surrounding waters, he called out to the sailors standing fore and aft.

"Deck party, stand by to cast off lines!"

Only when Samuel Fuller was certain that the tide was running with them did he order the sailors to cast off their lines. Once this was achieved, his next order was directed into a small hand-held microphone.

"Steer right ten degrees. All ahead slow."

The order was confirmed, and the captain began the delicate task of guiding the *Copperhead* to sea without the assistance of an accompanying tug. Working closely at his side was his XO. Vincent Coria had been the sub's second-in-command for over a dozen previous patrols, and never failed to appreciate the professional manner in which Samuel Fuller ran the *Copperhead*. Well aware that their captain was one of the most competent officers in the U.S. fleet, he knew that he was fortunate to have received this assignment slot. For attack-submarine duty demanded the Navy's elite, and Coria was proud to have been selected as one of his country's best.

The dawn continued to develop and both officers were afforded a spectacular view of Honolulu and its environs as the vessel steamed out of Pearl Harbor. Above, a huge 747 airliner descended toward nearby Honolulu International Airport, its seats filled with eager tourists from the mainland. Traveling in a vastly different element, the *Copperhead*'s rounded, teardrop-style hull bit into the warm waters of the Pacific, and the keelless vessel rolled lazily in response.

Fifteen minutes later, the captain ordered the sail vacated, and both officers climbed down into the central control room. From this equipment-packed compartment, all areas of the ship could be monitored. Efficiently scanning each station, Samuel Fuller proceeded to bark out the orders that would take the submarine down.

"Mark two degrees down bubble."

"Flood forward ballast tanks."

"All ahead, half speed."

"Stern planes down three degrees."

As this last command was carried out by the planesmen, the *Copperhead* angled downward and slid into

64

the depths with a surging hiss.

The crew's mess hall was located on the deck immediately below the control room. This brightly lit compartment was decorated much like a typical American coffee shop, and featured rows of four-man tables. Elevated television monitors were interspersed throughout the mess, and currently displayed the movie, *The Karate Kid*.

Seven hours out of Pearl, the *Copperhead*'s galley staff was just finishing up lunch. Only about a third of the tables were occupied, and most of those present were sipping coffee, and either reading or watching the movie that had started an hour before.

The booth nearest to the serving line was reserved for petty officers. It was here that Reginald Warner was currently holding court. His spellbound audience was Chief of the Boat Greg Meinert.

Between bites of his hamburger and French fried onion rings, and an occasional sip on a strawberry milkshake, Reggie was giving the brawny chief a blow-by-blow description of his affair with the Thai dancer. He had just gotten to the part where his new-found love had accepted his offer to check out the soul music collection in his apartment. So far, Reggie hadn't left out a single detail, and Chief Meinert seemed totally enthralled.

"I tell you, Chief, never did that Hawaiian air smell as sweet as when we began walking up Salt Lake Boulevard to my place. We were talking away like two long lost friends, and when a bunch of G.I.'s passed by and began whistling, I realized what a pair we must have made. If I only had a picture—a nigger from north Philly and a gorgeous long-legged Far Eastern beauty in a black leather miniskirt. My buddies back home would never believe it!"

An incredulous look crossed the chief's face. "Sometimes I don't know if you're shittin' me or what, Warner. You mean to say that she agreed to go to your place just to hear your soul records?"

Reggie flashed a smile filled with white teeth. "Like I said, my man, some of us got it, and some of us haven't."

Before continuing, he picked up his milkshake, and while spooning in a mouthful of strawberry ice cream, noticed that someone was headed toward them. From the newcomer's serious expression, Reggie just knew that Marty Stanfield was the bearer of bad news.

"Excuse me, Chief, but Lieutenant Commander Coria would like to see Reggie in his quarters at once."

The chief's eyes widened. "In his quarters, you say? Well now, Mr. Love Machine, what regulations have you broken this time?"

Puzzled by this summons, Reggie looked on the bright side. "Why do you say that, Chief? Who knows? Maybe the XO's got a fat promotion for me."

"Dream on, Warner," retorted the chief, who turned back to his own lunch while his dining companion rose and exited the mess.

Reggie headed straight to the ladder that would take him up to officers' country. Passing the vacant wardroom, he stopped before the closed door that led to the quarters of the *Copperhead*'s second-in-command. He knocked three times.

"Come in!" barked a deep voice from inside.

Taking a deep breath, Reggie entered. Vincent Coria had been sitting at his cramped wall-mounted desk working on a mound of paperwork. He looked up to identify his visitor.

"Good afternoon, Mr. Warner. Have a seat. I'll be right with you."

While the XO completed the requisition form he'd been working on, Reggie sat down on the room's only other chair, a small folding stool that was fondly known as the hot seat. A full minute passed before Coria finished his scribbling, put down his pen, and turned toward his guest.

"Well, Mr. Warner, how goes it?"

Relieved to see a pleasant smile on the XO's face, Reggie answered alertly, "Fine, sir."

Massaging his cramped writing hand, Coria said, "I understand you were a bit hung over when we pulled you on board this morning. Are those cobwebs in your head cleared out yet?"

"Most certainly, sir," shot back the completely sobered senior sonar technician.

"Good," returned Coria. "Because we're going to need a one hundred per cent effort on your part in order to successfully complete our current mission."

Turning back to his desk, the XO rummaged through the stack of paperwork and removed a folded bathymetric chart which he handed to Reggie.

"This chart is of the North Hawaiian Seamount Range, which is our immediate goal. Three months ago, we participated in an experiment that sent us into

67

this very same sector."

"I remember, sir," interjected Reggie. "We were testing out a new SOSUS grid for the wizards back at Barking Sands."

The XO nodded. "Precisely. At that time, the *Copperhead* was permanently fitted out with a special remote-control device, designed to trigger a prepositioned sonic buoy that had been anchored to the sea floor. It was hoped that such a system would give our subs the ability to safely transit waters that were previously too dangerous to travel while submerged, such as leaving harbors, patrolling the relatively shallow continental shelf zone, and penetrating friendly mine fields.

"Our patrol proved that this new grid indeed showed promise. Yet less than a week ago, the system unexplainably went down. Since the equipment back at Barking Sands doesn't seem to be at fault, Command is depending upon us to find the culprit."

"Could the Soviets be responsible?" Reggie queried anxiously.

The XO shrugged his shoulders. "Right now, your guess is as good as mine. But if we do find Ivan poking his nose where it doesn't belong, I'm depending upon you to smell him out long before he gets wind of our presence.

"You'll also be attempting to manually trigger that remote-control device. So dig into that console and make absolutely certain it's still operational."

"Will do, sir," replied Reggie, handing the chart back to Vincent Coria. "When will we be within the grid's range?"

The XO's glance went to the digital clock mounted

above his desk. "We estimate arrival at the activation point in another two and a half hours. That should give you plenty of time to make certain that the system is charged and ready to go."

"You can count on me," pledged Reggie boldly.

Certain that he could, Coria reached over to pick up his pen. "Now, I'd better get back to this confounded paperwork. I surely never dreamed that attack-sub duty would turn me into a damn pencil pusher, but just look at this mess!"

Aware that his audience was now over, Reggie stood and excused himself. A new surge of confidence guided his steps as he passed the still-vacant wardroom and headed forward to that portion of the *Copperhead* that he called home—the sonar room.

Captain Samuel Fuller had been in the maneuvering compartment, discussing the current state of their nuclear reactor with Master Chief Dennis Kerkhoff when the call arrived from the ODD informing him that they had reached the experimental SOSUS grid's activation range. Anxious to get on with the mission that had prematurely taken them away from family and friends, the captain used the intercom to inform the OOD that he would be stopping off at the sonar room before returning to join him in the central attack center. With this, Fuller left the maneuvering compartment and headed forward.

The sonar station was located amidships, in its own soundproof cubicle set snug against the sub's pressure hull. This was a portion of the ship that Fuller seldom visited—especially since Petty Officer Warner had joined them. Though the man certainly had a love for booze and women, his expertise as a sonar technician could not be questioned. Fuller had long ago learned to trust Warner's instincts explictly, giving him free rein whenever possible. One of their unwritten rules was that Warner would be allowed to run his station as he best saw fit, and the *Copperhead*'s officers had learned to respect his turf, often completely ignoring the sonar room during routine inspections.

As he entered the room's cork-lined doorway, the captain hastily scanned the cramped chamber. Three junior technicians currently sat before the keyboards of their tinted CRT consoles. A thick cork partition separated the seamen from their superior's workspace. Taking in the assortment of speakers and tape recorders that were mounted on the bulkhead, Fuller carefully scooted his way past the seated technicians and rounded the partition. Here, seated with his back toward him, was Reginald Warner. A pair of headphones was clamped over the black petty officer's ears, and the captain took a moment to further study the cubicle before announcing his arrival.

He visualized the series of highly sensitive twelve-inch microphones that were mounted on the sub's bow and sides. These hydrophones were part of their passive sonar system, and were utilized to listen for the advance of any object with a noise signature of its own. Such were the nature of the sounds that Reginald Warner was currently monitoring. Because the ocean itself produced all sorts of ambient sounds, it was Warner's responsibility to filter out the whale cries and

70

shrimp chatter, and concentrate on the distinctive racket of man-made machinery.

The air smelled of stale smoke and machine oil, and Fuller noticed a full-length poster showing the city of Philadelphia hung on the wall behind him. Remembering that this was Warner's hometown, the captain turned his attention back to the senior technician, who was bent intently over his keyboard now. Sensing that something was wrong, Fuller revealed his presence by loudly clearing his throat.

"Good afternoon, Mr. Warner. What have you got out there?"

Hardly affected by the captain's surprise appearance, Reggie's voice was tight with concern. "Afternoon, captain. It looks like you timed your visit perfectly, because if I'm not mistaken, we might have just caught Ivan napping out there.

"Take a listen for yourself. We were in the process of clearing our baffles when I noticed a faint electronic shadow on my screen. Just seconds ago, I picked up this submerged contact, at bearing two-two-zero."

Handing the captain a set of auxiliary headphones, Reggie proceeded to carefully turn up the volume gain. Behind him, Samuel Fuller listened as a loud hissing sound streamed into his eardrums. Closing his eyes, he concentrated on this noise, and soon picked out a distant pulsating throb that was somehow strangely familiar. A second later, he identified it as the type of sound a saltwater pump would make as it circulated seawater around a nuclear reactor's steam condenser.

"Jesus, Warner, have you notified control of this yet?"

71

"No, sir," Reggie shot back. "You're hearing it only seconds after I initially picked it up."

Snapping into action, Fuller picked up the intercom. "Sonar to control. We have an unidentified submerged contact, bearing two-two-zero, range twenty thousand yards."

A raspy nasal voice responded, "Control to sonar. Our repeater shows nothing on that bearing. Are you certain that it's a solid contact?"

Not believing what he was hearing, Fuller's voice rose. "Sonar to control. Of course, we're positive! Let me speak to the OOD."

After the briefest of pauses, a deep bass voice responded, "Control to sonar, this is the XO. We've just picked up a faint streak on that bearing. Captain, is that you down there?"

"That's positive," replied Fuller angrily. "Mr. Coria, have the quartermaster sound general quarters. I'm on my way to join you in the attack center a.s.a.p."

Hurriedly exiting the sonar room, the captain darted down the passageway just as the intercom sounded throughout the vessel, sending the crew racing to their battle stations. Several seamen sprinted past him carrying their white asbestos fire suits, and it took him less than a minute to reach the control room, which he breathlessly entered. Quickly positioning himself beside his XO, Fuller wasted no time taking control.

"Control to sonar, prepare to lock on weapons control. Do you have a signature on that submerged contact yet?"

Reginald Warner's response was clear and firm. "Sonar to control. Have locked on weapons. Big Brother shows a forty-seven per cent probability that we're facing a Soviet *Viktor*-class vessel."

With this disclosure, Fuller's face reddened and he turned to speak to Vincent Coria. "So the Russians have been down here all along. No wonder our SOSUS grid is down. God knows what those nosy bastards have done to it. But now we've got a chance to teach them a lesson. Let's load a Mark 48 just for safety's sake, and have weapons get a lock on sonar."

Surprised that the captain wanted to actually ready a torpedo, Coria was in the process of conveying this request to Lieutenant Costner when the line from sonar once again activated. This time, Reginald Warner's voice was frantic.

"They've tagged us, control! Picking up engine noise and increased propeller revolutions."

Not about to let the Russians get away so easily, the captain was quick to react. "The very least that we can do is give them a decent scare. Mr. Coria, let's crowd them. All ahead half!"

As the *Copperhead* picked up speed, so did the vessel that had been lurking in their baffles. In the sonar room, this mysterious contact expressed itself in a surging roar of grinding machinery. Having gathered up a head of steam quicker than Reginald Warner had anticipated, the bogey raced toward the deep, open seas lying to the northwest. Hardly believing its velocity, he watched the blip race across his screen at an amazing rate. Reggie calculated this speed to be well over forty-five knots, thus proving that the contact was not a Soviet *Viktor*, but one of their newer *Akula* or *Alfa*-class vessels. Well aware that if this was the case, the fourteen-year-old *Copperhead* would never be able to catch them, Reggie prepared to sit back and monitor Ivan's escape. Just then, the intercom activated.

"Con to sonar. Mr. Warner, this is the captain. I want you to go on active and hit those bastards with everything we've got!"

"Sonar to control. Aye, aye, sir. Switching to manual active override."

Efficiently attacking his keyboard, Reggie's gut tightened as a powerful surge of high-pitched sound shot from their bow and streamed out toward the fleeing Soviets. Known as a sonar lashing, this surge would be picked up in the Russian sonar crew's headphones as an ear-splitting, deafening blast. For if the *Copperhead* couldn't catch up with them, this was Captain Fuller's way of saying, "Until next time, Comrade!"

Having been lashed himself, Reggie knew that it was far from a pleasant experience. Since it was clearly a belligerent tactic, he wondered what had prompted the captain to go to such an extreme. Though the Soviets were in the vicinity of the experimental SOSUS array, the *Copperhead* hadn't really caught them tampering with the system. Assuming that his skipper had his reasons, the chief sonar technician listened as the sphere of energized sound bounced off the fleeing bogey with a distinctive ping. Their fire-control system would have a precise range and bearing now, yet Reggie doubted that even one of their Mark 48 torpedoes could catch the speeding enemy at this point. Resigned to being merely an observer, he sat back and listened as the Russian sub continued to gather speed and eventually fade off altogether in the distance.

Later that evening, well after the last dinner had been served, the control room watch found Lieutenant David Costner as the current Officer of the Deck. Still relatively new to attack-sub duty, the chubby blond-haired Missouri native was extra careful not to let a single detail of the *Copperhead*'s operational status get by him.

Standing behind the two seated planesmen, Costner eyed the depth gauge, then double-checked their course and bearing. Their patrol route was leading them in an elongated circle around the North Hawaiian Seamount Range as their wire-guided, remotely operated vehicle attempted to get some decent video tape of where the SOSUS grid had malfunctioned. Once this was in their possession, scuttlebutt had it that their course would then turn back to Pearl, and they'd be able to resume their disrupted leave.

It had been an exciting afternoon. This was the weapons officer's first real contact with the Soviets. It was also the first time that he had ever been ordered to actually load a torpedo offensively.

After the Soviet vessel had made good their escape with an incredible burst of speed, Samuel Fuller had called the officers together for a briefing in the ward-room. Their usually reserved captain was noticeably tense, and he castigated them for several minor proce-dural infractions which the crew had been guilty of during the alert. Later, Fuller had not been at his usual spot in the wardroom for dinner, and their table con-

75

versation had been limited to a light, nervous banter.

Costner was almost certain that he knew what was on his fellow officers' minds — which they were afraid to put into words. For surely the captain had over-reacted when they initially tagged the Soviet vessel. The sonar lashing was one thing: to actually load a torpedo was another altogether!

Still having trouble figuring out what had provoked their captain so, Costner turned away from the planes-men and walked over to the navigation station. Seated here sipping a mug of coffee, was the stout figure of Chief Petty Officer Greg Meinert. Costner had a genu-ine liking for this grizzled veteran, and had opened up to him on several previous occasions when he had sought another's opinion. Meinert was particularly versed in attack-sub lore, for he had served on such vessels exclusively for over fifteen years.

Careful to keep his tone low, the *Copperhead*'s cur-rent OOD nodded in greeting. "How's the coffee, Chief?"

Meinert made a sour expression. "If mud has a taste, I'd imagine that it's something like this. Still, it's drink-able."

Grinning nervously in response, Costner bent over the chart table, absent-mindedly scanning its contents. "How did the men take to this afternoon's excitement?"

Meinert grunted. "At least we know that some of them are still alive. A little action now and then helps to sharpen the edge."

"I must admit that my bunch did an excellent job down in the torpedo room," offered Costner. "What do you make of that order to load a Mark 48, and then to hit the Soviets with a sonar lashing?"

Aware now of what the young officer was getting at, Meinert caught his glance directly. "I'll make odds that you feel that the captain was overreacting."

Holding his ground, Costner retorted. "You don't really think that the Soviets did anything to provoke such an extreme reaction, do you, Chief?"

Meinert shook his head disgustedly. "Just being in the same water with the Russkies is provoking, Lieutenant. Though I haven't been on submarines as long as our skipper, I've seen enough in my decade and a half to back him all the way. We can all rest easier tonight knowing that somewhere in the North Pacific, Ivan is hightailing it home with a new respect for Uncle Sam in his memory banks."

"But what about the upcoming peace summit?" countered Costner. "Perhaps the Soviets are really serious about nuclear disarmament this time around?"

"The Russkies serious about peace with America? Oh, come now, Lieutenant! Marxist theory makes their opinion of us very clear. The Kremlin is not about to rest until the entire Western Bloc is in their deceitful grasp. Any compromise in the meantime is purely in their interest only. Just ask any senior Naval officer and I'll bet my pension that he'll tell you the same thing. As far as I'm concerned, the only good Red is a dead one!"

Impressed by the forcefulness of the chief's convictions, Costner reasoned aloud, "Then I guess that's the same school of thought that our skipper subscribes to."

The chief took a sip of coffee before responding.

"Though I'm certainly in no position to speak for Captain Fuller, believe me when I tell you that he has every reason to distrust the Russkies like he does. Not only has he gone eyeball to eyeball with them for the last twenty-five years, but he lost an older brother to them as well."

"No kidding, Chief. When did that come down?"

Meinert's voice dropped to a bare whisper. "It was two years ago. The way I hear it, Fuller's brother was a destroyer captain, and was in the midst of Fleet exercises in the Sea of Japan, when a Russkie *Viktor* snagged his ship's towed sonar array. The cable snapped, and the captain was cleanly decapitated in the resulting whiplash.

"At first, Command thought that it was all a mere unfortunate accident. But then a sonar tape surfaced, indicating that Ivan had been deliberately stalking the destroyer for a good quarter of an hour beforehand. Those bastards knew all along that we had an array in the water, yet they moved in to play chicken regardless of the risks involved. When Washington protested, the Soviets pleaded that their sub captain was lost and had no idea of his precarious position — even though he was almost up our destroyer's fantail. Somehow the Department of the Navy bought that load of crap, and Ivan got off the hook without even a slap on the hand. So as you can see, Lieutenant, it's going to take much more than a sham treaty to get Samuel Fuller to trust the Soviets."

Absorbing each detail of this startling tale, Costner was afforded a rare glimpse at a side of his present commanding officer that he never knew existed. Now he understood why the captain had taken the afternoon's encounter so seriously.

"Thanks for that, Chief. I guess that story tells it all."

Meinert shook his head. "I'm afraid it ain't that simple, Lieutenant. When you've got a couple of days free, I'll sit down and tell you a shitload of other horror stories that both me and the skipper somehow lived through. We've encountered Ivan in almost every corner of this planet, and each time it was far from pleasant. No, sir, as far as I'm concerned, the only good Red is a dead one!"

With these harsh words echoing in his mind, the OOD solemnly excused himself to get back to his duty. Turning his glance back to the helm to recheck their depth, speed, and course, the weapons officer found his previously well-ordered thoughts turned abruptly upside down. Things were not always as they seemed, and this was especially the case when dealing with U.S. Navy personnel.

CHAPTER FOUR

The Siberian air was frigid, the wind blowing in cold northern gusts. A storm front had passed sometime during the night, leaving in its wake several centimeters of freshly fallen snow. Thickly mantled in white, the forest of Kamchatka firs swayed in unison with the icy breeze.

A lone fur-coated figure walked briskly through the wood and momentarily halted when a raven cried out nearby. For Admiral Leonid Silka, who had grown up in nearby Chabarovsk, autumn in the Soviet Far East would always be an eagerly anticipated event. This season, and the surrounding forest, served as a link to a past that seemed to have occurred in another lifetime. Happy to see that the Arctic magic still existed, the seventy-two-year-old naval officer glanced up at the canopy of solid branches which crowned the forest. He had to look almost directly overhead in order to view a deep blue patch of cloudless morning sky. For a second, a huge eagle was visible, effortlessly soaring the gusting thermals. Wondering if this golden-feathered bird of prey had spotted him as yet, Silka marveled at the simplicity of nature's chain of survival. In nature, as in the military, only the strong prevailed. In this way, the remaining species reproduced and constantly evolved, the new generations comprising only the hardiest individuals.

A muffled, chopping roar in the distance broke the admiral's train of thought. Snapped back to thoughts of the present, Leonid identified this familiar racket as a circling helicopter. Suddenly aware of the time, he looked at his Swiss wristwatch and knew that it was time to move on.

His pace was swift, his step sure as he continued on in the direction that he had been heading. Having begun his hike over an hour ago, he was well accustomed to the frigid temperature, yet was looking forward to enjoying a hot brandy next to the blazing fireplace. In any case, the helicopter's presence surely indicated that his esteemed guest had arrived.

As supreme commander of the Soviet Pacific Fleet, Leonid Silka had a variety of privileges open to him. Never one to take advantage of his hard-earned position, one of his few pleasures in life was the sturdy wooden dacha that he was now approaching. Constructed of local timber, it was situated in the midst of a wilderness reserve. The nearest village was Milka, over twenty-three kilometers distant, with the naval base at Petropavlovsk another fifty kilometers away. Thus he could rest in this primeval, isolated world of his own, and merely jump in a chopper and return to his duty in less than an hour's time.

As he emerged from the forest, Leonid looked past a fleeing fox and set his glance on a thin column of smoke rising from his dacha's stone chimney. His beloved Katrina was surely in the midst of preparing their lunch, and he sighed contentedly, knowing that all the comforts of home awaited him on the far side of the snow-covered plain that lay before him.

He was halfway across this plain, when he spotted the distinctive fuselage of a Mil Mi-14 helicopter parked behind the cabin's far wall. Looking like some extinct prehistoric beast, the monstrous gray-skinned vehicle seemed strangely out of place here. Taking in its chin-mounted radome, five massive rotors, and the bright red star that was embossed near its tail, Leonid's thoughts instantly focused themselves. A new urgency guided his steps, and with the icy snow crunching beneath his boots, he wasted no time in closing the remaining distance between him and his dacha.

Waiting for him immediately in front of the cabin's main entryway was a tall, thin individual dressed in a stylishly cut black woolen greatcoat. Even though he had only met this man on one previous occasion, the Admiral could never forget his piercing dark gaze and movie-star good looks. Nearly half Leonid's age, Stanislaus Angara had requested this meeting less than twenty-four hours ago. One learned to take the words of their premier's chief of staff seriously, and the admiral had invited Angara to his humble dacha on the Kamchatka peninsula.

Considering that the young bureaucrat had traveled the entire night to get here from Moscow, Leonid supposed that he was acting as the premier's proxy. Anxious to know what this mission entailed, the admiral hastened to greet him.

"Good morning, Comrade Angara! Welcome to Kamchatka."

The young bureaucrat rubbed his gloved hands

together and answered, "Why, thank you, Admiral. This is my first visit to this portion of the Motherland, and I must admit that I am greatly impressed."

The two men hugged each other warmly, and Leonid stood at his guest's side, following Angara's gaze into the surrounding tree line. "It's indeed beautiful, isn't it?"

"I'll say," answered Angara. "For the past six months I've seen nothing but the cold gray walls of the Kremlin. My father used to say that a Russian is only half a man when separated from the earth, and now I know just what he meant."

A frigid northern gust sent a wall of blowing snow tumbling across the open field before them, and Leonid passionately observed, "Your father was a wise man, Comrade Angara. While you are here, you are free to make this humble abode your home. Stay as long as you wish. There's an extra bedroom and bath, and I believe you'll find the food satisfying — simple, yet hearty."

"The offer is very tempting, Admiral, but I'm afraid affairs of state cause me to reluctantly decline your gracious invitation. With the upcoming summit and all, there just don't seem to be enough hours in the day."

Noting the dark lines of exhaustion beneath his guest's eyes, Leonid suddenly felt sorry for the bureaucrat. "Well, the offer remains open if you change your mind. Now, how about joining me around the fireplace for a warm drink and a bite of lunch? I don't know about you, but I'm starving!"

Ten minutes later, both men were seated around the blazing hearth, sipping hot brandy toddies and nib-

83

bling on an assortment of goodies prepared earlier by Leonid Silka's wife. The admiral was consuming a herring sandwich — made with rye bread, sour cream, and chopped onion — while Stanislaus Angara worked on a finger-sandwich filled with cream cheese and black caviar. The fire snapped and crackled before them, and outside, the gusting wind could be heard howling unmercifully. Yet all was warm and cozy inside the expensively furnished dacha.

After exchanging the usual small talk, the young bureaucrat leaned forward in his high-back leather chair, and caught his host's steady glance. "Your hospitality is most appreciated, Admiral. But it's time for me to get to the matter that has called me these thousands of kilometers from the capital. I believe you have an elementary understanding of the treaty that we'll soon be signing with the United States."

"If you're referring to the nuclear arms accord, I most certainly do," offered Leonid solemnly. "I was recently given a draft of the treaty to study, and returned it along with my comments to Moscow."

Reaching into the briefcase that lay beside his chair, Stanislaus Angara removed a file-folder. "I happen to have a copy of that report right here, Admiral. If I'm not mistaken, in this same report, you make a strong case for abandoning the negotiations at once, before the treaty — which you call a useless, dangerous document — is signed and takes effect."

Leonid's face flushed as he put down his plate. "How did you get your hands on that report?" he demanded. "It was supposed to be highly classified, and read only by select members of the Politboro!"

Stanislaus Angara calmly shook his head. "Easy,

Admiral. You forget that I hold a position of utmost sensitivity. Because of the great demands of government, the premier relies upon me as an extension of himself. One man could never get through the workload with which he is burdened. Why, just reading the various reports and documents that find their way to the premier's desk would be a full-time job in itself!

"Now, I have been sent here at Premier Skuratov's direct request in an attempt to reply to your comments. For you see, your so-called heretical views are shared by more members of the government than you realize.

"The entire population of the planet is looking to the upcoming summit with the greatest of expectations. Even the headlines of *Pravda* herald it as the beginning of the end of the nuclear nightmare that has gripped the earth for the last four decades. Having taken the initiative in these discussions, the Motherland stands to gain the most once the treaty is signed. For then the entire world will know of our brotherly, peaceful intentions."

"But it's utter madness to even think of destroying our entire nuclear arsenal!" interjected Leonid. "We will be left practically defenseless!"

A sly gleam sparkled in the young bureaucrat's eyes. "Who said anything about destroying our entire nuclear arsenal, Comrade Admiral? Though the foolish Americans might be naive enough to do so, you can be assured that we will find a way to keep a vast number of warheads in secret, protective reserve. The *Rodina* has lost too many of its citizens to foreign invasions throughout history, and never again will we be put in a position of vulnerability.

"Why, the propaganda possibilities alone make the signing of this treaty a must! So we will implement it with the entire planet watching, and then sit back as the capitalist system continues to crumble. And once it inevitably collapses, the great theories of Marx and Lenin will be there to fill the void and calm the clamor, and our founder's dreams will at long last be realized. Just think of it, Admiral, the whole world united under Communism! And all for the cost of signing a ridiculous treaty!"

Calmed by what he was hearing, Leonid sat back and grinned. "I apologize for my arrogance, Comrade Angara. I didn't realize how close you were to the premier. Also, your astounding revelation does much to ease my fears. For a while there, I honestly thought that we were actually seriously considering destroying our entire nuclear deterrent, and I shuddered to think of the dangerous precedent that would be set by such a foolish move. Now, knowing that such a thing will never take place, I can rest more easily."

"I believe we can all rest easily once one other important element of your brilliant report is attended to," added the young bureaucrat.

"And what is that?" Leonid asked breathlessly.

Stanislaus Angara paused to take a long sip of his drink. "You stated that one of your greatest fears is that the Imperialists will take advantage of the lessening of tensions that have indeed preceded the treaty's signing, and will utilize this opportunity to launch a crippling nuclear attack against the Motherland. The premier agrees that such a possibility must be considered, and he has instructed me to personally ascertain what precautionary moves you have in mind to counter this threat."

A satisfied grin etched the corners of the admiral's mouth. "And to think that I actually had doubts as to our leader's competency. Why, I'd be happy to share my strategy with you, Comrade. But first, what do you say to a refill?"

With his last sip, the young bureaucrat had drained his mug. The hot brandy toddy, with just a hint of rich butter and cinnamon, was extremely tasty. Though not really a drinking man, Stanislaus Angara enjoyed the toddy's soothing warmth, and he readily agreed to his host's suggestion. The admiral himself rose to prepare their drinks, and minutes later, both men were sitting around the blazing fire with brimming mugs.

"Now, as to my tactics," continued Leonid firmly. "It is my belief that only one element of America's strategic triad gives us real concern—this being their Trident ballistic-missile submarines. Running silently submerged at their patrol stations, these vessels can strike the Motherland a crippling surprise blow. To effectively counter this ever present threat, I suggest immediately deploying our Navy's superb anti-submarine warfare units.

"As always, our first level of defense will be our attack subs. Designed specifically to hunt down and destroy other submarines, the attack vessels must be sent to seek out the Tridents as they reach their patrol stations. Then, if the Americans show the least hint of ascending to launch their lethal load of warheads, our boats must have the authority to sink the Imperialists before the first missile leaves its magazine."

"Are such American patrol stations known to us?"

countered Stanislaus. "I was under the impression that their Tridents currently sailed the seas invulnerable to detection."

"That is what we'd like the American navy to think!" returned Leonid. "And for a while, the Tridents were indeed undetectable. Yet, because of brilliant state-of-the-art advances by our scientists and engineers, our ASW capabilities have grown enormously. And today, not even their Tridents can escape us for long. Yet please remember that it will take time to prepare our attack subs for such a mission, and the summit is rapidly approaching."

Nodding his awareness of this fact, Stanislaus Angara absorbed the veteran naval officer's remarks. With his stare centered on the crackling embers, he found himself wishing that he could go ahead and personally authorize the release of the attack subs. But he could not do so without a direct order from the premier. Certain that Skuratov would give the admiral the go-ahead to begin tailing the Yankee Tridents, he looked at his wristwatch, and calculated that if he got going at once, he could be entering the gates of the Kremlin in less than twelve hours' time.

Approximately 2,400 miles to the southwest of Admiral Leonid Silka's wilderness dacha, a drama of a vastly different sort was unfolding. This one was taking place inside the gilded confines of Beijing's Celestial Opera House. Here, a standing-room-only crowd watched as the curtains of the central stage swung open to reveal a setting representative of the west side of New York City. There was the distinctive sound of snapping fingers, and as the music rose in volume, the gangs known as the Jets and the Sharks gathered before the various tenements and challenged each other to a rumble. And thus opened the first scene of Jerome Robbins' *West Side Story*.

Seated in a private box was a distinguished group of China's top leaders. Among them was the country's new Premier, Lin Shau-ping. This afternoon's matinee was an especially joyous one for the smiling leader of the world's most populous country. Not only was he watching a live performance of his favorite Broadway show, but this was also his forty-fifth birthday. In fact, the show had been brought to China expressly to celebrate this occasion, compliments of the United States government.

This unique gift genuinely thrilled Lin, and this was the third time this week that he would be watching the musical drama unfold. Particularly aware of the premier's joy was an attractive young Chinese woman seated in the back row of the three-tiered official box. Mei-li was a member of CITS, the China International Travel Service, and she was responsible for making the American cast and crew as comfortable as possible during their stay.

Tonight would be the last performance in Beijing, and Mei-li found it hard to believe that an entire week had gone by already. So far, except for an outbreak of influenza, which had played havoc with the cast, all had proceeded smoothly. The American actors were well behaved and extremely talented. Their versatility was displayed in the manner in which various members of the cast were able to take over for the leads when the flu had struck. Known as understudies, these actors and actresses were just as competent as the stars whom they replaced.

Scanning the stage, Mei-li saw the role of Bernardo, the Puerto Rican gang leader of the Sharks, was currently being played by such an understudy. A warm smile graced her lips as she watched Justin Pollock gracefully leap across the stage, with his trusty gang members behind him. The small, dark-haired, wiry actor was doing a most adequate job in this important role, and Mei-li was proud to know him. As the only member of the cast who could speak fluent Chinese, Pollock served as a convenient in-house translator, whom Mei-li depended on to properly communicate with his colleagues.

Mei-li had been privileged to attend each of the seven performances. She had already seen Pollock play the roles of Riff, the leader of the opposing gang, the Jets, and Tony, the all-important romantic lead, whose tragic love affair with Maria brought tears to Mei-li's eyes night after night. In each instance, Justin Pollock was most convincing, dancing and singing his way into the audience's hearts.

As she watched the Jets launch into the musical number extolling the particular virtues of their gang, Mei-li knew that she was very fortunate to be a part of this incredible cultural exchange. This had been the first time that such a modern play had been allowed into China.

It was in college that Lin Shau-ping first heard the soundtrack recording of *West Side Story* on a visiting foreign student's phonograph. It was by reading the liner notes in the album that he learned the story, and Lin was immediately fascinated. It was only when he attained high government office that he was able to get a video tape of the film version of the play from the American embassy. He watched the tape time after time, and was said to have developed a particular fondness for the American actress Natalie Wood, who played the role of Maria. Lin had even gone so far as to invite the actress to be his guest in China, and when he learned that she had died in a tragic boating accident, he took the news quite badly. He never dreamed of actually being able to see the play performed live, and when the U.S. ambassador arrived at his residence to personally convey America's willingness to bring the show to Beijing, he was ecstatic.

The local press had had a field day when the official announcement of the play's arrival was released to the public. The visit of a foreign theatrical troupe was big news in culturally starved Beijing, and the reporters did their best to find out what *West Side Story* was all about. Unbelievably, the distinctive, red-covered jacket of the movie soundtrack suddenly showed up at local stores, attractively priced and readily available for purchase. Beijing's young professionals swarmed to buy the album that was so beloved by their popular, dynamic new leader, and soon the tragic exploits of the Sharks and the Jets were the topic of many a spirited discussion.

Thus, by the time the production company arrived in Beijing, there already existed an audience who was familiar with *West Side Story*'s delightful music and clever lyrics. On the night of its gala première, the local critics were unanimous in their raves. Even the government's propagandists got into the act. For the musical's setting and theme played right into their hands. Under the leadership of Lin Shau-ping, America was painted as a benevolent ally of the People's Republic. As the world's high-tech leader, the U.S. was readily exporting advanced technology, which China desperately needed to take its proper place as a world superpower. Yet, as the play so graphically demonstrated, America was far from the democratic utopia it was rumored to be. Poverty, violence, and racial tensions ran rampant, and there was certainly much room for social improvement even within the materially successful confines of the bastion of capitalism.

Fortunately, the Americans took such criticism all in stride, and offered to move the show to Canton, once the seven Beijing performances were completed. Since this would allow audiences living in Southern China the opportunity to see the play, permission was gladly given, and the production company would be leaving for the south in two more days. At the request of Lin Shau-ping himself, Mei-li would be accompanying the cast to make certain that all continued to go smoothly.

As a native of one of China's southern provinces, Mei-li was excited by the idea of bringing such a unique event to the people of Canton. Certain that the cast would be warmly received there, she sat forward when the stirring strains of the twenty-five-piece orchestra signaled the beginning of one of her favorite pieces. "America" was the name of the song, and featured the Puerto Ricans, who both stressed the virtues of life in their new country, and poked fun at it at the very same time. This spirited number was over too quickly, to be replaced by a scene of a much more somber nature.

While the star-crossed lovers, Tony and Maria, sang the haunting melodies of "Tonight," Mei-li temporarily diverted her gaze from the stage to scan the members of the well-dressed group who sat spellbound in her box. Seated two rows in front of her, she took in the slim figure of their premier, whose eyes were opened wide in wonder. Beside Lin Shau-ping was a baldheaded, impeccably dressed gentleman, whom Mei-li knew was the troupe's U.S. State Department representative. His name was Ty Stadler, and he seemed delighted that his government's gift was so appreciated. She would be meeting with Mr. Stadler later that afternoon to discuss the company's travel plans.

Their first performance in Canton wasn't scheduled for five more days, and this would hopefully give the cast time to both rest and see a bit of the local countryside. They had seen practically nothing of Beijing, and if the weather cooperated, Mei-li planned to lead a group of them to the Great Wall tomorrow morning. With this hope in mind, she returned her gaze to the stage as the members of the Jets began the hilarious number "Gee, Officer Krupke!" It wasn't long before she was laughing uproariously, along with the rest of the audience, as the American gang amusingly expressed their feelings about the manner in which their country has treated them.

Twenty-four hours later, Mei-li was escorting seven

members of the cast to the mountain pass at Ba Da Ling. Some sixty kilometers from Beijing, the pass held a restored portion of the Great Wall, which was greatly favored by the tourists because of its relative closeness to the capital.

The weather had been most cooperative, and the dawn broke clear and cool. Because of the early hour of their departure, a good portion of the troupe decided to sleep in. Yet what her group lacked in numbers, they more than made up in enthusiasm. Intensely interested in each detail of Chinese history that Mei-li proceeded to share with them, the Americans were eager to leave their minivan and climb to the wall's top tower.

Though she was proficient in English, Mei-li was thankful that Justin Pollock was one of the seven sightseers who accompanied her. Having him along allowed Mei-li to often go into greater detail than her limited English vocabulary normally allowed. Always close at her side, Pollock was quick to help out when the proper descriptive word escaped her.

They were amongst the first tourists to arrive at the wall, which would soon be swarming with thousands of curious visitors. Taking advantage of the still-uncrowded trails, they wasted no time in ascending the footpath that led to the first of the accessible towers. She noted the collective look of wonder that etched her group's face as they finally reached the first scenic outlook. From this spot, on top of the wall itself, they were afforded a magnificent view of the surrounding countryside.

The sun was rising quickly in the clear blue heavens, and the air temperature was already rising. Before them was an immense ridge filled with thick green shrubbery, and beyond, a succession of rolling mountains. The wall continued well into this wild-looking range of hills, and Mei-li began a brief historical narrative.

"The first portions of the Great Wall were built in the fifth century B.C. to protect the locals from barbarian invaders from the north. It wasn't until 221 B.C. that the various sections of the wall were unified into a stretch approximately 3,700 miles long. It is recorded that over 300,000 laborers worked on this project, which took over a decade to complete.

"This section of the wall that we are currently standing upon has an interior formed from pounded earth, with an inlaid stone facing to protect it from erosion. The roadway extends the entire length of the wall and was built wide enough to allow a brace of five horses to gallop between the towers. It was used to efficiently convey troops, arms, and food to the various northern frontier outposts.

"Now, if you'd like, you're free to begin any individual excursions that you may have in mind. Please note that we'll be meeting at the bus an hour from now. This will give us time to continue on to the Ming Tombs. I'll be available to answer any questions that you might have, but for the next sixty minutes, you're on your own."

The majority of the group immediately took off for the central battlement, which crowned the summit of an adjoining hill. Mei-li was pleasantly surprised to find that Justin Pollock was the only one of the Americans to remain behind. Dressed in blue jeans, a denim jacket, and a cowboy hat, the handsome actor leaned over the wall's edge and peered out to study the wall as it snaked over the tops of the nearby mountains.

"It's truly magnificent!" observed the green-eyed understudy. "Now I understand why it's been classified as one of the wonders of the ancient world. Do you know that this wall was the only man-made object on earth that was visible from the moon?"

Nodding that she did, Mei-li walked over to stand at his side. "Each time that I come here, I can't help but find myself awe-struck. Sometimes I close my eyes and can just picture the Chinese defenders as they bravely faced the swarming barbarian hordes."

"I know what you mean," replied Justin Pollock. "For as long as monuments such as this remain, the past can be re-created by merely applying one's imagination. Back home in Manhattan I try my best to picture what New York was like when the first European explorers arrived there, four centuries ago. The only trouble is that the area is so built up now, there's not much left to remind you of what it was really like back then."

"What's it like living in such a place?" Mei-li asked.

Justin answered while scanning the surrounding countryside. "Visualize hundreds of chrome-and-glass skyscrapers extending high into the heavens, with just enough room inbetween them to hold millions of scurrying pedestrians and thousands of honking taxicabs, and you can pretty well picture what life is like there. It's a vibrant, crowded, colorful city, which bakes you in the summer and freezes your bones in the winter. Name your heart's desire and it's available there twenty-four hours a day, whether it be food, dress, or cultural pursuits. It also serves as the financial capital of the world, and when Wall Street speaks, the entire planet listens. But there are few places such as this, where one can really grasp a sense of history."

"China is an excellent place for such a thing," observed Mei-li. "Of course, our history goes back many hundreds of centuries. When Western man was just crawling from his caves, we were already living in great cities, practicing medicine and organizing our philosophy into poetry."

"Your cultural heritage is indeed a rich one," reflected Pollock. "My own mother was Chinese, and tried hard to give me a sense of her country's greatness."

Mei-li seemed surprised by this revelation. "I didn't realize that you had Chinese blood, Justin. Was it your mother who taught you to speak our language so expertly?"

"Yes, it was. I was thus lucky to learn Chinese as a child, when languages are easiest to master."

Looking at the actor with new eyes, Mei-li cautiously probed. "May I ask the name of the town of your mother's birth?"

"Why of course, Mei-li. If I remember correctly, it was Nanning."

"Why that practically makes us neighbors!" exclaimed Mei-li. "For I was also born in the south, in nearby Guilin. Did your father and mother meet during the war?"

Justin shook his head. "Believe it or not, they first met in Seoul, Korea. My father was an army doctor stationed there, and he met my mother at a local

97

hospital, where she was employed as a nurse. Her own family had been relocated to Korea by the Japanese ten years earlier. They say I was conceived in Asia, yet born in New York nine months later."

Mei-li blushed. "Did you always want to be an actor?"

"Not really," answered Justin, who was now focusing his gaze solely on his guide. "My dad wanted me to follow in his footsteps, and I was a pre-med student until my second year of college. I had enrolled in a drama course merely to satisfy an elective requirement, and found much to my surprise that I was a natural ham on stage. When it was discovered that I could dance and carry a tune as well, I was encouraged to try out for a part in a musical that the school was producing. To make a long story short, I got the part, and also a rave review. And from that day on, I knew that I had found my real calling in life."

"Well, although your father was probably disappointed, you certainly made the right choice," offered Mei-li. "I particularly enjoyed your performance yesterday. Why, I believe you played the role of Bernardo better than the actor who was cast in that part."

"Why, thank-you, Mei-li. I'm glad to hear that someone out in the audience bought my performance. I must admit that particular role gave me nightmares at first. It wasn't exactly written for a half-Jewish, half-Chinese actor." Grinning, he added, "Did I really make a believable Puerto Rican?"

Mei-li was quick to reply. "One thing that you can be certain of is that no one in the audience knew any different. In fact, I doubt if even a handful of those present know where the island of Puerto Rico is located, and even they wouldn't know what its people look like."

Appreciative of Mei-li's honesty, Justin took a moment to truly study his companion. For the first time since they had met, he saw her not as a foreigner, but as a warm, sensitive, intelligent woman, who had an exotic, natural beauty as well.

Conscious of the sudden gleam of interest in the actor's deep green eyes, Mei-li shyly lowered her glance and cleared her throat. "You know, yesterday I spoke to Mr. Stadler, your State Department escort, and he mentioned that the troupe would be free to travel in China, as long as they returned to Canton in time to prepare for the next show. My family still lives outside of Guilin, which is only an hour away by plane from Canton, and I was hoping to stop off and visit them during this hiatus. I know that it's sudden and all, but do you think you'd be interested in joining me? We occupy the same autonomous region as Nanning, and you'd get a chance not only to see how the real Chinese live, but also to explore the country where your mother's family originally came from."

Justin accepted without hesitation. "Why, I'd be honored to join you, Mei-li. But is such a thing permitted?"

"I don't see why not," answered Mei-li. "The government is just looking for an excuse to show off the commune on which my parents live, and there should be no problem getting you the proper traveling papers. Besides, judging by our premier's initial reaction to your company, all you have to do is ask, and the entire country will be at your disposal."

Thrilled with the idea of seeing a portion of China that the average tourist would never get the opportunity of visiting, Justin Pollock leaned forward and gave his escort an innocent kiss on the cheek. Though Mei-li's face reddened, she was surprised to find that she had not instinctively pulled back from the kiss. In China, such shows of emotion were usually kept far from the public's eye, yet in this instance, it all seemed so natural that she really didn't care who witnessed it. A carefree, joyous mood possessed her as she looked at her watch and saw that they had a full thirty minutes left in this magical spot before they would have to leave for the Ming Tombs.

Mei-li and Justin arrived at Guilin two days later. It was warm and humid as they left the airport, and the American wasn't surprised when he learned that Guilin was at approximately the same latitude as Miami. Since the commune that Mei-li's parents lived on was located on the outskirts of the city, they took a brief sightseeing tour of the town itself before hailing a taxi for the hour trip into the country.

Justin was particularly impressed by the solitary series of water-scarred limestone mountains that dotted the landscape. Their green peaks were veiled in a ghostly mist, and gave the actor the impression that he was looking at an artist's canvas. Several of these hills rose in the center of town. One was called Solitary Beauty Peak, which, Mei-li told Justin, had been her favorite as a child. Though the climb was a bit too arduous for them to presently undertake, Mei-li described the spectacular view that could be seen from its terraced summit. She went on to explain that the hill had once been surrounded by a wall enclosing a Ming palace, and she showed Justin the moat, portions of the wall, and a gate flanked by a pair of stone lions, which was all that remained of the palace.

Their next stop was a marketplace beside the river Li. To get there, they had to cross a series of narrow, crowded streets filled with scurrying locals. Justin noted that, unlike Beijing, there was a marked absence of tourists. Most of the surface traffic moved by bicycle, a vehicle used by individuals of all ages. Conspicuous in his cowboy hat and blue jeans, the American drew curious stares from almost all those he passed. Particularly fascinated with his presence were the children. Their eyes were full of wonder as they pointed to the foreigner, yet they politely kept their distance.

At the marketplace itself, the actor got a chance to see a bit of the varied produce grown in the surrounding countryside. Fresh corn, melons, stringbeans, rice, and tomatoes, sat beside stalls selling live poultry, squealing pigs, and freshly caught fish, many of which were still squirming. The delivery of a huge load of cabbage seemed to be causing a great furor, and shoppers rushed to be the first in line.

At a sidewalk stand they sampled some of the local cuisine. Influenced by the Cantonese-style of cooking, the food was moderately spiced and extremely tasty. Justin's favorite were the dim sum. Shaped into small dumplings, this dish came in a variety of recipes that included spring rolls, steamed fish balls, shrimp toast, and chopped pork that was formed into flowers. After indulging in a platter of such delicacies, he chose a handful of delicately-flavored lichees for dessert. Washing this mini-feast down with a cup of oolong tea, Justin and Mei-li left the market area to stroll beside the Li River.

An excursion boat was just pulling away from the pier. Mei-li explained that such day trips were extremely popular amongst the tourists. The standard cruise was five hours long and explored the southern reaches of the Li. This same river entered the Xi at Wachow, thus directly linking it with the great port city of Canton.

Justin felt strangely at home here. Well aware that his mother's birthplace was less than three hundred kilometers to the south of Guilin, he felt sure that many of his ancestors must have walked these same streets. With this intriguing thought in mind, he followed his expert guide to the nearest taxi stand.

The only vehicle that was available to take them to their ultimate destination was a battered jeep, which had once seen service with the People's Army. As it turned out, the driver knew the commune well, for his own niece currently lived there. This coincidence served to break the ice, and soon the old man was chattering away with the latest gossip. Justin found much of his rapid dialogue indecipherable, and was content to merely stare out at the passing countryside while Mei-li kept the conversation going.

As the city disappeared behind them, the landscape became increasingly beautiful. The limestone peaks rose from the ground here like ever-vigilant sentinels. Covered with thick green growth, each mountain seemed to have a personality of its own.

Set inbetween these hills were acre after acre of rich

farmland. An occasional hut was visible, set amongst the fields of rice, wheat, beans, and grapes. Working these crops were hundreds of simply dressed peasants. Tractors and other mechanical implements were noticeably absent. In their place, the peasants employed a variety of crude, hand-held tools, with an occasional mule or water buffalo taking on the more tedious tasks.

Their journey took them to the north, with thousands of cultivated plots visible from the narrow, asphalt pavement. After driving twenty minutes on this roadway, they pulled off onto a secondary road. This one was formed from packed earth, and was rutted with dozens of jarring potholes. It was all that Mei-li and Justin could do to hang on while the driver shifted the vehicle into four-wheel drive and followed the dusty trail to the east.

Ten minutes later, they were forced to slow down and move onto the shoulder of the road as a column of large green trucks passed them going in the opposite direction. Justin counted a dozen vehicles in this convoy, and was somewhat shocked when their driver identified them as belonging to the People's Army. The American struggled to interpret his reply as Mei-li sat forward and animatedly asked, "What is such a convoy doing in this valley?"

"They are with a mining expedition," the driver explained. "Rumor has it that a large vein of radioactive uranium was discovered in the nearby hills."

"How long have they been working it?" asked Mei-li.

As he steered the taxi back onto the road, the driver replied, "Less than a week, actually. Although a smaller detachment arrived much earlier in the month, the main force got here only recently. They have a large supply warehouse back in town, next to the railroad depot. It's most likely to this spot that the trucks are currently headed."

Having understood enough to get the gist of what the old-timer was talking about, Justin peered to his left when they passed by what appeared to be a central staging area. Here, on the floor of a broad valley, dozens of vehicles of all sizes were parked. The American spotted several pieces of modern earth-moving equipment, and a virtual mountain of stacked wooden crates. A long line of bare-chested figures could be seen working beside this cache, which they were in the process of carrying, piece-by-piece, up a narrow earthen trail. Dozens of green canvas tents dotted the valley, and Justin shifted his curious glance away from the scene only when he heard their driver issue a loud, crude curse. Looking up to see what had upset him so, the actor caught sight of a primitive roadblock set up immediately ahead of them. The jeep braked to a halt in front of this obstacle, and Justin looked toward his escort, his glance filled with concern as two armed soldiers approached the taxi's side.

"Don't worry, Justin," whispered Mei-li in English. "Just take off your hat, sit back, and leave all the talking to me."

The actor wasted no time taking her advice. With his cowboy hat now sitting on the worn floorboard, he took several deep, calming breaths as the soldiers positioned themselves one on each side of the car. Both sentries were young and stern-faced. Although there were no distinguishing insignia on their khaki uniforms, Justin supposed that the soldier standing beside their driver held the senior rank. With an eaglelike stare he studied the taxi's occupants.

"May I see your papers?"

Justin noticed that the driver's hands were shaking as he reached into the glove compartment and pulled out his internal passport. In contrast, Mei-li calmly reached into her bag and removed two sets of documents. While handing them over, she met the sentry's icy gaze of inspection without flinching.

The soldier ignored the taxi driver's papers altogether, concentrating instead on the documents that Mei-li had handed him. Quickly scanning their contents, his eyes suddenly opened wide, and he looked up to take another long look at Justin Pollock. Noting his new interest, Mei-li interceded.

"Excuse me, Comrade, but is there something wrong with our papers? I am a certified senior CITS representative, and my esteemed American guest here has an important appointment at the Blue Swan commune."

The sentry replied firmly. "I'm afraid that the only road leading to your destination is closed, Comrades."

"But that can't be!" dared the taxi driver. "Why, I drove out there only two days ago."

The sentry met this remark with a stare that caused the driver to cower in fear, and he immediately shut his trembling mouth. Not about to be turned away now that they were so close to their goal, Mei-li once again reached into her bag. This time she removed a single document that bore an ornate seal. Handing it to the sentry, she noticed that he only had to read a portion of this document before his expression and tone changed dramatically.

"I had no idea that you were personal guests of the premier, Comrades. You are free to continue. But please drive cautiously, for the route to the commune is an extremely rough one."

As he handed back their papers, he smiled politely and the mood inside the taxi significantly lightened.

"Thank you, Comrade," Mei-li responded. "Your competency has been noted."

With this, the soldiers turned to open the barricade, which the taxi wasted no time in passing through. It wasn't until they rounded a wide curve and left the camp well behind them, that the three shared a joint sigh of relief.

"I'm sorry, but I had no idea that the Army was restricting travel on this road," offered the still-shaken driver. "They certainly weren't doing so when I last traveled this route."

"It makes no difference now, Comrade," returned Mei-li. "How much farther do we have to go?"

"We have less than three kilometers left," answered the old-timer as he guided the jeep over a washed-out section of the roadway that was covered with loose gravel.

This news brought a smile to Mei-li's lips. Turning to face her traveling companion, she again lowered her voice to a whisper.

"Thank goodness I was carrying that document from Lin Shau-ping's office. Otherwise, I doubt that we would have been allowed to pass."

"Does such a thing occur often?" queried the

American.

"Not really. Of course, there are sensitive areas that the government keeps closed to all outsiders. But those are usually limited to military bases and experimental test sites. Unlike many Communist countries, internal travel within China is not restricted, though the cost of traveling itself serves to keep the average citizen close to home."

"Well, I'm also glad you were carrying along that document," added Justin. "I can't tell you how much I'm looking forward to staying with your family during these next couple of days. How long has it been since you've seen them last?"

"My last visit was over a year ago. With tourism vastly on the increase in our country, my days off have been precious few."

Justin nodded. "I know what that's like. Even living in the same city as my parents, I don't see them nearly as much as I'd like to. Why, just preparing *West Side Story* for the road took up most of the spring and summer. Things were so hectic at the end, I could scarcely find the time to phone them just to say good-bye."

As the jeep bounced over a particularly deep pothole, the two held on tightly to each other to keep from tumbling off the seat. They broke this hand-to-hand contact with a deliberate slowness, and both parties felt their pulses quicken in response to this brief touch. Awkwardly clearing her throat, Mei-li looked out the window as the vehicle began chugging its way up a steep hillside.

At the top of this hill, the taxi momentarily stopped. Proud of his driving skills, the driver pointed toward the broad green valley that now lay before them.

"There she is, Comrades. The Blue Swan commune, home of some of the best wine in all of southern China."

Leaning forward eagerly, Justin joined Mei-li in scanning the eastern horizon. Like a scene from a storybook, a range of craggy, green-encrusted limestone mountains sheltered a magnificent, wide valley. Nestled in this hollow was a tumbling stream and a small circle of whitewashed wooden cottages. Columns of smoke poured from several of the gray stone chimneys, and dozens of individual laborers could be seen working in the terraced fields that completely encircled the handful of man-made structures. As if he himself were returning home the American sat back in anticipation as their driver put the vehicle into gear and carefully steered the jeep down the scarred, dusty roadway.

CHAPTER FIVE

Samuel Fuller watched the breakers crash into the shoreline from a beachside deckchair. Though it was nine thirty in the morning, the sun was already hot, the muggy air made tolerable only by a stiff, northerly trade wind. Scanning the surf line, he watched as a young blond-haired surfer paddled furiously to catch a wave. Fuller had seen much greater swells pound this beach in the past, yet today's waves were more than adequate to allow the youngster a challenging ride.

Surfing was more difficult than it appeared, and Fuller remembered the last time that he had tried to ride the waves. It was last Christmas, and one of Peggy's teen-aged nephews was visiting from California. Somehow, Fuller had allowed the spirited lad to talk him into joining him on one of his new boards. A storm front had been passing well to the north of the islands, and the waves were arriving in massive, regular sets. The lad had promised that such seas would only make things easier for Samuel. Never known as one who turned away from a challenge, Fuller grabbed a fiber glass board and dove headfirst into the pounding surf.

His first lesson was in utilizing the board from a

prone position. Lying on his stomach, he quickly caught on to the intricacies of properly choosing and then catching a wave. He had body-surfed before, and the board, which could be controlled, made such sport only that much more enjoyable. After several such runs, it was time to attempt kneeling. Fuller soon caught a perfect wave, and he went from a prone position to his knees with little difficulty. Seeing no reason why he couldn't go all the way and stand, he decided to go for it and jumped to his feet. For a second, he felt the invigorating power of the wave pushing him at an incredible speed toward the distant beach. Yet his moment of control was brief, and the next thing he knew, he was flying awkwardly through the air. His board whizzed by only inches from his head, and he plummeted into the warm roiling surf with such force that his back actually scraped the sea floor.

After what seemed like an eternity underwater, he managed to surface. Choking from the water he had swallowed, he eventually made it to shore. Only when he was drying off, did he realize that his back was severely cut. His beach towel was covered with blood. He limped back home to let Peggy attend to these wounds, all the time swearing to himself that from now on, he would leave the surfing to younger, more fit individuals.

Grinning at the recollection, Fuller yawned and stretched his limbs contentedly. A sea gull cried overhead, and beyond, the surf crashed onto the beach with a soothing regularity. He had been home now for twenty-four hours and was already adjusting to life on dry land.

His condo's porch was directly behind him, less than fifty yards distant. He would be retreating there shortly, to escape the effects of the tropical sun, which all too soon would have his bare skin burnt to a lobster-red crisp. Even with the coconut oil sunscreen which he'd spread liberally over his body, he knew he could stay in the sun only another half hour at the most.

Later that day, he planned to take Peggy on a nature hike into the Ewa Forest Reserve. They would follow this excursion with dinner at the Crouching Lion Inn, one of their favorite North Beach restaurants. Aware that his wife had been unusually reserved when she'd picked him up at the base the day before, Fuller knew that she had something serious on her mind. Hopefully, their day together would break the ice, and she'd be able to get what was bothering her off her chest. He had a good idea what this something was. Most likely, Peggy would be bringing up the topic of his retirement once again. Still not certain how he'd answer her, Fuller scanned the ocean, his gaze finally coming to a halt on a distant, familiar shape a good mile from shore.

The twenty-five-year naval veteran identified the ship as a *Spruance*-class destroyer. He could make out its distinctive large hull, block superstructures, twin exhaust stacks, and the fairly large areas of empty space on its deck. When the Spruance boats were first introduced, many critics felt that they were too lightly armed. Fuller knew otherwise, for though the destroyer lacked great numbers of external guns, they were fitted with two five-inch Mk45 cannons, six torpedo tubes, twin Phalanx machine guns, and an

ASROC launcher, whose magazine carried no less than twenty-four reloads. The destroyer also carried a hangar capable of holding two SH-2F LAMPS helicopters. Four gas turbines gave the Spruances both the ability for rapid acceleration and a low noise signature. All of these features added up to a formidable platform, whose ability as a submarine hunter could never be doubted.

As Fuller watched the destroyer steam off to the northeast, his thoughts returned to the patrol from which he'd just returned. The *Copperhead*'s confrontation with the Soviet submarine was followed by a fascinating discovery on the floor of the sea. Here, in the southernmost quadrant of the North Hawaiian Seamount Range, their bottom-searching sonar chanced upon an unexplainable break in the experimental SOSUS grid. Seemingly the result of an explosion, the gap had apparently caused the entire system to fail. Since the SOSUS equipment carried no volatile substances, this blast had to have been triggered by an external source. As far as Fuller was concerned, it could only be attributed to the Russian vessel they had chased off. In his gut he knew that the Soviets were the culprits, yet so far, Command was completely deaf to that suggestion.

In the past, Fuller had always felt that Admiral Peter Lawrence, the current commander of submarines in the Pacific, had dealt with him fairly. Yet this time, when Fuller presented his case during the initial post-patrol briefing, the admiral seemed to immediately dismiss his suspicions. A hotshot commander from Washington, sitting at the admiral's side, was quick to launch into a sermon on the government's current view of U.S./Soviet relations. He painted a rosy picture of peaceful cooperation and new-found trust. Blaming the breakdown of the SOSUS grid on a physical anomaly such as an underground volcanic eruption, he then had the nerve to actually castigate Fuller for pursuing the Soviet submarine.

Before Samuel could defend himself, Admiral Lawrence interceded. Though he stopped short of directly criticizing Fuller's decision to lash the Russian vessel with the *Copperhead*'s sonar, he did advise that discretion was necessary in future confrontations of this nature. For after all, the United States was about to sign a comprehensive nuclear arms pact with the Soviet Union, which would be signaling a new era of relations between the superpowers. Lawrence then went on to reveal that as a gesture of good faith, the U.S. would be mothballing a third of its current force of strategic bombers, intercontinental ballistic missiles, and nuclear submarines. As one of the first generation of such vessels, the *Copperhead* was to be one of the ships retired. There would be one last patrol before the announcement was officially made and the boat stripped of its operational status.

Needless to say, Samuel Fuller was genuinely shocked by this revelation. Stunned into silence and swearing to keep the news to himself, he returned to the *Copperhead* to prepare for his present leave. He remembered his last view of the ship as Peggy guided their Chevy up Kamehameha Highway. Looking sleek and deadly, the sub still had many good years left. To mothball it now, along with dozens of other such vessels, was idiotic. For despite the fact that they were about to sign a treaty of peace, the Soviets could never be completely trusted. As long as Communist powers existed, the western capitalistic nations would be their sworn enemies. Of this fact, Samuel Fuller was certain!

Looking back on these events in the solitude of his beachfront retreat, Fuller felt both frustration and fear. Completely powerless to get his point across, he couldn't help but wonder what kind of fools ran the government. At the very least, the one area that they should be leaving intact was the submarine force. As the country's most effective deterrent, the subs could guarantee that both parties kept their word as promised. To prematurely dismantle such a force could very well be the worst decision since Roosevelt turned a deaf ear to Japanese Imperialism in the early 1940's. And this time they faced an enemy whose nuclear arsenal would make the sneak attack on Pearl Harbor look like a mere turkey-shoot in comparison. Why, the very survival of the American way of life would be directly threatened by such a move! What was Washington trying to do to them?

Pounding his balled right fist into the hot sand in response to this thought, Samuel Fuller sighed heavily. The powers that be had made their decision, and now he could only carry on as ordered.

It was times such as these that made retirement sound like the only course open to him. How could he fight to defend a government he no longer supported? Of course, his prayers were that real peace would be born out of the upcoming summit. But even with those hopes, he knew inwardly that the Soviets were just not ready for such a thing to come to pass. The very writings of Lenin proved that it would be through world class struggle that Communism would eventually triumph. Cutting America's strategic military strength was only the first step toward such a victory.

The grinding roar of powerful jet engines screamed overhead, and Fuller looked up to see where this throaty roar was coming from. Shading his eyes from the glaring sun, he caught sight of a pair of F-14 Tomcats streaking through the blue Hawaiian skies like a pair of howling banshees. While wondering how the young pilots of these aircraft would take the impending arms cuts, his train of thought was suddenly broken as a hand gently touched his shoulder. Fuller smiled as he turned to see his wife standing behind him.

"A penny for your thoughts, sailor," Peggy said innocently.

Reaching up to take his wife's hand in his, Fuller pulled her down into his lap. Their lips met, and they shared a long, sensual kiss. Hugging her tightly, he slowly drew his mouth from hers and only then responded to her question.

"You couldn't have arrived at a better time, Peg. Do you know that I was actually thinking about borrowing a board and trying my hand at surfing once again?"

"Oh, no you don't, Samuel Fuller. Don't forget who had to nurse you back to health after your last fling on the waves. Besides, I have something else in mind that's going to keep you well occupied for the rest of the day."

Noting the unusual twinkle in his wife's eyes, Fuller responded, "Just name it and I'm yours, my dear. Now, are you going to tell me where you ran off to in such a hurry early this morning? Before I could get out of bed, you were dressed and walking out the garage door."

Peggy grinned at her husband's questioning look. "Oh, it was nothing. I just had to go into Kahuku to get the results of a blood test."

Fuller's eyes suddenly narrowed in concern. "I didn't know that you'd been to the see the doctor. Aren't you feeling well?"

"To tell you the truth, I've been feeling a little dizzy in the mornings. But Dr. Kalena says that such a thing is only normal for a woman who's a good seven weeks pregnant."

This last word hit Fuller with the force of a punch to the jaw. "Oh, my God! Did you say pregnant?" he asked excitedly. "You mean we're going to be parents?"

Tears of joy welled up in Peggy's eyes as she fell into her husband's warm grasp. "Believe me, I'm just as shocked as you are, Sam. Why, it's almost like a miracle! After all these years of trying, God is finally answering our prayers. Isn't it wonderful!"

Struggling to control his emotions, Fuller fought back his own tears. "It's more than that, honey! Why, I had no idea."

The two embraced silently for several minutes before Peggy added, "The doctor says that everything appears normal, but he wants to pay extra attention to me because of my age. After all, it's not every day that a thirty-eight-year-old woman becomes a mother for the first time."

A swarm of thoughts clouded Fuller's mind, yet his supreme happiness couldn't be ignored. "I'll get you the finest specialist in the world, Peg. Vincent Coria's wife gave birth only three months ago, and I hear she swears by the delivery staff at the University hospital."

Smiling at his concern, Peggy shook her head. "Right now, Dr. Kalena is more than adequate. The local women go to no one else, and besides, his office is practically right down the street."

Barely listening to what his wife was saying, Fuller had already made up his mind that she would have the services of the finest obstetrician on Oahu. Anxious to get hold of his XO, to get the name of the physician who had delivered his child, Samuel Fuller suddenly found a new, vibrant purpose directing his thoughts. For at forty-six years of age, he was at long last about to have a real family!

Twenty-five miles due south of Fuller's beachside condo, Admiral Peter Lawrence sat behind his cluttered desk, his attention riveted on the report his secretary had just handed to him. Having originated with the Central Intelligence Agency, the document had disturbing implications.

It had all started ten days ago, when a Defense Department reconnaissance satellite was in the process of completing a routine infra-red scan of the South China Sea. Though the surface of the sea itself was veiled by fog, the red-hot plume of a ballistic missile's booster engine was picked up just north of Dongsha Island. After a brief flight into the far reaches of the earth's atmosphere, this signature then separated into six distinct entitites, each of which splashed down near the island of Hainan. Because the launch position was near no known land-based missile site, it was fairly obvious that it was test-launched from the bowels of a submarine. It was common knowledge that the Chinese Navy had successfully fired a submarine-launched ballistic missile some time ago. What was upsetting was the fact that this single missile most likely carried a MIRV'd warhead. For this had been a capability that had previously been outside the PLN's rather limited technology.

The second half of the CIA report was the by-product of a call from Taiwanese Naval Intelligence. Exactly three days after the suspected launch of the mysterious SLBM, a fisherman notified the Taiwanese Navy that he had actually witnessed the event. The Nationalist Navy had been on record as suspecting that the People's Liberation Navy was close to completing the development of a MIRV'd SLBM, and this incident only served to confirm their suspicions.

Admiral Peter Lawrence digested all these facts and calmly set the report down in front of him. Unconsciously, his gaze strayed to the large world map that hung on the wall to his right. While absent-mindedly scanning that portion of the map labeled *Asia,* he attempted to put the CIA document into its proper perspective.

In all the excitement caused by the soon-to-be-signed U.S./Soviet arms treaty, they had somehow forgotten that other countries had the ability to launch a nuclear strike. The most independent and enigmatic of these nations was the People's Republic of China. With no one really certain where the Chinese stood in the scheme of global relations, they were certainly a threat that had to be considered. If the PLN had indeed perfected the technology necessary to send a

MIRV'd warhead skyward from the magazine of a submerged submarine, such consideration was even more vital—especially if these warheads could be delivered with any degree of accuracy.

Lawrence shuddered to think what havoc such a platform could create. Though current political conditions inside China appeared to be stable, modern history showed that the world's most populous nation was too often subject to control by extremist factions. The Cultural Revolution of Mao, and the subsequent ascension of The Gang of Four had taken place less than two decades before. Their present premier, Lin Shau-ping, was young and a relatively inexperienced head of state. He had only to alienate any number of hard-line Maoists, who still held positions of power, to seal his doom. A fully loaded nuclear missile carrying submarine under the guidance of a reactionary Communist cabal would be extremely unpleasant to deal with. Such a threat would have worldwide implications, and directly involve the Soviet Union as well as the United States. Thus, such a weapons system had to be dealt with at the very inception of its deployment.

Lawrence knew that one of his first goals was to find out exactly where this submarine was harbored. The major Chinese Naval facilities capable of handling such a vessel were well known to the United States, and the Admiral foresaw no problem in determining the site of the installation.

Once the sub was pinpointed, their next task would be to secretly saturate the waters surrounding this base with submerged sonar buoys. This would be accomplished by either dropping them from the skies, or conveying the buoys into the proper chokepoints by submarine. With a recon satellite constantly watching from the heavens, and the sonar buoys listening for the least suspicious sound from the ocean's depths, the Chinese submarine would be detected long before it reached the shelter of the open seas. Once its general direction was known, an attack sub could be sent out to monitor its each and every movement, always ready to take out the Chinese vessel should it show the least hint of aggression.

Satisfied with this plan of action, Admiral Pete Lawrence reached for his telephone. His first call was to Commander Craig Benton at Pearl Harbor's Office of Naval Intelligence. Making certain to use a secure line, Lawrence went on to list the information that he would need from Benton to get the Chinese threat under control.

While the Commander of the U.S. sub force in the Pacific was making his top priority telephone call, his counterpart in the U.S.S.R. was absorbing the phone conversation that he only seconds ago had terminated. This had been the first time that the Kremlin had contacted him since Stanislaus Angara's visit, and Admiral of the Fleet Leonid Silka had been kept in suspense, wondering how his suggestions had been received.

Chief of Staff Angara had been full of apologies as he explained the delay. When he'd finally returned to Moscow, after traveling the width of the Motherland, his services were immediately needed elsewhere—to help smooth out a diplomatic snag that could have very well doomed the upcoming summit. Only after he had successfully negotiated a compromise with the American State Department, was he able to focus on the subject of his meeting with Leonid on the Kamchatka peninsula. As promised, Angara had presented the admiral's suggestions directly to Premier Skuratov. This briefing had taken place less than an hour ago, and the handsome bureaucrat had wasted no time in telephoning Leonid to let him know the results.

As Angara had expected, the premier agreed to allow Leonid to implement his suggested plan of action at once. Thus the admiral now had the authority to send his entire fleet of attack subs seaward, where they would seek out the American Trident vessels. Then, at the least hint of aggressive behavior from the Imperialists, the Soviet captains would have full authority to eliminate the Tridents as they saw fit.

Thanking the chief of staff for his support, the admiral hung up the telephone, and stifling the impulse to cry out in joy, mentally organized his next course of action. One of his first moves would be to call for his helicopter to take him to naval command headquarters at nearby Petropavlovsk. As much as he loved his wilderness dacha, it was no place to organize an operation of this magnitude.

With the help of his staff, he would determine the location of every single attack submarine under his command. All vessels currently in port would be rushed back to sea, while those boats already on patrol would be instructed to remain at their stations to the very limit of their endurance. Special attention would be given to adequately covering all known U.S. Trident sanctuaries. These subs were known to frequent the waters of the northern Pacific, in the seas directly south of the Aleutian Islands. Here, the waters ran deep and silent, the perfect environment in which to hide one of their ballistic-missile platforms.

Excited by the chance to prove the efficiency of his forces, Leonid Silka took a quick glance out the frosted window beside his desk. A compact patch of snow-covered evergreens beckoned in the distance. Though he would not get a chance to hike these woods this afternoon as he had originally planned, this new, challenging call to duty far outweighed that simple pleasure. Rubbing his hands eagerly together, he sat forward to pick up the telephone and arrange his transport to the port city of Petropavlovsk.

For Captain Anton Valerian of the *Akula*-class attack sub *Baikal,* it had been a most trying day. His problems had started twelve hours ago, when two members of the crew began arguing during breakfast. Both seamen were conscripts, and their heated words soon turned to actual violence as one of them pulled out a knife. It was the *Baikal*'s alert warrant officer who interceded, just in time to prevent bloodshed.

With a crew of only eighty-five men, Valerian couldn't risk losing a single individual to such foolishness, and he instructed the political officer to severely chastise both parties involved. Afterwards, he had each of the men brought to his quarters.

The captain soon learned that both sailors were from Odesssa, where they grew up only a few doors from each other. During their last leave, one of them had caught the other with his girlfriend in a compromising position, and had waited until today to vent his anger. Valerian wasted the entire morning establishing peace between the two headstrong conscripts, who eventually shook hands before the captain with a promise to behave themselves.

Not thirty minutes later, a primary valve in their reactor malfunctioned. Fortunately, the *Baikal*'s chief engineer had been close by to immediately scram the reactor and close the main steam feed. Though this prevented the reactor from cooling too quickly and cracking, which would have spewed radioactive material all through the boat, it also abruptly cut off the flow of steam needed to power the turbines. This left the *Baikal* without its main source of propulsion, and as the screw stopped turning, the sub lost its trim and slowly began sinking, stern down.

Valerian arrived in the control room in time to order engineering to rig for battery power. This afforded them just enough juice to blow the forward and after trim-tanks, and the *Baikal* quit sinking less than fifty meters from its crush depth. The rest of the day was spent repairing the broken reactor valve, and it wasn't until well after dinner that the boat was once more proceeding under full steam. Only when this was achieved did the exhausted captain hand the con over to his senior lieutenant.

In no mood to mix with the other officers, Valerian headed straight for his cabin. His neck ached from tension, and his stomach growled with hunger. Yet his first priority was to strip off his shirt and position himself in front of the compact sink mounted on the bulkhead. The cool water felt refreshing on his shoulders and beard-stubbled face. Deciding not to shave, he took a second to glance into the small mirror mounted above the sink.

Staring back at him was a familiar, grizzled reflection given additional character by a mop of close-cut pepper-and-salt hair and a black leather patch that covered his left eye. The day's tiring events seemed to have made him paler than usual, and he rubbed his high cheekbones and square chin in an effort to get the blood recirculating. After adjusting his eye patch — the by-product of a year of college boxing — Valerian turned from the mirror when a solid knock sounded on the cabin door.

"Come in!" instructed the *Baikal*'s senior officer.

With this, the door swung open to admit the corpulent figure of the sub's chief cook. "Please pardon the intrusion, Captain," he said somewhat sheepishly, "but I know that you missed both lunch and dinner, and I was wondering if it was my cooking that was at fault."

Valerian, who had always had a genuine liking for this pot-bellied Estonian, replied courteously, "Not at all, Comrade. It's just that this day has been such a hectic one, I didn't have time to leave the control room."

"I thought that was the case," returned the relieved cook. "Now, I hope I'm not being too forward, but I've taken it upon myself to prepare a dinner tray for you."

Without giving the captain time to respond, the *Baikal*'s head chef pivoted and reached out for the tray he had set down in the corridor. Grasping it firmly in his massive hands, he then returned to Anton Valerian's stateroom, where he carefully set the tray down on the captain's narrow desk.

An assortment of pleasing aromas filled the cabin,

and Valerian looked over to see what the cook had brought him. "Is that Ukrainian borscht, Comrade?"

Nodding that it was, the Estonian added, "I realize that today's events were most trying on all the crew, so I decided to whip up my specialty. Besides, our month is almost up, and this dish gives me the chance to utilize many of the assorted delicacies I have been saving."

Not bothering to put on his shirt, Valerian seated himself behind the desk, to more closely examine the large bowl of steaming borscht. As he picked up a spoon to sample the dish, the Estonian chef turned to exit.

"Enjoy it, Captain!"

The door slammed shut, and alone now, Valerian brought the first spoonful of borscht to his mouth. The soup was piping hot and had a delicious taste. Digging deeper into the bowl, he uncovered an assortment of delicacies that included cabbage, beets, potatoes, and huge hunks of tangy sausage. A heel of crusty black bread accompanied this simple feast, which Valerian washed down with a mug of heavily sweetened tea.

Burping and smacking his lips, he wished only for a good cigar and a snifter of fine cognac to make this meal complete. Unfortunately, he had smoked his last Cuban several days ago, and though he had no cognac on board, he did have a bottle of potato vodka stashed in his locker. It was reserved for special occasions, and Valerian could think of no better time than this to uncork it.

He was soon lying contentedly on his cot with his bottle in hand. The clear spirits burned his mouth and throat, settling in his stomach like a jolt of electricity.

Careful to limit his consumption, he drank barely a quarter of the bottle before capping it and putting it down. A soothing warmth possessed his worn body. He yawned, and was just about to nod off, when once again a loud knock sounded on his door.

Shocked into wakefulness, Valerian groggily called out, "You may enter."

This time a trim, baldheaded officer entered. Efficiently closing the door behind him, the *Baikal's zampolit,* Boris Glazov, positioned himself beside Valerian's cot.

"Sorry to disturb you, sir, but a matter of the utmost urgency has just presented itself."

Valerian reluctantly pulled himself up to a sitting position. "Now what, Comrade Political Officer?" he asked somewhat ungraciously.

Mindful of the captain's sour tone of voice, Boris Glazkov continued, "Only minutes ago, a top-priority Red Flag dispatch was received on the VLF band. As I am duly authorized to do, I proceeded to translate the message, which originated in the office of the Admiral of the Fleet himself."

"What does old Silka have to say for himself this time?" questioned Valerian bitterly.

Trying hard to ignore the captain's impertinence, the *zampolit* replied, "We have been ordered to remain on station indefinitely, sir, with a defense condition of level two prevailing."

These last words caused Valerian to awaken completely. "Did you say level two, Comrade?"

"That is correct, Captain. A proper authorization code followed these instructions. As it stands now, there is no reason whatsoever to question the legiti-

126

macy of these new orders."

His brow furrowed with concern, Anton Valerian pondered the nature of the dispatch that Command had just relayed to them. Having been on patrol for a solid thirty days now, the *Baikal* would normally be heading back to Petropavlovsk within the next forty-eight hours. Yet now they were being ordered to remain in their patrol sector indefinitely, entailing food rationing and all sorts of difficult morale problems.

Even more disturbing was the news that a level-two defense condition now existed. Only one step away from actual war, level two indicated that a state of increased world tension was causing Command to alert the Motherland's strategic forces to prepare for the possibility of an enemy sneak attack.

As an attack sub, the *Baikal* would be concentrating its efforts on searching out the enemy's Trident vessels. They would do so in a prearranged sector of the North Pacific, in which they would be the only Soviet sub present.

Once their elusive prey was detected, the *Baikal*'s next task would be to secretly monitor the Trident, ever vigilant for any aggressive moves on the part of the Americans. For if Valerian picked up the least hint that the Trident was about to launch its deadly load of nuclear warheads, level two gave him the authority to stop such a launch, using whatever force he deemed necessary. Well aware of the gravity of this situation, the captain was hardly aware that the *zampolit* was still talking away.

"I wonder what happened to that peace summit that everyone was talking about when we last left Petropavlovsk? I just knew that it sounded too good to be true."

Meeting the political officer's puzzled stare, Valerian responded, "You didn't actually believe that load of garbage *Pravda* was printing, did you, Boris Glazov? The capitalists might talk of peace, but their economic system depends on the production of armaments for its very survival. I knew all the time that this summit was nothing but a deceptive ploy on their part. And now they've apparently revealed their hand, and our esteemed premier has dared to call their bluff."

Impressed with this train of thought, the *zampolit* commented, "You might be on to something, Comrade. Most likely the imperialists were caught preparing their strategic forces for a sneak attack. I'll bet they thought they'd catch us napping, now that the so-called disarmament treaty is all but signed."

"The Americans make wonderful technicians, but poor chess players," observed Anton Valerian. "To insure that this is one game they won't win, I think that it's best to call a meeting of all the ship's officers. I will inform them of our new status and then put the entire crew on alert."

The *zampolit* nodded. "That is very wise, Captain. A united effort on their part will help greatly if we encounter the Americans."

"What do you mean by *if*, Comrade Glazov? The Motherland is counting on the *Baikal* to do its part in containing our sworn enemy. It is common knowledge that one of their Tridents is on continuous patrol in this sector. Thus it's imperative that we locate this vessel before the imperialists attempt their desperate, ill-conceived surprise attack."

"I will assemble the officers at once," returned the

zampolit.

Noting that the captain was absorbed in thought, the political officer pivoted smartly to get on with his duty. Alone once again, Anton Valerian stared across at the framed photograph hung on the opposite bulkhead. The scene showed a portion of the Ural Mountains. Having grown up in nearby Sverdlovsk, Valerian couldn't help but find himself inspired as he studied the massive snow-covered peaks in the photograph.

After decades of service, he sometimes wondered about the worth of all his efforts. He'd been particularly disturbed when he'd first heard of the soon-to-be-signed comprehensive disarmament pact. Yet now he felt encouraged. The very survival of the Motherland depended upon the *Baikal* and other vessels much like it. Regardless of the risks involved, they would not let their country down.

Rising to dress himself, the captain visualized his course of action. Presently cruising beneath the waters north of that geographical feature known as the Northern Hawaiian Seamount Range, the *Baikal* would have to prepare itself for the approach of the enemy. They would do so by implementing the tactic known as sprint and drift.

To cover as much territory as possible, their turbines would be operated at full power, to achieve massive bursts of forward speed. This would be followed by a sudden shutdown of the engines, during which time the boat would drift silently in the depths, allowing its passive sonar systems an undisturbed environment in which to listen for the approach of their adversary.

As Valerian tucked in his shirt, he knew that they would have to be extra careful to avoid the sort of unwanted confrontation that had occurred only last week. At that time, they had been tagged by an American attack sub. Although they were able to easily outrun this vessel, the *Baikal*'s senior sonar technician received a painful sonic lashing from the *Sturgeon*-class boat.

Fighting the impulse to turn the *Baikal* around and attack, Valerian and his crew had ached for revenge. Little did they realize that they would have that chance sooner than they anticipated.

CHAPTER SIX

Two hundred and ten kilometers due south of the city of Shanghai, the Kuocang mountain range extended to the very shores of the East China Sea. A rugged, inhospitable place, the coast here was home to only a few hardy fishermen. Two years ago a large contingent of naval engineers had arrived in the area. Soon afterward, huge numbers of construction personnel and heavy equipment followed. Content to mind their own business, the locals went about their daily routines, completely ignorant of the fact that a project of immense proportions was being undertaken right in their midst.

When it was eventually completed eighteen months later, the submarine base at Huangyan ranked as an engineering masterpiece. Situated in the base of a hollowed out mountain, a series of half a dozen individual sub pens lay completely hidden from detection by reconnaissance satellites or other intelligence apparatus. Because the entrance to the pens was cut into the side of the mountain itself, the vessels that were berthed here had instant access to the sea, while sheltered from above by millions of tons of rock and dirt.

Admiral Liu Shao-chi had been present on the day

when the base went operational. Since the white-haired naval officer had helped in the original implementation of the complex, he was especially thrilled when the first submarine steamed into the entrance of the mammoth man-made cavern. Afterwards, he went back to his command post in Shanghai content in the knowledge that the PLN now had the services of a most unique installation.

Today, as his helicopter touched down at Huangyan's airstrip, he was filled with the same sense of excitement. The day was cold and wet, yet the sixty-nine-year-old Liu barely noticed the raw weather as he rushed into a waiting jeep for the short ride to the base itself.

The vehicle disappeared into an underground tunnel and braked to a halt in a central staging area. Here, the base commander was waiting to escort Liu to the pen area. A massive stairway led down to the water line, and Liu took a moment to peer down at the amazing complex that lay before him.

Though not nearly as large as the recently discovered limestone caverns outside of Guilin, the area was large enough to hold six full-sized submarine berths, a refueling depot, and a main storage facility. Currently, only a single vessel lay tied to the pier—the ballistic-missile submarine *Red Dragon*, pride of the PLN. Its sleek lines were lit by a powerful bank of spotlights.

An assortment of uniformed personnel could be seen gathered on the deck of the boat, beside its elongated sail. One of these figures was several inches taller than his comrades, and Liu recognized him as the vessel's captain. A veteran officer, Chen Shou had once served on Liu's very own staff. They had shared

132

many an evening together, and there could be no ignoring both his expertise as a sailor and his firm political loyalties. Certain that he was the perfect man for the job at hand, the admiral resumed his careful descent to the sub.

The sound of his echoing footsteps and the gentle slap of seawater accompanied Liu as he made his way down to the concrete berth. A young sentry, who guarded the gangway, snapped to attention, and the admiral merely had to nod to gain entrance to the floating behemoth that lay beyond.

The *Red Dragon*'s design was loosely based on that of the Soviet Union's *Delta* I-class boats. One hundred forty meters long, the sub's characteristic feature was its humped missile casing, attached directly to the back portion of the sail. It was here that the vessel's sixteen *Xia*-class strategic missiles were stored in individual launch tubes laid out in two rows of eight.

Less than twelve hours ago, Liu Shao-chi received the telephone call informing him that the last of these missiles had been successfully loaded inside the *Red Dragon*'s magazine. Unwilling to let the vessel set sail without personally being there to witness this historic event, Liu timed his arrival at the pen to coincide with the change of the tide which would allow the sub to begin its first patrol. He could see that the deck crew was in the process of making last-minute departure preparations, and the admiral wasted no time approaching the group of officers who still stood beside the sail.

"Permission to come aboard?" requested Liu lightly.

As the khaki-clad sailors set their eyes on this newcomer, a collective look of disbelief crossed their faces.

133

Stiffening at attention, they allowed the tallest member of their group to respond for them.

"Welcome aboard the *Red Dragon,* Admiral!" greeted Captain Chen Shou animatedly. "Why, we had no idea that you'd be gracing us with your presence."

"I realize that," replied Liu, who walked over to hug his old comrade. "Yet I just couldn't resist paying my personal respects on this most momentous day. Will you be able to set sail as planned?"

The distinguished gray-haired captain promptly answered, "Why, of course, Comrade. All systems are fully operative, and the tide will allow us safe passage out of our subterranean berth any minute now."

Lowering his voice, Liu questioned, "Well, before I cause you a second's needless delay, is there somewhere close by where I can have a word with you in private?"

"If you don't mind a bit of a climb," the captain replied discreetly, "the sub's attack center is right below us. It should be vacant now, and our privacy will be assured there."

Nodding that this was fine with him, Liu motioned the captain to lead the way. After leaving his fellow officers with a series of last-minute instructions, Chen Shou walked over to the base of the sail. Opening a narrow hatch, he quickly ducked inside. Liu Shao-chi followed on his heels.

The smell of machine oil met the admiral's nostrils as he began his way down a steep tubular-steel ladder. This led directly to a cramped passageway. No stranger to the interior of a submarine, Liu followed his host forward. An assortment of pipes and cables lined the walls here.

Halfway down the corridor, the captain stopped and

turned to a closed hatchway on his left. This hatch was locked, and after the captain used his key to open it, he and Liu climbed through into an equipment-packed compartment dominated by several vacant computer consoles that were set up against the aft bulkhead.

Feeling as if he were in a research laboratory rather than on a warship, Liu shook his head in wonder. "So this is the *Red Dragon*'s attack center. Exactly what functions are performed here?"

"The main purpose of this compartment is tied to our missile magazine. From here the target coordinates are fed into the individual warheads, which are subsequently armed. This central station is our launch-control console. Once the proper "go" code has been authenticated, the missiles are released from this spot."

Paying particular attention to the array of instruments on this console, Liu remarked solemnly, "Though all of us hope that such a launch order will never be forwarded to you, it is reassuring to know that for the first time ever, enemy targets—no matter how hardened—can be eliminated by our warheads. Such a capability will do much to solidify our nation's position as a legitimate superpower. With the *Red Dragon* at sea, China will never again have to fear an aggressor's wrath.

"You have been personally chosen to command this inaugural voyage because of your years of excellent service, Chen Shou. We have been through much together, and have patiently watched the People's Navy go from a crude coastal fleet to a powerful nuclear armada, with ships such as this one leading the way.

"In the next couple of days, the heads of the United States and the Soviet Union will be meeting to sign an unprecedented disarmament treaty. As you well know, China was not invited to attend this event. We can thus only assume that this summit is being convened for purposes other than those being released to the public. For how can the powers of East and West discuss banning nuclear weapons from the face of the earth, with the planet's third largest possessor of such weapons not even present?

"You will be at sea as this summit convenes, and if the two superpowers indeed take this occasion to initiate hostilities against us, the *Red Dragon* will be China's last hope. Know that if the call to launch arrives, it has been conveyed only as a desperate last-ditch measure. If necessary, explain this to the crew, for once the first MIRV'd warhead streaks down from the heavens on its mission of revenge, the world will be changed for all time to come. Yet you and your men can rest easily, knowing that the *Red Dragon* acted solely in China's best interests. And if the gods so will it, perhaps the Republic will persevere in this time of chaos, and never again will such a drastic decision have to be made."

Emotionally drained by his discourse, Liu locked his serious gaze onto that of Captain Chen Shou. Without blinking, the tall, distinguished naval officer returned a look of equal concern. And with that glance, Liu Shao-chi was certain that his former staff member would carry out his orders, no matter how unthinkable they might appear to be.

* * *

Justin Pollock couldn't remember when he last enjoyed himself as much. Ever since he had arrived at the commune, it was as if he was discovering a natural, innocent side of life he had never known existed. It all started soon after the taxi dropped them off at the entrance to the central meeting house. His mind was full of all the sights that he had viewed since leaving Beijing earlier that morning, and he wasn't prepared for the reception that awaited them inside the white-washed structure.

With Mei-li leading the way, he entered the building and then froze as a joyful chorus of massed voices greeted them. Standing in the room's center, was a group of over fifty children, ranging from mere tots to teen-agers. Each was dressed in a spotless white uniform with matching red neckerchiefs.

A trio of adult supervisors raised their hands, and the children instantly began singing. Justin recognized the first song as a simple Chinese folk tune of welcome. He almost fainted from shock when he heard the next song, for it was a superb English rendition of "Oh, Susanna!" As soon as it was over, a wide-eyed, pony-tailed youngster of approximately three years of age, waddled out from the pack, and handed both Mei-li and Justin a bright red long-stemmed rose. The toddler then curtsied, and both newcomers fought to contain the tears of joy produced by this heartwarming welcome.

The next individual to greet them was the commune's director. He was a robust old-timer, who sported a full head of bristly silver hair and a Fu Manchu-style mustache, which extended well beyond his chin. It was most apparent that news of their visit had preceded them, and the elder apologized for the humble welcome, explaining that it was all that they had time to prepare.

Since most of the adults were still out in the fields working, Justin and Mei-li took this opportunity to take a tour of the compound area. They found the various buildings in an excellent state of repair, and the common grounds spotlessly clean. After visiting the auditorium, they moved on to view the cafeteria-style dining room, the day-care facility, the school, the infirmary, and, finally, one of the individual cottages where the commune members were housed.

By this time, Mei-li was anxious to see her parents, yet the director seemed a bit hesitant to let them out of his sight. He explained that Mei-li's father was a good distance away, planning a new series of terraced rice paddies on the commune's northern outskirts. Her mother proved to be a bit more accessible, for she was working in a nearby vegetable-sorting station. Though the director emphasized that the workday would soon be over, Mei-li persisted until he finally gave in and personally led them into the fields.

The sun was rapidly falling toward the western horizon, yet the heat and humidity showed no sign of letting up. They traveled by foot, following a packed-earth roadway through a broad, furrowed field that lay immediately behind the meeting house. The director explained that this field had just been harvested, and they soon caught sight of the crop as they approached a huge mound of dark green cabbage. Set beside this mound was a large corrugated-steel shed. Inside was a wooden sorting table, behind which five women were in the process of trimming cabbage heads. They did so with the aid of a cleaver-type knife. Justin was engrossed in watching the women expertly wield their razor-sharp implements when he heard an excited shout from Mei-li.

"Mother!"

Though each of the women raised their heads, it proved to be the figure working at the far end of the line whose face broke out in a warm smile. Dropping her cleaver on the table, she broke from the ranks of her coworkers as her daughter ran into her open arms.

Justin was touched as he watched this joyous reunion. Even though Mei-li was dressed in a bright yellow sun dress and her mother in a drab green apron and pants, the two looked almost like twins. They were the exact same height and had similar trim figures. Even their facial features were alike. Only the gray that streaked the mother's thick mane of black hair gave away her true age.

After giving the two women several minutes to get reacquainted, Justin sauntered over to introduce himself.

"Mother," said Mei-li, switching to English, "I'd like you to meet Mr. Justin Pollock, from New York City."

The actor was surprised when the older woman greeted him in perfect English. "Welcome to the Blue Swan commune, Mr. Pollock. It is an honor to meet you."

They shook hands and Justin knew in an instant that she was extremely well educated. "The honor is mine, ma'am. I can't tell you how exciting it is to be here."

He spoke this last sentence in Chinese, and Mei-li's mother grinned appreciatively and responded in the same language. "Your diction is excellent, Mr. Pollock. May I ask where you learned to speak our language?"

"Actually, my mother is Chinese. In fact, she was born in Nanning. And please, call me Justin."

"Only if you call me Shou," she replied in English. "I hope you don't mind my reverting to your native language, but I get so little chance to practice it, I have almost forgotten how to hold a proper conversation."

Justin shook his head. "Let me assure you that you're doing wonderfully."

"You're too kind," said Shou, who then looked to her daughter. "I hope our esteemed director hasn't bored you both to death with an endless stream of statistics. Did he offer you anything to eat?"

"We're fine, Mother," returned Mei-li. "The director has been most cordial. And both of us wouldn't exchange the greeting that we got back at the meeting house for anything in the world. Those children are just priceless!"

"Speaking of children, when are you going to have one of your own?" quizzed her mother. "It's time for you to settle down and have that baby you were always dreaming about when you were a teen-ager. Or have your goals changed since then?"

Mei-li could only shrug her shoulders and look toward Justin, who gave her a supportive wink. The American had recently heard these very same words from the lips of his own mother, and he realized that their two cultures weren't really that different after all.

A loud bell began tolling in the distance, and Shou explained that this signaled the completion of the workday. While her coworkers finished up their chores, she informed the director that she would be responsible for escorting the two newcomers back to the village. At first, the director protested. Then, deciding it wasn't worth the effort, he agreed to let them go.

Mei-li hadn't seen her mother in over a year, and the two chattered happily together, catching up with the latest family gossip during the hike back to the village. This was fine with Justin, who took the opportunity to study the dozens of returning workers with whom they now shared the road. In general, they seemed a healthy, contented group, sporting trim figures and tanned, weathered faces. Ages from young adult to senior citizen were represented, and each was dressed in a similar uniform of loose-fitting, drab-green cotton fatigues.

Because of their alien garb, Justin and Mei-li were instantly conspicuous as outsiders. Yet the curious stares that they drew were polite and brief. Justin was able to overhear several discreetly whispered comments. One of these remarks came from a group of young women who were admiring Mei-li's dress. Another came from the lips of a wizened elder, who recognized Justin's country of origin from the blue jeans that he wore. Wishing that he was wearing something less conspicuous, the American stepped to the road's shoulder as he heard a truck approaching from the rear.

The vehicle quickly passed them, leaving a cloud of dust in its wake. It was an ancient wood-paneled lorry, filled to the brim with ripe, green grapes. Its presence caused a ripple of excitement amongst the returning farmers, for this was the first grape crop of the year,

141

and tonight it would be turned into wine. Justin remembered that their taxi driver had mentioned something about the excellent quality of the local wine, and the actor wondered if this brew would be available for public consumption.

As they got closer to the village, the road split off into three separate paths. They turned onto the trail leading to the left. Little more than a footpath, it snaked its way past the meeting house, then crossed over a dike separating two immense, flooded rice paddies. Justin soon caught sight of their apparent goal in the distance, a compound comprising approximately three dozen whitewashed cottages set at the base of a solitary, jagged limestone peak.

Ten minutes later, they entered one of these compact structures. Shou gave them a quick tour of its interior. It reminded Justin of a cabin he'd once stayed in back in New York's Catskill Mountains. Simply furnished, it consisted of a combined living room and kitchen area, two tiny bedrooms, and a cramped bathroom. One of the bedrooms was being utilized as a study, and besides the mattress which lay on its floor, it was furnished with a cluttered desk and stacks of assorted books. Justin was surprised to find that many of these volumes were world history texts, printed in English. While Shou went off to prepare tea, Mei-li explained the presence of such a collection.

"This library is my father's most prized possession. His collection was once many times larger than what you see here, but during the Cultural Revolution, much of it was burned by the Red Guards.

"You see, Father was head of the History Department back at Peking Union University. He held this position from 1958 to 1966, when he was denounced as a bourgeois and sent here to learn proper Maoism from the peasants. Mother was an English professor at the University, and was also denounced. As it turned out, both were lucky to escape with their lives. I had an older brother who wasn't so fortunate."

Walking over to the desk, Mei-li picked up a small gilded frame which held a single black and white photograph. She handed it to Justin, who took in a bright-eyed Chinese lad about sixteen years of age.

"That was my brother Ping. The photo was taken three months before he was killed by a gang of Red Guards who had broken into our house to search for subversive materials. That same evening, we were arrested and led out of the capital. Not long afterwards, my mother and father were sent here to work the land, while I was assigned to a work detail in far-off Inner Mongolia."

"Those must have been nightmarish times," observed Justin as he handed the photo back to Mei-li. "But China has changed much since Mao's death. Why haven't your parents returned to Beijing to get their teaching positions back? I'm certain that their expertise would be most welcomed."

"You are probably right, Justin. But my brother's death affected my folks in such a way that they could never go back to life as it was before that fateful afternoon when the Red Guards stormed our house. Besides, I honestly think that they really enjoy working the land now."

"I bet that it was really hard for them to adjust to such a change in lifestyles," offered the American.

"You don't know the half of it," Mei-li said fer-

143

vently. "This land was raw and untamed in those days, and my parents were always given the hardest, most undesirable tasks of all. For the first several years, Father was confined to a detail whose only job was to treat human waste so that it could be used on the fields as a fertilizer. Mother had a pigsty for her exclusive domain.

"Just as unpleasant as these physical tasks, were the mental cruelties they were constantly subjected to. For after a full twelve hours in the fields, they were herded into a political indoctrination session, which often lasted into the wee hours of the morning. Thus it wasn't long until their spirits were broken as well as their backs.

"It wasn't until 1976 that the powers that be allowed my father to start collecting books once again. I was just starting my studies at the University at that time, and did my best to forward to him every available volume I could get my hands on. His whole outlook on life seemed to change soon afterwards, and the pall of gloom that had descended upon him during the Cultural Revolution slowly dissipated.

"Today, the entire commune comes to him for guidance and advice. Why, he even runs a lending library from this very room. Mother seems to have adjusted as well, although she does wish that she had more opportunity to practice her English."

"Did I just hear my name mentioned?" Came a voice from the other room. "I hope that whatever you were saying was complimentary. Now, how about joining me for some tea?"

Returning to the living room, Mei-li and Justin seated themselves around a small wooden table. Shou handed each of them a white porcelain cup filled with a steaming green brew. Justin carefully sipped this beverage, and found that it tasted vaguely of cinnamon. The subtle flavor was pleasing, and he was in the midst of sitting back to enjoy his drink when the front door swung open.

Entering with a lively step was a tall, well-built gentleman dressed in the customary green fatigues of a peasant. Justin was instantly reminded of the pictures of Mao Tse-tung that still plastered the capital. The newcomer shared the Chairman's full face and bright, inquisitive eyes. His mere demeanor commanded respect, and when his expression lit up upon spotting the figure of Mei-li seated at the table, there was no doubt as to his identity.

"Is that my Little Flower?" warmly greeted Mei-li's father, immediately wrapping her in his embrace. While still hugging her, he added, "Are my eyes deceiving me, or have you grown even more beautiful since I last saw you?"

Absorbing her father's standard salutation, Mei-li replied, "And you look younger and more fit than ever before. How do you manage it, Father?"

The elder's eyes sparkled with joy. "It's working the land that keeps the wrinkles of age away, daughter. That, a loving spouse, and faithfully practising Tai Chi are the secrets of longevity."

With this comment, Mei-li's mother loudly cleared her throat, and the two reluctantly broke their embrace. Only then did her father turn his attention to their guest.

"Ah, you must be the American actor who has honored us with his presence. Welcome to our humble

145

home. I am Wu Chiang-tzu, but please call me Chiang, as my friends do."

"Justin Pollock," returned the American, who stood and offered his hand. "But that's Justin to you."

"Very well. Justin it will be. I do hope that your needs have been taken care of."

Justin could tell that his host was sincere with his inquiry, and in replying he expressed himself as honestly as possible. "Everyone has been most thoughtful. In fact, I feel so comfortable here that it's almost as if I've found myself a second home."

Chiang beamed. "That's what I like to hear, my friend. What little we have is yours to share. Now, what's this I hear about a banquet being held in the central dining room tonight in our guest's honor?"

This was the first that Justin and Mei-li had heard of such a celebration, and Shou quickly apologized for her oversight. "In all the excitement, I completely forgot to tell you two about it. I do hope you'll forgive me."

"Why, of course we will, Mother," Mei-li replied. "But the commune didn't have to go to all this trouble just for us."

"What do you mean, trouble?" retorted her mother. "When we got word of your impending visit, the director immediately called a special meeting of the operating committee. When they learned that an American V.I.P. would be accompanying you, the committee unanimously voted to treat him as if he were the premier himself. After all, we are isolated here, and it's been almost a decade since the government last allowed a foreigner to visit us."

"I believe that the delegation was composed of a

group of agricultural specialists associated with your President Nixon," explained Chiang. "The commune was then barely a third of its present size, and we didn't even have the central meeting house built as yet. But even then we managed to scrape together a decent welcoming meal, which was served under a canvas awning. Thank the fates that it didn't rain!"

Justin still couldn't believe that all of this fuss was for him and he felt humbled. "This is a visit that I shall never forget. I'm afraid though, that I brought along nothing formal to wear."

Carefully eyeing his figure, Shou responded, "You have nothing to be embarassed about, for we dress very simply here. But if you feel uncomfortable, I do believe there might be a couple of suitable outfits in the spare closet that should fit you."

Mindful of the stares his blue jeans drew earlier in the day, Justin agreed to give the proferred clothing a try. It was Mei-li's father who led him to the closet in the extra bedroom, where Justin found a round-collared khaki Mao jacket and a pair of matching trousers that fit him quite well. A remnant of Chiang's university days, the outfit was spotlessly clean and kept stored in a heavy plastic garment bag. While Justin tried the outfit on, the elder remained in the room and asked him question after question. Chiang had a decent knowledge of the theater and wanted to know what it was like to work as an actor.

Justin liked the man instantly. His eyes glistened with intellect, and he listened carefully to each word of Justin's response before questioning him anew. The elder asked about America's current political, social, and economic condition. Justin began by describing how his countrymen were looking forward to the summit with the Soviet Union. This subject immediately caught the interest of Chiang, and soon both men were engaged in a spirited conversation regarding the wisdom of trusting the Russians when it came to treaty adherence.

They had just agreed that verification was the key to any successful treaty with the U.S.S.R., when Mei-li poked her head into the room to inform them that they would be leaving for the banquet shortly. Promising to continue their discussion at a later date, Chiang rushed off to clean up and change. A quarter of an hour later, they were on their way, by foot, to the central meeting house.

The banquet itself was held in the communal dining room. Here Justin Pollock was led to the seat reserved for the guest of honor, at the head of the main table. Mei-li was seated on his left, with the commune's director taking the seat to Justin's right. Mei-li's parents were seated at an adjoining table, made up exclusively of the commune's older members. By six thirty sharp, the room was filled with the remaining diners, who included members of every family currently living at the communal farm. All told, over one hundred individuals were in attendance.

The meal began when the director picked up a pair of chopsticks and used them to fill Justin's plate with an assortment of delicacies from a large bowl. The food had been brought to the table by several of the older students, who still wore their white uniforms. While the other diners began filling their plates, the actor sought Mei-li's help in identifying the composition of this first course. She explained that these were

148

the customary cold appetizers, all of which were products raised or grown on the commune. They included carp, chopped liver, minced quail eggs, smoke-cured ham, and chicken slices soaked in wine. The assortment was extremely tasty, and Justin needed no prompting to dig in with his own bamboo chopsticks. He was just finishing off the chopped liver, when the director picked up his wineglass and rose to offer the first toast of the evening.

"Workers of the Blue Swan commune, I am honored to officially welcome Mr. Justin Pollock to our ranks this evening. Mr. Pollock is an American actor who was invited to visit our country, along with the rest of his theater company, by none other than our esteemed premier, Lin Shau-ping. He is accompanied tonight by Mei-li Wu, whose proud parents, Chiang and Shou, have been invaluable members of our humble community since its inception.

"Please join me in raising your glasses in a toast. For all of us wish our guests a most pleasant stay and long, healthy lives."

He then made certain to click glasses with both Justin and Mei-li before taking a drink. The glass contained a delightfully smooth white wine, which Justin learned was the Blue Swan's own vintage. Understanding now why the taxi driver had raved about this wine, the American savored its delicate bouquet while turning back to his appetizers.

The meal continued in a succession of courses which included steamed trout, roast goose, fresh mushrooms sauteed in ginger and scallion sauce, sweet and sour chicken, and an assortment of cooked vegetables ranging from broccoli to crispy pea pods. Accompanying these dishes were bowls of rice and tangy Chinese noodles.

Halfway through the feast, Mei-li explained to Justin that it was customary for the guest of honor to return his host's toast at this time. The American took a few minutes to mentally compose his response, then picked up his wineglass and stood.

"I want to thank each and every one of you for this warm reception," he said in perfect Chinese. "I have been here only a few hours, but I already feel at home. You have graciously opened your homes and hearts to me, and I will forever be in your debt.

"I have been in China a little over a week. Most of that time was spent in Beijing. Your capital is magnificent, but I feel that the real soul of this country lies in communities such as this one. That is why I'm so grateful that I was allowed to visit you. You can be assured that I will take back to my own country a glowing report of your efforts here at Blue Swan. May you continue on in peace and prosperity in the years to come."

The room filled with warm smiles as Justin turned to click glasses with all of those seated at his table. As he finally sipped his wine, Mei-li bent over and whispered in his ear, "Well done, my friend. That toast will be talked about around here for years to come."

Beaming at this compliment, the American replied, "It was all meant most sincerely. Yet how can I ever properly repay them for all they've done for us tonight?"

Mei-li shook her head. "Don't even think about it, Justin. Just having you here is an honor. These hardworking people are proud of their efforts, and sharing their bounty with a respected foreigner is their way of letting the whole world know of their success."

The arrival of a platter of desserts diverted Justin's attention. Indulging an insatiable sweet tooth, he helped himself to a generous portion of delicious sweet cakes made with water-chestnut jelly and cold almond cream. Washing these pastries down with a cupful of green tea, he looked up when a loud gong suddenly sounded.

A large empty space had been left in the center of the room, and as the resonant sound of the gong faded, two robed figures appeared here holding musical instruments. Both were female and looked like mere teen-agers. Justin recognized the two-string, cellolike instruments that they proceeded to set up as being erhus. He had previously heard one played at an outdoor concert at Lincoln Center, in New York, and he would never forget its unique sound.

Using stringed, violin-type bows, the two musicians began a haunting, mournful melody, that had a slight atonal quality. The American was instantly captivated, and became even more so when another robed figure joined them at the room's center. Approximately the same age as the two musicians, this individual walked with the grace of a dancer. Her long black hair was braided in a bun on top of her head, and her face was made up in a most dramatic fashion. With thick lines of mascara emphasizing her eyes, cheekbones highlighted with contrasting rouge, and brightly painted red lips, she looked almost unearthly.

As she turned to directly face Justin, she raised her hands and began swaying to the music. The hypnotizing melody continued to develop, and the figure was soon caught up in an intricate interpretive dance. Justin was especially fascinated by the way the young dancer utilized her hands to tell her story. She moved with the grace of a delicate bird, and when the American caught sight of the life-sized blue swan etched in sequins on the back of her robe, he knew that this was indeed the effect that she wanted to convey.

Unaware of the passage of time, Justin looked on spellbound. Ballet had always been one of his favorite forms of entertainment, and this performance was a most unique one. It was evident that both the dancer and the musicians were trying to paint a somber picture, which had something to do with a tragic love affair. Ever mindful that the commune was also called the Blue Swan, the American wondered if this dance had anything to do with why the community chose this distinctive name. Hopeful that Mei-li would be able to clarify this later on, Justin sat forward as the music rose in a spirited crescendo. Following the melody's rising tempo, the dancer began a series of whirling pirouettes. All this came to a climax when the musicians struck their final chord, and the blue-robed figure slumped to the floor motionless.

Several seconds of stunned silence followed, after which the room erupted in a wave of rousing applause. Justin quickly joined in, and watched as the dancer rose to her feet, politely bowed, then exited with the musicians at her side. Sadly, there was no encore, and the banquet soon came to a conclusion after a platter of hot towels was passed around.

It was during the long walk back to the cottage, that Mei-li's mother explained exactly what the dance was meant to symbolize. Legend had it that long before the

Communists came to power, in an ancient time when an emperor still lived in the Forbidden City, a pair of young lovers lived in a village that was situated where the commune now lay. On the night before they were to be wed, a jealous suitor stabbed the groom-to-be to death. The bride didn't learn of this until the next morning, and after slumping to the ground completely heartbroken, she rose and ran off into the surrounding hills, where she killed herself by jumping off a lofty precipice. Exactly two weeks later, as the full moon rose over the village, a single blue swan was seen floating on the nearby Lijiang. Such a magnificent bird had never been seen in this region before, and the locals could only surmise that it was the spirit of the young woman who had taken her life fourteen days earlier.

Shou ended the tale with a curious side note. It was rumored that to this very day, if one hiked to the spot where the Lijiang cut through the surrounding mountains on the night of the full moon, this same blue swan could be seen floating on the waters, patiently waiting for her lover to join her.

Justin absorbed this fable, pleased with himself at having correctly interpreted the ballet merely by studying the dancer's movements and listening to the accompanying music. Of course, much of the credit went to the young performers, who so expertly played out their intended roles.

As they continued on to the cottage, an owl could be heard hooting in the distance. It was a warm, humid night, the cloudless sky was home to a myriad of twinkling stars. They were crossing a dike that separated two immense rice paddies, when the group temporarily halted to take in a breathtaking event occurring on the eastern horizon. Here, a luminous full moon was in the process of rising. As the glowing lunar orb broke over a ridge of craggy limestone peaks, the entire landscape was bathed in its radiance. By a light almost as bright as that of day, Justin scanned the lush valley and found himself wondering if somewhere in the hills beyond, the magical blue swan was indeed patiently waiting for its mate. Enchanted with this thought, the American reluctantly moved on when his hosts once again continued homeward.

The day had been a full and wondrous one, and Justin was exhausted by the time they finally reached the cottage. A bed was prepared for him in the living room, and as soon as his head hit the pillow, he was out. His sleep was deep and his dreams quick in coming. In one dream, he found himself on a small boat floating down a swiftly running underground river. Massive stalactites and stalagmites clung to the cavern's roof and floor, and all was quiet except for the mad rush of the tumbling water. He felt the heavy stirrings of fear settle in the pit of his belly as the current intensified, and soon he was shooting through a wild series of rapids.

Just as it appeared that he would never survive this passage, the melodious, haunting strains of a strangely familiar ehru solo rose above the roar of the stream. Calmed by this mournful music, he sighed gratefully when the small craft he had been traveling in emerged above ground. The current was much smoother here, and his way was now lit by a brilliant full moon. A collection of roughly cut peaks formed the river's banks, and as he peered downstream, he could just make out the figure of a massive blue swan effortlessly floating on the distant current.

He awoke eight hours later, his strange dream all but forgotten. The bare light of dawn filtered in through the curtained windows, and Justin rose from his mattress feeling rested and ravenously hungry. Careful to make as little noise as possible, he exited the cottage to watch the new day take shape.

Outside, the air was brisk and smelled of the earth and green growth. All was quiet except for the sigh of the gusting wind and the cries of the songbirds. Though the sun still wasn't visible, the dawn was rapidly developing. Puffs of white clouds drifted in the powder-blue heavens, and Justin gloried in the simple beauty of it all.

As he scanned the surrounding countryside, he spotted a thin trail of smoke rising from the chimney of one of the whitewashed cottages lying to his right. Set immediately in front of this simple structure was a broad green meadow, which was bisected by a narrow brook. Standing beside this stream was a lone figure doing his morning exercises. There was just enough light for Justin to see a head of long gray hair and a well-developed Fu Manchu mustache. Realizing that he had spotted the commune's director, the American watched as the elder raised his limbs and swung his body to and fro with the grace of a ballet dancer. Fully captivated by this sight, Justin was caught off guard when a deep male voice broke into his thoughts.

"Good morning, Justin. Would you like to join me in my own Tai Chi routine?"

Startled by this unexpected interruption, the American turned and set his eyes on Mei-li's father.

"A glorious morning such as this deserves a proper beginning," the elder observed. "That is why we practice the Tai Chi before getting on with the events of the day. It's really rather simple, and less than one half hour a day is needed to derive the benefits of this discipline.

"Did you know that Tai Chi originated many centuries ago, when a man watched a fight between a serpent and a crane? The crane attacked the snake repeatedly with stabs of his beak, but the snake merely shifted his body slightly at the proper moment, thus never letting his attacker touch him. When the mortal viewer grasped this fact, he came up with the idea of adapting it for human use. Thus we now have a method of dealing with an attack by using flexible maneuvers, correct timing, and sensitivity to avoid the aggressor's offensive moves.

"Later, Taoists tied the Tai Chi to their philosophy of life. I'm certain that you have knowledge of the yin and the yang, the so-called negative and positive aspects of the universe. The master of Tai Chi seeks to establish a method of living in harmony with the many overwhelming powerful forces of the world around him. He does so by avoiding extremes and creating a state of mental and physical balance, careful never to waste needless energy. Thus the practitioner of this art uses only that degree of strength necessary to perform a movement, thereby conserving energy and avoiding needless tension.

"We practice Tai Chi merely as an exercise. It has amazing results and can add many extra years to one's life. Now, what do you say to my sharing with you the first, elementary movements?"

Justin wasn't about to let such an opportunity pass him by, and instantly accepted Chiang's offer. The elder proved to be an excellent teacher and began by instructing him in the proper posture and breathing techniques. Only then, did he demonstrate the first movement, a flowing shift of weight from right foot to left, which led to a gradual raising of the arms until one limp hand was in front of each shoulder.

This basic movement was surprisingly complex, and Justin continued to work on it while the elder went on with his daily routine. This continuous sequence was made up of a variety of different positions with exotic names such as Grasp Bird's Tail, Stork Spreads Wings, and Carry Tiger to Mountain. Altogether there were some sixty separate movements, which took approximately ten minutes to complete.

By the time Chiang had finished, the sun had risen. There seemed to be a new closeness between the elder and his guest as Chiang led the way back to the cottage for breakfast. Mei-li was busy in the kitchen, working beside her mother as the two entered. As before, Justin made himself right at home, sitting down to a meal that had been prepared especially in his honor.

They started off with freshly squeezed mandarin orange juice. This was followed by a heaping platter of scrambled eggs, ham, and steamed rice. Mei-li had baked some American-style corn muffins, which went perfectly with the commune's own guava jelly. All this was washed down with copious amounts of piping hot oolong tea, which Justin sweetened with clover honey.

After all had eaten their fill, Chiang invited his daughter and Justin to join him in the fields. Today he would be working in the commune's extreme northern outskirts, where they were seeking out new land to develop for their ever increasing rice crop. Mei-li and Justin eagerly agreed to accompany him, and the elder instructed his wife to pack a picnic lunch and meet them at noon beside the mango grove.

Faced once again with being conspicuous in his blue jeans, Justin asked if there was any extra native attire that he might wear. Once more the spare closet was tapped, and soon the actor was decked out in the homespun drab-green fatigues worn by the average peasant. When a straw hat was added to this costume, one would have had to look extremely close to identify the American as anything but a local.

With Mei-li and her father dressed in similar attire, the trio went outside and headed for the central meeting house. Here they joined up with two other men, who would be accompanying them on their mission. A horse-drawn flatbed cart, mounted on huge truck tires, was appropriated to carry both themselves and their surveying equipment. And shortly thereafter, they began to make their way down a narrow earthen roadway headed due north.

It took the better part of an hour to reach the end of the road. During that time they passed fields full of cabbage, wheat, taro, and sugar cane. After parking the wagon in the shelter of a mango grove, they shouldered their equipment and continued northward on foot. Now, they traveled along a simple trail that led straight up into the green scrub-filled foothills. The going here was rough, and Justin could feel the full heat of the morning sun as they began climbing a series of steep switchbacks.

By the time they reached the summit, the American was soaked in sweat. This was in striking contrast to the three commune workers, whose foreheads were completely dry, even with the extra burden of the equipment they were carrying. Mei-li was also winded, and struggled over to Justin's side to catch her breath. When she could speak, his attractive traveling companion pointed out the adjoining valley where the path now led. Cut by a good-sized stream, this clover-filled plain appeared untouched by the hand of man.

"That stream is a tributary of the Lijiang," offered Mei-li between gasps. "Its source is deep in the mountains."

Before Justin could fully absorb this magnificent pastoral scene, the sound of a muffled explosion rumbled in the near distance. It was Mei-li's father who identified the source of this blast.

"As you can hear for yourselves, we are not so alone here. Several days ago, the Army began a mining operation in the hills just east of this ridge."

"I believe we encountered elements of this detail while we were driving in yesterday," offered Mei-li. "We saw all sorts of heavy machinery and men, and it took every bit of official clout that I had to get us past their checkpoint."

"Our taxi driver said something about their searching for uranium in these hills," interjected Justin.

Chiang shook his head. "That's what they say, but for the life of me, I never heard of anyone finding a decent deposit of uranium in these parts. It's just not compatible with the local geological makeup."

As another explosion sounded in the distance, Mei-li looked in the direction of the blast. Following her gaze, Justin picked out the bare outlines of a goat track that crossed over the ridge on which they now stood, and merged with the eastern horizon.

"Would it be all right if we hiked over there and took a look?" he asked hopefully.

Scanning the trail, Mei-li's father answered cautiously, "I'm not really certain how far that goat track extends. It might afford you a decent look at this so-called mining operation, and then it might not. If you want to take a chance, then it's fine with me. Only, be careful not to show yourselves if you come upon any of the soldiers. I'm certain that they're armed and they hate to be spied upon."

Excited by this opportunity to do some real exploring, Mei-li beamed. "Thanks, Father. We'll be extra certain to proceed cautiously."

"I thought that you two couldn't resist such a thing," returned Chiang. "I'd join you, but we've got our work to do. Meet us back here in three hours, and we'll hike back to the mango grove to join Mother for lunch. And remember, keep to that trail and be alert for any patrols! I'd hate to have to spring you two from jail."

Taking this last comment as the joke that it was meant to be, Justin and Mei-li laughed, waving to the trio of commune workers as they quickly descended into the adjoining valley. Moments later, the young couple were all alone on the ridge, with only a circling hawk as a companion.

"Well, I guess it's just you and me, kiddo," offered Justin playfully. "Shall we be off to see what the People's Liberation Army is doing out here in this gorgeous spot?"

Signaling him to lead the way, Mei-li fell in behind

her American companion, who from the rear looked like any other native Chinese peasant. The goat track proved to be a bit more difficult to negotiate than the trail that had carried them up to the ridge. In many places it snaked precariously around various obstacles such as exposed tree trunks and rocky outcroppings. Its surface was often littered with small pebbles which made descents particularly dangerous. While following the track into one hollow, Mei-li lost her footing altogether, and managed to stay upright only by grasping at a nearby bush for support.

They also encountered a variety of wildlife on this trail. Lizards, rabbits, and large coveys of quail were the most frequent animals spotted. Justin caught sight of a full-grown buck charging off into the thick underbrush, and Mei-li arrived at his side in time to see the wildly shaking tree limbs that were left in the deer's wake.

As the sun rose higher in the heavens, the temperature rose proportionately. Fortunately, a stiff wind continued to blow in from the southwest, which served to make the humid conditions a bit more tolerable.

Justin had just stopped to take a look at his watch, noting that they had been on this path for almost three-quarters of an hour, when another explosion sounded. This blast was much louder than the others they had heard.

"It can't be much further now," Justin observed. "Perhaps over the next rise."

"Remember what my father warned of," cautioned Mei-li. "The PLA is no organization to be taken lightly."

"Don't worry. We're only going to take a look. What

harm is there in that?"

Though Mei-li had plenty of horror stories regarding unintentional confrontations with the Chinese military, she decided to keep them to herself for the time being. With Justin again taking the lead, they followed the trail up a steep hillside. Mei-li was just approaching the top of this rise, when her companion suddenly crouched down and motioned her to do likewise. She did so without question.

"I can see them!" exclaimed the American, who gestured for her to join him.

Mei-li reached his side on her hands and knees. Her heart was pounding away in her chest as she cautiously peered over the ledge that topped the rise. Visible below was a broad, tree-covered valley, much wider than the one her father was presently surveying. She gasped upon viewing the hundreds of bare-chested soldiers working at the base of the hills forming the valley's opposite ridge. Interspersed amongst these swarming figures were dozens of pieces of heavy equipment, including bulldozers, tractors, and canvas-sided trucks. Most of the activity was centered around a central supply depot, where an immense stack of wooden crates was being transferred, piece-by-piece, into a massive entrance way cut into the rocky base of the opposing ridge.

Taking in this back-breaking process, Justin observed excitedly, "They aren't digging a mine! It looks like they've uncovered the entrance to a cavern which they're filling with the contents of those crates."

This indeed seemed to be the case, and Mei-li looked puzzled. Nowhere in the acacia-lined valley was there any drilling equipment visible. The heavy machinery that was on hand was being utilized solely to widen the cave's limestone entrance. It was soon apparent that the blasts they'd heard were detonations of dynamite, which was also being used to widen the entrance to the cave. This was made obvious when a series of shrill whistle blasts sent the men scrambling for cover. Minutes later, a deafening explosion echoed down the valley, causing a cloud of crushed rock and dust to temporarily veil the cavern's entrance. Hardly had the air cleared, when the men were seen crawling from their hiding places to return to work.

"I wonder what this whole thing is all about?" asked Justin, his curiosity now fully aroused.

Though Mei-li's interest was also piqued, she responded guardedly, "Whatever it is, it's certainly none of our business. Let's go back and tell Father."

Hardly paying attention to her reply, Justin scanned the eastern wall of the scrub-lined ridge on which they stood. "It looks like the trail we've been following continues on down this hillside. Since there's plenty of natural cover, what do you think about seeing how much closer we can get to that clearing? Surely those crates are labeled, and that means that we'll be able to find out what's inside of them."

"But Father warned us!" cautioned Mei-li.

"We'll make certain to keep covered," retorted the actor. "If there's the least bit of risk involved, I'll be the first to turn back. All right?"

Mei-li took one more look at the swarming mass of soldiers before shrugging her shoulders and replying, "I would like to know exactly what they're doing down there if it isn't a mining operation. But first promise me that you really will turn back if there's the least

163

possibility that we'll be discovered."

Tracing the outline of a cross over his chest, Justin said, "Cross my heart and hope to die."

When Mei-li seemed puzzled by this response, the American explained, "That means that I definitely promise. Now, come on and let's get to the bottom of this mystery. Your father will never believe it."

Even though it was against her cautious nature, Mei-li accompanied Justin over the ridge's summit and through a thick stand of fragrant acacias. This put them on a portion of the goat track that led directly into the valley. The downward track followed a series of switchbacks that made descending somewhat easier to manage. Though narrow, the trail was bordered by thick stands of vegetation which often veiled even the sunlight. Thankful for this cover, Mei-li nevertheless felt her pulse flutter when the sound of voices was suddenly heard nearby. Without a moment's hesitation, Justin grabbed her hand and pulled her into a particularly dense patch of shrubbery. Seconds later, a trio of khaki-uniformed soldiers sauntered up the trail and halted right in front of this same clump of undergrowth.

Silently cursing their bad luck, Justin peeked through an opening in the bushes and watched as one of the soldiers pulled out a package of cigarettes, which he proceeded to share with his comrades. They didn't appear to be armed, and it was evident that they had merely sneaked off into the cover of the hills to grab a smoke. Resigned to waiting them out, the American looked to his right to see how his companion was doing. At that moment his eyes caught a sudden movement in the tangled web of greenery that hugged the ground.

Following the direction of his startled gaze, Mei-li froze as she spotted the writhing body of a huge snake. The serpent's skin was patterned in bright green and yellow diamonds, yet it wasn't until Mei-li sighted its triangular head, that she identified it as a deadly poisonous Guangxi rattler.

It was far from being one of her favorite creatures and Mei-li's heart pounded madly away in her chest. Her limbs shook as she vainly attempted to control the fear generated by this unwelcome visitor. Her companion seemed to be silently imploring her to keep her cool, and she actually thought that she could do so, when a heavy object plopped onto her head. She felt a rustling sensation in her hair, and gingerly reached up to identify it.

It took merely a touch of this creature's hairy body for her to know that it was a monstrous spider. As much as she feared snakes, spiders were the cause of her worst nightmares, and she instinctively acted to rid herself of it. Smashing the flattened palm of her right hand down onto her scalp, she squashed the spider. At the very same moment, the snake let out a loud hiss and began rattling its tail. This combination of events proved too much for Mei-li's fragile state of nerves and she screamed, darting from the bush with her hands madly swatting at her scalp. The American merely had to take a single look at the massive brown tarantula that fell from Mei-li's head to let out his own scream and quickly join her in flight.

The three soldiers reacted to this commotion in a most unprofessional manner. As Mei-li darted out into their midst, the trio's first reaction was pure self-preservation. Yet when they turned to scatter, they ended up tripping over each other's limbs, with Mei-li falling down right on top of them. By the time Justin joined this tangle of human bodies, a whistle-toting officer had arrived at the site, drawn by Mei-li's screams. With three shrill blasts of his whistle, he cautiously moved forward to identify the mass of bodies that now lay squirming in the narrow earthen clearing.

CHAPTER SEVEN

From the moment Petty Officer First Class Reginald Warner heard that they would be returning to port, shortly after their encounter with the Soviet sub, he could think of but one thing. The Thai dancer had cast a spell on him, as surely as if she were a witch. Each spare moment, when he wasn't involved with his official duties, his thoughts went back to their evening of shared pleasure. Recalling her gorgeous body and sensual, caring ways, Reggie found himself infatuated. He had certainly been with his fair share of women in his time, but Kim was unique.

They arrived back in Pearl on a stormy wind-swept afternoon, and Reggie was forced to stay on board until well after dinner. It was rapidly approaching nine o'clock when he was finally allowed to leave the *Copperhead,* for six days of precious R and R. After stopping off at his apartment to shower and change into his civvies, he headed straight for the Doll House. Like a child on Christmas Eve, he found his pulse pounding away in anticipation as he scrambled down Salt Lake Boulevard and ducked through the tavern's padded leather doors.

It took several seconds for his eyes to adjust to the

dim red lighting inside. The air was heavy with smoke, and a good-sized crowd sat around the central stage waiting for the next dancer to appear. Reggie was walking over to ask the bartender if Kim was working this evening, when the pounding strains of Ted Nugent's "Little Miss Dangerous" issued forth from the elevated stereo speakers. Instantly turning toward the stage, he looked on as a tall, familiar figure in a black miniskirt strutted out and began swaying her hips rhythmically to the music. A chorus of spirited applause greeted the big busted Thai beauty as she teasingly began fingering the zipper of her dress.

It was like a dream come true as Reggie slowly walked over to the stage area. Still standing in the shadows, he watched his new-found love expertly work her appreciative audience. It was during the song's raucous guitar solo that Kim ripped off her abbreviated skirt and displayed her exquisite body for all those present to see. Whistling and howling in response, the sailors pressed forward to stuff their hard-earned dollar bills into her sequined G-string.

Reggie waited for her to complete her rounds before he advanced to the edge of the stage. Trying hard to keep his cool, he dug into his pocket and pulled out a crisp fifty-dollar bill. Seconds later, she was dancing directly in front of him

For an instant, their eyes met, and much to his horror, she didn't even seem to recognize him! The expressionless, bored look that had masked her face all through her act remained unchanged and Reggie felt his gut tighten. He had been so confident that his great attraction for her was mutually shared, he was totally unprepared for such a cold reception. It was as if she had already completely forgotten that he existed!

Unable to hide his disappointment, he pocketed the fifty, and was in the process of turning from the stage, when a firm hand on his shoulder kept him from doing so. Looking around, he found the dancer standing on the platform's extreme forward edge, her hand still gripping him. His pulse raced, and tears actually formed in his eyes as she winked and broke out in a warm smile. Pulling him forward, she kneeled down and kissed him passionately on the lips. This was more like the welcome that the sonar technician had expected, and he felt his loins instinctively stiffen in response.

A chorus of catcalls broke their embrace, and Kim motioned him to have a seat while she completed her act. Reggie planted himself in one of the back booths. He ordered a pair of mai-tai's, and sat back as his Far Eastern beauty danced her way through two more songs. Her G-string, which had a small American flag sewn on its crotch, was filled with bills by the time she finished her numbers.

She joined him ten minutes later. Wasting no time with pleasantries, she fell into his lap and immediately began kissing him. Her tongue probed urgently, and Reggie now knew without a doubt that she was his.

With Mick Jagger wailing out the lyrics to "Jumping Jack Flash" in the background, they embraced. After they hurriedly tossed down their drinks, Kim excused herself to get the manager's permission to leave early. Since she didn't ask for favors often, her request was promptly granted.

A light drizzle was falling as they left the club and began walking up Salt Lake Boulevard. Completely oblivious to the rain, they held each other's waists and chattered away like long lost friends. They were soaked by the time they finally reached the apartment, and it was Kim who suggested that they take a shower together.

Before ducking into the bathroom to get the shower ready, Reggie poured two long Scotches and put Otis Redding's last album on the stereo. Steaming hot water was pouring forth from the shower head as he called his love to join him.

It was as if they had never been apart. Their lips met, and as their naked bodies touched beneath the hot spray, the passion that had possesed both of them during their initial coupling instantly overtook them. Reggie needed no coaxing to get himself rock hard. Hungrily, he slurped her full breasts. Tweaking her nipples erect with his lips, he heard her sigh urgently, and knew that it was time to satisfy his lover's rising need.

Her body felt smooth and supple as he reached down to part her thighs. Wrapping one of her legs around his buttocks, she positioned herself to accept the throbbing, stiff black snake that she had missed so, these last few days. Reggie found her depths wet and primed for action. Under the soothing spray of the shower, he cautiously guided his phallus into her love channel, taking care to enter her slowly. Pushing his hips forward, he felt himself being swallowed by a pulsating, hot void that demanded all of him. Kim whimpered when this gift was given, and urgently sought out his mouth as his hips began an undulating, in-and-out movement. She cried out in ecstasy when this rhythm quickened, and seconds later, her body

170

trembled in the throes of orgasm. Reggie felt his own seed rise, and joined her in bliss as his juice squirted deep inside of her. They lay in each other's arms, temporarily spent and satiated. Only then did either one of them realize that the shower was pouring forth a torrent of cold water.

So began six of the most glorious days that Reginald Warner had ever spent. The current owner of the Doll House was an ex-submariner, and Reggie had no trouble convincing him to let Kim have a few days off. This left their days free for sightseeing, and their nights open for endless sessions of ferocious lovemaking.

What had started as a purely physical attraction was rapidly developing into something deeper. They found that they had similar interests ranging from science fiction movies to sushi and long walks on the beach. The island of Oahu was a virtual paradise, much of which neither one of them had ever seen. To explore it properly, Reggie rented a bright red Suzuki Samuri convertible. The small open car proved to be a perfect way to cover the island.

For one full day they toured Honolulu, sampling its fascinating shops, museums, and excellent restaraunts. They even managed to get tickets to see Don Ho, and capped off the evening with a luau on Waikiki Beach.

Subsequent trips took them to Diamond Head, Hanauma Bay Underwater Park, the Waimanalo Forest Reserve, and even included a tour of an operating pineapple plant. It was while strolling through the pineapple fields, that Kim opened up to him and explained the circumstances that had brought her to Hawaii only three months before.

171

Her father had been a colonel in the Thai Air Force. Eighteen years ago, while stationed in Bangkok, he had an affair with a young nightclub hostess, and Kim was born nine months later. Her father was already married, and could have easily abandoned Kim to go his own way. Fortunately, he had not. He secretly supported both mother and child, making certain that when Kim was of age she was enrolled in a Catholic school run by a group of American nuns. Kim enjoyed school, and it was here that she learned to speak English. She was even preparing to enter the University, when her father was killed in a helicopter crash near the Cambodian border. This tragic event had occurred only six months ago, and Kim and her mother were stunned to find themselves penniless.

One of her father's associates learned of Kim's plight, and offered to send her to Hawaii to escape the squalor of Bangkok. Though she hated to leave her mother, this was a once-in-a-lifetime opportunity that she couldn't easily refuse.

She arrived in Honolulu with just enough money to get a small hotel room in Pearl City. Dancing had always come naturally to her, and she had obtained her present job from a newspaper ad. The sailors proved to be a likable audience and they tipped quite generously. Kim's current plan was to save as much money as possible to enroll in the local university. Then she would secure more respectable employment as a translator, with the ultimate goal of becoming an American citizen and eventually sending for her mother.

As Reggie listened to her story, he acquired a new respect for this beautiful courageous girl. Though his own childhood, spent in the ghettos of Philadelphia, certainly hadn't been easy, Kim had been raised in an entirely different world, where hardships were all that was known. Instead of merely sitting back and accepting her fate, she worked hard to better herself. How very frightening it must have been to leave her mother and friends behind to begin a new life here in America. And listening to her ultimate goal was nothing short of inspiring!

That night over dinner, Reggie began to see her in a whole new light. Fate had brought this exquisite, brave, intelligent woman to him. She was unlike any girl he had ever met, satisfying needs deep within him that he'd had since childhood. Not only was she a tigress in bed, she was also a delightful companion to share his innermost dreams and aspirations with. Wondering how he'd gotten along without her, he hated to think what would happen if they should break up. This mere thought caused a shiver of dread to streak up his spine, and Reggie reached over to squeeze her hand. This innocent gesture caused a warm glow to paint his love's exotic face, and his fears were temporarily calmed.

They soon found themselves with only one day to go until Reggie would be going back on duty. This time the *Copperhead* would be going on a full-scale patrol, and it could very well be a month before he'd see Kim again. A new urgency guided his lovemaking as he considered this somber thought. Pledging to make their last day together a memorable one, he stayed awake long into the night, considering his options. As the first streaks of dawn filtered into the bedroom, he made the decision to ask her to marry him.

They had decided to spend their final day together

touring Waimea Falls Park. The morning broke clear and warm, and after a hearty breakfast of grits, scrambled eggs, pancakes, and sausage, they climbed into the Suzuki for the trip across Oahu's breadth.

Kim had been uncharacteristically quiet over their morning meal, and Reggie supposed that this had something to do with his call to duty in less than twenty-four hours. Snapping a Temptations tape into the car's cassette player, he proceeded to drive northward up the Kamehameha Highway. The traffic was light, and after passing Wheeler Air Force Base, they crossed a broad, rolling plateau filled with pineapple fields. Twenty minutes later, they reached the coast and turned right on Highway 83. The blue Pacific was now visible, crashing onto the beaches that lay to their left. Dozens of surfers could be seen braving the waves, which often reached gigantic proportions.

They followed the beach for six more miles, to Waimea Bay. Here, a sign reading *Waimea Falls Park* guided them inland. The roadway narrowed and led them eastward, beside a tumbling stream. Hundreds of coconut palms lined this route which cut into a steep, tree-lined valley.

The road ended at a large asphalt parking lot. Because of the still-early hour, the first tour bus from Honolulu had yet to arrive. Still, there were several dozen cars parked here. Leaving the Suzuki beside a battered Chevrolet Jimmy, they hiked to the park's main entrance.

Reggie bought them each tickets and magnificent leis. Kim was particularly impressed with her floral wreath and stroked it lovingly. The first cliff-diving exhibition of the day would be taking place in fifteen

174

minutes, and they hopped on a tram to get to the falls in time to witness this event.

Their tram driver explained that the park was situated on a 1,800-acre site that was famous for its arboretum and extensive botanical gardens. Over 3,500 varieties of plant life flourished here, while more than 30 species of birds roamed freely throughout the grounds. They were soon passing through a dense forest of ferns. A stream tumbled beside the roadway, its banks covered in brilliantly colored bougainvillea, hibiscus, and oleanders. In a clearing a little bit farther down the road, an ancient Hawaiian village had been re-created, complete with several grass huts situated in front of a hillside covered in snow-white gardenias. This would be the setting for a hula show, which would begin right after the cliff divers did their thing.

Halfway through a thick stand of Kukui trees, the tram was forced to brake to a halt when a flock of Hawaiian geese chose that moment to cross the road. The birds, whose fat bodies were covered with black and white feathers, strolled along with all the majesty befitting the official state bird of the Islands.

Kim's eyes were wide with wonder, and Reggie marveled at her innocence. The tram was soon moving once again, and they linked hands and briefly kissed.

The roar of a distant waterfall directed their attention back to the passing countryside. This distinctive surging rumble intensified until it was almost deafening. Its source still wasn't visible as the tram pulled into a circular clearing, where a small refreshment stand was located. The passengers were instructed to leave the vehicle here, and hike up a stone pathway that would take them to their immediate goal.

After stopping at the stand to share a bowl of tart pineapple spears, Reggie and Kim continued on up the trail. The roar of tumbling water was all-encompassing here, and they soon caught sight of the falls for which the park was named.

Over fifty feet high, the waterfall cascaded down a smooth stone face to a crystal clear pool of frothing water. As the two dozen or so tourists gathered beside an iron railing overlooking this pool, a drum began beating. This was followed by the appearance of four divers, two male and two female, who emerged from the thick forest of ferns opposite their audience, and dove into the pool. All four were in their late teens and wore colorful native swimwear over their deeply tanned bodies.

The drum beat quickened as they swam to the rocky wall that undercut the falls, and began climbing up its sides. This feat alone was daring, for the rock was wet and covered with slippery green moss. Yet they proceeded without incident, and gathered on a narrow ledge halfway up the wall. A young Hawaiian boy dressed in a grass skirt came out onto a clearing at the base of the waterfall, and put a conch trumpet to his lips. He blew a series of seven shrill notes, and one by one, the divers plunged headfirst into the pool below. They surfaced to a round of applause and quickly began scaling the wall once again. This time though, they stopped at various heights, and dove into the pool, with a variety of complex somersaults and flips.

Finally, one of the female divers climbed to the very summit of the waterfall. Again the conch trumpet sounded as the girl balanced herself precariously on a narrow tongue of rock. A collective gasp came from the audience as she jumped from this perch, gathering her body in a tight, spiraling ball, only to enter the water headfirst, with hardly a splash.

This incredible exploit signaled the end of the cliff-diving performance, and the audience was invited to the old Hawaiian village for the hula show. They had a half hour before this demonstration was scheduled to begin, and Reggie and Kim decided to walk to the site instead of taking the waiting tram.

A good portion of this stroll took place beside the quick-moving stream created by the waterfall's run-off. Flowers grew everywhere, and Kim became excited when she spotted a clump of blooming ginger, a variety of plant native to her homeland. As they stopped to take a closer look at the ginger, a peacock strolled out of the adjoining fern forest. The bird's plumage was spread in all its colorful glory, and Reggie cursed inwardly for forgetting to bring along his camera.

Kim seem anxious to see the hula show and Reggie obliged by finding a shortcut to the Hawaiian village. This route took them away from the stream and up a steep flight of stone steps. Once on top of the hill, they passed a collection of moss-covered volcanic blocks which centuries ago belonged to an ancient temple. An atmosphere of reverence pervaded this site, and they found themselves lowering their voices as a gesture of respect.

The village was set in an adjacent clearing. A large number of tourists had already arrived there, and were noisily congregating around the clover-filled stage area. A solid wall of white gardenias served as a backdrop. The scent of these flowers permeated the air as Reggie and Kim sat down on a log bench located in the rear of the viewing area. This vantage point kept them well away from the crowd, yet still afforded a decent view of the festivities, which began soon after they were seated.

Once again it was the pounding beat of a drum and the shrill cry of a conch trumpet that signaled the beginning of the show. Several other drums joined in, and a pulsating, hypnotic rhythm was generated. There was a loud shout and suddenly the dancers appeared. The first chorus line was formed by four native Hawaiian women. Dressed in grass skirts, brief halter tops, and leis, they easily matched the pulsating drumbeat with their swaying hips, arms, and hands. As this beat intensified, there was another loud shout, and four male dancers entered. Teaming up in pairs, they quivered and shook wildly to the intense, jungle-like pounding of the native drums. The number ended with a rousing climax as the drums abruptly stopped, and the dancers froze in midstep. It took the spellbound audience several seconds to react with a hearty round of applause.

Kim was especially appreciative of their efforts and was one of the last to stop applauding. Seated now on the edge of the bench, she looked on expectantly as a ukulele player took stage center. This portly Hawaiian officially welcomed them to the park, and announced that the next number would be an interpretation in dance of the "Hawaiian Wedding Song." Hearing this, Reggie sat forward anxiously, for this could very well prove to be the opportunity he had been waiting for.

As the musician began strumming the familiar chords of the wedding song, Reggie reached into his pants pocket and pulled out a small ring box. Though he had planned on waiting until dinner to give it to Kim, he couldn't resist opening the box and removing the gold engagement ring which had belonged to his mother. Gripping this cherished keepsake in his hand, he reached over and guided Kim's left hand into his lap. It was just as one of the female dancers emerged to interpret the song with the movement of her body and hands, that he slipped the ring onto Kim's finger. She was puzzled by his actions at first, and had to look twice to figure out what he had just done. Tears fell from her eyes as she took in the golden ring and cried out, oblivious to the crowd that was gathered around them, "Oh, Reggie!"

She was quickly in his arms, and from the mere force of her kisses, he knew that she had accepted his proposal. By this time, the audience had gotten wind that something unusual was occurring in their midst, and soon all eyes were on the two lovers, who were still deep in a passionate kiss. Only when the onlookers broke out in applause, did Reggie look up and realize that he and Kim were the cause of this commotion. He blushed, and was glad when the crowd eventually turned its attention back to the stage.

Yet one member of the audience, seated on the ground to their right, failed to return his attention to the hula dancer. Reggie caught a brief glimpse of this stranger's ruggedly handsome, weather-worn face, and realized with a start that the man was none other than his commanding officer, Captain Samuel Fuller! A pert, blond-haired woman sat at his side, and Reggie recognized her as Fuller's wife. They had never met, but the sonar technician had seen her on several occasions from a distance. Only when the grinning captain saw that Reggie had recognized him, did he nod and finally turn his gaze back to the stage.

The two numbers that followed passed in a dream, and the show was soon over. Kim still had trouble believing that the ring she was now wearing was real, and kept looking at the fourth finger of her left hand as if to be sure the gold band was still there. They remained seated as the audience broke up around them to head for the park's other attractions. Content to stay right there on the bench, Reggie looked on as Samuel Fuller and his wife rose and turned toward them. The Petty Officer First Class had never seen their skipper in shorts and a polo shirt before. Dressed as he was, he looked like any other civilian, here for an innocent day of sightseeing.

As Peg and Samuel Fuller neared them, Reggie took in a deep breath and addressed his bride-to-be. "Heads up, my little beauty. Here comes the boss and his wife."

Not really certain what he was talking about, Kim looked up in time to see a good-looking American couple headed straight for them. The man appeared older than the woman, his bearing suggesting that he held a position of great responsibility. The blonde at his side seemed vibrant and full of life, her wide grin instantly setting Kim at ease. Before Kim could question Reggie, his voice rose in greeting.

"Good morning, Captain!"

Samuel Fuller extended his hand and responded, "And to you, Mr. Warner. I'd like you to meet my wife, Peggy."

While Reggie shook hands with the vivacious blonde, Samuel Fuller added, "Chief Petty Officer

Warner here is a very important part of my staff aboard the *Copperhead*. As the senior sonar technician, he is our eyes and ears out there beneath the silent sea."

Ever mindful of his own companion, Reggie cleared his throat. "And this beautiful creature at my side is my fiancée, Kim."

Taking Kim's hand gently in his own, Samuel Fuller grinned pleasantly. "Why, I didn't know that you were engaged, Mr. Warner. My, she is a pretty one."

With this comment, Kim blushed, while Reggie quickly interjected, "Actually, I only just asked her less than ten minutes ago."

"So that's what the audience caught you in the midst of," observed Fuller with a wink. "Well, let me be the first to congratulate the two of you. You can rest assured, Kim, that Reginald here is one of the best at his job that I've ever seen. I'm certain that as long as he desires it, the U.S. Navy will be proud to employ him."

Kim nodded shyly. "Thank you, Captain. Even though we've only know each other for a few short weeks, it didn't take me long to realize how very special my husband-to-be is."

"Have you set a wedding date yet?" asked Peggy Fuller.

Reggie shook his head. "I'd like it to be as soon as possible, but it looks like we'll have to wait until we get back from patrol. Are we still going out tomorrow as scheduled, Captain?"

"That we are, Mr. Warner," retorted Samuel Fuller. "All crew have been ordered to be aboard the *Copperhead* by 0600 hours."

Peggy caught the somber expression that painted

Kim's exquisite face, and the veteran navy wife turned to the young woman sympathetically. "He'll be back safe and sound before you know it, Kim. In the meantime, you can plan the ceremony. Why don't you have it right here in Waimea? As neighbors, we visit the park often, and have seen some lovely weddings take place here."

Kim's grim look quickly dissipated. "I didn't realize that such a thing would be allowed. Why, I'd love for the ceremony to take place in such a spot. But how does one go about planning such a thing?"

"It shouldn't be too difficult," returned Peggy. "Your fiancé knows how to get hold of us. Just give me a call, and I'll be happy to help you with the arrangements."

Kim smiled warmly. "That is most kind of you. You've made a memorable day only that much happier."

Impressed with Kim's sincerity, Peggy took her husband's hand. Well aware that they had brunch reservations at the Turtle Bay Hilton, Samuel Fuller initiated the good-byes.

"It's time that we left you two lovebirds on your own. Tomorrow morning will be upon us soon enough. See you then, Mr. Warner."

"Don't forget to call," added Peggy, who shook hands with the beaming couple before turning to join her husband.

Reggie watched them leave the clearing and climb onto a tram that would take them to the parking lot. Oddly affected by this surprise confrontation, he took Kim in his arms and squeezed her fondly.

"I guess the Old Man's not so bad after all," he

muttered softly.

"What old man is that?" questioned his fiancée.

Unable to control himself, Reggie broke out into a loud laugh. His mirth was contagious, and Kim joined in his laughter, her spirits buoyed with the realization that one of her most cherished dreams had at long last come true.

The Turtle Bay Hilton was located approximately six and a half miles north of Waimea Falls Park. Set on Kahuka Point, Oahu's northernmost extremity, the beachside resort offered championship golf, tennis, comfortable accommodations, and superb dining. Far from the hustle and bustle of Honolulu, Turtle Bay had a restful, native pace of its own. In fact, it was this feature that originally drew the Fullers here seven years before, to celebrate their honeymoon. Instantly charmed by this rustic portion of the island, they bought a condo on nearby Kuilima Point, and had been living there happily ever since.

Even though they now lived nearby, each time that Samuel and Peggy visited the Turtle Bay Hilton, they couldn't help but remember those first glorious days of marriage. Samuel had waited to the ripe old age of thirty-eight to tie the knot. And from the moment she'd first set eyes on him, at a USO Christmas benefit, Peggy had been certain that the dashing naval officer was the man she'd been waiting for. A storybook romance followed, all culminating here at Turtle Bay.

Feeling as if they were entering their second home, the Fullers strolled through the open lobby and made their way to the dining room. The hotel was crowded with gaudily dressed tourists, and Samuel noted several strangely familiar figures dressed in golf clothes. His suspicions were confirmed when he learned that the resort was hosting a celebrity golf tournament in which dozens of the biggest names in Major League baseball were participating. Looking on as the League's current Most Valuable Player passed them flashing a tooth-filled smile, Samuel explained to his wife the nature of the amazing assortment of superstar athletes who were assembled here.

As always, the dining room was full, yet their reservations granted them instant access. They even had their favorite table, a cozy little booth set near the room's huge picture window. Palm trees and blooming hibiscus plants beckoned outside, while the surging Pacific lay immediately beyond. The sun was almost directly overhead now, the deep blue sky painted with cottony puffs of drifting clouds.

Their visit to Waimea Falls Park did much to stimulate their appetites, and both chose to have the buffet, for which the restaurant was famous. They started off with freshly cut pineapple spears and tart guava juice. This was followed with oatmeal, eggs Benedict, home-fried potatoes, and a bowl of poi. Peggy had a particular liking for this last dish, a local food composed of cooked taro root kneaded into a delicately flavored paste. Samuel watched his wife consume this native staple while he sipped a mug of strong black coffee made from beans grown on the Kona coast of the big island of Hawaii. The couple then splurged on a pastry, and only then pushed away their plates.

They decided to walk off their meal by hiking along

the beach to Kahuku Point. The volcanic sand was firm, the air balmy, as they proceeded to their goal, which was a good quarter of a mile distant. With the roiling surf crashing on their left, and a line of stately coconut palms hugging the beach to their right, Peggy Fuller took her husband's hand in hers.

"Thank you for a most wonderful six days, Sam," she said with affection. "I can't tell you how much I've enjoyed myself."

"The feeling's mutual," returned her husband. "As always, you've been a joy to be with. And by the way, thanks again for offering to help out my petty officer's bride-to-be back at Waimea. Your compassion never fails to astound me."

"I appreciate that, Sam, but I genuinely felt for that girl. It's obvious that she hasn't been in this country long, and anything that I can do to assist her will be a labor of love."

"I knew when I first met you that you'd make a perfect naval officer's wife. You really care about people, and it shows. I just hope that Petty Officer Warner will be so lucky."

"What kind of man is he?" queried Peggy as she stepped over a fallen palm frond.

Samuel shook his head. "Believe it or not, I was under the impression that Warner was a confirmed bachelor. His exploits as a womanizer are well documented, and his ability to consume vast amounts of alcohol reigns unchallenged. Yet even with these vices, Warner shows great promise. As far as I'm concerned, he's the best sonar operator I've ever sailed with, and that's quite a statement. He's got an uncanny instinct for sensing the enemy's presence long before Ivan shows himself. During our last patrol, I witnessed this ability firsthand, and how he does it still puzzles me.

"Until this day, he's refused any offer to better himself in rank. I always thought that with a little maturing he could make an excellent officer. Perhaps this marriage will help settle him down."

"A steady woman tends to do just that," offered Peggy lightly. "You just concentrate on successfully completing your upcoming patrol, and I'll take care of the bride-to-be. She's a doll, and I have a feeling that we'll get along just fine."

A sea gull cried overhead, and Samuel temporarily halted to look out at the surging sea. "Lord, this place is beautiful! It's going to be a perfect spot to raise a child. And speaking of children, how are you feeling? Is this hike too much for you?"

"Of course not!" Peggy shot back. "I've never felt better in my life. But I could have done without that last pastry."

Samuel patted his own bulging stomach. "I know what you mean. But what fun is a brunch if you don't stuff yourself? Now, are you going to promise to make an appointment with that specialist the Corias told us about? I know that you're comfortable with your doctor, but I'll rest easier just knowing that the university clinic has looked you over."

Catching her husband's concerned glance, Peggy nodded. "Don't worry, Sam. I'll try to see the Corias' doctor while you're away. You've got enough things on your mind without losing sleep over me."

Samuel placed his arm around his wife's snug waist. "You know, lately I've been considering ways to simplify my life. Fatherhood at my advanced age isn't something to be taken lightly, and I want to make certain that I'm in a position to spend all the time that I want with my family. So, you'll be happy to know that after this patrol, I'll be seriously considering retirement. The Navy's had me for twenty-five years. I've done my bit for God and country, and it's time to see what life on the outside is all about."

Hardly believing what she was hearing, Peggy stammered, "Are—are you really going to do it, Sam?"

"You know me, once I've made up my mind," he replied. "I love you, Peg, and I'll be counting the days until we're together again."

He took her in his arms, and they kissed, long and deeply, oblivious to the crashing surf and the advancing tide that soon covered their feet and ankles.

Lieutenant David Costner was the assigned OOD as the *Copperhead*'s full crew began reporting for duty. The men filtered onto the vessel slowly, yet by 0530 hours, the entire complement had arrived. This included their chief sonar technician, Reginald Warner. Not only was the black petty officer amongst the first group to log in, he was alert and sober as well.

Though Costner was only the sub's junior officer, he could never understand why his superiors put up with Warner's antics. As far as the chubby blond-haired weapons officer was concerned, such men couldn't be relied on and served as a poor example to the rest of the enlisted men. Thankful that Warner had finally gotten his act together, the lieutenant made certain to log his impressions in the daily record.

The control room crew was busy preparing to get

underway, and Costner made his rounds, careful not to let a single detail escape him. As low man on the totem pole of command, this attentiveness was of paramount importance if he had hope for future advancement. Thrilled with having secured a position on an attack sub, he wasn't about to allow a lax crew member to slip up while he was officer of the deck. For Costner was third generation navy, and had his family name to live up to.

He started his rounds at the fire control panel. The planesmen had already seated themselves in their upholstered chairs, and Chief Meinert had taken up his position behind the diving console. Satisfied that all appeared to be going smoothly, Costner walked over to the navigation table. Here, Lieutenant Jeff Mathison was putting the finishing touches on a chart showing their course out of Pearl. This was a routine procedure, yet Costner double-checked the navigator's work just to make certain that his plots were correctly drawn.

The intercom sounded, and it proved to be the XO requesting that the OOD proceed at once to the officer's wardroom, where the captain was waiting for his readiness report. Instructed to bring along the chart of their exit route as well, Costner wasted no time doing the Lieutenant Commander's bidding.

The weapons officer followed a long, equipment-packed passageway that led aft from the control room. He passed the locked doors of the sub's radio room, the cramped cubicle reserved for the boat's office, and the all-important space reserved for the sonar monitors, before ducking through the hatchway that led to officers' country.

The captain was seated at his usual place at the head of the wardroom table. He looked tanned and rested, and had been sipping a mug of coffee, with the XO seated directly opposite him. Costner proceeded straight to Fuller's side.

"Sir," he reported succinctly, "the *Copperhead* is ready to get underway. I have the readiness log and the exit chart as requested."

"Very well, Lieutenant. Let's see the chart first."

While Fuller studied their preplotted course, and eventually signed the chart in the lower righthand corner, his XO silently appraised him. Samuel Fuller seemed like a new man when Coria first bumped into him on the docks over an hour before. He was genuinely interested in the state of the XO's new family, and was more relaxed than Coria had seen him in months.

Of course, the man was about to become a father for the first time. Remembering the high that he had experienced when his own wife revealed that she was expecting, the XO silently prayed that all would continue to go smoothly for the Fullers. From what Coria understood, Peggy Fuller was in her late thirties, and although she was perfectly healthy, a delivery at that age could prove to be difficult. That was why he'd been happy to share with the captain the name of the specialist who had delivered his first baby boy, only three months ago.

Fuller hastily scanned the OOD's readiness log, and the XO listened as the captain routinely questioned the *Copperhead*'s youngest officer as to the state of a radio component that had given them trouble during their last patrol. The alert OOD efficiently showed Fuller the portion of his log that documented this component's repair, and only then did the captain excuse him. With the approved chart in hand, Costner returned to the control room while an alert orderly refilled Samuel Fuller's coffee cup.

"That kid certainly has a no-nonsense attitude," observed the XO, who accepted a refill himself. "So far, I'm impressed with his work."

"I am too," offered Fuller. "Once he gets his feet wet, he's going to make one damn fine officer. Never have I seen such a stickler for detail. You should see this readiness log."

"I read his last one," revealed Coria. "It was like something out of a Navy textbook. Afterwards, I pulled his personnel jacket and reread it. Seems his old man was a tin can driver in World War II. Before that, his grandfather was a liason officer with the Navy Department, and helped organize our naval forces during the First World War. So I guess he's got a lot to live up to."

Fuller shook his head. "I just hope he doesn't expect too much of himself. I've seen it before — a hotshot like that, with all the potential in the world — completely burnt out before he's thirty."

"I hope you're wrong with that projection, Skipper. The sub force needs smart ones like Costner. By the way, there's been some interesting scuttlebutt coming out of COMSUBPAC lately. My source tells me that there could be a real bloodletting here soon, complete with personnel layoffs, forced retirements, and even the possibility of the early deactivation of more than one warship. Seems it's all tied in with this treaty that the President is about to sign with the Soviets."

Well aware that the *Copperhead* was to be one of

these deactivated ships, the captain probed carefully. "What do you think of this upcoming summit, anyway?"

The XO had read much about this meeting between the President and the General Secretary in the newspapers, and was quick to express his opinion. "I'm all for opening a dialogue between our two countries, but at the same time my gut tells me to be ever watchful that the Soviets don't try to pull the wool over our eyes. A treaty is still mere ink on paper, and although handshakes, smiles, and promising speeches look great on television, on-site verification is still the key to any disarmament treaty's real success.

"The Russians say that they'll be allowing our inspection teams onto their military bases, but the U.S.S.R. is a huge country, and who's to say that they haven't a store of nuclear warheads concealed somewhere. And for us to even think about cutting our conventional forces is sheer madness! After all, the Soviets have the largest standing army that this world has ever known. If we destroy our nuclear deterrent, what's to stop them from marching into Europe, the Middle East, or Asia? I'm certainly no warmonger, but what I've personally seen of the Russians only serves to substantiate my opinion that to merely trust them without concrete verification is foolishness of the first degree."

Absorbing this passionate discourse, Samuel Fuller thoughtfully responded, "As you well know, I have my own reasons to distrust the Soviets. During the investigation into my brother's death, I saw how Ivan was always quick to distort the truth for his own purposes. At that time we even had sonar tapes proving that they

191

were lying. Yet they stuck to their story, and somehow our government bought their line of b.s., and dropped the inquiry without so much as a hand slap.

"One thing I'm certain of is that the Russians respect strength. That's why when we caught that sub messing around with our SOSUS array last week, I made certain to give them a little something to remember us by. If the United States starts pulling it's warships from the seas as a mere goodwill gesture, I just know that Ivan will rush in to take advantage of the situation. This is especially the case with our submarines, which we can't afford to do away with."

"Do you really think that any of these deactivated vessels will be subs?" quizzed Vincent Coria. "Why that's almost unthinkable!"

Realizing that he had said too much already, Fuller abruptly changed the course of their conversation. "Did you get a chance to read our orders yet, Mr. Coria?"

The XO nodded that he had and added, "At least Command is being consistent. By this time, the *Copperhead* should know the waters surrounding the North Hawaiian Seamount Range by heart. Why in the hell do they always give us that particular sector to patrol? It would be a different story if we had a Trident there to keep watch over, but from what I gather, they've moved all of our missile boats back, closer to port."

"Who knows?" countered the captain. "Maybe Command is afraid that as the summit approaches, Ivan might pick this as an opportune moment to move their own missile boats onto our turf. That would be a real shocker—a sneak nuclear strike on the day before the so-called peace summit is about to convene."

Such a possibility had also crossed Vincent Coria's mind, and he nodded his head in agreement. "I wouldn't put it past them. That's why I think it's best that we keep the men extra sharp these next couple of days."

"Sounds good to me, Mr. Coria. Now, how about our going topside and getting this show on the road? If Ivan is indeed preparing some shenanigans out there, now's the time for us to show them that Uncle Sam has still got some bite left."

CHAPTER EIGHT

Lately, there didn't seem to be enough hours in General Huang Tzu's days. This had been the case for practically the last two and a half weeks, ever since he had picked up Admiral Liu Shao-chi at the Guilin airport. From that day onward, his every waking hour had been dedicated to readying their vast subterranean home before the leaders of the United States and the Soviet Union met in New York City to seal China's doom. This summit was to convene in three more days, and as it looked now, Huang Tzu's troops would complete their herculean task just in time for him to welcome the first group of VIP's who would be making this cavern their temporary home.

The other half of their operation was also proceeding right on schedule. The *Red Dragon* had set sail from its top-secret sub pen four days ago. Liu Shao-chi had been in Huangyan to personally witness this historic event, and conveyed to the general daily updates of the sub's progress. So far, the vessel had crossed the China Sea, successfully penetrated the Ryukyu Islands, and was currently heading due westward into the central Pacific. This would put the *Red Dragon* at its desired launch point, in the waters immediately north of the Hawaiian Islands, in approximately forty-eight hours.

Once the sub attained its patrol sector, it would drastically cut its speed and loiter silently beneath the sea's surface. Meanwhile, the cavern would be receiving its hand-picked guests. Pledged to secrecy, this assemblage of China's most loyal supporters had already been invited to the hills north of Guilin, to share in their country's rebirth. Only when they were safely sequestered inside the limestone grotto, would the emergency war orders be sent to the *Red Dragon*. The crew would then release its load of *Xia*-class ballistic missiles at targets located in both the U.S.S.R. and the United States. The two superpowers would inevitably blame each other and order immediate counterstrikes. Their populations would soon be utterly decimated, and China's select group of cave dwellers only needed to wait for the air to clear of radioactive debris before emerging victorious.

Glorying in the simplicity of this plot, the general prepared to get on with the day's business. He had set up his personal office deep in the cave's interior, in a cathedral-like room decorated with hundreds of glittering stalactites. The complex's portable generator provided illumination for the many documents that presently cluttered his desk. He had been studying a report showing the amount of decontamination gear in their possession, when his aide entered. A look of concern etched the aide's face, and the general prepared himself for bad news.

"Excuse me, sir, but a man and a woman have just been captured on the trail leading up the valley's western ridge. They have no identification on them, and say that they're inhabitants of the Blue Swan commune."

Having anticipated just such an occurrence, the baldheaded general vented his anger. "Damn it! I knew that we should have closed that place down and moved those peasants out of this sector. They are just too close to us, and make our security efforts here only that more difficult. What have we done with them?"

"In accordance with your standing orders, they were immediately blindfolded and their hands bound. They are presently being held under armed guard in Captain Han's tent."

Staring off into the cave's black depths, the general replied, "I think that it's best that you bring them in here for me to properly interrogate. Though they very well might be two innocent farmers, there's always the possibility that they could be spies. This fact must be ascertained before we make any decision to release them."

Saluting in response to this directive, the aide exited and General Huang returned his attention to the report he had been reading. Then minutes later, two blindfolded figures were escorted into his cavernous room. Both wore baggy green fatigues, the customary dress of the communal peasants in this region, and silently waited while Huang finished the memo that he was writing. After hastily scribbling his signature on this document, he addressed the pair of soldiers who had escorted the prisoners inside.

"Please be so good as to convey this order to Captain Han at once. Tell him that the Geiger counters were missing from the last shipment, and that I want an adequate stock on these premises by nightfall. I will handle the questioning of our intruders here on my own."

Pivoting to carry out this order, the soldiers left Huang alone to begin the interrogation. The general's first order of business was to stand and approach the two figures. They were approximately the same height, and seemed content to let their captors do the talking. This was fine with the pot-bellied senior officer, who slyly began to probe.

"So you two are from the local commune. May I ask what you were doing in this valley? I thought that we had made it clear to your director that there was important government work taking place here, and that this site was strictly off-limits to civilians."

"We are humbly sorry, sir," the young woman answered. "But we were working in the adjoining valley, and when we heard the sound of explosions coming from this direction, we couldn't resist checking it out for ourselves."

"It's my fault, sir," interrupted her male companion, who seemed to be about the same age. "Father always did say that my curiosity would get me in serious trouble sooner or later."

The general's interest was piqued by a strange inflection in the young man's accent. "So you two are shirkers as well as trespassers," Huang observed coolly. "What will your supervisor say when your work quota is not met today, Comrades?"

"It won't be the first time," offered the young man. "My ineptitude seems to constantly get us in trouble."

"Shame on you," reflected Huang as he positioned himself behind the pair and yanked off their blindfolds.

Circling in front of them, the general studied their faces. Both appeared to be in their mid-twenties and seemed to be having trouble adjusting to the rather dim light that illuminated this portion of the room. As he expected, the male didn't appear to be of pure Chinese ancestry. Though his straight black hair, slight physical build, and general facial features hinted of Oriental blood, his green eyes were strictly Western. On the other hand, there could be no denying his attractive companion's country of origin.

Watching as they stood there humbly with their eyes focused on the ground, Huang resumed his interrogation. "Why don't you start off by telling me your names. Then I can send one of my men over to your community to inform them of your presence here."

"I am Mei-li Wu," offered the girl. "My father was one of the commune's original founders."

"And I am Lo Kuan, her fiancé," added Justin.

The general grinned. "Ah, so you two are to be married. Are you from these parts, Comrade Lo?"

The green-eyed suspect answered him smoothly. "No, I'm not, sir. My place of birth was outside of Kashgar, near the Chinese-Soviet border. I have been living at the Blue Swan for only a couple of months."

Realizing that his place of birth in the Far West could have indeed been responsible for his green eyes and strange accent, Huang tried a different tack. "Tell me, Comrade Lo, did you have any idea what you'd be encountering in this valley when you sneaked down here?"

The young man looked him right in the eyes as he responded, "Rumor had it that you were in the midst of a mining operation. One of the commune's elders told us that several decades ago, a farmer in these parts pulled a golden nugget from the Lijiang and was able to move his entire family to Hong Kong, to live a life of luxury as a result of this single find."

"And you thought that we had discovered the mother lode here in this valley," continued the general.

As both suspects nodded that this was the case, Huang forcefully added, "I should have realized that material greed would be at the root of your irresponsibility! What if everyone in this nation looked to satisfy their own selfish needs? Would we ever be able to realize the great Socialist dream of our glorious founder, Mao Tse-tung, if that were the case? Of course we couldn't, Comrades!

"It will take a united effort of all those concerned to make this vision come true. I'm afraid you youngsters have had it too easy. You don't know what it's like to truly sacrifice your efforts for a brighter tomorrow. I pity your ignorance, and only hope that it isn't too late to lead both of you back to the path of Communist redemption."

His spellbound audience looked on sheepishly. Both of them looked like naughty children who had just been castigated by their teacher. Almost certain they weren't spies, the general still proceeded cautiously.

"I will leave the rest of your reeducation in the hands of your commune's political instructor, for unfortunately, I have my own work to get back to. For your own safety, we will keep you confined to this cavern, pending verification of your identities. Once this is obtained, you will be free to go."

As the general pivoted to return to his desk, the girl cleared her throat and meekly questioned, "May I ask what it is that you're doing here, sir? Why, we didn't know that such an immense cavern like this even existed here."

Hardly believing her audacity, Huang nevertheless answered her. "It didn't, until last month's earthquake opened its entrance to one of our surveyors. It wasn't long afterwards that a mineral was indeed discovered here. You can relax, Comrade Lo. This substance is uranium, not gold."

"Isn't such a radioactive element dangerous?" dared the green-eyed intruder.

Enjoying the young man's discomfort, Huang took his time in answering. "Have no fear, Comrades. We will make certain that you don't get a fatal dose while you are our guests. Now, I'm afraid, our little meeting must come to an end. As senior officer in charge of this operation, my responsibilities are many, and my superiors demand results."

Reaching for his intercom, the general took one last look at the pair of young trespassers before calling his aide to place them in detention.

Justin Pollock couldn't believe their good fortune. Fearing that they would be executed without question soon after being captured, he knew that they had much to be thankful for.

Ever since their discovery by the startled squad of soldiers, their captors had been more than fair with them. After they'd been led into a large tent, their hands had been loosely bound and blindfolds placed over their eyes. No real effort to question them had been made until they were taken to the general's subterranean lair. And now it appeared that once the director of the commune vouched for them, they would be free to go.

Until that time, they were to be held in a stone alcove, located deep in the cavern complex, not far from the general's office. The only cave that Justin had ever toured before was Carlsbad Caverns in New Mexico, and the grotto in which he currently found himself easily matched Carlsbad in sheer size and majesty.

Their containment cell seemed to be primarily some sort of storage area. Hollowed out of solid rock, it was a good-sized room, about the size of a large garage. A locked gate of iron bars guarded its entrance. An armed sentry was stationed outside as an additional security measure.

Though the captives' hands were still bound, the soldiers had not replaced the blindfolds. This allowed them to get a better idea of the awesome nature of the cavern complex as they were led to the holding cell and locked inside.

In the illumination provided by a single light bulb, Justin scanned the collection of crates stored in this room, before joining Mei-li on a smooth rock-bench. The air was musty and damp, and had a noticeable chill to it. Yet things could certainly be worse.

"Well, Mei-li," the American said, "it's certainly a fine mess that I've gotten us into. But look on the bright side. At least we won't die of thirst."

"Whatever are you talking about?" the downcast tour guide asked.

Justin pointed toward the pile of nearby crates. "If those boxes are marked correctly, they're keeping us in the liquor cabinet. I believe I know the Chinese charac-

201

ter for brandy when I see it."

Unable to coax a smile out of his companion, the actor shrugged his shoulders. "Okay, so I was an idiot for even suggesting that we go and poke our noses where they don't belong. Surely the commune's director will vouch for us, and we'll be out of this mess soon enough."

Mei-li shook her head. "I only hope that he remembers you, Lo Kuan. How in the world did you ever come up with that one?"

"Improvisation, my dear," retorted Justin. "It's an actor's best friend when he finds himself without legitimate written lines. And besides, what was I to tell him—that I'm a visiting American? I guarantee you that if I did, they'd be readying the execution squad as we speak."

"Who's to say that isn't the case," offered Mei-li gloomily.

Upset with her grim attitude, Justin responded, "And here I thought that I went and gave the performance of my life. I just know that the general really bought my identity. Good old Kashgar. Remind me when we get out of this place, to send the commissar there a bottle of rice wine and some flowers."

This last remark produced the desired effect, and the barest of smiles crossed Mei-li's face.

Noting this, Justin added, "Can you believe that we actually took cover in a bush with a rattlesnake and a family of tarantulas? I never saw anybody move as quickly as you did when that spider plopped on your head."

Grinning as she recalled this horrifying moment, Mei-li countered, "If I remember correctly, you came charging out of that thicket right at my side, Comrade. Did you catch the look of astonishment on the faces of those soldiers as we plowed into them? I thought they were going to faint from shock!"

She was actually giggling by this time, and Justin did his best to keep the mood light. "That will be one smoke that those boys will remember for a while. What do you make of this place, anyway?"

A serious expression once again crossed Mei-li's face. "If it is indeed a uranium mine, it's the strangest operation I've ever seen. Where are all the ore cars and drilling equipment? All I've seen are endless caches of supplies."

"I noticed that, too," said the American. "I also couldn't get over the general's office. Why, he had a desk, file cabinets, and all the comforts of home within reach. If you ask me, whatever they're doing here, they plan to stay for quite a long time."

"Maybe it's an underground fortress of some sort," offered Mei-li. "Or it could be just a storage site."

Justin shook his head. "This is a strange place just to store something. Unless it's extremely valuable, such as nuclear warheads, or even currency for that matter."

"There you go with your treasure stories again, Justin. For a moment, back in the general's office, you actually had me convinced that we were out here looking for gold. That lie made a wonderful story, and gave the old-timer a perfect excuse to straighten us out with a dose of Communist doctrine. The way we both stood there with our heads hung in shame, he couldn't possibly have seen through our cover."

The actor grinned. "We did look like a couple of

pouting miscreants, didn't we? And your performance was simply wonderful. Did you ever think about going into the theater?"

"Except for a handful of classical opera companies, there's not much call for actors in my country, Justin. Anyway, when I was growing up, it took acting ability just to get through school and cope with the system.

"Mao was still alive in those days, and the Cultural Revolution was at its height. If you think today's lecture was something, how would you like to sit through such an indoctrination for three solid hours, each and every day? And the exams were even worse. For to graduate, you had to first pass a test of political doctrine. Why, we even had to know portions of Mao's infamous *Red Book* by heart, and had to commit to memory pages of boring Socialistic theory, none of which ever made any sense to me. No Justin, for me, my everyday life was a play, which I somehow managed to act my way through without even the benefit of a script."

Mei-li really hadn't opened up to him until this moment, and Justin was impressed with what he heard. A sudden itch on his cheek caused him to instinctively reach up to scratch it, yet his bound hands kept him from doing so. Turning to his companion, he asked for her assistance. "Do you mind if I borrow your shoulder? I've got an itch on my cheek that's driving me crazy!"

Nodding agreement, Mei-li scooted to the side so that Justin could rub his cheek against her shoulder. His physical closeness affected Mei-li strangely, as did the light kiss he placed on her cheek as he brought his head up.

"Thanks for the shoulder to lean on in my time of need," jested the American, who now leaned forward and attempted to jiggle his wrists, which were bound behind his back. "You know, I think I can get our hands free. It sure would be a lot more comfortable, if we're going to be confined here much longer. Do you want to give it a try?"

Mei-li halfheartedly nodded that it was okay with her, and Justin looked up to check the position of the sentry before continuing, "This might sound silly, but I saw this trick in an old Western movie on television. We scoot up back to back, then try using our fingers to loosen each other's bonds. It might take some time, but I've yet to see it fail."

The young soldier who was left behind to keep an eye on them, had just lit up a cigarette and was watching the efforts of several of his coworkers on the cave's far side. His inattentiveness gave the two prisoners the perfect opportunity to attempt Justin's Hollywood escape-act. Placing themselves back to back, they wriggled their fingers in a spirited effort to loosen the bonds around their wrists. When several minutes passed without any progress, Justin turned his head and whispered, "Damn it, anyway! This always looks so easy in the movies."

This time it was Mei-li who had a suggestion. "I think if we back up to this shelf of rock behind us, we can break the rope by rubbing it up against the serrated limestone."

Justin, who was just about to make this suggestion himself, quickly retorted, "I've seen this one on television, too, but it sure doesn't hurt to give it a try."

Their sentry had closed his eyes and was dozing as

they turned around to look for a suitable spot to begin rubbing up against. It didn't take them long to find a promising ridge of rough rock, and less than a half an hour later, they both had their hands free.

"Now what?" whispered Mei-li guardedly.

The young soldier was snoring away soundly by this time, and Justin beckoned his companion to join him by the stack of crates.

"Why don't we see what's really inside of these crates? Because whatever it is, it must be damn important to keep it locked up in here like this."

This was fine with Mei-li, who helped Justin find a hand-sized splinter of rock to use in prying out the nails in the crates. A perfect fragment was spotted, and the American began the tedious job of removing the nails one by one. His tireless effort eventually paid off, and soon he and Mei-li were peering down into a crate filled with bottles of brandy.

"I thought I read that stenciling correctly, but I guess I just didn't believe my own eyes," observed Justin as he reached down to examine one of the bottles. "Good Lord, it's even a French vintage, and a damn good one at that!"

Mei-li studied one of these bottles herself, then looked up to take in the collection of over fifty similarly marked crates that filled the rest of the alcove. "Whatever they plan to do in this cavern, someone could sure throw an awfully nice party with this stash."

Absorbing this thought, an idea suddenly dawned in the actor's mind. "Speaking of parties, what do you say to making a little offering to our alert protector out there? It will probably be some time before that army messenger gets back from the commune, and if our luck holds, perhaps we can finally find out what the hell is going on down here."

Mei-li responded cautiously, "And just how do you plan to get that information, Comrade?"

The American's eyes gleamed as he lifted one of the brandy bottles. "We're going to throw a little party of our own, that's how. All we have to do is place one of these bottles on the floor beside the iron gate. Then, using your most seductive smile, you're going to invite our hard-working comrade out there to share a little toast to the People's Republic. This stuff is almost one hundred proof, and it won't take much to have him talking away like an old hen."

"I don't know, Justin. I think that you're only asking for more trouble by attempting such a thing."

The actor had a quick comeback. "What ever happened to those inquisitive Oriental minds I've heard so much about? Don't you want to know what your government is doing down here? Surely we didn't go to all this trouble, just to be released and then leave this valley, none the wiser for our efforts. Why, that would be the ultimate waste!"

Though Mei-li's common sense still told her no, her companion's zeal was infectious, and she couldn't help but find herself weakening. "But what's he going to say when he sees that bottle just sitting there out of nowhere?"

"Bottoms up, I imagine," offered the actor with a wide grin. "Look, I know it's not the most logical plan, but what good is logic in a situation like this? He's a young soldier, for goodness' sake, who's not about to kill the goose who's laid the golden egg. Give him your best wink, and just let nature take its course."

Taking a moment to deliberate, Mei-li sighed. "You're going to get me thrown in prison yet, Justin Pollock. I still don't know why I bother listening to you."

"Aw, you're just a glutton for punishment, darling," returned the American with a wink. "Now, let's get going with our little party before the general decides to crash it. I'll set the bottle where he can reach it, and you just sit close by, looking your normal sexy self. Why, he'll be talking away in no time flat."

Signaling him to get on with it, Mei-li prepared herself for the worst. Only when Justin had placed the brandy bottle beside the gate and then lay down in the alcove's shadows, pretending to be asleep, did she make her way over to the entranceway and loudly clear her throat.

"Excuse me, Comrade. Are you awake?"

At this unexpected query, the young soldier's eyes popped open, and it took him a moment to orient himself. His startled expression softened when he spotted the female captive sitting seductively on the other side of the security bars.

Seeing that she had his complete attention, Mei-li continued, "I'm sorry to disturb you, Comrade, but I was wondering if you'd care to join me in a drink."

Completely caught off guard by this inquiry, the soldier scanned the cell, taking in both the bottle of brandy and the just visible outline of Justin's prone body in the distance. Realizing that they were, for all practical purposes, alone here, he smiled, licked his dry lips, and quickly reached out for the bottle.

The sentry seemed to have an insatiable thirst, and he gulped down the liquor as if it were water. He consumed a good quarter of the bottle before passing it through the bars to Mei-li. Careful not to appear unsociable, she managed to swallow some of the fiery spirits herself. She had never been a lover of alcohol, and the brandy hit her stomach like a jolt of lightning. When she belched, the soldier broke out laughing, and gladly took the bottle back to show her how a man held down his drink.

It didn't take long until the alcohol went to his head, and he sidled up to the bars to share his troubles with his attractive drinking companion. Mei-li soon learned that he was only nineteen years old, and had been drafted into the People's Army nine months ago. Born in the Manchurian town of Harbin, he had been a coal miner before being called to serve his country.

Hearing this, Mei-li knew that she had the perfect opportunity to inquire about the nature of his current duty. With eyes wide with innocence, she asked him if it was true that the Army was interested in the massive cavern as a source of uranium.

A wide grin split on his face, and after taking another swig from the bottle, he lowered his voice to a whisper. "Uranium? You've got to be kidding! Why, there's nothing of value inside of this hellhole but tons of fossilized limestone."

"Then what in the world are you doing down here?" dared Mei-li.

Only when he was absolutely certain that there was no one within hearing, did he beckon her closer and whisper in her ear, "I've got a friend on the captain's staff, and he says that what we're building in this cavern is a huge fallout shelter. It struck me peculiar at first, but ever since I've been stationed inside, I think that's indeed the real purpose of this place. You should just see the huge amount of supplies that we're storing in here! They include foodstuffs, medical supplies, clothing, bedding, and even a complete library of books. Why, there's enough material in this cavern complex to see to the needs of a small city for months on end. And what's even more disturbing is the vast amount of radiation decontamination gear that's also being transferred inside. It's almost as if they were expecting World War III or something!"

Contemplating this last statement, Mei-li looked up as the sound of advancing footsteps echoed in the distance. The sentry also heard this noise, and after making certain that the brandy bottle was hidden behind the rocks, struggled to stand up and straighten his uniform. Meanwhile, Mei-li returned to the rock bench and seated herself, just in time to view the approach of the portly baldheaded general who had interrogated them earlier.

The sentry snapped to attention, instantly sobered as the general's voice boomed forth authoritatively, "Miss Wu, is Comrade Lo Kuan available?"

Justin, who had heard this summons — and most of the drunken guard's disturbing revelation — rose stiffly to show himself.

Quickly spotting him, the general continued in a tone that was now tinged with sarcasm. "I hope I haven't disturbed you, Comrade Lo. Or should I say, Mr. Justin Pollock? Yes, I'm afraid your little charade has been exposed, my American friend. Now, if both of you will just accompany me back to my office, perhaps we can get to the bottom of this foolishness, before any more of my valuable time is wasted!"

It was most obvious that they had worn out their welcome, and Justin watched as two burly sentries emerged from the shadows to unlock the iron gate. Taking in a deep breath, he caught his companion's concerned glance, and could only offer a brave smile in response.

"Why has your government sent you here to spy on us?"

The general's question boomed out firm and clear, and Justin found his throat unnaturally dry as he attempted to respond.

"I swear to you, sir, I am not a spy! I'm nothing but an actor, who's been admitted into China at the personal invitation of your very own premier."

"I have documentation that will prove that fact," offered Mei-li frantically. "All of this is but a tragic misunderstanding. We only wanted to see what the dynamiting was all about."

Unmoved by her plea, General Huang Tzu studied his prisoners from the vantage point of his cluttered desk, and commented icily, "So it appears that the American CIA has even infiltrated our travel service. Why, your audacity sickens me!"

"We are not spies, General!" shouted Justin, who was very close to losing his control. "This whole thing is ridiculous, and I demand that you notify my embassy of my detention at once."

A sly grin painted the general's face as he responded to this outburst. "You are in a poor position to issue demands, Comrade. Let me remind you that you were caught red-handed, trespassing on a top-secret military site. Why you've even gone to the trouble of disguising yourself in native clothing, and you had the nerve to lie to me regarding your proper identity. Do these sound like the actions of an innocent foreigner? Of course they don't! With such evidence I could have you immediately shot if I so desired. But as matters now stand, I think I'll keep you locked up here until you properly confess. Then, perhaps, a phone call to your embassy might be allowed."

"But we are not spies!" cried the American vainly. "What must we do to prove this fact to you?"

The general massaged his forehead. "You disappoint me, Comrade. Do you really think that I'm stupid enough to fall for any more of your lies? Your deceitful ways might work on one of my conscripts, like the young guard whom you succeeded in plying with liquor in a vain attempt to escape. Yet I can assure you that I've seen too much in my time to fall for such petty, amateurish antics. No, Comrades, my mind is made up. You will remain in this cavern complex until you confess to your crimes. And if you continue to resist, you can rot away down here for all I care. The decision is solely yours now."

"You really can't be serious," countered Mei-li. "Since we failed to show up for lunch with my parents, I'm certain that the commune has already sent out search parties to track us down. When we don't show up, the authorities will be informed that an American is one of the missing, and you'll soon enough have all hell to pay."

Huang Tzu couldn't help but chuckle. "And what authorities are you referring to, Comrade Wu? You forget that you're speaking with a general in the

People's Liberation Army. I am the sole authority here, and your precious commune has already been dealt with. Since it appears that they were involved in this plot, I've had no choice but to put the entire community under protective custody. A squad of armed men is down there right now, and the members of the Blue Swan commune will be confined to their quarters until you have the decency to admit your crimes. Thus, for all practical purposes, the outside world will merely know that a CITS guide and an American tourist were lost in the rugged hills north of Guilin, in a remote region notorious for its landslides and other geological instabilities."

With this, Justin and Mei-li were finally made aware of the true seriousness of their predicament. A nightmare of the worst order had somehow come true, and having no one but themselves to blame for their situation, they could only consider their present options. One thing they were certain of: They would not sign any confession until they had time to contemplate the consequences of such an act. So far, their rash action had gotten them nothing but trouble, and this time they intended to fully think out any moves on their part before proceeding. Locked up once again in the stone alcove, they had a perfect spot to ponder their problems.

Mei-li noted that two alert sentries were now posted outside their cell. Much older than the teen-ager with whom she had shared the brandy, they had a strict, no-nonsense attitude. Surprisingly, the soldiers hadn't bothered to tie their hands again, although one of the guards was positioned so that he could watch their each and every movement. From the look of the rifle that this soldier expertly held in his hands, neither one of the prisoners dared make the least suspicious move anyway.

Seated at Mei-li's side on the rock bench, Justin looked uncharacteristically grim. He had barely spoken a word since leaving the general's office, and when he eventually did express himself, his tone was far from cheerful.

"It's a fine mess that I got us in, Mei-li. I take full responsibility, and will forever be in your debt."

"Nonsense," retorted his cell mate. "I'm a full grown woman and you didn't force me against my will to accompany you. We got caught where we had no business being, and instead of telling the truth, we made the mistake of trying to lie our way out of it. And now we have to pay the consequences."

"Do I have any choice but to sign that confession?" quizzed the American.

Mei-li shook her head thoughtfully. "At first I thought that was our only course of action, but now I wonder if it's a good idea at all. What's to keep them from executing us as soon as they have that confession in hand? It's obvious that we've stumbled onto something extraordinary down here. That poor lad that we got drunk was certain that there was no mining operation going on in this cavern. He believes it's an enormous fallout shelter of some type, and I tend to agree with him. But why would the army construct such a complex here, in this desolate wilderness? And why this rush to complete it? It's almost as if they were expecting a full-scale nuclear war to break out in the next couple of days!"

This last observation tended only to blacken Justin's

mood and he grimly voiced his frustrations.

"If we could only get out of this damn place! I feel like we've been buried alive beneath the earth."

Mei-li did her best to keep a positive frame of mind. "I find it hard to believe that the army was able to round up and contain the members of the commune so quickly. If there's any way possible, my parents won't let us down. Father's butted heads with the authorities before, and he's not the type to merely sit back and let them have their way. The odds are that he's planning to help us escape even as we talk."

Unable to share her optimism, Justin sighed heavily. "I hope to God that you're right, Mei-li. Otherwise, it's going to take a virtual miracle to get us out of here safely."

The seconds turned to minutes, and the minutes to hours as the two prisoners settled themselves into a confined, boring routine broken only when one of the guards was replaced, or a simple meal of overcooked rice and water was served.

Neither Justin or Mei-li had the strength to raise their voices in complaint, and were content to pass the time sitting patiently in silent contemplation. Since no bedding had been provided, it was difficult to sleep. Eventually, however, the day's emotionally trying events took their toll, and they lay down on a relatively smooth portion of the floor beside the stack of wooden crates. It was dank and chilly, and Mei-li gratefully snuggled up into her cell mate's arms. There was a primal innocence to this embrace, and both young people were soon sound asleep.

Justin was in the midst of a wild dream, in which he found himself alone on the open sea, fleeing an approaching tidal wave in the flimsiest of canoes, when he awoke with a start. The very ground beneath him seemed to be vibrating, and an alien, resonant rumble rose in the distance. At first he thought that this was all still part of his nightmare, but when Mei-li snapped from her sound sleep beside him, he knew otherwise.

The shrill electronic sound of an alarm awoke them completely, and both sat up, frantically scanning their cell for some clue to the source of the disturbance. Above them, the alcove's single bare light bulb swayed to and fro as the tremors seemed to be intensifying. There was the distinct, rending sound of falling rock, and Justin could think of only one thing.

"One of their dynamite blasts must have caused a cave-in! Let's get over to the wall by the bench!"

Taking Mei-li's hand in his, he managed to get them both on their feet. Yet the rocky ground beneath them was undulating so badly that crossing the alcove proved most difficult. Like a pair of drunken sailors, they used each other's bodies to keep standing upright, and only after the greatest of efforts, reached their goal.

They crouched beside the thick rock ledge that they had previously used to sit on. Desperately hugging each other for protection, their combined glances turned to the alcove's locked entrance way as one of the sentries screamed out in terror.

"Earthquake!"

This horrified exclamation raised goosebumps on Justin's skin, and he instinctively looked up to check the alcove's roof. His heart pounded away madly in his

chest as he took in a massive stalactite swaying precariously above them. With no time to shout a warning, he
took hold of Mei-li's arm and abruptly yanked her
forward up against the iron gate. Oblivious to her
words of shocked protest, he then jumped on top of
her, using his own body as a protective shield.

No sooner did he wrap his arms around her, than a
splintering crack sounded from up above. This was
followed by a deafening, explosive concussion as the
stalactite fell from the roof and smashed into the
ground below. Conscious that only seconds ago they
had been crouched in that very spot, Justin held his
breath and looked upward. He breathed freely again
only when he found that there were no stalactites
suspended above them in this spot.

Shaken by this close call with death, Mei-li cautiously poked her head up and caught Justin's glance.
He had saved her life, but before she could express her
gratitude, another, even more intense tremor shook the
earth, and she found herself grabbing onto the American. Like sailors adrift on a stormswept sea, they
struggled to ride out the undulating waves that the
earthquake was sending through the earth's crust. All
around them there was the crashing sound of falling
rock, while the warning siren still wailed away in the
distance.

When somewhere close by a man screamed in pain,
they were reminded that they were not the only ones
inside the cave. The still-swaying light bulb provided
just enough illumination for them to peer outside and
catch sight of one of the sentries kneeling beside the
body of his fallen comrade. Through a thick haze of
dust, Justin and Mei-li could see that the guard's prone

217

body was covered almost up to the neck in fragments of rock. With no time for pity, Justin called out forcefully.

"Please Comrade, unlock this gate and let us out of here! Otherwise, we'll all needlessly share your co-worker's fate!"

As another powerful tremor arrived with an ear-splitting rumble, the surviving guard turned to face his prisoners. His eyes were wide with horror, and it was clear that he was out of his mind with fear as he reached for his rifle and pointed it toward the alcove.

"You are the reason that my dear friend had to die in such a horrible manner!" cried the maddened sentry. "May your own deaths be as painful as his was!"

"My God, he's going to shoot us!" screamed Justin. "Please Comrade, we meant you no harm. Get control of yourself!"

Completely deaf to the American's pleas, the soldier rammed a bullet into his assault rifle. He had to kneel on one knee to keep his aim steady as he struggled to get the two spies within his sights.

Inside the alcove, Justin continued looking on in disbelief. He had never looked down the barrel of a rifle before, except once in a play. Yet this was harsh reality, and as the soldier's finger went to the trigger, Justin prepared himself for the pain that he knew would soon follow. Mei-li's hand squeezed his tightly, and he found himself saying the twenty-third Psalm, when the strongest tremor yet knocked them completely over. This was followed by a loud explosive crack, and the now familiar sound of the splintering rock.

Justin managed to look up just before the overhead

light began blinking on and off erratically. Barely visible through the thick veil of swirling dust was a scene he would remember always.

Lying on the ground before them, the rifle-toting sentry was trembling in the last throes of death, his back cleanly pierced by a razor-sharp stalactite. This macabre sight was followed by a more cheering one. For Justin next saw that the falling debris had also served to smash the lock on the iron gate to their cell. His trembling hand was just pointing this out to Mei-li, when the overhead light failed altogether, plunging them into total darkness.

Groping for each other, they embraced, and looked around blindly as a final tremor violently shook the walls of the cavern. As the last aftershock rumbled in the distance, Justin once again found himself in silent prayer, to a God he was only just now rediscovering. It was Mei-li's trembling voice that brought him back to thoughts of a more immediate nature.

"Do you really think that it's over for good, Justin? What are we to do now?"

The American squeezed her shoulder tenderly. "It appears that for at least the time being, the earthquake has spent itself. But before we learn otherwise, let's take advantage of this lull and see about getting out of here. Those sentries are certainly in no shape to stop us and the others surely have more immediate concerns. This is the perfect time to make good an escape, don't you agree?"

"Yes, Comrade," Mei-li replied. "But how are we going to find our way out in this blackness?"

Justin sighed heavily. "It's not going to be pleasant, but I noticed that both of those guards had flashlights clipped to their belts. I should be able to crawl out of here and find the body of that poor twisted soul who was about to do away with us. If Lady Luck is still around, his flashlight will be working and that will give us some illumination."

Unable to come up with any better plan, Mei-li nodded agreement. "Then do it if you must, Justin. But please get back to me quickly. This place gives me the creeps!"

Squeezing her hand in response, the American began the dangerous job of exiting the alcove in the pitch blackness. Proceeding on his hands and knees through the rubble, he was cut and bruised by the time he got through the gate and reached the sentry's side. Reaching out in the darkness, he found the body still warm and sticky with blood. He fought off the urge to retch, and using his shaking right hand, followed the outline of the guard's corpse, from his limp neck to his belted waist. Unclipping the flashlight, he made no attempt to turn it on until he had crawled away from the body.

As a narrow beam of light shot from the lens, he gave a silent prayer of thanks, then directed the beam to the alcove, where Mei-li could be seen crouching with hands raised to shield her eyes against the sudden brightness. Picking his way carefully through the debris, he helped the shaken young woman to her feet and they left the cell together.

Once they were past the two fallen soldiers, they traveled down a narrow tunnel that snaked its way farther into the cavern's dark recesses. Mei-li followed close on Justin's heels, ever watchful for the tons of rocky debris strewn on the ground. The route was familiar, leading to the immense, cathedral-like room they had previously visited. The general's office had been located not far from here. Wondering if the portly, baldheaded senior officer had survived the quake, Justin switched off the torch and beckoned Mei-li to join him. As they knelt behind a fallen shelf of rock, several frantic voices could be heard up ahead. Seconds later, the darkness on the opposite side of the grotto was pierced by several shafts of bright light. The voices continued, and Mei-li quietly translated.

"They're with a rescue party, sent from outside to check for survivors. So far, they've found nothing but corpses. At least we're not completely sealed off from the outside world. Do you think that we should surrender, or try finding another way out of here?"

"I'm afraid that we don't have much of a choice," answered the American. "Regardless of the tragic quake, they still think that we're spies. It's apparent that they've got their work cut out for them, and if we suddenly show up, we'll only serve to get in the way. An execution would solve that problem real quickly."

Somewhere in the area immediately before them, other lights flashed on, accompanied by a deep, firm voice.

"It's the general!" Mei-li gasped. "He's asking the rescue squad for the preliminary damage reports, and wants to know if anyone has thought of checking to see if we survived the tremors!"

A new sense of urgency could be heard in Justin's response. "That settles it. We're going to have to try to find another way out of here. A complex this immense must have a number of different exits, and we're just going to have to do some exploring on our own. What do you say to trying that tunnel that leads off to our right?"

Shrugging her shoulders, Mei-li motioned for the actor to lead the way. Justin took her hand, and not daring to switch on the torch, groped his way in the dark along the wall to find the passage. Once in this tunnel, which led away from their pursuers, they were able to use the flashlight again.

There was a virtual labyrinth of passages to choose from and Justin tried to pick those which had the least amount of earthquake damage. Even then, many tunnels that looked promising initially were blocked by fallen debris, forcing the couple to backtrack and find a clearer route.

In the midst of their travels, they passed through several immense rooms, most of which had streams running through them. Though the flashlight's beam lit only a tiny portion of these vast, cathedral-like spaces, the little that they were able to view was most impressive. In several places the stalactites and stalagmites were so thick they appeared like the mouth of a predatory fish. In other places these calcite formations, which hung from the roof and grew up from the floor, joined together to form single columns or—as they did on one wall—a huge stone curtain composed of thousands of individual icicles.

One route showed particular promise, for it followed the meandering path of a well-developed stream. The earthquake damage was at a minimum here, as they passed down a wide tunnel and crossed through a room dominated by a single, monstrous stalactite. It appeared that several of the streams joined here, and after Justin checked the direction of their flow, Mei-li scanned the surrounding walls.

"There are some more crates over there," she shouted excitedly, "on that ridge of smooth rock!"

Justin also caught sight of this collection of carefully stacked wooden boxes, and led the way to them. It was Mei-li who kneeled down and translated the stenciled lettering.

"It says that they contain decontamination equipment and Geiger counters. Each crate is also marked with the official seal of China's Civil Defense organization. That first guard must have been right. This complex is being developed as a massive fallout shelter! Buy why did they pick this desolate spot, and what's the big hurry to complete it? If anything, with the upcoming summit and all, the world has never been so safe from nuclear war as it is today."

"It appears that way on the surface," Justin replied. "But don't forget that there are other countries besides the Soviet Union and the United States that are very capable of starting a nuclear war. Even your own country has such a capability."

"Surely we would never even think of such a thing!" retorted Mei-li.

"I realize that," answered Justin. "But what if a demented minority of powerful military figures, such as our current hosts, were able to gain control of enough nuclear warheads to launch an attack of their own? This secret subterranean complex would serve as a most convenient refuge in which to wait out hostilities until it was safe to go back above ground."

"That's a most astute observation," broke in an icily cool male voice from behind.

Turning instantly to see who had uttered these words, Justin gasped when he spotted the corpulent

223

figure of the general, standing on a raised ledge of rock immediately behind them. Mei-li also saw him, and held tightly to her escort's waist as the general fingered a pistol at his side.

"I'm impressed, Comrade Pollock," Huang commented. "You have figured out something that even my staff have yet to comprehend. For this complex is indeed being developed as a shelter, to protect China's most loyal subjects from the horror of nuclear war. This same conflict will wipe out the decadent powers of East and West, and we will climb out from these walls as the ultimate rulers of the planet!

"Don't look so shocked, Comrades, and never doubt the abilities of a determined foe. Even as we speak, the submarine carrying the warheads which will initiate this final apocalypse is approaching its missile release point. It will reach this predetermined spot in the Pacific in exactly two more days. Can you imagine the looks of horror on the faces of the American president and the Soviet premier when they sit down to talk peace at their sham summit, and then get the news that half of their respective countries have been destroyed? How very ironic it is that they will proceed to wipe each other out only hours after they were to sign the treaty that was supposed to make such a conflict impossible. The Chairman will surely be smiling from his grave!"

"Surely you could never get away with such a sick scheme!" cried Mei-li. "Someone's bound to stop you!"

"It certainly won't be you, Comrades," retorted the general, who raised his pistol to take aim. "I should have done this hours ago, instead of fooling with you two."

For the second time in his life, Justin found himself looking down the barrel of a gun. But this time, there wasn't any fortuitous earthquake to save them. Conscious that their lives are solely in his hands now, the actor decided to at least go down fighting.

The general pulled back the pistol's hammer, and as the metallic clicking sound echoed through the cavernous limestone chamber, Justin diverted the beam of his flashlight to hit their captor full in the eyes. At the same time, he roughly pushed Mei-li aside, diving to the ground himself just as the explosive crack of a pistol shot rang out. A split second later, there was the high-pitched whine of a ricocheting bullet, and three more deafening blasts followed in quick succession. More bullets ricocheted overhead, and a deep voice screamed out angrily, "Die, you traitorous fools!"

Taking advantage of the general's blind fury, Justin picked up a rock and tossed it toward the stream. When it struck the ground with a loud clatter, the general diverted his aim and fired two more quick shots. Again, the American picked up a rock and threw it in the direction of the stream, but this time the distinctive clicking sound of a pistol's hammer hitting an empty chamber echoed forth from the elevated ledge. Swiftly calculating that the general had fired six times, Justin jumped to his feet and grabbed Mei-li, who had been huddled behind a thick stalagmite.

"He's got to reload!" yelled Justin. "Come on, now's our chance!"

Pulling her by the arm, he sprinted back toward the path that followed the stream's meander. Beyond, another tunnel was visible, this appearing to be the direction in which the tumbling current now flowed. Their only chance was to duck into this dark, narrow passageway for cover, for surely their pursuer had reloaded his gun by now. This was indeed the case, for a second later, two shots were fired in rapid succession, one of the bullets striking the rock wall only inches from Justin's head. With his heart pounding wildly, the actor grabbed Mei-li and scrambled down toward the stream bed. He halted only after viewing an object that set his pulse beating even more quickly. Incredibly, someone had left a two-man kayak tied up here!

Another bullet whined overhead, and Justin leaped into the fiber glass boat. By the time Mei-li climbed in behind him, the actor had already untied the vessel and with the help of a double-bladed paddle, had pushed it into the rapid current. And the tiny vessel plunged into the darkness.

CHAPTER NINE

Seaman Pavl Petrovka was not a happy man. His current duty inside the *Baikal*'s forward torpedo room was tediously boring, and got him covered from head to toe in thick black grease. It was not his fault that the torpedo loading mechanism had failed like it had. Yet the way the *michman* was ranting and raving, you would have thought that Pavl had been responsible for sabotaging the device. Of course, all the loud-mouthed warrant officer had to do was scream out order after order. It was Pavl who had to carry out these directives, which obliged him to completely take apart the rail system on which the torpedos were conveyed to their firing tubes.

Currently in the process of regreasing each of the hundreds of ball bearings that were set into each rail, Pavl silently cursed his misfortune. His father had been right. He should have enlisted in the Air Force. At least he would have been treated like a gentleman in that respected service, and got a breath of fresh air whenever he liked. But no, he had to be the smart one, and listen to his old friend Vitaly Bolgrad. Join the navy and see the world, advised Vitaly, who had been his closest friend all through primary and secondary schools. And when the day came for enlistment, Pavl had taken Vitaly's advice, and like him, joined the elite force of the Soviet Navy — its submarine corps.

At first such duty indeed appeared exciting. Both enlisted men were sent to the Frunze Naval School in far off Leningrad. This had been their first real trip away from Odessa, and Pavl's eyes were wide with wonder as they boarded the northbound train that conveyed them across the legendary Ukraine region. They had even spent a night in bustling Kiev before continuing on to Leningrad, the city founded on the banks of the Neva River almost three hundred years ago by no less than Peter the Great.

Leningrad was a wondrous place. The second largest city in the Motherland, it was home to over three million people. Hundreds of bridges and canals connected dozens of wide boulevards, magnificent palaces, and public buildings. The city was also the site of the Hermitage, the most beautiful art museum Pavl had ever visited.

Leningrad was to be their home for the next six months as they learned the elementary principles of engineering and seamanship required of all those allowed to go to sea on submarines. Pavl and Vitaly were in the same classes, and even lived in the same dormitory. On those rare occasions that they were given leave, they stuck together like brothers, one rarely going into town without the other. They were thus thrilled when command assigned them to the same vessel. But then, during their last period of R and R, their relationship underwent a drastic change when Pavl learned what kind of man his old friend Vitaly really was.

228

Just thinking about their last trip back home to Odessa caused Pavl's pulse to accelerate. His face reddened in anger, and his hands trembled, causing him to drop the handful of ball bearings he had been coating with grease. As the tiny spheres of steel dropped onto the deck with a loud metallic clatter, the entire compartment seemed to echo with the sudden racket. Instantly dropping to his knees to begin picking the ball bearings up, Pavl froze when a resonant, deep-toned voice boomed out behind him.

"Damn you, Seaman Petrovka! You are as clumsy as you are stupid. Why the sound of those falling bearings was probably heard all the way to Pearl Harbor!"

It was most evident that the *michman* was in one of his sour moods again. Fighting the impulse to turn on the fat warrant officer and give him a piece of his mind, Pavl inhaled deeply and tried to calm himself. Discretion eventually prevailed, and he turned to humbly express himself.

"I'm sorry, Comrade *Michman*. It won't happen again."

"It better not, Petrovka," warned the warrant officer. "Otherwise Captain Valerian will have your head as well as mine. Must I remind you that we are still under a Red Flag alert? And here we are with one of our torpedo tubes inoperable! So if you value your life, get back to your work. And concentrate, Comrade. Concentrate!"

Nodding that he would, Pavl turned his attention back to the task at hand. It took him a good five minutes to gather all of the dropped bearings, which he proceeded to hastily grease and replace in the rail.

Throughout this tedious task, he found himself inwardly fuming. After all, this was to be his second consecutive four-hour work shift. And they wouldn't even send along another seaman to assist him! Pavl was well aware that with a crew of only eighty-five men aboard, the *Baikal* was hard pressed manpower-wise. But a malfunctioning torpedo tube loading system was not something to take lightly. Why should he get the responsibility of repairing it alone?

Pavl supposed that his current duty draw was a direct result of his recent altercation with Vitaly Bolgrad. At that time, he had uncharacteristically lost all self-control, and was only seconds away from stabbing Vitaly, when the *michman* intervened. A series of severe reprimands followed, and Pavl was rebuked by both the *zampolit* and the captain himself. Until this time, Pavl hadn't had much contact with the *Baikal's* commanding officer, and didn't know what to expect as he and Vitaly were ordered to Anton Valerian's cabin. The captain seemed genuinely incensed that such a violent argument had occurred on his boat, and wouldn't quit preaching until they shook hands and swore that such a thing would never happen again. With no available alternative, Pavl took his old friend's clammy hand in his, but still found it hard to look him full in the eye. Pavl's current duty must have been the captain's way of further expressing his displeasure.

To make matters even worse, ever since the *Baikal* had gone on alert, their meal portions had been severely cut down. As a result, Pavl's stomach gurgled with hunger. For breakfast, the cook had served nothing but a bowl of tasteless oat gruel and a weak cup of tea, while their lunch consisted of a stale hunk of bread and a serving of vegetable soup, which was short on vegetables and long on broth. Thus not only was he tired and frustrated, but starving to death as well!

Join the navy and see the world, thought Pavl to himself sarcastically. So far on this cruise, all that he had seen were the snow-covered shores of the Kamchatka Peninsula, as they initially set sail from Petropavlovsk. Since then, over a month had passed, and not once during this time did the *Baikal* even break the ocean's surface. No exotic ports were visited. All that they had to look forward to was one weary day after another locked within this one hundred-meter-long sphere of steel, with eighty-four equally bored fellow submariners. And all to what purpose. To prevent a war that would never occur anyway?

Struggling to contain his frustrations, Pavl dipped a new group of bearings into the grease pot. The oily lubricant had a disgusting odor to it, and he controlled his rising nausea by trying hard to think of a more pleasant subject. Thoughts of his hometown rose in his mind, and as he pictured the streets of Odessa, he couldn't help but think of Katrina. The shapely redhead had been his only love ever since primary school. A passionate, creative soul, Katrina was a talented artist, who had already received local acclaim for her superbly rendered landscape paintings. Pavl had always encouraged her to pursue a living in this field, and today her paintings were being purchased by some of Odessa's finest families. They had talked of getting married as soon as Pavl got out of the Navy, and though he had yet to give her an engagement ring, he took it for granted that she was exclusively his.

During his last leave, he had returned home with the intention of officially asking her parents for her hand. Then they would be able to set a wedding date and begin planning their future together. He had only been in Odessa for a few hours, and after visiting his own family, had eagerly taken off for Katrina's house. It was her mother who informed him that she was out painting in the woods nearby.

The afternoon was a warm, gorgeous one as he crossed the wheat field that bordered the wood, whistling gaily in anticipation of seeing his soulmate. He was well acquainted with the section of the forest that Katrina's mother had directed him to, for he and his love had explored this area extensively as children. Hoping to surprise her with his presence, he crept cautiously down the trail leading into the thick oak wood. He crossed a narrow footbridge, which spanned a gurgling stream where they used to catch frogs, and slowed his pace even more as he approached the clearing where she was supposed to be working. The unexpected sound of laughter met his ears, and crouching down, he made his way over to a fallen tree trunk which overlooked the clearing he was bound for. Pavl poked his head over his trunk, and what he saw in the clover-filled clearing sickened the very pit of his soul. For there was his beloved Katrina, rolling on the ground with Vitaly Bolgrad, their lips merged as one, their passions obviously shared.

Somehow, Pavl had kept himself from storming out into the clearing and beating Vitaly's brains out. He had even managed to keep his discovery to himself during the rest of his grim leave. In fact, it wasn't until last week that they'd had it out, when Pavl's frustrations finally reached their bursting point. What angered him even more, was that Vitaly had the nerve to disavow any knowledge of the event that Pavl had witnessed. Blaming his poor memory and uncontrollable passions on too much vodka, Vitaly explained that Katrina was just one more whore whom he had long ago added to his collection. Hearing this, Pavl exploded in rage and pulled out his knife, with every intention of killing his old friend. Only the *michman's* swift intervention kept him from doing so.

By the time Pavl had replayed this scene that would stay with him to his grave, he had successfully completed replacing the defective ball bearings. As he turned to find a rag with which to wipe his grease-stained hands and face, the sound of voices suddenly came from the aft hatchway. He looked up in time to view a single figure duck through the hatch and greet the *michman*. Pavl's stomach tightened as he recognized Seaman Vitaly Bolgrad.

Looking his usual cocky, self-assured self, Vitaly crossed by the rack of torpedoes that took up most of the compartment. Halting only when he reached the side of the just-repaired loading rail, he turned his head to address the warrant officer.

"Why, I didn't know that we had any blacks on board, Chief. It's about time that Command gave us a couple of darkies to do the menial work."

Obviously referring to the black grease that still stained Pavl's hands, arms, and face, Vitaly had intended merely to make a joke. But Pavl was in no mood for his humor, and he found himself bursting with anger.

"Why, you lecherous bastard! How dare you make

fun of me. It's time that someone around here taught you some manners, Vitaly Bolgrad."

Tossing his grease-stained rag to the floor in disgust, Pavl picked up a large wrench that lay on the rail, and began crossing the room toward Vitaly. Instantly sensing trouble, the *michman* ran to intercept him.

"For goodness sake, Pavl, stop this madness at once! Have you already forgotten your promise to Captain Valerian?"

From the other side of the compartment, Vitaly spitefully responded, "Have no fear, Chief. This spineless coward doesn't have the balls to follow through with his threats. From what his girlfriend tells me, he's not much of a man in the lovemaking department either."

This last remark proved to be the one that sent Pavl completely over the edge. Totally out of control now, he raised the wrench over his head and continued toward his adversary.

"You son of a bitch," he screamed. "You'll eat those words! You seduced my Katrina, and now you have the nerve to belittle my manhood as well. I'll show you who's the real man around here!"

By this time, Vitaly could see that Pavl was deadly serious, and for the first time he felt concern. Pavl was less than a dozen meters away from him now, his eyes glazed with anger, his face a brilliant beet red. Conscious that he had nothing to defend himself with but his own hands, Vitaly softened his tone.

"Easy now, Pavl! I was only joking with you. I meant you no harm!"

Oblivious to these words, Pavl continued his approach, and once again it was the *michman* who got

234

between them.

"Now, that's enough of this nonsense, Seaman Petrovka!" shouted the warrant officer. "Lower that wrench and stand aside this instant!"

A tortured, animal-like expression came over Pavl's face as he drew the wrench back and then smashed it firmly into the side of the *michman*'s skull. There was the sickening sound of fracturing bone, and the warrant officer slumped to the deck unconscious. Vitaly looked on in disbelief as blood began gushing from the *michman*'s head wound.

"Have you gone totally insane, Pavl? Stop this madness. I beg of you!"

Looking on impassively as his old friend began trembling with fear, Pavl spat, "Even this is too good for you, Comrade. You deserve to die in the gutter like a dog!"

Unable to stop his limbs from shaking, Vitaly lost control of his bowels as he dropped to his knees and pleaded again, this time with tears rolling from his eyes. "Please, I beg of you, Pavl. Come to your senses and get control of yourself!"

A sardonic sneer twisted Pavl's lips as he lifted the blood-stained wrench and smashed it downward, time after time, into the skull of Vitaly Bolgrad. By the time his former friend's head was smashed to a bloody pulp of broken bone and torn skin, Pavl Petrovka was completely insane.

Captain Anton Valerian was in the midst of his routine late-afternoon tour of the control room, when the intercom sounded and he was informed that one of

235

his men had just barricaded himself in the forward torpedo room. Cursing in response, Valerian called the crew to general quarters, then rushed down to the deck below to learn the facts of this incident firsthand. The sweating figure of the *Baikal's zampolit*, Boris Glazov, was waiting there to brief him.

"It's Seaman Petrovka, Captain. From what we've gathered, he's already killed Warrant Officer Silka and Seaman Bolgrad. And now he's threatening to blow up the ship by activating one of the torpedoes."

"Damn it!" Valerian shouted. "Has the man gone mad?"

The political officer nodded grimly. "It appears that he has, Captain. He's in there alone, with the door sealed shut from within, and our full load of weapons to do with as he pleases."

"We should have put that man in irons last week, when he first pulled that knife. Now look at the mess that he's gotten us in. And to think that all of this is occurring while we are still under a level two Red Flag alert!"

"Perhaps we should inform Petropavlovsk of our unfortunate situation?" dared the political officer.

The captain fixed the *zampolit* with an icy stare. "Don't tell me that you've also gone insane, Comrade Glazov. We won't go to any such extreme until we have exhausted all efforts in defusing this crisis ourselves. A proper first step would be for you to call an immediate meeting of all available officers in the wardroom. By putting our best minds together, we're bound to come up with some sort of solution to this problem."

"I'll do that at once, sir," retorted the *zampolit*, smartly pivoting to carry out the captain's bidding.

Seven minutes later, the *Baikal*'s wardroom was crowded with eight anxious figures representing the vessel's senior-officer staff. Anton Valerian presented the initial briefing, during which time he explained the nature of the crisis they presently faced. It was their chief engineering officer, who came up with a suggestion. Since Pavl Petrovka apparently could not be talked into surrendering, perhaps a group of volunteers could crawl through the main ventilation shaft to gain access to the torpedo room. Once inside, they would proceed to disable Seaman Petrovka, using whatever force might be necessary. With few other options open to them, this plan was adopted, with the political officer volunteering to lead this squad into action.

The *zampolit* prided himself on his superb physical conditioning. Too often, the confined environment of the *Baikal* made proper exercise difficult, and he therefore looked forward to the upcoming mission as a definite physical challenge. He picked two individuals to accompany him. One was a petty officer, the other a senior seaman. Both were tough, wiry figures, who could hold their own, and then some, when it came to a fist fight.

The captain was anxious for them to get started, and they wasted no time positioning themselves in front of that portion of the ventilation shaft that could be accessed from the passageway immediately aft of the torpedo room. Armed with sturdy hard-rubber truncheons, the *zampolit* disappeared into the shaft first, with the petty officer and the senior seaman following.

It was dark and cramped inside the shaft, which was just wide enough for the *zampolit* to crawl through on his hands and knees. Glazov's heart was pounding furiously, and he found his thoughts returning to the quick briefing that the chief had given him only minutes before. Above all, they had to keep Petrovka away from the torpedo activation switch. Though he would be unable to actually launch a weapon, he could arm one and start its motor. Since the torpdoes were programmed to explode once their propellers had stopped turning, the demented seaman could instantly doom all of them, if he so desired.

They were relying on the element of surprise to keep this worst-case scenario from occurring. Thus, they had to make certain to strike quickly and surely. Boris Glazov had no doubt in his mind that they would be able to get to Petrovka long before he'd be able to do them further harm. In a way, the *zampolit* was actually looking forward to this confrontation. For the routine of submarine duty was by it's very nature boring, and here was a chance for him to experience real action.

Proceeding as quietly as possible, he continued crawling down the cold metal shaft. Behind him, he could hear his teammates grunting and groaning as they followed close behind. Boris had to stop only once, when a painful cramp gripped his right calf. He had to bite his lip to keep from screaming out in anguish as he reached down awkwardly to massage the knotted leg muscle. It seemed to take an eternity before the spasm lessened and he was able to go on.

As the barest of flickering lights beckoned up ahead, he found himself wishing that his schoolmates at the Nakimov Institute could see him now. *Zampolits* were said to have inactive, sedentary duties aboard the Motherland's warships, and here he was, proving otherwise. Just because his primary job was to monitor the political reliability of the crew didn't mean that he couldn't play an active role in the ship's day-to-day functions. In this way, he showed the men the true meaning of socialist doctrine.

Even here in the submarine force, every man was equal, sharing responsibilities no matter how unpleasant they might be. Boris would never forget the look of shocked surprise that came over the faces of his fellow officers when he immediately volunteered for this assignment. He knew that most of them considered him to be mere excess baggage, a remnant of the past, when political officers were needed to keep the crews from defecting. But now he was showing them otherwise. Proud of his courage, Glazov eagerly pushed on as the distant light grow brighter.

It didn't take him much longer to reach the metallic grate from which this light emanated. Cautiously peeking through this screen, he was able to see a portion of the torpedo room below. From his current vantage point, he could make out an empty fire control console. A man's inert body lay at the foot of this station. Though he could only see this figure's back, it was completely soaked in bright red blood. From its slight build, the *zampolit* assumed that this was the corpse of Seaman Vitaly Bolgrad.

A new sense of urgency guided his movements as he edged forward to check out the view from a different angle. His glance narrowed as he spotted a single figure seated in front of the room's main hatchway. Constantly slapping the flat head of a large wrench into his open palm, Pavl Petrovka sat there staring at the hatch with wide, vacant eyes. It was obvious that he was concentrating his attention solely on this accessway, thus giving Boris and his teammates the opportunity they needed to take him by surprise.

Signaling his men that he had spotted their quarry, Boris Glazov prepared for the initial attack. The shaft was just wide enough for him to pull his knees up to his chest and gather himself into a tight fetuslike ball. This allowed him to place the soles of his feet up against the grate. Taking in three, deep calming breaths, he then pushed forward with his legs. With this, the screen popped out and fell to the deck below, with the figure of the *zampolit* not far behind.

The drop was only a few meters, but Boris landed awkwardly, causing him to sprain his left ankle. Trying to ignore the excruciating pain that coursed up his leg, he did his best to limp out of the way as his teammates proceeded to join him. They dropped onto the deck uninjured, and immediately set out to capture the still-seated figure of Pavl Petrovka.

Cursing his misfortune, Boris Glazov could only watch as the startled Petrovka reacted to the seamen's presence with a shocked gasp. Quickly standing with his wrench cocked menacingly, Petrovka raced to the side of the nearby torpedo rack. By this time, his pursuers were less than three meters away from him. Yet they were forced to instantly freeze when Pavl's hand went to a bright red switch set beneath the propeller of the topmost torpedo. A look of pure madness shone in Petrovka's eyes as he dared them to take a single step further.

The *zampolit* and his team knew that this was the same switch that the chief had warned them of earlier. A manual override that would simultaneously arm the torpedo's warhead and activate its propeller, it was designed as an emergency system which could be triggered if the main fire control computer malfunctioned.

As Boris Glazov spotted the bloody corpse of the *michman* on the other side of the rack, he decided to try one more verbal plea. For it was either this, or try to take the demented seaman by force.

"Please, Comrade Petrovka, we mean you no harm. I realize that things have gotten out of hand down here, and we've been sent to help you with your problems. So stand away from that torpedo, Pavl, and your shipmates here will assist you in sorting this mess out."

There was a strained smile on the political officer's lips as he slowly signaled his teammates to lower their truncheons. They did so, yet Petrovka failed to step aside.

Again the *zampolit* pleaded, "I beg of you, Pavl. Step away from that torpedo! Have you forgotten your sworn duty to the Motherland?"

With his right hand still fingering the red trigger mechanism, Pavl responded irrationally, "If I can't have Katrina, no one will have her! You're all the same. All you want to do is satisfy your animal lusts. Why, you're no better than a pack of wild dogs!"

"Whatever are you talking about, Comrade?" quizzed the puzzled *zampolit*. "We don't want your girl. All we want is for you to stand aside so the *Baikal* can once more fulfill its obligation in defence of the Motherland."

Pavl seemed to completely ignore this comment, and his limbs began to shake nervously. Realizing that he was too far gone to reach with mere words, and fearing that his shaking hand would hit the trigger switch, Boris Glazov decided that there was only one thing left that they could do. Ever so cautiously, he caught the attention of his two teammates and silently signaled them to take Petrovka by force.

It was the petty officer who made the first move. Lunging forward, he used his extended truncheon to push Pavl away from the weapon's metal storage rack. Though the blow made solid contact, Pavl was just able to push down on the trigger before being sent to the deck unconscious. A deafening high-pitched whine sounded as the torpedo's motor was activated and its propeller spun into action. Cursing at this sickening noise, Boris Glazov screamed out at the top of his lungs.

"He's done it now, Comrades! Break the seal to that hatch and get the chief in here! We've got exactly six and a half minutes before this baby runs out of fuel and the warhead blows, so move it!"

Needing no more motivation, the petty officer rushed to the hatchway and unlocked it. The first one into the compartment was Anton Valerian, with the *Baikal*'s chief engineer close on his heels. Both men heard the screeching whine, and were aware that their worst fears had been realized.

"What can we do about it, Chief?" asked the captain frantically.

The *Baikal*'s senior engineer had already grabbed a tool box and was on his way over to join Valerian at the torpedo's side. "We've got to pull off the engine cowling and yank out that armament pin before it triggers," he said breathlessly.

Coolly using a screwdriver to begin this process, the

chief concentrated on the task at hand while Valerian's eye went to his wristwatch. They had approximately six minutes left before the engine ran out of fuel and the warhead exploded. Since it would take several minutes just to remove the torpedo's protective cowling, the captain reached for a screwdriver to help the chief in this crucial race against time.

In a nearby portion of the Pacific, Petty Officer First Class Reginald Warner was about to begin his first sonar watch of the day. He had just polished off a Sunday dinner consisting of fried chicken, mashed potatoes and gravy, corn, biscuits, and hot apple pie with a scoop of vanilla ice cream for dessert. The guys had been giving him the business ever since they learned of his wedding plans, and Reggie took their good-natured ribbing all in stride. In fact, he couldn't remember when he last felt so sure of himself.

Since Kim had accepted his proposal during their unforgettable outing at Waimea Falls Park, his whole outlook seemed to have changed for the better. For the first time in much too long, he felt as if his life had some real purpose. Never one to spend much time pondering the future, Reggie now had a new family and home to plan for. This was a great responsibility, yet it was one that he undertook quite willingly.

As he left the mess hall and began his way forward to the sonar compartment, Reggie seriously considered his career possibilities. Just last month, the XO had talked to him about seeking a position as a commissioned officer. Lieutenant Commander Coria had emphasized that his work was excellent, and that the

Navy was looking for talented individuals like Reggie for promotion into the upper ranks. Such a position had never before been important to him, and fearful of any increased responsibilites, Reggie politely turned the XO down. Now he was beginning to wonder if he should reconsider the offer.

Higher rank would mean increased pay and benefits. It was evident that Kim would lose her current source of income once they were married, and this meant that he would have to take care of the two of them. In the past, money had never really mattered to him. As long as he had enough to pay his half of the rent and cover his bills, he was content. But a family would quickly change all that. He wanted to kick himself for not having put away a good portion of his salary in a savings account as his mother had advised. But he hadn't, and now he would have to face the consequences.

A commission would bring with it a big fat raise. Then he'd be able to start his new family off in comfort, and have a little to put aside for the future as well. Wondering when the best time would be to talk with the XO about his real chances of becoming an officer, Reggie ducked into the cramped compartment where he would spend the next six hours on watch.

Sonarman Second Class Marty Stanfield had been seated at the CRT screen nearest the hatch and was the first to spot Reggie. He cleared his throat loudly, and together with the two technicians seated beside him, began whistling the wedding march. Reggie let them continue for a full minute with this song before interrupting.

"Real cute, guys. I get the message, but I think you'd

better turn your attention back to your work. This would be a hell of a time for Ivan to pick to sneak up on us."

"Aw, for Christ's sake, Reggie, lighten up," came a deep bass voice from behind the supervisor's partition. Seconds later, Chief Meinert stood and stretched his cramped limbs, while continuing, "After all, how many time does our favorite sonar technician get married?"

A wide grin lit up Reggie's face as he walked toward the cork-lined partition to relieve the chief. "I appreciate the thought, but you're on watch now. What do we have out there?"

Handing Reggie his headphones, Meinert replied, "We're just entering the southern portion of the seamount range, and picked up a school of whales about an hour ago. They sound like grays and they're really singing up a storm."

"Great," reflected Reggie, who knew that this would make listening even more difficult for their enemy.

Chief Meinert patted his gurgling stomach, obviously having a more important subject in mind. "Did you leave any chicken for the rest of us, Warner?"

Reggie scooted by the hefty chief, to take his place at the supervisor's console. "Don't sweat it, Chief, the last I looked there was plenty left to go around. Cooky really did a number with his biscuits this time. They're as light as Seaman Stanfield's brains."

Stanfield had turned back to his CRT screen and failed to hear this comment, but it coaxed a brief chuckle out of the chief. "I'll be sure to grab a couple," he added as he turned to exit.

This left Reggie alone to get settled behind the

245

console. He seated himself in the padded leather chair and carefully fitted on the headphones. A virtual symphony of mournful, drawn-out cries met his ears, and he knew that he was listening to the strange chatter of the whales that Meinert had warned of. They seemed to be all around the *Copperhead*. Most of the huge mammals were near the surface, though several were deep in the black depths, searching for the squid that was their favorite food.

Reggie was no stranger to such cries, and found it somewhat comforting to know that they weren't so alone here after all. Yet he only wished that he had an understanding of their language. He knew that scientists were currently working on unlocking such secrets, and that hopefully some day soon, man would be able to comprehend just what the whale sounds really meant. Looking forward to that day with great anticipation, the senior sonar technician sat forward to initiate a comprehensive hydrophone scan of the surrounding waters.

He was nearly halfway through his watch when his headphones conveyed to him a distant sound, on a completely different frequency than that of the still-singing whales. Though it was barely audible, even under maximum amplication, this noise had disturbing implications. Belonging to a submerged contact, some 10,000 yards off their starboard bow, it had all the high-pitched, whirring characteristics of a torpedo's engine. Yet it was severely muffled, and since there was no sound of a weapon having actually been launched — and certainly no active search on its part apparent — Reggie seriously doubted that they were currently under attack. Strangely enough, by the time he informed the control room of this contact, the sound had abruptly terminated, leaving nothing in its place to even hint that another sub had been the cause of this mysterious racket.

Samuel Fuller had been in the attack center when the call from sonar arrived. With his XO at his side, the captain immediately sounded general quarters. As the men scurried to their battle stations, he hurriedly conferred with Vincent Coria to formulate a proper plan of action.

"Well, what do you think we've got out there, Mr. Coria," quizzed Fuller, his glance riveted on the instruments that showed their current depth, course, and speed.

Following the captain's line of sight, the XO responded, "Sonar mentioned that the contact's signature resembled the high-pitched whine that a torpedo would produce. Since it's evident that we haven't been fired on, maybe we've chanced upon some sort of remotely operated vehicle that utilizes a torpedolike propulsion system."

"That may very well be the case," reflected Fuller. "But where in the hell did such a platform come from? If it is an ROV, it had to be launched from a mother vessel, most likely a Soviet submarine."

"But why did the contact dissipate so abruptly?" questioned Coria.

The captain scratched his jaw thoughtfully. "Perhaps it malfunctioned, or maybe it simply ran out of fuel. Whatever the case, my instincts tell me that the mother ship is nearby. Let's load a couple of fish and a decoy, just to be safe. If Ivan's indeed out there, this time he's not getting away so easily."

Anton Valerian knew that they had been extremely lucky. The chief engineer had been able to disarm the torpedo with a full thirty seconds left before it was programmed to explode. Only when the captain was certain that the *Baikal* was safe from this threat, did he turn his attention to the man responsible for this nerve-racking mess.

Pavl Petrovka was just returning to consciousness when the torpedo propeller he had triggered spun safely to a halt. The alert *zampolit* was quickly at his side, ever ready to physically restrain the fallen sailor should it be necessary. Strangely enough, Petrovka awoke from his knockout blow as if nothing out of the ordinary had happened. Rubbing the back of his head where it had made contact with the deck, the conscript scanned the torpedo room with puzzled eyes. A look of genuine horror possessed him as he spotted the blood-soaked corpse of the fallen *michman* lying close-by.

"What in the world has occurred here?" he asked groggily.

The *zampolit,* who had an elementary knowledge of that serious mental disorder known as schizophrenia, answered guardedly, "There's been a tragic accident here, Comrade Petrovka. You have been seriously injured yourself, necessitating your immediate confinement to sick bay."

Slowly sitting up, Pavl caught sight of the assemblage of grim-faced figures now gathered around him. They included the political officer, the chief engineer, and even their captain. A splitting pain coursed through his forehead as he noticed another bloodied body lying on the room's opposite side. This corpse's slim figure was most familiar and his voice quivered with disbelief as he recognized it.

"Vitaly Bolgrad? Oh, it can't be! What has happened to my old friend?"

This time it was the captain who kneeled down beside Pavl and addressed him cooly. "Don't upset yourself, Seaman Petrovka. As the *zampolit* said, there's been an accident here, and we must confine you to sick bay for your own welfare."

Looking up to beckon two medical orderlies forward, Anton Valerian fought back the urge to slap the disturbed seaman in the face. Beside him, Boris Glazov could sense the captain's upset.

"Come now, Captain," the *zampolit* said firmly, "There's nothing else that we can do down here but get in the way. I've instructed the chief to see to the removal of the bodies. The weapons officer will get to work refueling the spent torpedo, and all will be back to normal by the next watch."

Watching as the still-babbling figure of Seaman Pavl Petrovka was led out the aft hatchway, Anton Valerian shook his head and somberly commented, "Do you realize that I actually wanted to beat that man's face in? Do you think he's merely acting, or does he really have no recollection of his actions?"

"That's tough to say," returned the political officer. "But in his case, mental illness could have indeed been the cause of his violent outburst. I guess we won't know for certain until we get him back to Petropavlovsk. Meanwhile, the orderlies have plenty of tranquilizers to keep him calm."

Valerian still had trouble accepting the reality of the entire incident. "In all my twenty years of dedicated service, nothing like this has ever taken place on one of my commands. You can rest assured that I will take all the responsibility for this tragic accident when we return to port."

"Nonsense," retorted the *zampolit*. "Don't forget that I am equally at fault here. One of my direct responsibilities is to enforce discipline, and I'm afraid that I seriously misjudged the depth of Seaman Petrovka's instability. Anyway, I doubt that even a trained therapist would have been able to foresee this tragedy. If anything, it's the navy recruiters who are at fault, for allowing such a disturbed man to become a submariner. You just watch. We'll walk out of this whole thing without so much as a blemish on our records."

Anton Valerian watched as two members of the *Baikal*'s security squad began placing the limp corpse of the *michman* into a heavy plastic body bag. "That might be so, Comrade Glazov," the captain responded, "but we still have to live with the fact that two brave men were beaten to death by Seaman Petrovka. Damn it! I should have placed him under arrest the moment he pulled that knife on Vitaly Bolgrad. Such stupidity on my part cannot be excused!"

"Easy now, Captain," cautioned the political officer. "What's done is done, and however badly you feel about this incident, it won't bring those two sailors back to life. Besides, we still have a level two Red Flag alert to be concerned with."

No sooner were these words out of Glazov's mouth, than the intercom chimed three times. Anton Valerian swiftly crossed the compartment and picked up the nearest handset.

"This is the Captain!" he barked into the transmitter.

The voice on the other end was excited and strained. "Sir, this is Senior Lieutenant Karmonov. Sonar reports an unidentified submerged contact, bearing two-zero-zero, at maximum range."

Hearing this, Valerian's stomach instinctively tightened. "Very well, Senior Lieutenant. Keep the men at battle stations, and have the sub remain in a state of ultra quiet. I'm on my way to the attack center, and by the time I meet you there, I want a computerized I.D. on this contact's signature."

Reaching to hang up the handset, the captain hurriedly turned to address the curious *zampolit*. "You are right, Comrade Glazov. Life does go on, and unless sonar is mistaken, it appears that our enemy has finally showed himself."

"Is it a Trident?" quizzed the anxious political officer.

Valerian was already heading for the aft hatchway. "We will soon see, Comrade. We'll soon see."

The *Baikal*'s attack center was located amidships, directly beneath the vessel's elongated sail. Illuminated by its red battle lights, the equipment-packed room took on a sinister appearance. Working intently before their various consoles, the staff hardly noticed when two figures entered the compartment and proceeded immediately to the station reserved for navigation. Here, the vessel's second in command stood with an intercom handset at his ear. Anton Valerian waited for the blond haired officer to conclude his conversa-

251

tion before questioning him.

"Well, Senior Lieutenant Karmonov, what type of vessel is currently approaching us from the south?"

This was Karmanov's first patrol as second in command, and he answered somewhat nervously. "Sonar reports that upon signature analysis, the computer shows a sixty-seven per cent probability that this submarine is an American *Sturgeon*-class boat, sir."

"Ah, so our nosy Yankee friends have returned!" exclaimed the captain. "This time we will not only easily escape them once again, but give them a dose of their own medicine as well. Have engineering prepare for flank speed. We will put a knuckle in the water that they'll never be able to follow. Then instruct sonar to ready the active transmitter. As soon as we get moving, I want to hit them with every available decibel of sonic energy that we've got. Now move it, Senior Lieutenant! We've got the Motherland's honor to uphold!"

Ever since they had picked up the mysterious motorized whining noise, Samuel Fuller had ordered the *Copperhead* to proceed cautiously. This decrease in speed was much appreciated by Reginald Warner and his sonar staff, who were able to utilize their sensitive hydrophones that much more effectively. Unfortunately, they had absolutely no success in determining if an enemy vessel was responsible for this brief racket.

Reggie's instincts told him that a Soviet sub was most definitely nearby. Even though his headphones picked up nothing that could prove the platform's presence, he knew that it would show itself eventually. Patience was the name of the game in cat and mouse chases such as this one. Only by keeping a cool head, would a winner prevail.

It was times such as these when Reggie really loved his job. With the entire crew depending upon him to determine if a threat existed, he was responsible for their very lives. There was no doubt in his mind that he was the best sonar operator in the entire navy, and now was his chance to do the thing that he did best.

He leaned forward expectantly when a low pitched bass groan emanated from the waters before them. But he sat back in relief after identifying this sound as the cry of a surfacing whale. A shrill clicking sound indicated that a colony of shrimp were feeding nearby, while from another direction, came the distinctive cries of a pod of frolicking dolphins. The successful sonar operator learned to distinguish such natural noises, and to listen solely for those sonic disturbances that were the direct by-product of man.

Certain that such prey was close, Reggie once again scanned the surrounding waters. This time as he manipulated the amplifier gain, he closed his eyes to better aid his concentration. The sea's local inhabitants greeted him with their normal symphony of sound. This shrieking chorus seemed to engulf them, yet his instincts limited his search to a relatively small portion of the ocean lying off the *Copperhead*'s starboard bow. Like a blind man, who relied upon his other senses to see him across a busy city street, Reggie absorbed the racket that was directed into his headphones. In such a way, he painted a mental picture of each individual sound's source.

The minutes passed by unnoticed, and his vigilance finally paid off when a far away throbbing sound suddenly caught his attention. This time as he sat anxiously forward, his hand was already reaching for the telephone that would connect him to the control room. Just as he was about to activate the intercom, the noise he had been monitoring drastically increased. A split second later, after he had already figured out that this was the sound of a nuclear propulsion unit going on-line, an ear-splitting blast of high-pitched noise streamed into his headphones. Ripping them off his head, Reggie cried out in excruciating pain.

Sound could be a most powerful, tormenting weapon. This was especially the case when it was intentionally being utilized to cause injury. Like a youngster who had stuck his ear up against the P.A. speakers at a heavy-metal concert, Reggie found his entire being racked in pain. Completely deafened, his head splitting in agony, the senior sonar operator still managed to summon the self-control to scream out to his associates.

"Somebody call control! Ivan is dead ahead of us!"

Marty Stanfield carried out this frantic directive. Only after he had completed this task, did he stand to help his injured coworker.

Meanwhile, in the *Copperhead*'s attack center, Samuel Fuller was quick to react to the enemy's surprise appearance. As the vessel's own water-cooled reactor snapped back on-line, the ship's steam-driven turbines began revolving more rapidly, and the *Copperhead* began steadily gathering forward speed.

Anger flushed the captain's face as he turned to address his XO. "Now you know what it's like to trust the Soviets, Mr. Coria. Those bastards have been

254

sitting out there waiting for us all along. From that lashing they just gave us, I've got a pretty good idea that we've encountered this same vessel once before. I guess they didn't get the intended message during our last meeting after all. This time we've got to be extra certain to get our point across. Do you read me, Lieutenant Commander?"

Vincent Coria watched as an almost maniacal gleam flashed in Fuller's eyes. Nodding silently in response, the XO listened as the captain urgently continued.

"All ahead full! Tell engineering to open those throttles all the way. Then prepare to activate the target-seeking sonar. I want to have a clear shot if we need it!"

Without hesitation, Coria relayed the order to engineering, requesting flank speed. Back in that portion of the ship reserved for its turbines, this directive was received by the *Copperhead*'s head nuc, Master Chief Dennis Kerkhoff. Minutes later, the temperature inside their work space rose to a sweltering ninety-five degrees. Trying their best to ignore this heat, which was being conveyed by the red-hot steam lines, Kerkhoff's sweating staff stripped to their waists and began double-checking the intricate system to make certain that every available ounce of power was being fed into their propeller shaft.

Back in the sub's attack center, this effort began to show results as the *Copperhead* picked up additional speed. Soon, they were surging forward with a velocity of over thirty-five knots, yet still the Soviet sub continued to pull away. Genuinely upset that their best wasn't enough, Samuel Fuller perched anxiously above the seated planesmen. With one eye on the digital counter indicating their speed, and the other on the dial showing their current depth and course, the captain seemed to be silently willing his ship forward. Having been foiled by this same elusive enemy vessel once before, his frustration built as sonar reported that the Soviets were now in the midst of a steep spiraling dive.

"Take us down after those bastards, Mr. Coria!" commanded Fuller. "Stern planes down maximum angle. Prepare the boat to attain test depth!"

The XO relayed these orders and the *Copperhead*'s bow dipped downward in response. So steep was the angle of this descent, the crew had to brace themselves to keep from falling over. At a depth of sixteen hundred and fifty feet the boat had to level out. They could only be observers as the Soviet sub continued on to a depth of more than twice this level. To add insult to injury, the Russians made good their escape at a speed of almost fifty knots, over ten knots faster than that achieved by the *Copperhead*.

Smacking his balled right fist into the side of his thigh, Samuel Fuller monitored the fading Soviet vessel and could only mutter in response, "Until next time, you Red bastard. Then we'll see if you can outrun an Mk 48 torpedo!"

CHAPTER TEN

The kayak surged down the swiftly moving current. Their way lit by only a single, hand-held flashlight, it was all Justin could do to keep them from smashing into the jagged walls that lined each side of the subterranean tunnel. It was while Mei-li was fumbling through the vessel's cramped interior, that she accidently triggered a metal switch, activating a pair of powerful spotlights mounted on the boat's bow. A wide beam of bright light clearly illuminated the rapidly advancing waters.

"Wonderful, Mei-li!" Justin cried out. "Now we can see where the hell we're going."

Using the double-bladed paddle to steer around a huge, half-exposed boulder, he added, "I bet they were preparing to use the kayak to explore this river. Thank God, it was waiting for us back there. Otherwise the general's shots were bound to eventually hit their intended mark!"

Even though Mei-li was seated directly in front of him, Justin had to scream out at the top of his lungs to be heard. For the water smashed against the rocks that formed the stream's channel with a deafening intensity. Like the roar of a passing freight train, the sound of the cascading current echoed off the walls of the underground tunnel. Its thundering resonance was all-pervading.

Justin had done a bit of collegiate rowing back at New York University. Yet the current was so swift and the channel so narrow, his main objective was merely to keep the vessel's bow headed in the right direction. For if they were to get turned around here, the danger of swamping would be greatly increased. The water was icy cold, and he doubted that they'd be able to take but a few minutes of exposure if such a disaster occurred.

One thing he remained thankful for was that the explosive crack of gunshots no longer sounded behind them. Lady Luck had been with them as their pursuer's bullets went astray and the waiting kayak took them quickly out of the cathedral-like room where they had been held prisoner. Since that time they had been traveling through a limestone tunnel, hollowed out solely by the river's pounding force. Because of the swiftness of this current, there were few obstacles blocking its meander. Justin was quite aware of this fact, yet still kept a careful watch for any threatening rock formations.

He sat forward when their lights illuminated a break in the tunnel up ahead. The current seemed to widen, and soon they were passing through another massive chamber. This one was given additional character by the hundreds of spiky stalactites that projected from its domed ceiling.

Seconds later, they passed through an auxiliary chamber dominated by a wall of calcified rock which sparkled with a jewel-like iridescence. Mei-li angled the torch's beam toward this glimmering sheet of limestone and oohed in delight.

"Oh Justin, it's absolutely gorgeous! Why it's like we've entered a fairy tale world."

The American couldn't help but agree, but failed to vocally respond when an ominous roar was audible in the distance. They followed the stream's meander around a wide bend, and as the current narrowed, Justin sighted a rippling expanse of white water up ahead. The kayak seemed to suddenly surge forward and the actor called out in warning.

"Hang on, Mei-li! I'm afraid it's going to get a little rough soon."

As she responded by tightly gripping the sides of the fiber glass vessel, Justin took a deep breath and prepared the paddle for action. It was all too soon in coming.

The rapids were formed by a portion of the streambed that was made up of a series of terraced limestone plateaus. The water was in the process of wearing this rock even. Yet for now, the current could only smash onto the exposed rock with a thunderous roar, and the rapids were the result.

Justin tried to follow the channel that offered the deepest water for their hull to safely travel over. Because of the poor lighting conditions, the meander of the wildly cascading stream was almost impossible to read. Thus for the most part, he had to be content to let fate be their guide.

He did spot one chute that looked promising, and utilized the paddle like a rudder to turn the kayak hard to the right. The vessel instantly responded, and the foaming current did the rest. The streamlined craft bounced off the rippling waves, and shot forward, successfully passing through the chute with a minimum of contact with the rock below. This put them a good two-thirds of the way through the rapids. Justin was in the process of steering them back into the current's central channel, when they struck a submerged shelf of limestone. This collision caused the kayak's bow to ride up on the shelf, while the stern was swept on. Much to their horror, they now found themselves going backward down the rest of the rapids.

It would be impossible for him to turn them around until they passed the last of the white water. Since the spotlights were mounted on the bow, the only illumination he had to light their way was the torch that Mei-li shakily handed him. Twisting his upper torso, he used the flashlight to gauge the stream's future meander. He then turned his attention back to his paddle, in an effort to keep them in the middle of the stream for as long as possible.

After what seemed like an eternity, the boat surged through a final chute, bounded off a steep shelf of rock, and landed with a splash into a wide pool of calm water. Justin's limbs were trembling with cold wet shock as he dug the paddle into the water to turn them around. With the way once more illuminated by the spotlights, he sighed heavily, and only then remembered his passenger.

"Hey, lady, are you all right?"

Mei-li's teeth were chattering as she responded, "I just got a little wet, but other than that, I can make it."

The American felt the damp chill pervade his bones also, and knew that hypothermia could kill them just as quickly as drowning could. Knowing there was

nothing else he could do for them but to keep paddling, he dipped the double-headed oar into the current and pushed them farther downstream.

This portion of the subterranean complex had a
noticeable absence of stalactites and stalagmites. In
their place were vast walls of smooth rock which
seemed to have been worn down by the constant rush
of hundreds of centuries of running water. After the
thunderous roar of the rapids, this section of the river
was ghostly still. All that could be heard was the sound
of the paddle as it dipped into the gentle stream.

They turned a wide bend, and Justin gasped upon
spotting a huge cloud of roiling white vapor that
completely veiled what lay beyond. As they approached this wall of mist, the temperature suddenly
rose and the damp chill dissipated. Soon, blessed
sweat was actually forming on their brows. It was the
American who identified the source of this unexpected
warmth.

"There must be a thermal spring entering into the
river here. That mist up ahead must be nothing but
steam!"

This indeed proved to be the case, and soon a
saunalike atmosphere prevailed. The thick mist
hugged the surface, and they found it impossible to
view the banks of the river, let alone that which lay
beyond. Yet the current was virtually nonexistent here,
and the obstacle-free water ran deep and hot.

For the first time since beginning their unscheduled
underground river journey, both passengers found
themselves relaxing. Calmed by the tropical heat, and
soothed by the gentle sway of the waters, they sat back
and put the frantic events of the past few hours into

their proper perspective.

"You know Justin," Mei-li said reflectively. "If that general was really serious, we've stumbled upon something that could affect the entire planet. But could such an operation actually be possible? I mean, no one in their right mind would purposely go and start World War Three, would they?"

"When it comes to the military, anything is possible, no matter how irrational it may seem," retorted Justin grimly. "No, from what I've seen, I feel that the general is quite serious. Both of us know for certain that there is no mining operation going on down here. It's obvious from the supplies they've already carted in, that the cavern's sole purpose is to serve as a nuclear fallout shelter."

Even though the air remained stifling hot, Mei-li shivered. "I still can't believe that my government could support such a warped plan."

"Who's to say that they even know anything about it," replied the American. "It sounds to me like this whole thing is a scheme dreamed up by the general and a select group of his twisted cronies."

Mei-li nodded. "I have heard rumors about the existence of a group who is violently opposed to our premier's liberal, democratic ways. Most of these individuals are old-timers, survivors from the ranks of Mao, whose hard-line policies they still swear allegiance to. As you very well know, things take much time to change in my country. This is especially the case with political loyalties."

"It's the same in America," added Justin. "But I'm afraid that the general and his supporters are taking this whole thing to an extreme. Hopefully, that earthquake has slowed them up a bit. It's now up to us to get word of their mad scheme out to the public — before those submarine-based missiles he spoke of are launched and the world that we know is no more."

Again, Mei-li shivered in shocked realization. "But who's to say where this stream leads, or if it even flows above ground for that matter? Why, we might never get out of this place!"

"Easy now, little one. I got you into this mess and I swear that I'll get you out of it. This stream has got to flow to some river above ground eventually, and we're not leaving it until it does. Now get hold of yourself, and help me figure out where we'll head once we get out of this subterranean hell. After all, we've got an entire planet to save!"

Justin's firm words hit home, and following his example, Mei-li took a series of deep, calming breaths. New purpose filled her being when she spoke again.

"Chances are that this stream is a tributary of the Lijiang. That should put us close to my parent's commune. My father will know what our next stop should be from there."

"Then the Blue Swan commune it will be," returned the American, who dipped the double-headed oar into the gentle, mist-covered water with a new sense of urgency. Stroke after stroke followed, and soon the roiling veil of steam dissipated and the familiar roar of white water sounded in the distance.

Mei-li's stomach tightened as the current increased and the kayak began progressively picking up speed. Confident of Justin's abilities, she still held on firmly to the vessel's gunwales as the first shelf of exposed limestone passed on their left. All too soon the frothing white water was all around them, it's thunderous roar rising to almost deafening intensity. The tiny boat shook and bobbed, its fragile hull at the complete mercy of the jagged rocks lining the narrow chute which Justin had chosen to guide them through. They rounded a narrow bend, and much to Mei-li's horror, the rapids rose even more violently. Twice, they hit submerged boulders and almost turned over. Once again they were completely soaked, and because the water had long ago cooled, their wet limbs trembled with an icy chill.

Ahead, the channel seemed to be further narrowing, and even Justin doubted that they would be able to pass through it safely. With no other choice, he aimed the kayak's pointed bow toward the exact center of the two massive shelves of rock that lay just ahead. There was no turning back now, and having made his commitment, he dug the paddle into the water and screamed wildly, "Ya hoo!"

The speeding kayak glanced off a boulder, righting itself in just enough time to penetrate the exact center of the two limestone shelves. Propelled by the full force of the current, the boat shot through and plunged downward into a pool below. The water here was deep, and though they both got thoroughly soaked, the kayak bobbed to the surface in an upright position.

As Justin was wiping the icy water from his face, he suddenly spotted an extraordinary sight up ahead. In the distance, the entire tunnel seemed to be glowing with a soft light of its own. It was Mei-li who sat forward and identified the source of this illumination.

"It's moonlight!" she cried joyously. "You've done

it, Justin. We're back above ground level!"

As the tunnel walls continued to take on additional definition, the American knew that Mei-li's observation had been correct. He increased the pace of his strokes, and within a short time the mouth of the channel was visible.

Their relief was great when the kayak finally shot through this formation and they emerged into the warm, humid night. They found themselves on a wide, slowly moving river. Above, the stars twinkled invitingly, while behind them, the jagged mountains from which they had just emerged filled the entire horizon like a menacing behemoth.

Momentarily putting down the paddle, Justin reached forward and gave his passenger a warm hug. "Thanks for not giving up on me, little one. Though I didn't want to admit it, even I wasn't sure if we were going to be able to pass through that last series of rapids."

Mei-li responded by turning her head and giving the actor a deep, passionate kiss on the lips. At first, Justin seemed shocked by this sudden show of emotion, but he quickly adjusted and returned the kiss warmly. He was breathless when they eventually parted, and reluctantly turned his attention back to the river.

"I take it that someone is happy to be out of that grotto," observed the American lightly. "Well, the feeling is mutual. Now tell me, do you have any idea where in the hell we are?"

"This could be the upper reaches of the Lijiang, but I'm still not certain, Justin. It's best if we continue downstream until I spot something familiar."

To a chorus of chirping crickets and frogs, the actor guided them down the center of the wide channel. Thick stands of reeds hugged both banks, and when the full moon broke over a distant hillside to their left, a good portion of the surrounding landscape could be seen. Much to their disappointment, there was no evidence of any cultivated fields, or anything else to suggest the presence of man nearby.

Soothed by the comforting night sounds, they floated silently on the gentle current. Mei-li's eyes were heavy with exhaustion, and she found it increasingly difficult to keep them open. Justin was equally tired, and it wasn't long before both of them surrendered to the call of a deep, dreamless sleep.

With no one to guide it, the kayak continued floating downstream, eventually coming to a halt in a clump of reeds. They were thus situated when Justin awoke with a start. Needing a few moments to orient himself, he looked to his left and jumped, startled, when a pair of glowing red eyes stared back at him from the grass on the nearby bank. Two pointed horns capped this mystery creature's skull, and the American sighed in relief only when he identified it as a water buffalo.

Laughing to himself, Justin picked up the paddle and quietly guided them back into the main current. The moon was high overhead by now, the night warm and cloudless. Determined not to awaken his still-slumbering passenger, he used the oar with care, soon establishing an easy, near-silent rhythm. This was more like the sculling he'd done at college, and Justin was able to make excellent progress.

The moon had just disappeared behind a limestone

peak to his right when he spotted a footbridge up ahead. It was a simply built suspension affair, which crossed the river at a narrow bend. This was the first evidence that man was nearby, and though Justin hated to do it, he gently shook Mei-li's shoulder.

"Hey, wake up, sleepyhead. I want you to take a look at something."

His passenger awoke, groggy at first. But when Mei-li realized where she was, she came fully awake with eyes wide open.

"I'm sorry, Justin. How long have I been out?"

Justin pointed toward the narrow span that lay before them. "It doesn't matter, little one. But tell me, does that bridge look familiar?"

Still wiping the sleep from her eyes, Mei-li looked in the direction that he had indicated. Her voice rose in instant recognition.

"I know this place! Father used to take me down here to see the swans. It's only a couple of kilometers from their cottage."

Justin was greatly relieved to hear this news. "That's music to my ears, my dear. What do you say to hiding our kayak beneath the bridge and then heading straight to their house?"

"But didn't the general say something about stationing troops in the commune?" Mei-li countered.

Justin was already steering them toward the bridge's bamboo abutments as he answered, "Don't worry, if we could steer our way through those rapids, a couple of soldiers won't stand in our way. Besides, we'll proceed very cautiously."

Calmed by the actor's optimism, Mei-li shrugged her shoulders and watched as the bridge grew closer. A thick clump of blackberry bushes provided excellent cover for their vessel, and they quickly exited the fiber glass craft. The solid ground felt good beneath their feet, and they wasted no time in climbing up the bank. Mei-li scanned the countryside and directed them over the bridge. A narrow cart path led them over a series of terraced paddies.

Dawn had not yet broken and the fields were empty, except for numerous crickets and frogs, and an occasional hooting owl. After their confinement in the cramped kayak, the simple act of walking felt good to both of them, and they quickly established a spirited stride that took them past the last paddy and up a steep hillside. From this vantage point, a good-sized valley was visible. Even Justin recognized it as the same one that they had traveled just yesterday while accompanying Mei-li's father to work. They turned to the south here, using a wide earthen roadway.

The eastern horizon was just lightening with the first hint of dawn as they spotted the cottage compound. Leaving the road here, they took a shortcut that led them through a grape arbor. This proved to be a wise decision, for only minutes later a truck rumbled down this same roadway. It was headed away from the compound, and its cab was embossed with the distinctive red star of the People's Liberation Army. Undaunted, the couple merely ducked down until the vehicle had passed, then continued on their way.

They reached the edge of the compound ten minutes later. Once again, it was the grape vines that provided them with cover as they worked their way over to Mei-li's cottage, which was set off by itself, near the base of a limestone peak. Just as they were preparing to make a dash for the front door, a rifle-toting soldier rounded the far corner of the house. Looking tired and bored, he seated himself on a low-lying rock ledge and pulled out a cigarette.

"Damn it!" whispered Justin angrily. "To think that we're thwarted now that we're this close."

Before Mei-li could reply, the front door suddenly swung open and her father strolled out. By the first light of dawn they could see that he was dressed in his green work fatigues. He greeted the soldier and astonishingly enough, continued on straight toward the grape arbor.

"I bet he's headed this way to practice his Tai Chi in private!" Justin exclaimed excitedly. "Just wait till he sees who's waiting for him."

Wu Chiang-tzu did not proceed all the way into the arbor, but halted in an adjacent clearing. His hidden audience watched as the oldtimer began his exercise sequence. He flexed his knees, and was just beginning to swing his arms upward, when Mei-li whistled softly in perfect imitation of a bird. It took several additional calls to get the elder's complete attention. Only when he was certain that the sentry was still absorbed in his smoke did he cross into the first row of grape vines. When he saw who awaited him there, his round face lit up with an expression of pure joy.

"Are my eyes deceiving me?" he whispered excitedly. "Or perhaps this is all a dream?"

"I wish it was but a bad dream for all of us," said Mei-li, who ran into her father's arms.

By the time Justin reached his side, the old-timer's face had turned quite serious. "Now, what's this I hear about you two being CIA spies? And what in the world

269

are you doing here, anyway? The last we heard, you were under lock and key somewhere inside the mine complex."

"That's no uranium mine," returned Mei-li. "Justin, you tell him, because I still have trouble believing what we've seen."

Accepting the elder's warm handshake, Justin took a deep breath and started speaking softly. "I know that it was foolish of me, but my curiosity caused us to be captured while we were checking out the so-called mining operation from afar. The soldiers immediately blindfolded and bound us, and led us inside the cavern to be interrogated. Though the details of how we did it are unimportant, we soon learned that the underground complex is being developed as a nuclear fallout shelter. We met a crazed army general inside, who's actually planning to precipitate a full-scale war between the United States and the Soviet Union. While their warheads wipe out the world's population, the general and his cronies plan to wait out the apocalypse from the safe confines of the cavern. Then they'll emerge to rule what's left of the planet."

A skeptical look crossed Wu Chiang-tzu's weather-worn face, and Mei-li was quick to add, "You've got to believe us, Father! Not only did we hear this mad plan revealed from the general's own lips, but we saw the preparations as well. There are tons of foodstuffs stored away in that cave, as well as clothing, medicine, and vast amounts of radiation detection gear. I know that it sounds absolutely absurd, but such a thing is really happening in the valley just north of here."

Well aware of the sincerity of his daughter's emotional plea, Wu Chiang-tzu nevertheless replied cautiously. "I believe that what you experienced indeed occurred, daughter. There are many sick individuals in our country who are very capable of formulating just such a dastardly plan. But I'm afraid that the very general of whom you speak is also responsible for the company of soldiers currently occupying our compound. In fact, if I don't get back to the cottage shortly, you'll be meeting one of these young fellows face to face. Right now, it appears that you are in a better position to inform the outside authorities of this plot than I am. By the way, how did you make good your escape?"

"We used a kayak to float down a subterranean stream which eventually flowed into the Lijiang," answered Justin.

"Do you still have this vessel?"

"That we do, Father," Mei-li replied. "It's currently hidden beneath the footbridge where we used to watch the swans from."

"Good," returned the old man thoughtfully. "The river offers you the most inconspicuous route away from this place. As you well know, the Lijiang continues on to the south from here. You should be safe from detection until you approach Guilin. From there, it would be best if you left your craft and hitched a ride on one of the many barges that make the city their port. Such a means of transportation can take you all the way to Canton if you wish."

"Canton!" exclaimed Justin. "Why, that's just perfect. A representative of my government is waiting for us there at the U.S. consulate. He'll know what to do with this information."

"That is most fortunate," observed the elder. "With

a plot the likes of which you've stumbled upon, there's no telling who's involved in our government. So you must be extremely careful!"

Nodding that he understood, Justin look on as Mei-li and her father once more embraced. Good-byes were tearfully exchanged, and Justin left the oldtimer with a promise to take good care of his daughter.

They arrived at the footbridge just as the sun was breaking the eastern horizon. Not another soul was encountered during this hurried trip across the many open fields, and they were greatly relieved when they found the kayak just where they had left it. They gratefully climbed aboard and were soon once again floating down the river southward.

The current remained slow, and Justin resumed his rhythmic paddling. A mist had formed, veiling the surrounding landscape. Yet as the sun continued to rise in the sky, it slowly evaporated, revealing several water buffalo wallowing in the shallow water to their left. Stringy tendrils of grass hung from their mouths as they looked up to watch the kayak pass. Behind these beasts, there was a ridge of tall, craggy hills with stunted pine trees growing out of the rock crevices. A golden hawk circled above, and Justin felt as if he had just stepped into an artist's canvas.

As the day developed, he made certain to hug the river bank whenever possible. They had been extremely lucky so far, and it would be foolish to tempt fate by unnecessarily drawing attention to themselves. This cautious attitude paid off toward mid-morning, when a sudden chopping roar signaled that a helicopter was close by. Justin quickly guided the kayak into a stand of tufted marsh plants at the river's edge. Just as they reached this cover, a large green helicopter swooped in from the south. The copter, which had an elongated fuselage and a large red star near its tail, was less than two dozen meters above the water's surface, and appeared to be following the river's northward meander.

"I wonder if they're searching for us?" Mei-li asked as she watched the chopper quickly fade in the distance.

"If that's the case, we'd better be on the lookout for ground and boat patrols as well," Justin replied. "Though it would be safer to pull up somewhere and wait for the cover of night, I'm afraid we just don't have the time to spare. Besides, they still don't know if we even made it out of that subterranean complex. If they are searching the Lijiang for us, they'll most likely give it a couple of passes with the helicopter, and if we don't show by then, they'll go back to working on their precious fallout shelter."

Aware that they'd better get moving if they hoped to reach Canton before any planned attack might take place, Justin guided the kayak back into the current. It wasn't long afterward that they encountered their first bit of local river traffic. The craft was a simple bamboo raft, propelled punt-style by a grizzled, white-haired elder. It was headed downstream slowly, overladen and awash. Yet it's cargo of cabbage was stored safely above the water level, in several large wicker baskets.

As they passed this raft and nodded in greeting, a group of women could be seen on the western bank, pounding their washing on the rocks. They barely seemed to notice the two young occupants of the kayak, so busy were they with their chores and gossip. This was fine with Justin, who applied himself with a new urgency to his paddle strokes.

A broad bend was navigated, and a village loomed in the distance. Clusters of fishing barges were moored beside the river here. It was obvious that many of the fishermen lived on these barges, which had spacious hulls and awnings made of straw. Fishing nets and laundry were hung out to dry on the bamboo railings, and stacks of firewood took up most of the open deck.

Justin watched one of these fishermen working from his raft. Most of his efforts were concentrated on a circular net, which he threw into the water with a professional expertise. The American's curiosity was aroused when a dark-skinned bird popped out of the water and the old fisherman bent down to pull it toward him. Angling a basket beneath the bird's beak, he then proceeded to pull a fish out of its long throat. Mei-li was quick to explain.

"Those birds are specially trained cormorants, Justin. The fishermen in these parts have been using them to catch fish for centuries. That collar on the bird's lower neck keeps it from swallowing the catch before the fisherman retrieves it."

"Why, that's one of the most incredible things I've ever seen!" Justin said in astonishment. "It sure beats the old hook and worm."

As they passed the village on their left, Mei-li pointed downstream. "I believe that we're approaching the outskirts of Guilin now. We must keep our eyes peeled for the motorized barges that Father spoke of."

There was a good deal of river traffic now, and the banks on both sides were bustling with all sorts of activity. Feeling very conspicuous now, Justin sighed in relief when they rounded another broad bend and Mei-li shouted, "There are the docks now, to our right! It looks like there are quite a few barges there."

Justin had no trouble spotting them, approximately a quarter of a kilometer further downstream. Following Wu Chiang-tzu's suggestion, he steered the kayak into a thick stand of marsh plants on the righthand bank of the river. They jumped out of the craft, and Justin searched the ground until he located a heavy, jagged boulder that he was just able to lift. He grunted loudly as he picked it up and carried it toward the river's edge. Momentarily setting it down on the sandy bank, he turned to Mei-li.

"Well, I hate to do it, but it's really best if we destroy this last bit of evidence. This kayak has sure been good to us. In fact, I guess you could say that we owe it our lives."

Pivoting to face the streamlined, fiber glass vessel, Justin once again lifted up the boulder, this time wading out into the water and dropping it squarely into the boat's interior. There was a loud cracking sound as the hull split. Only when the kayak was completely filled with water did it sink beneath the surface.

Wading back to the bank, Justin joined Mei-li and commented, "So much for our kayak. Now, what kind of line are we going to use to get us passage on one of those barges?"

Mei-li replied while leading them toward a footpath that followed the river downstream. "It's obvious that we can't pay our way. That means that we're either going to have to find someone who's willing to give us free passage, or better yet, work off our fare. Let me do the negotiating. You can once again be Lo Kuan, my fiancé from Kashgar."

"I hope that I can give a more convincing performance than I did for the general," offered the actor with a wink. "Otherwise, we'll have to swim the rest of the way to Canton."

Mei-li shook her head. "If that's the case, you'll be going southward alone. You see, I never learned how to swim."

Justin seemed astonished by this disclosure. "Do you mean to say that you allowed me to take you down those rapids, knowing all the time that you'd most probably drown if we overturned? Why didn't you say something?"

"What was I to say, Justin? It wasn't as if we had a whole lot of alternatives back in that cave. Believe me, I was plenty scared. But somehow, I just knew that you'd successfully get us out of that place."

"Little one, you're indeed one of the bravest women that I have ever met."

"I don't know about that, Justin. I'm just a survivor, who loves life as much as you do."

Their discussion was interrupted when a mule-drawn cart filled with straw passed them. A young boy in ragged shorts prodded the mule incessantly with a reed stick, hardly paying any attention to the couple in his path. A market was set up on the river bank up ahead, and very soon they found themselves in the midst of a jabbering mass of humanity. Farm produce, fish, and poultry of all types were being haggled for, and both Justin and Mei-li realized how hungry they were. After all, their last meal had been the tasteless gruel served to them in their cavern prison over sixteen hours before. It had been less than a satisfying repast, and the two tried their best to ignore the food that now surrounded them.

Dressed as he was in his grubby fatigues, Justin felt right at home with the locals. He greeted several elders, joked with the children, and even wished a pair of stern-faced policemen a hearty good morning. Remembering that his mother's ancestors came from a village much like this one, he absorbed the strange sights and sounds around him, wondering idly if any of the peasants might in some way be related to him. The shrill blast of a boat whistle diverted his attention to the docks. With Mei-li leading the way, he found himself walking down a wooden-slat pier. A half dozen, large motorized barges were moored here. He had seen similar vessels plying New York's East River, and was impressed with their modern construction and excellent state of upkeep.

Only one of the barges currently had smoke pouring from its exhaust stack. This proved to be the same vessel that had previously blown its whistle, for three more shrill tones followed. A group of figures stood on the dock beside this barge, frantically loading a pile of cabbages into the hold. A white-haired man was supervising this hurried effort, and it was this elder whom Mei-li chose to approach.

"Excuse me, sir, but would you happen to be the captain of this vessel?"

The elder totally ignored her, his attention focused solely on a deckhand who had tripped and dropped an armful of cabbages into the river. Spewing forth a stream of invective, in which he questioned the legitimacy of the clumsy deckhand's maternal heritage, he waved his hand disgustedly and only then turned to see who had the nerve to disturb him.

It was only because he liked the look of the young girl's face that he even bothered answering her. "That I am, Comrade. Why do you ask?"

Mei-li took a deep breath and then continued, "My fiancé and I are looking for passage downriver to Canton. We are both students, and are willing to work in exchange for the fare."

Once again the elder was distracted when the deckhand who had tripped earlier, once more stumbled. This time he collided headfirst with one of the other crew members, causing him to go flying off the pier and into the river below. As this startled figure—and the cabbages he had been carrying—plopped into the water, the other deckhands began roaring with laughter. Hearing this, the white-haired elder lost his temper completely.

"Get back to work this instant, you shirkers! What am I running here, a circus filled with clowns? Must I remind you that we are already running eight hours late? If we don't get to Canton by tomorrow, this entire load will be rotten, and then there will really be all hell to pay!"

As the men turned back to their work, the captain took a closer look at the two newcomers who were requesting passage. "So you're willing to work off your fare, are you now? Have either one of you worked on a barge before?"

Mei-li and Justin shook their heads that they hadn't, and the elder continued, "Well, you certainly couldn't be more incompetent than this bunch of scallywags

278

that currently man my boat. Why, they've already dropped just as many cabbages into the river as they have into the barge's hold.

"You know, I envy the two of you. You've got your whole lives ahead of you. Keep studying and make something of yourselves. Don't end up like me, stuck with this clumsy lot of clowns for the rest of my years."

"Don't underestimate yourself, Comrade," offered Justin in fluent Mandarin. "The Republic flourishes because of the unselfish efforts of men such as yourself. After all, the workers is the backbone of our country. Without you, China would be but a weak country, still threatened by foreign invaders."

"My fiancé is right," added Mei-li. "We salute you, Captain, as a hero in your own right. For we never forget that our university education would be impossible without your hard work and sacrifices."

Pleased by what he was hearing, the elder hardly noticed it when one of the deckhands, who had been trying to help his hapless coworker climb out of the river, slipped into the water himself. Even when the rest of the men broke out laughing, he went on speaking equally to the newcomers.

"It is refreshing to hear such wise words coming from the mouths of two so young. It is a tribute to your maturity and the success of our educational system. It's not often that I get a chance to talk with really intelligent people, and I'd be honored if you'd join me on my humble ship.

"We will be leaving within the half hour. Things are a bit cramped on board, but the ship is clean and the engines most capable. By running at full power, I hope to be approaching Canton by tomorrow at this time.

Meanwhile, you will be afforded an intimate look into the minds of my crew, this so-called backbone of China that you speak of. I'm anxious to see if you have the same lofty opinion of them twenty-four hours from now."

Thanking the captain for his offer, Mei-li and Justin willingly helped load the rest of the cabbages. A quarter of an hour later, the last head was passed aboard, and the whistle sounded four times. It was only as the American helped untie one of the lines which held the vessel to the pier, that he noticed the name of the boat stenciled on its stern. He shivered in sudden awareness that they would be carried southward to safety on a barge called, quite appropriately, *The Blue Swan*.

As the noon sun rose high above the Lijiang, General Huang Tzu nervously paced that portion of the acacia-lined valley which lay immediately in front of the cavern's entrance way. His day so far had been a virtual nightmare of damage reports and the inevitable delays occasioned by necessary repairs. But as Captain Han had so wisely observed, the earthquake could have very well been even more destructive. Though a dozen men had been killed as a direct result of the tremor, and tons of supplies ruined, the cavern complex itself was still intact. The lost men and supplies could be replaced with a minimal amount of delay. Then Operation Red Dragon could get back on schedule.

Surprisingly enough, Liu Shao-chi had taken the news of their unexpected setback without so much as a whimper. Huang had only just gotten off the telephone with the esteemed First Admiral. During the course of this conversation it had been agreed that the launch would have to be delayed only another twenty-four hours at most.

Liu seemed relieved that the subterranean complex hadn't suffered major structural damage, and went on to convey other news of great importance. Far out in the Pacific now, the *Red Dragon* was well on its way to its launch point. So far, the submarine had been operating perfectly. Not a single Soviet or American vessel seemed aware of its passage, and the all-important element of surprise was thus still with them.

Liu signed off in a most optimistic manner. He would be greeting Huang personally in forty-eight hours, when he would arrive in Guilin with the first group of handpicked VIP's. Thus, the General would have a full two days to clean up the damage done by the quake and restock the ruined supplies. This seemed most reasonable, and Huang felt a bit relieved as he hung up the receiver and stepped out of the tent where the telephone conversation had taken place.

It was another cloudless, muggy day. Most of his men were inside the grotto, clearing away debris. A supply convoy was due in shortly, at which time several squads would have to be pulled out of the cavern to help unload the trucks.

Manpower had previously not been much of a concern to him. Yet all of this had changed when the two spies were caught and the earthquake struck. To maintain security, it had been necessary to send a full armed detachment into the Blue Swan commune. They would remain in the community until zero hour, when they would be recalled to the cave.

Huang was angry with himself for not foreseeing this difficulty from the beginning. He should have cleared out the commune from the very start. Then there would have been no CIA spies poking their noses where they didn't belong.

As a direct reminder of these two intruders, a muffled, chopping roar sounded in the distance, sending the general's glance skyward. He had no trouble spotting the helicopter responsible for this noise as it swept in from the south. Inside its green fuselage, Captain Han was waiting with the results of his morning's search of the Lijiang and its environs.

So far, the young American and his Chinese cohort had yet to show themselves. Though the odds were that they never made it out of the cavern alive, General Huang couldn't rest until he knew this for a fact. Just in case they had managed to escape, he had sent the captain skyward to scour the river. Meanwhile, another security detail had been sent down the underground river itself, in an effort to uncover any evidence of their fate.

Cursing the fates that had so conveniently provided the kayak in which they were last seen, Huang turned his back to the clearing where the helicopter was now landing. He held his palms over his ears, and closed his eyes tightly as the powerful down draft of the rotors created a gusting wall of dust. He turned only when the whine of the turbines faded, and the rotors slowly spun to a halt.

The chopper's main hatch opened, and the tall, distinguished figure of Captain Han stepped out to greet him with a salute. Huang was anxious to know the results of the search, and quickly took him aside.

"Well, Captain, what did you find?"

"As we anticipated, absolutely nothing, sir," retorted the senior officer. "We checked the surrounding countryside, and made a particularly intensive search of the Lijiang north of Guilin. If you'd like, we could give it another try. Perhaps that portion of the river south of Guilin will prove more productive."

"That's really not necessary, Captain," replied Huang. "I am certain that the two escapees never made it out of the subterranean river, let alone all the way to Guilin. Besides, there's much to do here in the compound."

"When we were flying into the valley, we spotted a motorized convoy turning off from the main road. They should be here shortly."

Already focusing on matters other than the two missing prisoners, Huang beamed. "That's excellent news, Captain. The trucks are carrying medicine and spare decontamination gear. Such supplies are extremely important, and must be stored away without delay. Since my office area was the least affected by the quake, we will be securing these supplies in that portion of the cave. I am placing you in charge of seeing that everything is stacked away safely."

Saluting in response to this directive, the captain turned to get on with his new responsibilities. This left Huang alone on the clearing once again. Confident that he'd be able to meet the timetable that he had discussed earlier with Admiral Liu, he decided to return to the cave himself to get a firsthand assessment of the quake damage. Also anxious to get out of the hot sun, he turned toward the grotto's entrance way.

Here he donned a miner's helmet, switched on its battery-powered lantern, and gratefully entered the cool dark tunnel.

In forty-eight hours, the first elements of their new society would be filing through this same rock-lined passageway. Then, less than twelve hours later, the *Red Dragon* would be ordered to spit forth its load of strategic nuclear death, and the world would be consumed in a holocaust. The next time that they walked out of this same tunnel, it would be to rule an entire planet! And at long last the wisdom of their beloved Mao could be shared by all of mankind, as China's ten thousand years of divine rulership came to fruition.

CHAPTER ELEVEN

The rains came down in heavy tropical squalls. Peering out his office's central picture window, Admiral Walter Lawrence could barely see the line of coconut palms set outside the building, let alone the boat docks beyond. Yet the precipitation fell with an almost mesmerizing force, and he found himself unable to break away from watching it and return to to his desk.

With the bit of his favorite Canadian clenched solidly between his lips, Lawrence contemplated the phone conversation that he had only moments ago concluded. It wasn't every day that he personally spoke to the Chief of Naval Operations, or the CNO as he was commonly called. Even more unusual was the nature of the news that the CNO had to relay. Having initiated the call to Pearl Harbor from the secured confines of the White House Situation Room, the CNO divulged an incredible tale, one that could very possibly lead the world to the brink of nuclear destruction.

It had all begun in Canton, China, when a young American actor on tour in the People's Republic, burst into the American consulate and demanded to speak to a State Department representative. What followed was an astonishing tale of international intrigue, which, if it could be believed, revealed a fiendish plot to initiate World War III.

The conspiracy was traced to a certain unidentified general in the PLA, who had actually captured the American actor several days earlier. The entire incident had taken place in southeastern China, near the city of Guilin. Here, according to the American, the general was in the midst of developing a massive underground city in a series of interconnecting caverns, with the ulterior motive of utilizing this subterranean world as a fully stocked nuclear fallout shelter. Such a shelter would be needed when the second portion of his plot unfolded.

This would come to pass when a Chinese submarine, loaded with ballistic nuclear missiles, reached its launch point in the mid-Pacific. A faked war alert would then be conveyed to this vessel, which in turn would proceed to release the missiles, whose warheads were targeted at sites in both the United States and the Soviet Union. The conspirators were apparently gambling that the two countries would inevitably blame each other for this surprise attack, and immediately retaliate against each other. This exchange would quickly escalate, and within a short time both superpowers would be completely annihilated. Only when it was safe to do so would the Chinese general and his followers emerge from the cavern complex, to rule that portion of the world that still existed.

In his thirty-seven years as a naval officer, Lawrence had certainly heard his fair share of wild stories, but this one was in a league all its own. Even though on the surface it merely sounded like a fantastic fabrication, there were some elements of the account that were genuinely disturbing. This was especially the case when the CNO had mentioned that a mysterious Chinese ballistic-missile submarine was involved. For Lawrence had actually been tracking such a vessel for almost seven days now.

It had all started three weeks ago, when one of their surveillance satellites caught sight of the launch of a suspected Chinese submarine-based missile in the South China Sea. This launch was also verified by Taiwanese Naval Intelligence, and proved to be particularly significant since it involved the accurate delivery of a MIRV'd warhead. This was a capability that the Chinese, had heretofore not acquired, and Lawrence knew that if the launch had taken place, it would signal a dangerous new development in the nuclear arms race.

On the same day that Lawrence had learned of this launch, he had met with Lieutenant Craig Benton, one of his own intelligence officers here at Pearl. It was with Benton's invaluable assistance that he was to learn of a newly developed, top-secret Chinese naval anchorage located outside the port city of Huangyan. Designed to service a limited number of submarines, this installation was set inside the hollowed-out confines of a sea cave. The Soviets were in the process of building similar bases on the Kola peninsula, and Lawrence guessed that it would be this kind of protective spot that the PLN would choose for this missile-carrying submarine's port.

To find out if this was the case, Lawrence dispatched one of their 688-class submarines to the waters off Huangyan. Here the vessel proceeded to litter the seabed with a series of sonobuoys. A fiber-optic link connected this array with one of the constantly patrolling P-3 Orions based out of the U.S. Naval base at Sasebo, Japan.

Six and a half days ago, this array picked up the passage of an unidentified submerged vessel headed straight for the open Pacific. The submarine's sound signature was a unique one, never showing up before in their computer's memory banks. In an attempt to determine its precise class and purpose, Lawrence assigned a P-3 to secretly monitor the sub's patrol route. It did so by anticipating the boat's course and sowing sonobuoys in the ocean before it. For almost an entire week now, they had been able to keep tabs on the vessel, which was last heard approaching the waters just west of the North Hawaiian Seamount Range.

Lawrence knew that if the Chinese had a plot to launch a submarine-based missile attack against both superpowers, the North Hawaiian Seamount Range would be the perfect release point. From this position they could hit targets throughout the Soviet Far East, and up and down the west coast of the United States as well. Thus, if such a threat really existed, this mystery sub, which they had been following for the better part of the week, had to be the same platform from which the strike would originate.

Thankful for his foresight, Lawrence continued to look out at the falling rain, all the while contemplating his next move. If these were normal times, he would only have to make a single call to insure that the threat was countered. For this same portion of the Pacific was the current patrol sector of one of his most capable attack submarines, the USS *Copperhead*. With Samuel Fuller at the helm of the *Copperhead,* the suspect Chinese vessel would be easily tagged and monitored. Then if they showed the least hostile move, the *Sturgeon*-class sub would eliminate them.

Unfortunately, it wasn't going to be this simple, for the President of the United States had picked this moment to intervene. Only twenty-four hours away from his scheduled summit with the Soviet Premier, the President had decided to share the news of this Chinese plot with the Russians. Not only would this be a supreme gesture of *glasnost,* or the openness and trust that was to symbolize this new era of superpower relations, but since targets inside the U.S.S.R. were also at risk, it was only fair that they work with the U.S. to eliminate this shared threat. Thus the CNO had only moments ago ordered Lawrence to telephone his counterpart in the Soviet Union, Admiral Leonid Silka, and ask for his assistance in tracking down the Chinese sub.

It was this portion of his recently concluded phone call with Washington that truly upset Lawrence. He was all for peace with the Soviets, but it went against every principle he believed in to have to trust them in this instance. Regardless of his own feelings, he could just see Samuel Fuller's face when he learned that he would have to work with his sworn enemy to eliminate a common threat. The veteran sub commander would be absolutely furious!

Lawrence couldn't blame him. Besides the tragic incident involving Fuller's brother, he had every reason to still distrust the Soviets. Though their smooth-talking leaders might talk of peace, their submarine fleet had yet to get the message. Almost every day of the week one of their vessels attempted some sort of tomfoolery, whether it was secretly trailing in a U.S.

sub's baffles, or trying to sneak into America's territorial waters.

Samuel Fuller and his colleagues were firsthand witnesses to actual Soviet policy application. Aggressive by its very nature, the Russian Navy would still do anything it could to get the advantage. From industrial espionage to sonar lashings, they still played the part of the enemy—no matter how much their premier might argue otherwise.

Of course, Lawrence was always looking to the day when this foolishness would stop. So far, it hadn't. That was why he was so upset with Washington's attitude in the matter.

To prematurely disarm the United States, merely because of a treaty, was madness of the first degree! At the very least, the Soviet's publicly declared attitude should be reflected in the day-to-day actions of its fleet. That was only one of the reasons that Lawrence had been so upset when he'd been instructed to prepare a third of his submarines for early retirement.

How were we ever to know if the Russians were doing likewise, if our eyes and ears beneath the sea were severely restricted? And more importantly, why ask for their help in the elimination of a target that could be just as readily tracked down by one of our own subs? Surely this whole thing was nothing but a ridiculous public relations scheme. It was political grandstanding of the worst kind!

Besides, the Russians would only get in the way of a routine interception. American attack-subs still operated under the lone wolf principle. A single platform was solely responsible for patrolling its preassigned sector. Aware of this, captain and crew could be assured that any unidentified contacts they encountered were not their countrymen. Thus if a shooting war ever did break out, they could proceed without fear of attacking one of their own submarines.

The *Copperhead* was such a lone wolf. To ask it to play nursemaid to a Soviet vessel was sheer stupidity! Yet if the CNO hadn't been able to convey this point to their Commander-in-Chief, how was Lawrence to get his argument across? The President still had the last say, and Lawrence, being the loyal officer that he was, could but do his duty.

The rain had yet to slacken and he sighed heavily. Knowing that he had already delayed the inevitable long enough, he reluctantly turned back to his desk. He eyed the red telephone, which lay beside a cluttered mess of documents and reports, and prepared to make two calls. Both of these conversations would be transmitted from the Navy's satellite relay station located on the hills above Oahu's north shore. Yet how very different were their destinations! For one would be projected into the silent depths of the North Pacific, while the other would travel far to the northwest, to the Soviet naval base at Petropavlovsk.

Admiral Leonid Silka had just awakened, and was in the midst of his early morning toilette, when the top-priority call arrived from Pearl Harbor, Hawaii. Hastily wiping a good portion of shaving cream from his face, he crossed into his nearby office to take the scrambled call in private. By the time he completed this conversation, seven minutes later, he was wide awake.

The seventy-two-year-old senior officer digested the amazing contents of this conversation while sipping on a cup of piping hot tea, which an alert orderly had set before him. Still wondering if this wasn't all some sort of terribly realistic nightmare, he pondered the words of his American counterpart, Admiral Walter Lawrence.

Leonid had previously read the man's dossier, and had even seen recent photographs of this distinguished naval officer, yet this was the first time that they had spoken with each other. Impressed with Lawrence's mastery of the Russian language, Leonid listened as the American admiral explained the nature of the supposed crisis that currently faced them. Well aware that the leaders of their two countries would be meeting soon to initiate the so-called summit of peace, he still couldn't believe that the aftereffects of the yet-to-be-signed treaty were already being applied. With a minimum of interruptions, he listened as Walter Lawrence, the current commander of U.S. submarines in the Pacific, actually asked for Soviet cooperation in tracking down the outlaw Chinese vessel.

At first, Leonid was virtually speechless. After all, it wasn't often that an American admiral called him asking for assistance. In fact, it was unprecedented! Yet as the nature of the crisis sank in, he formulated a cautious response, well within the scope of current Soviet Naval policy. He even offered the services of one of the Motherland's most advanced attack platforms, which just happened to be training in the same portion of the Pacific that the Chinese sub was supposedly headed.

Promising to get back to Walter Lawrence as soon as

the details were worked out, Leonid broke the connection. Of course, his first priority would be to notify the Kremlin of this strange request. Only after getting clearance from above would he proceed as promised.

He couldn't help but laugh to himself at the irony of it all. For it wasn't that long ago that he had met with the premier's personal representative, Stanislaus Angara, to discuss this upcoming summit. At that time, while nestled cozily inside Leonid's dacha, the handsome, young bureaucrat had revealed the Soviet Union's true intentions. Their crafty premier was prepared to obtain a major propaganda victory, for the price of a mere signature.

Surprised that Angara had been allowed to read Leonid's initial opinion of this disarmament treaty, their discussion next turned to tactics. The Kremlin was sincerely interested in what he had to say, and Leonid reiterated his belief that the Soviet Union faced a grave danger from a U.S. sneak attack in the days just before the treaty was signed. Not long after Angara returned to Moscow, Leonid was even given the premier's blessing to send their fleet of attack subs into the Pacific to monitor the American Tridents. As it turned out, the very Soviet vessel that was responsible for patrolling the sector that Admiral Lawrence had mentioned, would have been well on its way back to port if the premier hadn't permitted Leonid's plan to be implemented.

But who would have ever dreamed that the adversary Captain Valerian and the crew of the *Baikal* would be sent to hunt down wouldn't be a Trident at all, but a Chinese vessel? And to think that they would be doing so wish the full assistance of a U.S. Navy

293

attack sub was even more astounding!

The American mind continually baffled him. Alternating between ingenious deception and utter naiveté, there was no telling if the imperialists were really serious or not. That was why Leonid had to keep his mind open to a Yankee trick.

Though he would certainly double-check, his intelligence people hadn't heard a word that the Chinese were considering such a desperate sneak attack. Not only was it highly improbable, considering the present liberal-minded Chinese premier, but Leonid seriously doubted that they even had the MIRV'd capability Admiral Lawrence had spoken of. If the Chinese had really already tested such an accurate weapon, why hadn't the Soviet surveillance satellites picked it up? Could this all be some sort of American hoax, created to lead the Soviet Union into a trap? For what if the mysterious missile-carrying submarine was of American origin and not Chinese? Then this same platform could release its load of warheads, and take out cities all over the Soviet Far East, with the devious Yankees all the time blaming this attack on the Chinese. Only after the missiles that had been targeted for Russian soil were released, would the Americans sink this so-called outlaw sub, just before it was scheduled to launch those warheads supposedly aimed at the U.S. And they would thus hit the Motherland a crippling blow, without anyone being the wiser!

Though he had no concrete proof that this was what the Americans were up to, Leonid activated the telephone line to Moscow with just such a possibility in mind. His call traveled by satellite, crossing the vast breadth of the Motherland in a matter of seconds.

After briefly explaining the situation to the Defense Minister, who was at his desk even though it was past midnight in the capital, Leonid was transferred directly to the office of the General Secretary. A full minute later, he was greeted animatedly by Premier Skuratov's trusted Chief of Staff, Stanislaus Angara.

"Good morning, Admiral Silka! Let me guess, you're calling as a result of a conversation that you just completed with the commander of the American submarine force in the Pacific. I do hope that our old friend Admiral Lawrence is well."

Leonid should have anticipated that the Kremlin would be aware of the situation before he was, yet he was nonetheless surprised. "Then you know about the supposed crisis he related to me?" Leonid asked.

"Most definitely," retorted the young aide. "The President called Premier Skuratov over forty-five minutes ago. It was only after we approved his suggestion, that Walter Lawrence was given the okay to make the phone call to you. Now tell me, Admiral, what do you honestly think of this unusual situation that we find ourselves in?"

"I don't like it one bit," shot back Leonid. "It has all the makings of a Yankee trap."

"Come now, Admiral. What way is this to react to our new American friends?"

"You might see them as friends, Comrade Angara, but I still view them as our only true enemy."

"We were expecting as much," returned Angara. "Yet please bear with us, Admiral, for there is more here than meets the eye. After a bit of checking with the KGB, it indeed appears possible that the threat they have warned us about could be a very real one.

Does the name Liu Shao-chi ring a bell?"

Leonid deliberated a moment before responding. "Do you mean First Admiral Liu of the People's Liberation Navy?"

"He's the one," returned the alert bureaucrat. "And if our KGB lead proves to be correct, this same naval officer appears to be the one responsible for sending the submarine they call *Red Dragon* into the North Pacific. Though you're certainly entitled to your doubts, we believe that the Americans are playing their cards above the table on this one. It is Premier Skuratov's express with that you cooperate with them fully. What vessels do we have available in the area to begin this chase with, Admiral?"

Upset that the premier was so readily falling for the Yankee line, Leonid responded somberly, "We have only one submarine in the vicinity, Comrade. It is one of our newest *Akula*-class vessels, the *Baikal*."

"An Akula you say? Excellent! In the spirit of *glasnost*, we will work with the Americans to hunt down and destroy this common threat."

"But what if it's a Yankee trick?" countered Leonid passionately.

The chief of staff replied firmly. "Trust us, Admiral. Premier Skuratov has agreed to cooperate fully with the Americans in this matter, and that's the way that it shall be! Now, can we count on you to inform the captain of the *Baikal* of his new orders?"

Leonid's voice was heavy with disappointment as he answered, "Of course you can, Comrade Angara. You can notify the premier that I will contact the *Baikal* at once."

"That's more like it," said Angara. "After notifying

296

our submarine, you are to telephone this office before initiating the call to Admiral Lawrence. Let me remind you that soon the whole world will know that the Soviet Union and the United States of America have worked together to stamp out a common foe, for the first time since World War II. This will be a momentous day, and the propaganda benefits alone will be enormous. So, wish the crew of the *Baikal* good hunting from all of us, Admiral, and may the fates be with them."

With this, the line went unceremoniously dead, and Leonid fought the urge to scream out in anger. How dare that young pup treat a veteran officer in such a highhanded manner! Why, Angara wouldn't even take the time to listen to Leonid's well-founded suspicions. And now he had no choice but to do the Kremlin's bidding.

From what Leonid knew of Anton Valerian, the *Baikal*'s captain, he was sure that the directive ordering him to work with the Americans would be met with disbelief, suspicion, and fear. Valerian, who had been trained all his life to regard the Yankees as the only enemy, was now being asked to alter his deepest beliefs to satisfy the whim of a bunch of idiotic politicians. Yet, having sworn his allegiance to the Motherland, he would ultimately obey his orders, no matter how confusing they might seem.

To insure that this was the case, Leonid would direct his communiqué to both the captain and his *zampolit*. Through this tactic, the political officer would be close by to offer Valerian his valued opinion should it be needed. Already in the process of mentally preparing this message, Leonid Silka reached out to notify the communications supervisor that he would soon have a VLF transmission to project into the black depths of the North Pacific.

Pavl Petrovka snapped into waking consciousness feeling dazed and confused. A horrible ache pounded in his head, and for a moment, he didn't know where he was. Yet as his eyes adjusted to the sudden brightness, he identified the cot he was lying on as belonging to the *Baikal*'s supply officer. Lieutenant Rostov himself could be seen sitting at his cramped desk, with his back toward Pavl, busily sorting through a pile of paperwork.

Try as he could, Pavl couldn't remember what he was doing here. His own cot was in the crew's quarters on the deck below. Though this space was utilized as a sickbay when needed, he certainly didn't feel ill except for his persistent headache and clouded thoughts.

It was only when he attempted to sit up that he realized both of his wrists were chained to the steel frame of the cot. His confusion deepened and, clearing his dry throat, he lifted his head to address the supply officer.

"Excuse me, Lieutenant Rostov. What in the world am I doing here?"

The supply officer seemed startled to hear his voice, and turned around quickly. "Why, Comrade Petrovka, welcome back to the world of the living! How are you feeling?"

Ignoring the question, Pavl continued, "Lieutenant, what are these chains doing on my wrists? Is this some sort of sick joke?"

"Not at all," responded Rostov as he stood and made his way over to Pavl's side. "Actually, they are there for your own protection. Don't you remember anything about what took place in the torpedo room earlier, Comrade?"

A look of true concern crossed Pavl's face as he shook his head that he didn't. With this, Lieutenant Rostov guardedly added, "You were involved in a terrible accident several hours ago, in the torpedo room. Both our *michman* and Seaman Vitally Bolgrad were killed during that same incident. You were fortunate to survive, and have been in a deep coma since. So that you wouldn't accidentally fall out of your bunk, we utilized the chains as a primitive yet effective containment system. I hope that they're not too horribly uncomfortable."

Still not having the slightest idea of what had happened in the torpedo room, Pavl was genuinely upset to learn of Vitaly Bolgrad's death. "Did you say that Vitaly Bolgrad is no longer alive? Why, that's terrible news! We were the best of friends, and practically grew up together. We even enlisted in the navy at the same time, and were like brothers."

As Pavl's somber face clouded over with emotion, the supply officer, who was also the *Baikal*'s medic, realized the true extent of the young seaman's mental illness. Schizophrenia was a dangerous psychotic disorder characterized by the disintegration of the patient's personality. It demanded serious respect, and Rostov responded most carefully.

"All of us mourn their passing, yet life goes on. Now, you just lie back and relax while I go out to the ship's safe and get you your medicine. You suffered a nasty concussion that resulted in a severe memory loss, and I happen to have just the pill to make you feel better."

This so-called medicine was actually a powerful tranquilizer, which the captain had ordered the medic to administer as soon as Petrovka awoke. It would ease his anxieties, and hopefully keep him under control for the rest of the patrol.

While Rostov left the cabin to get this drug, Pavl lay back and tried to clear his mind. The news of Vitaly's passing greatly upset him, and he searched his clouded thoughts in vain effort to remember any details of this mysterious accident. Still drawing a complete mental blank, he redirected his ponderings to the fond memories that he had of his old friend.

Sure, he and Vitaly had their differences, but this was only natural. Growing up only a few doors away from each other, they were inseparable. They played and ate together and even shared the same career goals. Actually, the only time that they seriously argued was when he caught Vitaly making love to his beloved Katrina.

Thinking about that fateful day caused Pavl's pulse to quicken. Though he still couldn't remember events of only a few hours ago, he was able to re-create, with startling clarity, the moment when he'd caught Vitaly and Katrina in their shameless embrace. Would he ever forget the animal grunting sounds that passed Vitaly's lips as he lay on top of Katrina and lustfully dipped his phallus deep inside her? And was he mistaken, or didn't Katrina respond with deep, urgent sighs of her own as she parted her shapely thighs for him? He had been cold to both of them since catching sight of their lovemaking in that clover-filled glen, and now he couldn't help but wonder if this had been a tragic mistake on his part.

Life was too short to hold foolish grudges. Vitaly was a passionate person, who made no bones about his sexual drives. Both of them had only just recently returned to Odessa from almost two months at sea, and it was only natural that Vitaly was aching for a woman. Sadly enough, he had to choose the girl whom Pavl was about to propose to.

And now Vitaly was gone. With nothing left but fond memories, Pavl realized how foolish he had been. Though it might be too late to make his peace with Vitaly, this wasn't the case with Katrina. In a way, she was all that he had left of the past, and to lose her in a fit of jealousy would be the greatest waste of all.

It was while he was recalling her exquisite face, dark soulful eyes, and full-bosomed body, that the idea came to him. He would call her, in far-off Odessa, and beg forgiveness. Then he would ask her to marry him. She wouldn't dare refuse his offer, and they would be happy for the rest of their lives.

Yet there was one major obstacle to this plan. How was he to contact her from his present location, somewhere beneath the waters of the Pacific? Wouldn't he have to wait until they returned to Petropavlovsk?

The patrol had already been extended, and there was no telling how much longer they would be away from land. Time was of the essence, for with Katrina still unspoken for, any number of suitors could be pursuing her while he lay here. This meant that he would have to act now, or risk losing her forever. Thus he had no choice but to make this call from right here, beneath the silent sea.

On their last patrol, he had looked on as such a call was placed from the *Baikal*'s radio room. They were cruising beneath these same waters at the time, and as the captain ordered the *Baikal* to communications depth, satellite contact was made with Petropavlovsk. A free telephone line was then made available so that their anxious Senior Lieutenant could call his home in Kiev, to check the condition of his wife. How he had celebrated when he learned that only hours earlier, she had given birth to their first child, a healthy baby boy!

Since such a call was possible, he only had to work out the details of somehow getting into the radio room alone. Since he seriously doubted that the captain would grant his request, no matter how urgent it might be, Pavl knew that his first task was to free himself from confinement. He made his first tentative move to gain his freedom when the supply officer returned with a medicine bottle in hand.

"Here you go, Comrade Petrovka. These pills will relax you and have you feeling like your old self again in no time flat."

As Rostov removed two of the large white pills from the bottle and reached over to fill a glass with water, Pavl spoke out, "Thank you, Lieutenant Rostov. Your assistance is most appreciated. Yet would it be too much to ask if I could visit the head? My bowels feel like they're about to explode."

"Why, of course not," returned the supply officer. "Just take your medicine, and I'll remove those constraints and escort you to the bathroom."

Pavl had never been a lover of medicine, and though he pretended to swallow the two pills that Rostov

302

handed him, he slyly spit them out instead. Soon afterwards, the constraints were unlocked and Pavl was able to sit up fully erect. As he did so, a wave of dizziness swept over him. His forehead pounded, and for a second he thought that he would vomit. But the spell passed, and with his ulterior motive firmly in mind, he allowed the supply officer to lead him by the arm to the nearby head.

As they entered the cramped cubicle, they were greeted by a noxious, sour odor. This smell was coming from one of the open toilet stalls, where Vasili Sasovo, their chief radio operator, sat with a painful grimace.

"Oh, Comrade Rostov, I'm glad to see you. Is there anything you can give me to control these cramps? I've been running to and from this crapper for the last quarter of an hour." After passing a resonant blast of gas, he added, "It must be Cooky's stew that's causing me to shit my insides out."

Fighting to keep from laughing, the supply officer playfully held his nose. "For the safety of all aboard, I'll see what I can dig up, Comrade Sasovo. Heaven help us if anyone lights an open flame nearby. Why, this whole ship will blow up!"

As Pavl slowly approached the urinal, the supply officer addressed him before turning to exit. "Go ahead and do your thing, Comrade Petrovka. I'll return in a moment to escort you back to sick bay."

Nodding obediently, Pavl relieved himself while the radio operator continued moaning in pain beside him. As Pavl activated the flush mechanism, he listened to what Vasili Sasovo was saying between grunts.

"So you're not feeling well either, Comrade Petrovka? I sure hope you didn't eat any of that slop

303

Cooky calls Estonian stew. Why, the man could have poisoned the entire crew! Oh, does it hurt! I only wish that the *Baikal*'s complement was large enough for me to have an assistant. For the very minute I return to my post, the cramps send me running back here, as quick as I can travel. What if a war alert arrives at this time? Why, I shudder to even think of such a thing!"

Once more, Sasovo released a resonant blast of gas, and Pavl wasted no time heading straight for the exit. Only after making certain that the supply officer was nowhere to be seen, did he turn down the passageway and duck into the vacant radio room.

The narrow compartment was packed with sophisticated gear. Thankful for his extensive training in Leningrad, he easily picked out the transmitter. Pavl seated himself in front of this console and fingered the plastic frequency dial. A diagram taped to the bulkhead showed that it was set up to communicate with their home port. But before switching the transmitter on, he searched for the button that would launch a specially designed buoy stored behind the vessel's exterior sail. This device was attached to the transmitter by way of a fiber-optic link, and was used like an antenna to send the intended message skyward while the boat was submerged.

Pavl had just spotted this trigger switch and was reaching out to depress it, when the hatch swung open and in walked Vasili Sasovo. A look of pure puzzlement came over the radio operator's face as he confronted the intruder.

"Pavl Petrovka, what in Lenin's name do you think you're doing here?"

Completely ignoring Vasili's presence, Pavl hit the

switch releasing the buoy. Not believing what he was seeing, the astounded radio operator quickly approached the console.

"Damn you, Petrovka! Do you know what you have just done? Why the captain is going to have your hide, and mine as well! What's gotten into you, Comrade? Have you gone crazy or something?"

Not realizing that the junior seaman was in fact out of his mind, Vasili could hardly believe it when Pavl reached out to switch on the transmitter. But this time he moved to stop him.

"Oh no you don't, Petrovka! Your foolishness has caused me enough trouble already. Now get out of here, and pray that I can reel in that buoy before anyone in the control room notices that it's been released."

Seemingly unaware of the senior technician's warning tone, Pavl merely brushed Vasili's hand away to again reach for the transmitter's activation switch. It was the straw that broke the camel's back.

"That does it, Petrovka!" Sasovo screamed. "I've tried to be patient, but your idiotic game has gone too far. I don't know what you've been drinking, or what pills you've been taking for that matter, but you're seriously endangering all of us by acting in this irresponsible manner. So stop this insolent behavior at once!"

When Pavl once more attempted to reach out to activate the transmitter, the radio operator stopped talking and went into action, delivering a powerful karate chop to the seaman's wrist. This painful blow immediately diverted Pavl's attention. His heartbeat quickened, and he only then realized what his attacker

305

was attempting to do.

The radio operator must have had his eye on Katrina himself! No wonder he didn't want Pavl to contact her. He had almost lost his beloved to another once before, and he swore that he'd never let it happen again. Thus he had only one option, and that was defend her honor with his very life if necessary.

Pavl's breaths were coming in quick, short gasps as he sprang forward to take the offensive. There was a loud grunting sound as his shoulder made solid contact with the radio operator's lower torso. Striking out blindly with fists flailing, Pavl's punches hit solid bone, and for one glorious moment his adversary actually took a step back and shouted out in pain. But it was only a brief respite, for Vasili Sasovo swiftly recovered and countered his attacker's continued advances with a series of expertly placed karate blows. The last of these forceful punches caught Pavl full in the throat, crushing his windpipe. He was already choking to death as the force of this last blow sent him crashing into that portion of the radio console where the receiver was situated. A minute later, Pavl Petrovka was stone dead.

Vasili had little time to mourn his shipmate's passing, for Pavl's limbs had barely stopped twitching, when the captain came storming into the room. Close on Anton Valerian's heels were the panting *zampolit* and the red-faced supply officer.

"I tell you, I don't know how he ever managed to escape," whined the supply officer. "All I did was turn my back on him for a couple of seconds, and off he went."

The captain had more important things on his mind

306

as he looked at the corpse sprawled on the cracked console. "Is our radio still functioning?" he asked.

Vasili's hands and voice were trembling. "I — I don't know, sir," he stammered.

"Well damn it, don't you think that you'd better find out!" screamed Valerian. Then, turning to the supply officer, he ordered, "Lieutenant Rostov, get this corpse out of here at once, and secure it in the freezer with the others."

"Yes, sir!" retorted the supply officer, who proceeded to get on with this rather unpleasant task.

Grasping the corpse by the shoulders, the lieutenant managed to lift him off the console. It was in this same manner that he dragged Pavl out of the narrow cabin. Meanwhile, the radio operator anxiously seated himself behind the console. Several of the glass dials were cracked, and the steel cabinet itself was stained with blood. Expertly activating a series of toggle switches, Vasili studied the instruments.

"It doesn't look good, Captain," he reported somberly. "The VLF receiver doesn't seem to be getting any power."

"That's just wonderful," spat Anton Valerian sarcastically. "Can it be repaired?"

Vasili reactivated the toggle switches. "I believe so, sir," he replied as he searched in his desk drawer for a screwdriver. "Hopefully it's only a broken connector. I'll pull off the panel cover and have a look."

"Please do that, Comrade," returned the Captain impatiently. "For as it now stands, the *Baikal* is completely deaf to any transmission on the Very Low Frequency band."

Standing at Valerian's side, the *zampolit* silently

307

absorbed this grim observation and shuddered to think what it meant. The VLF band was the primary frequency which Command used to communicate with them. Without this band, the *Baikal* had no way of knowing about any change of orders. This capability was vital now that they were under a level two Red Flag alert. At such a time, any delay in receiving a change of orders from Petropavlovsk could have disastrous implications for them all.

Standing to the right of the political officer, Anton Valerian couldn't help but notice the scowl on Boris Glazov's face. Lowering his voice, the captain discreetly addressed him.

"Why the serious look, Comrade *Zampolit*? Believe me, things could have been much worse."

"I don't know about that, Captain," replied Glazov, his gaze locked on the radio operator's repair efforts. "How are we to continue without the ability to monitor the VLF band? Command could be trying to reach us even as we speak."

The captain's tone seemed a bit brighter as he replied, "We'll soon know if our problem is repairable. Until then, think positive, Comrade."

This last suggestion did little to alter the *zampolit*'s grim outlook. "That's easy enough to say, Captain, yet what if the receiver can't be repaired? We will then be forced to return to Petropavlovsk, our mission still incomplete. And to think that this is all happening during a Red Flag alert!"

"Easy now, Comrade Glazov. Your pessimistic outlook upsets me. And besides, why would a malfunctioning radio receiver send us packing for port with our tail between our legs? Have you forgotten that there are other ways for Command to communicate with us?"

"I doubt you would risk sending the *Baikal* to the surface just to listen for incoming messages," said the *zampolit*.

Valerian shook his head. "Who said anything about having to go to such extremes? Please don't forget that if the world should pick this inopportune moment to go to war, we still have the full use of our ELF communications system. Though granted, any message sent on the Extra Low Frequency band must be brief and to the point, it will be sufficient to inform us when a state of hostilities indeed exists. Then we can go on with our primary mission, which is to sink American submarines. No Comrade, not even an inoperable VLF radio is going to keep me from this most anticipated task."

A slight ray of hope was glimmering in the *zampolit*'s eyes, when the radio operator suddenly broke in. "I believe I see the problem, Captain. Several of the transformer connectors have broken. Though it could take some time, it appears that I can repair them."

"Wonderful!" exclaimed Valerian. "Whatever assistance you need, just name it, Comrade Sasovo. I knew that you wouldn't let us down."

No sooner were these words out of his mouth, than a piercing electronic buzzer sounded. Valerian's pulse instinctively quickened at this call to battle stations, and he swiftly reached for the intercom.

"Control, this is the Captain. What in the world is going on up there? I didn't order any drill."

The steady voice of the *Baikal*'s senior lieutenant answered. "This is not a drill, Captain. Sonar reports an unidentified submerged contact, bearing one-seven-zero, at maximum range. The computer shows a sixty-three per cent probability that this signature belongs to an American *Sturgeon*-class attack sub."

"Then our Yankee friends have returned for more punishment!" reflected the joyous captain. "When will they get it through their thick skulls that their antiquated vessel is no match for the *Baikal?*"

"Shall I order an immediate intercept, Captain?"

"Absolutely not!" retorted Valerian. "I want this ship buttoned down in a continued state of ultra quiet. We will remain hovering under battery power only. This way our adversary will never know that we're out here. Only after they have passed us by will we secretly follow in their baffles. And I guarantee you, Comrade, that they'll lead us right to one of their Tridents."

"Very good, Captain. I'll inform you when they've safely passed us."

With this, the intercom went dead, and Valerian turned to address the *zampolit*. "Didn't I tell you that everything would work out, Comrade Glazov? Who needs a radio, when our prey has wandered right up to our front door?"

Noting a maniacal gleam in the captain's eyes, the political officer nodded soberly, then turned his attention back to the radio console, where Vasili Sasovo was busy removing various components. Silently praying that his efforts would produce quick results, the *zampolit* pivoted to follow Anton Valerian as he ducked out the hatchway and turned toward the boat's bow.

CHAPTER TWELVE

One of the things that Reggie Warner liked best about the *Copperhead*'s current complement, was the way the cooks prepared chili. The head chef was a native Texan, and his recipe was right out of a cowboy's chuck wagon. At the crew's request, he prepared this dish at least twice a week, in generous enough quantities so there was always enough for seconds.

This would be the second afternoon in a row that chili was being offered for lunch, yet Reggie was grateful to get one of the last bowls. With a thick piece of cornbread and his usual strawberry milkshake, he went to work wolfing down a meal that he felt was fit for a king.

"I don't know how Tex does it," he said between spoonfuls. "This stuff ought to be patented. You know, somebody could make a fortune putting it in a can. I can see the label now — *Copperhead* Chili, the brand that keeps America strong."

Well into his own serving, Marty Stanfield

grinned. "It probably couldn't miss in the Southwest, but would it sell in Philly?"

Taking a second to savor a spoonful of the tangy, tomato-based sauce, Reggie replied, "Anything will sell in Philadelphia if it's promoted properly. That, my friend, is the key to a successful American business."

"Don't tell me that you're seriously thinking about starting your own company?" quizzed Stanfield as he broke off a piece of cornbread and squirted some honey on it.

"Why not?" answered Reggie, between sips of his milkshake. "After all, I've got to start thinking about the future. You know, it hit me soon after I received that sonar lashing. It was only by the grace of God that I didn't have my eardrums perforated. That would have been the end of my naval career. As it turned out, I was lucky, and I've only got this damn buzzing that Pills says will go away soon. But what if Lady Luck wasn't with me? I mean, what else am I good at except for listening to those friggin' hydrophones? Without my full hearing, the navy would drop me as quick as a hot bowl of Tex's chili."

Stanfield shook his head thoughtfully. "I don't know about that, Reg. If I remember right, you're pretty handy in the kitchen. Maybe Tex could share some of those recipes with you, and you could become a cook. You won't make admiral, but as long as you don't poison anyone, you'll most likely

312

get in your twenty years."

"Real cute, Stanfield. I don't know why I bother trying to have an intelligent conversation with you."

Realizing that his shipmate was in no mood for levity, Marty Stanfield countered, "Easy does it, bro. I was only having some fun. Don't forget that I was down there in the sound shack with you, and got the tail end of that lashing myself. It made me realize that it's certainly no game that we're playing down here. Why, instead of that burst of sound, we could have just as easily been hit with a Russkie torpedo. And who would ever be the wiser? The *Copperhead* would take the deep six, and back home they'd blame it on an improper weld, letting Ivan off the hook to do it to the next crew of suckers. They certainly couldn't get away with such a thing if they took out one of our surface ships."

Reggie nodded in agreement. "You're absolutely right, Marty. We live constantly on the edge down here. Though there's currently no declared war between us and the Soviets, and even with that peace summit and all, a different set of rules exists beneath the ocean's surface. We don't make headlines, or the evening news, but we do our bit for God and country just the same. And you know, that's kind of what makes this job so exciting. Because just about anything could be waiting for us beyond the next seamount. And if it's indeed a Russkie torpedo with our name on it, I just hope to God that the crew of this old tub is capable of getting us out of harm's way."

"The old man will see to it," said Stanfield, after spooning in the last bite of chili. "In my book, Captain Fuller is the best."

Reggie was quick to agree. "The skipper's certainly a tough one, all right. You know, I didn't tell you before, but I bumped into the captain and his wife on the morning that I popped the question to Kim. We were sitting there at Waimea Falls Park watching the hula show, and when I first saw the skipper in his civvies, I did a double take. In his shorts, he looked like any other tourist. When I introduced him and his wife to Kim, I got the distinct impression that they really cared about us. Do you know that Mrs. Fuller actually volunteered to help Kim with the wedding details? That was certainly beyond the call of duty, and I'll never forget her for that.

"Yet I can't help but wonder if Mrs. Fuller knows just what kind of man her husband really is. The skipper might look like an easygoing guy, but in a fight, I'd sure want him on my side."

"I'm with you, bro," returned Stanfield. "As I said before, our skipper is tops, and I'm proud to serve him." After finishing off his cornbread, he added thoughtfully, "So you're really going through with those wedding plans, huh Reg?"

Reggie's eyes were sparkling as he answered his shipmate. "I most certainly am, my man. I guess I knew from the first time that I saw Kim that she was everything that I could possibly want in a woman. Not only is she a stone fox, but she's bright and caring, too. If you only knew what she went through to get to America. Why, it made growing up in the ghetto look like kid stuff."

"Jesus, bro, you are hooked," observed Marty Stanfield. "Pardon my doubtful nature, Reg, but don't forget that I've seen you in action before. Do you remember that little Hawaiian chick you met on Waikiki a couple of months ago? Why, you were so hot to trot with that babe you even dragged me along to look at engagement rings. No offense, but I could have sworn that your latest flame would share her fate, along with all the dozens of others."

"I hear you, Marty. But Kim's different than all the rest of them. I guess you could say that I finally found my soulmate. She's what I need to make my life complete. Did I ever tell you that a psychic once told me that I was an Oriental in a past life? Who knows? Perhaps me and Kim knew each other then, and fate has miraculously thrown us together once again to fulfill our destinies."

"You're not going to start with that spiritual stuff again, are you, Reg? You know that kind of talk scares the wits out of me."

Marty Stanfield was saved by the sudden appearance of Chief Meinert. The burly petty officer crossed the mess and headed straight to their table. There was a no-nonsense expression etched on his face and Reggie sensed trouble. Smiling, he looked up to greet Meinert, in an attempt to defuse what appeared to be an unpleasant situation.

"Afternoon, Chief. Sorry we weren't able to save you a bowl of Tex's chili. Guess you'll just have to wait until Friday to satisfy your chili addiction."

The chief had other things on his mind. "No time to think about food now, Warner. We've got a damn hydraulics leak back in maneuvering that's turned out to be a bitch to plug. I was just on my way aft to pull some schematics, and I have a little message to convey to you. Seems that the captain and the XO want to have a word with you in the officers' wardroom. Good luck, Warner. I just left those two, and they were as solemn as a couple of funeral directors."

With this, the concerned chief shook his head and turned to leave via the aft hatchway. Only when Meinert's hefty frame had disappeared from sight did Reggie push back his chair and stand.

"Well, bro, I guess this is it. Fifty bucks says that I'm going to get my ass chewed out for letting that *Akula* sneak up on us. I guess I'd better be looking into the chili business after all."

"You never know with officers, Reg. Just keep your cool and stand your ground."

Accepting a supportive slap of his shipmate's up-turned palm, Reggie left the mess hall. He traveled forward, toward the boat's bow. As he moved down the cable-lined passageway, he barely acknowledged his passing shipmates. His thoughts were turned

316

inward, to the meeting that he had been abruptly called to.

Certain that he was being called to the wardroom to be castigated for allowing Ivan to get the drop on them, Reggie wondered how this would affect his service record. If he was written up by the *Copperhead*'s command staff now, he might as well flush down the toilet any hopes that he might have had of getting an officer's commission. It would mean a certain end to any promising naval career plans, and would thus leave his future much in doubt.

Such was the grim nature of his thoughts as he ascended the ladder leading into officers' country. Waiting for him at the wardroom table were the *Copperhead*'s two senior officers. Both were in the midst of a spirited discussion when Reggie entered. It was the XO who signaled the captain that they had company, and Samuel Fuller abruptly cut off their conversation.

"Petty Officer Warner reporting as ordered, sir."

Reggie could hardly believe it when the captain caught his gaze directly, and displaying a slight smile, greeted him with a voice full of concern. "Glad that you made it up here so quickly, Mr. Warner. Please grab a seat, and tell me, how are you feeling? Are those eardrums of yours still vibrating?"

The sonar technician felt awkward seating himself beside the captain, but he did as he was ordered.

Noting that the XO also had his attention riveted on him, Reggie cleared his throat nervously before responding.

"Actually, my hearing has substantially cleared up already, sir. Like Pills said, the discomfort was only temporary. Right now, all that I have is a little buzzing, and a slight bit of tenderness inside the ear itself."

"Thank the Lord that it wasn't more serious," returned the captain. "Why I've known men who have had their eardrums perforated by lashings half the strength that you took. That would have been a hell of a way to lose the best sonar man in the entire U.S. Navy."

"Why thank you, sir," responded Reggie, who was unprepared for this compliment.

Samuel Fuller nodded. "And I mean that in all seriousness, Mr. Warner. I can't tell you how much your expertise is appreciated. Just knowing that you're on duty substantially eases my apprehensions. And believe me, I have enough to worry about.

"Now, Lieutenant Commander Coria here mentions that you've expressed some interest in a commission. That's wonderful news, and I want you to know that you have my full support. The navy needs more men like you. Having worked your way up through the ranks, you will, as an officer, have a much greater understanding of those you're responsible for. After all, you know what it's like being on the other end. Have you given any thought to possibly going into teaching? You would make one fine sonar instructor."

"I've considered that, sir," answered Reggie shyly. "But for now, I like being out here, where all the action is."

The captain sat forward. "Speaking of action, something's recently come up that should keep us plenty busy these next couple of hours. Mr. Coria, why don't you brief Mr. Warner on the exact nature of our new assignment."

Reggie turned to face the XO, who was seated opposite the captain. Vincent Coria took a long sip of coffee before speaking.

"First off, I want to join the captain in support of your commission, Mr. Warner. We appreciate your efforts, and are ever thankful that Ivan wasn't able to take out one of our best. Since it appears that you're fit to return to duty, I think you'll be interested in the contents of a top-priority dispatch recently conveyed to the *Copperhead* by COMSUB-PAC. In this communiqué, we have been ordered to hunt down a boomer belonging to the People's Republic of China. This vessel was last monitored entering our patrol sector from the southwest. It is believed to be carrying a full load of ballistic missiles which are targeted at locations in both the United States and the Soviet Union. Command believes that a plan exists that will authorize the Chinese to release these weapons sometime within

319

the next forty-eight hours. Our duty is to insure that such a nightmarish thing doesn't come to pass."

As the XO paused briefly, Reggie quickly broke in. "Excuse me, sir, but I didn't realize that the Chinese had submarines capable of launching strategic missiles."

It was the captain who answered. "Although they've had this capability for some time now, the accuracy of their delivery systems has always been suspect. But it appears that their scientists have solved this problem, and the threat we face is a very real one."

"And Command really believes that they're serious about using them?" quizzed Reggie.

"I'm afraid so," answered Samuel Fuller. "That's why it's imperative that we have our best man down in sonar listening for their advance. Are you up to the challenge, Mr. Warner?"

Nodding affirmatively, Reggie voiced another concern. "You mentioned that this Chinese boomer has targets located in both the U.S. and Russia. I thought that the Chinese and Soviets were allies."

Again it was the captain who replied. "Though both countries are founded on Socialist theory, China had developed its own unique brand of Communism, as envisioned by Mao. If anything, the Chinese feel that the Russians have strayed from the true path of Socialism, and that China's model is the correct one."

"From what I hear, they've got serious border problems as well," added the XO. "The Soviets have just as many troops stationed along their shared border as they do in Eastern Europe. Besides, Ivan has always had the hots for Manchuria, and the Chinese know it."

"But why launch an attack against both the world's superpowers?" questioned Reggie. "Surely they can't hope to win such a war."

"I don't think that they do," retorted Fuller. "COMSUBPAC believes that this whole thing is coming down to get the U.S. and Soviet Union slugging it out between themselves. Then the Chinese merely have to wait for the two nations to destroy each other before emerging uncontended. I know it sounds sick, but there's no telling how either country will react once the first warheads start descending. That's why the *Copperhead* must act to nip this mad plan in the bud, before things get out of hand and millions die needlessly."

"You can count on me," offered Reggie wholeheartedly. "It's best if I get down to the sound shack as soon as possible. What search technique will we be utilizing?"

The XO gave him the details. "The last P-3 bearing showed the bogey just entering the western edge of the seamount range. We shouldn't be more than one hundred nautical miles from them presently, and we're continuing to close in at a prudent speed."

As Reggie prepared to stand he dared to ask one more question. "And what happens if we chance upon Ivan along the way?"

Samuel Fuller took a long look at his XO before replying. "That's a good one, Mr. Warner. Believe it or not, Command has dealt with that possibility by informing the Soviet Naval hierarchy of our shared situation. It's hoped that they will offer their cooperation in hunting the Chinese boat down and destroying it if necessary."

Reggie was genuinely astounded. "Let me get this straight. We're actually going to be working with the Soviets on this one? Oh, Lordy, and here I thought I'd heard almost everything. Pearl Harbor doesn't really think that this so-called cooperation will amount to anything, do they? How in the hell can you trust the Russians?"

Surprised by Reggie's emotional outburst, the captain responded guardedly. "I understand how you feel, Mr. Warner. I must admit that I don't like the idea of having to work with Ivan either. But we are in this one together, so to speak. Right now, Command has yet to confirm that the Soviets have even offered us any assistance, and for all I care, it can stay that way. So until we learn otherwise, you will remain alert for all unidentified contacts, treating each one as a possible threat.

"Now, I'm sure that you're anxious to get back to work. Please keep all that we discussed here to yourself. And, good hunting!"

Reggie's mind was spinning as he rose and exchanged handshakes with the two senior officers, after which he headed straight for the sonar compartment.

How very different was the nature of his thoughts from the last time he had climbed the ladder leading to the next deck. No longer was he preoccupied with his own selfish concerns, but with the world's very survival!

The possibility that he might be involved in a full-scale nuclear war was always at the back of his mind. Such was the nature of his daily duty. Yet somehow he had never really believed that such a horrifying event would ever take place. Surely the world's leaders were too intelligent to let such a thing happen. The nuclear bomb had been an effective deterrent for over four decades, and it was common knowledge that a conflict in which such devices were used would have no winner. The entire planet would be destroyed, and the few survivors would envy the dead.

In the past, Reggie had been solely concerned with countering the Soviet threat. Russia was the evil empire, whose leaders swore in public that they would bury the United States in a cloud of radioactive dust. Now, a new enemy had emerged, one who threatened to break the fragile peace with a fatal surprise strike.

China had always been an enigmatic country. Reggie had never taken the Chinese seriously, even though he knew very well that they were the earth's most populous nation. He liked their spicy food and exotic women, yet believed they were only second rate as a military power. In all his years of naval study, he had heard their fleet mentioned only as a mere coastal defense force. This included their submarines, which were mainly obsolete Russian copies, powered by diesel-electric drive and designed for limited, shallow water operations only. Just to hear that the Chinese had a sophisticated ballistic-missile vessel was astonishing news in itself. This put them in an elite club, composed of the world's most technologically advanced countries. China was thus a power to be respected, and now the rest of the world was about to pay the price for ignoring them all these years.

Reggie shuddered to think what would happen if a missile launch actually occurred. Even if it was only a limited strike, surely one of the first targets eliminated would be Pearl Harbor. Well aware that Kim lived only a few short blocks from ground-zero, he approached the attack center with a new sense of urgency guiding his steps.

Oblivious to the fact that the afternoon watch still had more than an hour to go, he ducked into the sonar room's hatchway. Barely giving his eyes time to adjust to the compartment's dim red lighting, he scooted past the three seated junior ratings, whose eyes remained glued to their blinking CRT screens. Reggie sighed in relief only after rounding

324

the cork-lined partition that separated the supervisor's console from the rest of the compartment. Seated here, unexpectedly, was the chubby blond-haired figure of Lieutenant David Costner, the *Copperhead*'s weapons officer. Not certain what the lieutenant was doing at this station, Reggie tapped him on the shoulder.

The officer had been completely absorbed with the variety of sounds conveyed by his headphones, and was momentarily startled by this unexpected interruption. His body jerked, and he turned quickly to see who was behind him. As he caught sight of Reggie, he broke into a grin and reached up to pull off his headphones.

"Hello, Mr. Warner. Don't tell me my watch is over already? I was just starting to get the hang of this stuff once again."

"May I ask what you're doing down here, sir?" Reggie asked directly.

"Why, of course. Chief Meinert was called away to help stem a hydraulics leak, and I volunteered to replace him. I was fully qualified on the BQQ-5 back at sub school. You know, it's amazing how quickly this stuff comes back to you, even when you haven't sat on a sonar watch for a while."

Conscious of the young officer's enthusiasm, Reggie interjected, "It certainly is an amazing field, sir. Now, if you don't mind, I'd be more than willing to take over for you."

Having been on his way to lunch when his serv-

325

ices were needed, Costner readily pushed his chair back. "That's most kind of you, Mr. Warner. This stuff is best left to the experts anyway. By the way, I understand that you took the brunt of that sonar lashing that the Russians sent our way earlier. Are you sure you're okay to get back to work?"

Unclipping the headphones from Costner's thick neck, Reggie replied, "Don't worry about me, Lieutenant. My ears have taken a worse beating at a rock and roll concert. Besides, I know just what to listen for. I'll find them, and you can finish them off with one of your fish."

"That's a deal," responded the weapons officer as he stood to let Reggie replace him at the console. He exited unceremoniously, and Reggie immediately got back to work.

This was his first official watch since suffering the sonic lashing, and Reggie's ears were a bit tender as he fitted on the padded headphones. This soreness, and a soft buzzing hum, were all that remained of his injuries, and he successfully compensated for these handicaps by concentrating all the harder on the important job at hand.

It felt good to get back to work once again, especially when he knew how desperately his services were needed. As he carefully turned up the amplifier gain and listened as the sounds of the sea filtered in through the sub's hydrophones, he found his thoughts returning to the unexpected compliments the two senior officers had thrown his way. It

326

felt good to receive praise from the two men whom he respected most in this world. Of course, he had worked hard to perfect his craft, yet just hearing that his efforts had been recognized and appreciated was most satisfying. Now that his future advancement in the navy was all but assured, he had much to be thankful for. An officer's commission would soon be his, and he would be in a much better position to provide for his new family. But at the moment, there was still one thing that could get in his way.

Somewhere in the black depths, approximately one hundred nautical miles from their current position, a vessel supposedly existed that could end all of his dreams with a single push of a launch button. Regardless of this adversary's identity, only one thing mattered, and that was to stop this launch before it took place. Everything else was immaterial.

With this single goal in mind, Reggie leaned forward and focused his total concentration on the sounds that were being channeled through his headphones. With his eyes tightly shut, he existed for one purpose only—to tag this vessel the moment that it came within range.

Completely unaware of the passing minutes, Reggie's consciousness was elevated to an almost transcendent state of awareness. Thus he really wasn't surprised when a barely audible pulsating hiss sounded in the distance. His eyes snapped open, and only then did he realize that two and a half hours had gone by since he had sat down to initiate this watch.

Ignoring his cramped, uncomfortable position, Reggie proceeded to analyze this unidentified mechanical signature. The sound was fed into the BQQ-5's computer, whose memory banks held the identities of over one hundred different classes of submarines. Less than a minute later, the results of this search showed up on his monitor screen. It simply read "Submerged contact, unknown."

After double-checking the bogey's course and bearing, he reached out for the plastic intercom handset that hung on the bulkhead beside him. He punched in three numbers, and waited anxiously before his call was answered after the third ring.

"This is the Captain."

Breathlessly, Reggie responded, "Sir, this is Petty Officer Warner speaking. Bingo!"

Powered solely by the near-silent propulsion of its batteries, the *Akula*-class attack submarine *Baikal* surged forward, following almost soundlessly in the *Copperhead*'s baffles. From its own sonar compartment, located amidships immediately beside the attack center, an alert junior officer also picked up the faraway, pulsating hiss of yet another submerged contact. This mysterious ship was still over one hundred and fifty kilometers distant, and strangely enough, its signature was not included in the sonar computer's sound library.

The Ukrainian technician supposed that this vessel was still too far away to get a proper signature reading. Otherwise this would indicate that they faced a new class of submarine which not even the intelligence programmers at Petropavlovsk were aware of. Anxious to inform the *Baikal*'s command staff of this sighting, he used the sound-powered telephone to contact the bridge.

Senior Lieutenant Viktor Karmanov was the current officer of the deck, and it was to him that the sonar technician's call was relayed. Proceeding quickly to the navigation station, the senior lieutenant plotted this new contact. He couldn't help but grin as he noted that the American submarine they had been following for the last three hours was apparently headed to an exact intercept with this still-unidentified contact. It was thus with great satisfaction that he notified the captain.

Two and a half minutes later, Anton Valerian stormed into the control room. Close on his heels was the *zampolit*. Both these somber-faced figures went straight to the navigator's station, where they joined the senior lieutenant.

"So, the chick is leading us straight to the mother hen," Anton Valerian exclaimed triumphantly. "I just knew that the attack sub would rendezvous with the Trident sooner or later."

"But, sir, we still don't know the identity of this

newest contact," interjected the senior lieutenant.

"Nonsense," countered the captain. "It's only too obvious what is occurring out there. We already know for certain that this so-called mystery vessel is not one of ours. Thus it has to be a Yankee platform. Don't forget, we've witnessed such encounters before. The attack sub will proceed to carefully scan the waters surrounding the Trident to insure its safety. Little do they realize that the big bad wolf is following them right through the chicken coop's front door!"

The captain chuckled at this analogy, his previously solemn mood significantly lightened now. The *zampolit* noted this change in attitude, yet found himself still gripped by an unnatural tension.

"If only we had the radio receiver on-line once again," observed the tense political officer. "Who knows if the level two Red Flag alert even still exists?"

"Must you always be the consummate worrier, Comrade Glazov? Trust in your captain's judgment, and know that this is not a time for anxiety, but celebration! Don't you realize that this is every attack submariner's dream? We've got two of the enemy's most sophisticated platforms sitting practically right in our sights. And incredibly, they don't even know that we're here! The *Baikal* still has the ability to receive brief ELF transmissions. Thus we will know the minute our alert status is altered. Meanwhile, we will proceed as last ordered.

330

"I think that it's best to immediately inform the crew of the exact nature of the two contacts we currently face. Their continued cooperation will be needed greatly in the hours to come. Our ultra quiet integrity must not be compromised as we continue following in the *Sturgeon*-class vessel's baffles, while simultaneously closing in on the patrolling Trident. Then it will be up to our sonar operators to closely monitor the missile-carrying sub's status. Let it show the least hint of aggression, and we will blow it to the bottom, with the attack sub sharing its fate seconds later. The *Baikal* has been given this opportunity to act in the defense of the Motherland, and as fate so wills it, we will not let our countrymen down!"

The captain's stirring words did little to loosen the knot of worry that continued to tighten in the *zampolit*'s gut. Though Valerian's reasoning seemed most logical, something about their current situation still made him uneasy. Hoping that this feeling was merely the aftereffects of the watered-down stew he had eaten for lunch, Boris Glazov looked on as the captain picked up the intercom to share his insights with the rest of the crew.

Completely unaware of the two vessels that approached from the south, the *Red Dragon* plunged ahead at flank speed. The pride of the Chinese Navy had enjoyed an uneventful passage across the

331

Pacific. With men and equipment functioning perfectly, the ship prepared to end that part of its voyage dedicated to pure transit, and begin a vastly different task. For soon the patrol portion of their mission would begin. Then the *Red Dragon* would drastically cut its forward speed and, utilizing the ocean's silent depths to insure their anonymity, they would wait for orders instructing them to ascend and launch their load of *Xia*-class ballistic missiles.

Captain Chen Shou was proud of his boat's performance so far. He was particularly impressed with the efficiency of his hand-picked crew. Chosen from the ranks of the PLN's finest, the one hundred and ten enlisted men and officers had exceeded his highest expectations. Since their high-tech equipment was only as good as the men who maintained and operated it, the personnel factor was crucial. Satisfied that he had made the right choices, Chen continued with his afternoon rounds.

He had started off in the *Red Dragon*'s forward torpedo room, and was progressively working his way through the ship. Currently he was heading down a passageway that led to the sub's largest single compartment. This area of the *Red Dragon* lay behind a locked hatchway, and he had to use a key to gain access. This put him in the sub's missile magazine.

The cavernous room was dominated by sixteen launch tubes, laid out in two rows of eight silos apiece. A single metal catwalk separated these two rows of tubular steel canisters. It extended the length of the compartment, leading eventually to another locked hatchway that guarded the ship's nuclear reactor.

Chen Shou stood at the head of the catwalk and peered down its well-lit length. This part of the boat always had a special significance for the veteran naval officer. Spotlessly clean, it had a temple-like quality, inspiring reverence. The deadly load of warheads stored here made him as powerful as a god!

This was the *Red Dragon*'s first operational cruise, and the reality of their new capabilities was still just sinking in. For the first time ever, each of the sixteen missiles was capped with six MIRV'd warheads, giving them a total of ninety-six in all. Not only could each of these 50-kiloton warheads be guided to their targets independently, they could be delivered with an amazing degree of accuracy over 5,000 kilometers away.

Chen was thus well aware that this voyage signaled a momentous new chapter in the history of the People's Republic. They were a full-fledged superpower now, and very soon would gain the respect that had been so long in coming. Admiral Liu Shao-chi had made it a point to emphasize this fact when he had arrived at Huangyan to wish them a safe voyage. This unannounced visit had caught Chen by surprise, but he couldn't help but be pleased with the senior officer's presence.

Their brief conversation had taken place within the private confines of the *Red Dragon*'s attack center. Having served on Liu's staff for a full two years, over a decade ago, Chen knew the grizzled old-timer well. He wasn't the type who would make the arduous trip to Huangyan just to make idle talk. Each move that Liu made was always carefully thought out and had a definite purpose.

The *Red Dragon* wouldn't even exist if it wasn't for Liu. And it was only natural that he would want to be present when it departed on its maiden operational voyage. Yet Chen couldn't ignore the lines of worry that lined the elder's heavily jowled face. He seemed particularly preoccupied with the upcoming summit between the Soviet Union and the United States. Upset that China hadn't been invited to participate in this all-important conference—whose ostensible purpose was to ban all nuclear weapons from the planet—Liu had expressed his innermost fears. They centered around his belief that the two superpowers would use this occasion to initiate hostilities against the People's Republic, in an attempt to rid themselves of the China problem once and for all. Thus, as the time for the summit approached, the *Red Dragon*'s mission took on an even greater degree of importance.

Chen listened respectfully to the admiral's suspicions, and used this opportunity to reaffirm his loyalty. He was but an extension of the PLN, and if the homeland was threatened, Chen would make certain that the missiles went skyward on their flights of revenge just as ordered. Liu seemed most satisfied with this response, and hugged Chen warmly before departing. As Liu Shao-chi stood on the dock waving good-bye, he looked old and fragile, but Chen knew that the admiral's iron will would fade only with his death.

Wishing that he could break radio silence for just a few minutes to let the admiral know how well everything was functioning, Chen began to slowly make his way down the compartment's central catwalk. All was deathly silent, except for the sounds of his echoing footsteps and the distant, muffled hum of machinery. A faint scent of warm oil was perceptible in the air as he carefully examined each of the passing silos.

He visualized the shiny white *Xia*-class missiles stored inside. They were the product of thousands of hours of tireless research and development. Designed by China's most brilliant scientists, they were certain proof that the People's Republic could hold its own in a world of super computers and high technology. He could hardly believe that forty years ago they had trouble producing such simple items as rifle ammunition and light bulbs. Why, just feeding themselves was a full-time effort. How very quickly they had proceeded to develop since then!

It was in 1949 that Chen enlisted in the new Republic's fledgling navy. Barely seventeen at the time, he couldn't wait to do something with his life.

The sea had always fascinated him. Even though he had grown up far inland, in distant Kunming, as soon as he was of age he headed straight for the naval base at Shanghai. The Nationalists had only just been driven from the mainland at that time, and everything was in a state of chaos. They inherited a pitiful navy composed of only a few rusty surface combat vessels, which were barely capable of patrolling the coasts. Yet these worn relics of World War II were to provide the base on which the new PLN would grow.

It was largely with the assistance of the Russians that the navy was able to develop so rapidly. Quick to provide the necessary technology, the Soviets helped organize a suitable master plan. During the 1950's, Chen found himself enrolled in the Naval Academy, and it was in a class taught by a Russian adviser that he became particularly interested in submarines. Soon after he earned his commission, he was sent to sea aboard a crude diesel-electric sub which the Soviets had kindly given to them. Though this vessel was badly outdated, it afforded them invaluable experience. Chen had an opportunity to apply this expertise firsthand when, in 1962, he was transferred to Albania. Here, on the distant shores of the Mediterranean, he helped the Albanians refit four W-class submarines which the Soviets had unwillingly left behind. It was immediately after this successful mission that Chen first came under the scrutiny of the esteemed Admiral Liu

Shao-chi. Already rising quickly through the ranks, Chen was chosen to help organize a program whose goal was the production of a nuclear submarine.

On January 14, 1981, the first Chinese nuclear-powered attack sub was launched, with Captain Chen Shou at the helm. After almost two decades of exhausting, often frustrating effort, this voyage signaled the birth of the modern Chinese Navy. Chen spent a year on this vessel, working out the bugs, before being transferred to yet another new R and D project. It was as a result of this next effort that his present command came into being.

He had seen much in his forty years of service, but the *Red Dragon* was the most sophisticated platform yet. It was everything that a submariner could ask for. Silent and quick, it could evade the enemy while proceeding to deliver a punishing load of nuclear death to targets thousands of kilometers distant. It was the culmination of his long career, and it made all the thousands of hours of selfless toil worthwhile.

Because of his loyal service, Chen had no time to devote to a wife and family. He was married to the PLN, and his children were the submarines he helped to design and send to sea.

As he passed the last of the launch tubes, the captain contemplated the awesome amount of firepower stored around him. Surely Mao and his early supporters never dreamed that such a platform could, by itself, be capable of wiping out a good portion of North America. Though it was comforting to know that this capability was theirs, Chen inwardly doubted that it would ever be utilized. Even taking into consideration Admiral Liu's ominous warning back at the sub pen, a nuclear conflict was fraught with too many horrifying unknowns. Beyond the immediate destructive effects of the initial bomb blast, there was the terrifying specter of radiation poisoning, and unknown environmental consequences, such as the possibility of a "nuclear winter" to follow. Thus more than actual weapons of war, his load of missiles served as a deterrent, something for other nations to think twice about before threatening China's sovereignty.

For hundreds of centuries, China had been subjected to one foreign invasion after the other. In ancient times, devices such as the Great Wall had been built in an effort to keep these invaders out. In the last two hundred years, various enemies had swarmed to their shores, with advanced weaponry and greedy, imperialistic aspirations. To the south it was the French, who robbed them of Indochina, while from the southeast came the English and the Americans, who occupied their ports as if it were their right to do so. Advancing from the northeast was an even more dangerous enemy—the Japanese, who had their eyes on Korea, Manchuria, and the rest of Northern China for hundreds of past decades. And, of course, one could not leave out the Russians, who waited to the north and west, hungry for the rich steppes of Mongolia and Kunlun. Yet somehow, throughout all this exterior chaos — and internal dissension as well — China had persevered.

It was under Mao's tutelage that the foreign invaders were expelled for the final time. Under the guidance of the Republic's glorious founder, China's internal wounds were healed as well. Sweeping the countryside clean of unproductive dissidents, the new Communist leadership planted the seeds of true equality and pride. And today, forty years later, China had emerged like a stately oak tree, her roots nourished by the blood of those who sacrificed their lives so that the Republic would never have to fear for its integrity again.

The *Red Dragon* served as the ultimate deterrent, insuring China's security in the years to come. And if another nation dared challenge their right to exist in peace, Chen Shou could only pity them. For the *Xia*-class missiles that currently surrounded him would streak into the heavens and descend with a mushroom-shaped cloud of instant death.

Yes, he was like a god of old — all-powerful, with the ability to wreak havoc upon those who broke the law of peaceful coexistence. Like this vengeful god, his fury knew no containment once his country's safety was threatened. And deep in the enemy's homeland, the living would envy the dead.

Absolutely certain that he would follow through with the launch sequence if this black day ever came to pass, Chen sat down to check the console mounted on the aft bulkhead. He swiftly addressed the keyboard, and waited as the monitor screen displayed its response. As of this moment, the sixteen missiles were ready for flight. The ninety-six independently guided warheads had only recently been retargeted. He had supervised this process himself, from a top-secret directive that had originated in Admiral Liu Shao-chi's office.

As it now stood, half the warheads would eliminate targets up and down the West Coast of America. If the order to launch was received right now, cities such as Seattle, Portland, San Francisco, Los Angeles, San Diego, and Honolulu would no longer exist in their current forms. Their destruction would take but a scant thirty minutes. The other forty-eight warheads were programmed to fly in the opposite direction—and the cities of Petropavlovsk, Vladivostok, Chabarovsk, Irkutsk, Seoul, Tokyo, Osaka, and Taipei would likewise disappear in a radioactive cloud of death and destruction. Thus, the entire Pacific rim was currently within their sights.

He was using the computer to check the integrity of the ship's inertial navigation system, which insured that these warheads hit their targets accurately, when the intercom buzzed. He was startled at first by this unexpected interruption, but managed to pick up the plastic handset on the second ring.

"Captain here," he announced curtly.

"Captain," came a distinctive bass voice at the other end, "this is the senior lieutenant. I wanted to inform you that we have just crossed into our patrol sector."

"That's wonderful news!" returned the captain, who shifted his gaze to the line of missile silos that lay behind him. "You are hereby authorized to initiate our prearranged random patrol sequence."

"Very good, Captain. I'm instructing maneuvering to stand down from flank speed. We will proceed at loiter velocity. By the way, sir, we've located a distinct thermocline zone some fifty meters beneath us. Shall we utilize it to further veil us?"

"Why, of course!" returned the captain. "We must use every trick available in order to keep our presence here a secret. But since such a new depth will be beyond the range of our VLF receiver, please inform me when the next prescheduled transmission from Command is due. I'd like to join you when we launch the communications buoy."

"I will do that, sir."

With this, the line went dead, and Chen replaced the handset. Seconds later, his practiced ear noted that the muffled hum which had prevailed for the last twenty-four hours abruptly ceased. This meant that the senior lieutenant's directive had reached the engine room, and the *Red Dragon* was no longer traveling at flank speed.

They would remain in this patrol sector for the next three weeks, or until Command ordered them either to return to port or go elsewhere. Their current sector was ideally situated so that targets on both North America and Asia could be readily reached. It also had a varied bathymetric composition, created by that geological feature known as the North Hawaiian Seamount Range. Such subterranean mountainous terrain could prove invaluable should it be necessary to further veil their presence from an approaching enemy. Hoping that it wouldn't come down to such a dangerous game of cat and mouse, the captain rose and took one last look at the missile magazine before heading for the aft hatchway.

Before unlocking this hatch, he made certain to pull out his radiation badge and pin it to the front pocket of his coveralls. He would be entering the reactor room next, and such a precaution was necessary to insure that he wasn't exposed to any excess radioactivity. Only after the badge was firmly in place did he proceed to unlock the hatch and duck into that portion of the *Red Dragon* where their power was generated. This part of the ship always fascinated him, and he found himself anxious to see how the reactor had held up after spewing out twenty-four hours of flank speed.

The reactor room was barely one-tenth the size of the missile magazine. Yet it was completely filled with dozens of gauges, dials, and various digital monitors. Seated before this assortment of instruments were the four current members of the maneuvering watch.

Quick to react to Chen's entrance, baldheaded Chief Wu gave the captain an animated greeting. "Well, look what the wind has blown in. To what do we owe this honor, Captain?"

Chen had been to nuclear power school with the amiable chief, and the two shook hands warmly as the captain replied, "I'm just making my rounds, Chief, and wanted to see for myself how our engines held up to the strain of constant flank speed."

A broad grin lit the chief's face. "As promised, the turbines surged away without a single glitch. Why, it's almost unbelievable, Captain. We didn't even have a minor steam leak."

Chen returned the chief's smile. "Our engineers have outdone themselves this time, old friend. Wait until Admiral Liu reads our report. He is going to be absolutely thrilled!"

"Let's hope so," said the chief, whose eyes drifted downward to scan the digital readouts of their power surge monitor. "That old salt is hard to please, even when we give him perfection."

As he inspected the power surge figures himself, the captain commented, "Don't let our esteemed First Admiral fool you, Chief. Believe me, his bark is worse than his bite. That tough exterior of his is only his way of getting things done."

Satisfied that the reactor was cooling down properly, the chief turned again to the captain. "Well, however tough he may appear to be, Admiral Liu is certainly a miracle worker. I don't think that anyone else would have been able to get the *Red Dragon* to sea as quickly as he did. Although I must admit that your own efforts didn't hurt either."

"All of us pitched in to make this vessel a success, Chief. In a way, the efforts of the entire Republic put this ship to sea. And now it's our responsibility to treat the *Red Dragon* with the respect it rightfully deserves. How about escorting me into the reactor vessel? I'd like to see just what makes this boat tick."

Motioning for the captain to precede him, the chief stood and joined the distinguished senior officer as he ducked through a hatch marked with a series of bright red characters reading *Danger, No Admittance!* Well aware that this warning was only to keep unauthorized curiosity seekers from trespassing in this sensitive area of the ship, the chief joined Chen Shou on the rest of his rounds as the *Red Dragon* silently descended into the icy Pacific depths.

CHAPTER THIRTEEN

The first group of guests began arriving at Guilin in the morning, and General Huang Tzu made certain there was adequate transport awaiting them for the short trip to the cavern complex. He had obtained a dozen large buses for this purpose, and by mid-afternoon each of these vehicles was on the road with a full load of passengers.

The publicly announced purpose of their visit was to attend a retreat, where the future direction of the Party would be discussed in a relaxed, wilderness setting. Fearing leaks regarding the real nature of their stay, the general disclosed the truth to only a few respected individuals. Thus, the rest of those chosen were indeed expecting to merely attend a political seminar.

Fortunately, the weather cooperated and the new arrivals were conveniently processed in a large tent that had been set up outdoors. Lunch was served and afterwards, a series of lectures was scheduled. Most of the speakers were political officers who were members of Huang's staff. The discussions centered around the value of hard-line Maoist theories in an age of rampant liberalism, and the general loss of direction of the Chinese people. Since the hand-picked audience was extremely supportive of just such beliefs, these lectures served to reaffirm their viewpoints, and were also helpful in passing the time until all were assembled.

General Huang greeted his guests personally toward late afternoon. They were over a thousand strong and represented a comprehensive cross section of the Republic's population. From eager teenagers to inquisitive white-haired elders, they had one thing in common: a firm belief that the liberal policies of their young Premier, Lin Shau-ping, were taking the Republic in a dangerous direction. Many of those invited had been amongst Mao's earliest supporters. The younger ones had been involved in preserving the Maoist tradition as a base on which modern China would grow and prosper.

Toward dusk, when the last busload of guests pulled into the valley, the general was relieved to see that one of the new arrivals was Admiral Liu Shao-chi. He arrived along with several dozen top military officers and their families. These individuals knew the real reason for their being here. As they left the cramped confines of the bus and began the brief walk to the central tent, General Huang quickly advanced to greet them. Only after the last hand was shaken, did he take Liu by the arm and lead him into a grove of nearby acacias. Here, amidst the blossoming trees, the two had a chance to properly greet other in private.

"Well, Huang Tzu, it looks as if we've done it!" observed Liu triumphantly. "Has everyone arrived?"

An excited gleam sparkled in the general's eyes. "Your bus was the last one, Comrade. Other than a few security patrols that I still have to pull in, we are ready to proceed into the cave as planned."

"Excellent!" retorted Liu. "All continues to go smoothly on my end as well. At last report, the *Red Dragon* had successfully reached its patrol sector. We only have to broadcast the war alert to initiate the next stage of our historic operation. Is the communications gear ready?"

"Your men arrived two days ago to set up the transmitter. They chose the top of the ridge behind us to position the satellite up-link dish. A subsequent test transmission showed it to be completely operational. All that we need now are the current alert codes, and the apocalypse shall begin as scheduled."

Liu smiled as he patted the breast pocket of his Mao jacket. "Today's alert code just happens to be in my possession. As it looks now, we will be initiating our strike just as the superpower summit officially convenes. The U.S. President and the Soviet Premier have already arrived in New York City. How fitting it is that our first warheads will descend just as they sit down to divide China up between them. If I could only see their faces when their aides inform them of these incoming missiles. What a poetic way to begin a peace summit!"

"I wonder if the Soviets will wait for their premier to leave New York before they order the first counterstrike?" quizzed Huang.

"If I know the Russians, I doubt it," observed Liu. "The generals in the Kremlin aren't about to hold back merely to save one individual, who is just a figurehead, and not too popular at that. No, my friend, the moment the first atomic warhead explodes over their territory, they'll hit the U.S. with everything that they have."

A serious expression settled over Huang's face. "I imagine you're right," he reflected grimly. "The Soviets will retaliate quickly, with the Americans answering only seconds later. What a horrible mess will soon be unleashed upon the earth!"

"You're not having second thoughts about this strike, are you, Comrade?" asked Liu cautiously.

"Of course not," retorted the general. "It's either them, or us. And no matter the cost, China must persevere."

Liu nodded in support of this statement. "That's more like it. Now tell me, is our cavern shelter ready for us?"

Huang's spirits were already lightening as he answered. "That it is, Comrade. It might not have all the comforts of home, but I believe that we've included all the necessities to insure our survival."

348

"I understand that a little earthquake paid you a visit recently," probed Liu slyly.

Huang nodded vigorously. "Little did you say? Why, it was one of the strongest tremors I have ever experienced. Yet fortunately we escaped with a minimum of damage."

"Speaking of escapes, what news do you have of the two spies you caught several days ago? Did they ever show up?"

"We're almost positive that they never made it out of the cavern alive," answered Huang. "Though their bodies have not yet been found, we'll come upon them sooner or later. You may be sure of that."

Satisfied that the general had everything under control, Liu glanced down at his pocket watch. "The hour's getting late, my friend. Shall we get on with it?"

Huang nodded solemnly and proceeded to lead Liu Shao-chi out of the acacia grove. The sun had long since dipped beneath the western ridge, and the sky was just coloring with the first hint of dusk. It proved to be another warm, humid evening, and as Huang Tzu took in the vast crowd assembled on the floor of the valley before him, he was thankful it wasn't raining. They were currently between lectures, and the excited murmur of voices could be heard clearly even from this distance.

At his side, Liu also viewed this huge assemblage. Momentarily halting to scan the surrounding valley, the white-haired senior naval officer then turned to Huang.

"It's time that we shepherded our esteemed guests into what will be their home for the next couple of weeks. As planned, you will make the announcement informing them that a military crisis has just arisen in the Republic. You will then order them to proceed immediately into the cavern complex, which has been conveniently prepared as a fallout shelter. Meanwhile, I will join my staff at the radio transmitter and release the alert code to the *Red Dragon*. By the time the cavern is sealed, the first missile should already be on its way into the heavens. With a flight time of less than thirty minutes, a full-scale nuclear war will not be long in following."

Huang's voice was calm as he replied, "So it shall be, Comrade. May the gods be with us."

He then beckoned Liu forward, hardly affected at all by the fact that they would soon be witnessing the end of the modern world as they knew it.

Approximately 4,500 miles east of the Guilin complex, Captain Chen Shou sat in the *Red Dragon*'s wardroom, expertly using his chopsticks to consume a light meal of steamed shrimp and vegetables served on a bed of soft noodles.

Their head cook was a genius at making do with a rather limited larder. He was a former gourmet chef, originally trained in Hong Kong. When he returned to Shanghai to lend his support to the new government, Chen had offered him a position in the navy—as head instructor of mess hall personnel. He accepted instantly, and launched an intensive program to improve the quality of food preparation in the entire PLN.

Such a program was important to Chen, for unlike most of the world's navies, the PLN had never been known for the quality of its meals. This would have to change if they hoped to enlist—and keep—a better class of personnel in their ranks.

When the *Red Dragon* was initially outfitted, Chen had asked the chef to accompany them. He took this invitation as the challenge that it was meant to be, and got to work at once preparing a balanced menu.

Life aboard a missile-carrying submarine was not the most interesting of duties. Most of the crew's time was spent monitoring the equipment and doing maintenance when necessary. To break the dull routine and give the men something to look forward to, Chen was hoping that the chef would be able to come up with something special that could be used as a standard to be followed on future patrols. He had not been disappointed.

Making the most of his limited storage and preparation facilities, the chef stocked the galley with a well-thought-out selection of foodstuffs. Just the basic feeding of one hundred and ten men for a period of two months was no easy task. Yet, by careful and imaginative planning, he succeeded in making mealtime something to look forward to.

Chen's present meal was a good example of his excellent work. The shrimp and vegetables were cooked to perfection, with just the right amount of spices. Chen had already asked for his recipe for noodles, which the chef made by hand and smothered in a rich and tangy soya-based sauce.

The men were equally enthusiastic, and Chen was pleased to note their high level of morale. Ever thankful that he had asked the chef to join them, the captain chewed up his last shrimp and washed it down with a drink of piping hot green tea. He was just refilling his cup when the ship's quartermaster entered the wardroom. The veteran officer was a big-boned Tartar from Yumen, and a superb radio man. Customarily he was an emotionless individual, yet as he hastily crossed to the captain's side, Chen could sense that something had occurred to upset him.

"Sir," said the quartermaster tersely, "This dispatch was just received on the emergency, extra low frequency band."

Scanning the folded piece of paper that had just been handed to him, the captain took in a typed message that read simply, "Long March." This was obviously a code of some sort, and Chen was somewhat puzzled.

"Are you certain that this was the extent of the message?" he asked.

"Absolutely," returned the quartermaster. "I even took the liberty of launching a VLF buoy to check for transmissions on the more standard frequencies, but to no avail. Isn't an ELF message of this type most unusual, sir?"

Chen was oblivious to this question as, deep in thought, he rose to make his way to his cabin. Sensing the captain's preoccupation, the quartermaster merely shrugged his broad shoulders and returned to his station in the radio room. If the message was really that important, he'd be hearing from the captain soon enough.

In a world of his own now, Chen Shou ducked into his cabin and closed the door behind him. He went straight to his desk and unlocked the top drawer, where his code book was stored. His hands were trembling slightly as he opened the red leather-bound book, which only he and the boat's senior lieutenant had copies of. He was disturbed to find the two code words under the heading *Strategic Alert*.

It was a simple call to war. Though Chen was certain that this was no more than a drill, he found his gut tightening. A series of fail-safe measures had been incorporated into the system to insure that a missile couldn't be released by mistake. Thus, his next task would be to contact the quartermaster to see if a series of numerals had been subsequently relayed to them via the ELF receiver. Such a sequence would be needed to actually initiate a launch, and would signal that the supposed exercise would take them to yet another level of realism.

His call to the quartermaster found the Tartar in the midst of recording this second transmission. An actual launch-release code was soon conveyed to him, and Chen knew that if this was indeed only a drill, it was distressingly close to sounding like the real thing. Until otherwise informed, he could only proceed as if a state of war actually existed. Thus, he hit the wall-mounted alarm that sent the crew scrambling to their battle stations. Next, he called the senior lieutenant and ordered the sub's second-in-command to meet him in the attack center at once. Then, with the code book and launch-release sequence gripped tightly in his hand, he left his cabin.

His pulse was beating madly as he rushed through the cramped passageways and ducked into that portion of the boat where the sub's weapons systems were controlled. Lit by the dim red battle lanterns, the attack center's digital consoles seemingly glowed with a life of their own. Orchestrating the activation of these monitors was the senior lieutenant, who sat before one of the keyboards preparing the ship for battle. Chen Shou hastily sat down beside him, and it was only then that the senior lieutenant realized he was no longer alone.

"I've activated the fire-control system and loaded a full complement of torpedoes and decoys, Captain. I'm in the process of integrating these systems

354

with sonar."

Taking in the senior lieutenant's words, Chen began addressing the keyboard of the console that he now faced. "Very good, Comrade. I'm going to need to you to ready your launch key."

As the captain reached for the key that he always kept hung around his neck, his second-in-command questioned, "Why is that, Captain? Is this an exercise that I wasn't told about?"

Chen answered while the senior lieutenant removed his own key from his pocket and placed it on the counter. "Minutes ago, we received a go-to-war alert. The code was subsequently verified, and a secondary release sequence conveyed to us soon after the initial ELF contact. As far as I know, this isn't an exercise."

"You've got to be kidding!" exclaimed the senior lieutenant. "Do you mean to say that we're actually going to go ahead with a launch? Why, that means that it's the end of the world!"

Chen fitted his key in the proper slot on his console, and signaled his second-in-command to do likewise. "I wouldn't go so far as to say that, Comrade. But it does appear that we are at war. At least, that's what I've been led to believe. So until we are told otherwise, we're going to prepare the ship to launch its missiles. On the count of three, we're going to unlock the missile firing system. One . . . two . . . three!"

Both officers turned their keys simultaneously,

and a digital counter set above the two locks, instantly lit up.

"Proceeding to input the secondary release code," continued the captain. "One, zero, one, nine, three, two. I repeat. One, zero, one, nine, three, two."

As these numerals flashed into the display, a red light was triggered beside both lock mechanisms.

The senior lieutenant now spoke out, "We have an authentic release code, Captain. The missiles are go for launch."

A thin line of sweat had formed on Chen's forehead as he double-checked the various readouts. "I concur. We have a go for missile release. But before we inform the bridge to take us up to launch depth, I'm going to break with procedure and give the quartermaster one last call. This whole thing has just got to be an exercise!"

Chen's hand was shaking quite badly now as he reached out for the intercom handset. He punched in a series of three digits, and waited until a familiar gruff voice answered.

"Quartermaster speaking."

Chen anxiously inquired if any subsequent directives had been received. When he was curtly informed that they had not, he sighed heavily and hung up the handset. A look of pure disbelief etched his face as he turned to his equally concerned associate.

"I still don't believe it, Comrade, but Command has actually ordered us to launch our missiles!

356

What in heaven's name has occurred to prompt such an unthinkable thing?"

The senior lieutenant's deep bass voice was cracking nervously as he attempted to respond. "All I can surmise, sir, is that the Republic must be under a direct attack for Command to go to such an extreme. Yet, thank the gods that we are here to avenge this senseless aggression."

Snapped back to his senses, Chen nodded his head in agreement. "You are right, Comrade. Though none of us wanted to admit it, this day was bound to come. We can only be thankful that the *Red Dragon* exists to show the world that China still has some fight left in her after all.

"You may ring the bridge, Comrade. Instruct the chief to bring us up to launch depth. Then we will do our sworn duty, and release those missiles!"

Since his conversation with the captain and the XO in the wardroom, Reggie Warner had practically lived in the sonar compartment. Breaking only to go to the head or grab a catnap, he even took his meals at the console. There were others aboard the *Copperhead* who were qualified to take Reggie's watch, but now that the mystery sub had been tagged, he wanted to be close by to monitor its each and every movement. Just knowing that it was out there, lurking in the depths nearby, would keep him from properly resting anyway.

They continued approaching the still-unidentified target from the south. It was some fifteen nautical miles away from them now, its unique signature barely audible through the hydrophones. Because of its slow speed and random course, Reggie was certain that it was a missile-carrying vessel. Such a platform would attempt to loiter as quietly as possible, utilizing both mechanical stealth and the ocean's environmental qualities to remain undetected. Several hours ago, he had monitored the sub as it descended several hundred feet to take advantage of a well-developed thermocline. This clever tactic would have succeeded if it hadn't been for a noisy engine bearing, which continued emitting a constant hum even from this layer of deeper, cool water.

The *Copperhead* was still at general quarters, with the captain and the XO currently on duty in the control room. Reggie sensed that the crew was ready for some real action, and his instincts told him that it would be soon in coming. Almost one hundred per cent certain that the sub they were facing was the outlaw Chinese boat Command had warned them of, the senior sonar technician had his three assistants focusing their attention solely on this contact. Occasionally, Reggie would scan the surrounding waters for any other unwelcome visitors, but most of his attention was concentrated on the rapidly approaching bogey.

He had been seated at his console for three solid

hours since taking his last break, and decided that he could spare a few minutes to relieve himself of some of the coffee he'd been constantly pouring into his body. It was with great relief that he pulled off his headphones and massaged his sore ears. The buzzing had all but stopped now, and his only real discomfort was coming from his tense upper back and neck muscles. He stood and stretched his cramped limbs, then scooted out of the narrow cubicle where his console was located.

Of his three current assistants, Marty Stanfield had the senior rating. Gently tapping him on the shoulder, Reggie waited for his roommate to remove his headphones.

"Hey bro, I'm off to the head and to get some more java. How about minding the store while the boss is away?"

"No problem, Reg," replied Stanfield. "Would you mind bring back a thermos of coffee for the rest of us working slobs?"

"I think that can be arranged," returned Reggie as he exited the sonar room.

Once in the passageway, Reggie had a chance to stretch more fully. He did a couple of deep knee bends, then walked over to the nearby head. He felt much better after relieving himself and splashing cold water on his face and neck. Barely taking time to wipe himself dry, he took off for the galley.

The smell of frying bacon greeted him as he entered the *Copperhead*'s mess hall. The cooks were just preparing breakfast, and only then did Reggie realize what time it was. He was in the midst of filling a thermos with hot black coffee, when a deep voice came from behind him.

"Good morning, Mr. Warner. How goes it?"

As he screwed on the lid of the thermos, Reggie turned and set his eyes on the grease-stained face of Greg Meinert. "Good morning to you, Chief. Why, you almost look like a brother with all that gook on you. Don't tell me you're still working on that hydraulics problem?"

"The very same," answered the burly chief petty officer. "But luckily for us, it looks like we've finally got it licked. Are you still keeping my seat warm in sonar?"

Nodding that he was, Reggie watched as Meinert poured himself a mug of coffee. "Actually, Chief, I haven't left that station since I relieved you. We've got us an unidentified bogey nearby that the skipper wants us to keep tabs on."

"So I understand," retorted the chief, who took a sip of the steaming hot brew. "If things get out of hand, just give me a call. Meanwhile, I'd better wash up and get off to my assigned battle station. There's certainly no rest for the wicked in this man's navy."

Reggie stopped off at the galley to appropriate a handful of crisp bacon before returning to the sonar room. He was walking down the passageway that led to this compartment, when a familiar figure scrambled down the corridor from the opposite direction and intercepted him.

Marty Stanfield's face was shiny with sweat. "Jesus, Reg," he called out breathlessly. "You'd better get back to the sound shack at once! Something funny is happening out there."

Without waiting to hear anything further, Reggie took off running down the passageway. His roommate led the way as they ducked through the hatch and entered the sonar compartment. The other two technicians were hunched anxiously over their consoles as Reggie hurriedly positioned himself behind his own station. Clipping on his headphones, he directed the hydrophone array to monitor that portion of the ocean immediately to the *Copperhead*'s north. His pulse was still racing as he picked up the distinctive sound of venting ballast. This was followed by a dreaded, grating metallic noise, which sent Reggie reaching out for the intercom.

"Con, this is sonar. Contact is ascending! I believe we're also picking up the sounds of its missile magazine being opened to the sea!"

Samuel Fuller and Vincent Coria had been at the navigator's station when the frantic call from sonar arrived. With his eyes still glued to the bathymetric chart on which this same contact was represented as a large red X, the captain shouted out commands.

"Mr. Coria, have weapons load tubes one, two,

361

and four with Mark 48's! Conventional warheads, wire-guided. Load three with a decoy."

As the XO conveyed this order to the torpedo room, Fuller visualized the frantic action that this directive was producing on the deck below. Here, their young weapons officer, Lieutenant David Costner, would be supervising his torpedomen as they unbolted the torpedoes from their storage racks and slipped them into the tubes. The inner doors would then be locked, and the targeting computer would begin feeding data into the on-board computers located behind each warhead. To insure that their aim would be true, Fuller barked out additional orders.

"Control to weapons, lock on sonar and proceed to flood tubes!"

As the signature of the bogey was fed into each torpedo, the distant sound of rushing water meant that the weapons were ready to fire. Taking a deep breath, Samuel Fuller prepared to deliver the order that would send the Mark 48's surging out toward their target.

From the silent seas behind the *Copperhead*, the Soviet *Akula*-class attack sub *Baikal,* also heard the threatening sound of venting seawater in the distance. Mistakenly, the crew attributed this racket to a missile-carrying vessel of American origin.

Gathered in the boat's hushed attack center, with

362

his senior staff surrounding him, Captain Anton Valerian nervously paced the room's crowded confines. Having just ordered the boat's six bow tubes loaded with an assortment of weapons, he readied himself to convey his own firing orders. Yet before he did so, he took a moment to reconsider the situation that faced them.

The *Baikal* currently had two contacts in its sights. They had been following one of these vessels for several hours now. The American *Sturgeon*-class attack sub was an old adversary. They had tangled several times before, and nothing would gratify Valerian more than sending this ship to the bottom. Fortunately, he had held himself back from doing so prematurely, and now the Yankee attack platform had led them right to the ultimate prize of all.

They had first heard the supposed missile-carrying vessel as it was quietly loitering in the distance. Though their computer had yet to verify this boat as a Trident, its random course and slow speed indicated that this was surely the case. Most likely they were facing a specially adapted boat, one that was as yet unknown to Intelligence. One thing was apparent — the Trident was working in tandem with the *Sturgeon*-class sub to insure that it wasn't attacked. This was fine with Anton, who was now in a position to take out both submarines with a single salvo.

All that Valerian needed to order the torpedoes released was evidence indicating that the Trident was about to initiate a missile launch. As far as he knew, they were still in the midst of a level two Red Flag alert. The *Baikal*'s VLF radio receiver had yet to be repaired, but subsequent ELF transmissions indicated that a state of heightened tension continued to exist between the two superpowers. Thus he was fully authorized to eliminate the two American vessels should they show the least bit of hostile movement.

With this contingency in mind, the captain continued his nervous pacing. The attack center was bathed in red light, and all was quiet except for the plastic chatter of a computer keyboard being accessed. An open line with sonar had been routed through the compartment's mounted public address speakers, and Anton awaited anxiously for it to once again activate. As he looked up at one of these speakers, set on the opposite wall, he noted a trim baldheaded figure watching him from this corner of the room. The *zampolit* had been unusually quiet ever since the second American vessel had been discovered, and Anton crossed the room to see what Boris Glazov had on his mind.

"Why the long face, Comrade Glazov? Things can't be that bad, can they?"

The political officer sighed heavily. "It's just this infernal waiting, Captain. It can make a man go gray before his time."

"That's one thing you won't have to worry about," jested the captain.

This failed to elicit even a faint smile from the *zampolit*. "I wish the Americans would go ahead and make their move," he grunted. "We've been very fortunate to remain undetected for as long as we have. And once we've lost the element of surprise, our little ambush will be ruined."

"I don't know about that," countered the captain. "Even if discovered, the *Baikal* is a formidable adversary. Of course, it would be to our advantage to get off the initial shots. That way, the Yankees would be put on the defensive, while we continue to move in and make good the kill."

"Something about this whole setup still bothers me," reflected the *zampolit* solemnly. "I'd feel much better if our VLF receiver was back on-line, and we knew for certain that the alert still existed. An unauthorized attack would trigger the very war that we have been sent out here to prevent."

Anton had guessed that this was the reason for the political officer's grim mood, and he moved to reassure him. "Must I remind you once again of the results of our last ELF transmission, Comrade? Less than forty-five minutes ago, our emergency communications buoy clearly relayed to us an extension of the level two alert. Though I, too, would like to have our normal communications gear back on-line, we must make do with what is available.

"Don't forget, somewhere in the waters nearby a vessel lies waiting with a load of nuclear death locked inside its missile magazine. If only a single

365

one of these warheads hits its intended target in the Motherland, it will result in hundreds of thousands of casualties. We exist solely to make certain that such a nightmarish thing will never come to pass. If the Americans dare to choose this moment to unleash their imperialistic aggressions, the *Rodina* can be assured that the *Baikal* will be there to do its duty, no matter how unpleasant!"

No sooner were these forceful words out of Valerian's mouth, than a loud electronic chime sounded and the intercom was abruptly activated. The worried voice that came through the speakers was noticeably strained.

"Captain, this is sonar. Our primary target has just blown its main ballast tanks. A sound followed which could very well be that made by its missile-superstructure's outer hatch opening."

"And the secondary target?" quizzed the anxious captain, his finger on the intercom transmit switch.

"The attack sub continues its cautious approach, sir," returned the voice of the sonar operator.

Taking a moment to contemplate this new information, Anton crossed to the console where his senior lieutenant was seated. With the worried *zampolit* close at his side, the captain decided that the time had come to act. Scanning the faces of his officers, Anton took a deep, calming breath.

"It's obvious that the Trident is ascending to launch depth and is preparing to unleash the first salvo. Thus, under the rules of engagement as spelled out under our current level two alert status, we are within our rights to eliminate this vessel without further delay. Now, I realize that we haven't received a formal declaration of war as yet. But since we are obviously witnessing one of the first aggressive moves in this conflict, I feel it is my duty to order an immediate torpedo release, targeted at both contacts. Does anyone feel otherwise?"

Quickly taking in their stares once again, Anton sensed that his staff was solidly behind him. Only the *zampolit* seemed to be vacillating. Briefly meeting the political officer's pained expression, the captain cleared his throat and continued.

"Very well, Comrades. The *Baikal* shall do its sworn duty and eliminate the enemy without further delay.

"Senior Lieutenant, prepare tubes one through five for firing. Tubes one, two, and three shall be reserved for the primary target, with tubes four and five targeted at the attack sub. You are to flood all tubes and initiate a signature interface. Then you shall fire on my command."

Looking on as the senior lieutenant readied the fire-control panel, Anton Valerian found his nerves steady and his confidence level high. After decades of meaningless patrols and boring exercises, the time had finally come for action. Thankful that he had lived to see this day, he listened as the *Baikal*'s second-in-command spoke out excitedly.

"Tubes one through five ready for firing, Captain!"

Savoring this triumphal moment, Valerian firmly responded, "Fire!"

The senior lieutenant hit the release switch, and seconds later the entire sub shook as the first torpedo shot out of its tube, propelled by a powerful blast of compressed air. Four other torpedoes followed in quick succession, and the *Baikal*'s diving officer had to take on additional ballast to compensate for the sudden loss of weight.

Watching all of this as if in a dream, Anton Valerian anxiously waited for the next sonar report, at which time he would most likely know if their quarry had reacted quickly enough to escape them. Once again he found himself possessed by an unnatural calmness that genuinely surprised him. For he could have very well just fired the first shots of World War III!

CHAPTER FOURTEEN

In the *Copperhead*'s sonar room the approaching torpedoes sounded like a runaway freight train. Hardly believing what he was hearing, Reggie pressed his headphones closer to his ears. Slowly but surely the grim reality sank in. They were under attack themselves—from an adversary who had caught them completely off guard! A cold sweat formed on his forehead as he reached out for the intercom to inform the control room staff of this new threat.

"Sonar to control. Incoming torpedoes, bearing one-six-zero!"

Sitting forward anxiously to monitor the approach of these weapons, Reggie silently cursed his own inefficiency. He had been paying so much attention to the vessel they had been stalking, he had missed detecting still another submarine, which had been apparently following in their baffles. Assuming this was a Chinese attack sub which had been sent out to protect its boomer,

Reggie could only pray that the skipper would be able to see them out of harm's way. Otherwise, he could only look forward to a couple of more minutes of life at most.

"Fire that decoy!" ordered Samuel Fuller, his voice strained with tension.

As the Mk-70 mobile submarine simulator surged out of its torpedo tube, the entire *Copperhead* shook. Designed to fool an attacking torpedo into believing that it was its real target, the decoy plunged into the surrounding waters and was soon traveling at a speed of over twenty-five knots.

Satisfied that this last-ditch defensive system had deployed properly, Fuller nevertheless ordered the sub into a deep dive. "Planesmen, take us down, maximum angle! Engineering, for our very lives, give us everything she's got!"

In response, the *Copperhead's* bow angled sharply downward, and the crew had to brace themselves to keep from falling. Quickly picking up speed now, the sub shot into the cold black depths, in a race against death itself.

With his right hand firmly gripping one side of the chart table, Samuel Fuller looked over at the seated planesmen, who were firmly restrained in their padded chairs by shoulder harnesses. Their airplane-type steering wheels were pressed all the way forward, and the digital depth gauge mounted on the bulkhead before them indicated a depth of six hundred and thirty feet, and constantly dropping.

An explosion suddenly sounded in the distance, and Fuller diverted his glance to silently meet the concerned stare of Vincent Coria, who was also holding onto the chart table. Seconds later the intercom activated, and the excited voice of Reggie Warner echoed forth from the wall mounted speakers.

"Sonar to control. Scratch one torpedo and a decoy! Other weapon continues to close."

Noting that they were below seven hundred feet now, Fuller addressed his XO. "I hope to God that we cross into that thermocline soon."

"Where in the hell did those torpedoes come from, anyway?" questioned the XO.

"I'll lay odds that it was a Chinese attack sub," replied Fuller, who continued monitoring their desperate dive. "They must have been following in our baffles, under battery power. Damn those bastards! A couple of seconds more and we could have taken out that boomer. Now, not only are we running for our lives, but we've got to start the hunt all over again."

The deck beneath them shuddered, and the two senior officers locked their gazes on the digital depth gauge, which had just passed seven hundred and fifty feet. The very hull around them groaned under this increased pressure, and a new concern

371

arose in Fuller's mind as they began to approach their crush depth.

"Torpedo continues to close," came Reggie's strained voice over the loudspeaker.

"Where in the hell is that damn thermocline?" exclaimed the captain angrily.

With no time left to load and launch another decoy, Fuller was depending upon the cold layer of water known as the thermocline to confuse the torpedo's sonar. Acting almost like an impenetrable wall, this dense layer would hopefully veil the fleeing *Copperhead* from further detection. But it would have to be encountered soon, for the boat was rapidly reaching its depth limit.

"Eight hundred feet and dropping," reported Chief Meinert, the current diving officer.

The boat shuddered once again as it continued to slice downward at a speed of over thirty-five knots. Visualizing the streamlined weapon which was following them into the depths, the captain considered his options. He could continue guiding the *Copperhead* down through the one thousand-foot threshold, and pray that their hull would remain intact and that they would be able to eventually outrun the torpedo. Or he could halt their descent, and begin a series of last minute evasive actions, in the hope of losing the torpedo in the resulting turbulence.

As it turned out, it proved to be the composition of the sea itself that guided their fates. For as

372

the *Copperhead* reached a depth of eight hundred and seventy-five feet, Reggie Warner's voice once more broke forth from the intercom.

"Sonar to control. The torpedo is holding at eight hundred and fifty feet! I believe its sonar is confused by the well-defined thermal layer we just crossed into."

"All right!" exclaimed the joyous XO.

The rest of the control room staff joined in a brief cheer. Exhaling a deep breath of relief himself, Samuel Fuller allowed the *Copperhead* to break the nine hundred-foot level before ordering the planesmen to level out. Only when he was absolutely certain that the pursuing torpedo was no longer a threat, did he allow himself the barest of resolute grins.

"Well, Mr. Coria, that was a bit too close for comfort. What do you say to turning the tables and showing our attackers what this little lady is really made of?"

Flashing Fuller a firm thumbs-up, the XO replied, "I'm with you, Skipper. I just hope we can get back to that boomer before it launches."

With this same hope in mind, Samuel Fuller ordered the *Copperhead* to take the offensive. With its full complement of sensors scanning the seas above, they rose from the depths on a new mission of revenge.

Captain Chen Shou had found himself only thirty-five seconds away from releasing the first ballistic missile, when the frantic call from sonar arrived, informing him that they were under torpedo attack. His first thought had been that such a thing wasn't possible, yet as the reality sank in, he cursed their bad luck.

Seated beside him at the launch console, his senior lieutenant listened to him vent his anger. With his eyes still glued to the sixteen separate launch release switches placed alongside his keyboard, the *Red Dragon*'s second-in-command addressed his captain.

"Shall we go ahead and initiate the launch, sir? At the very least, we should be able to send half of our load skyward before the first torpedo reaches us."

Though he was tempted to agree with this suggestion, the captain shook his head solemnly. "I'm afraid that such a move would defeat the purpose of our true mission, Comrade. For it would still leave half of our targets unscathed, while condemning us to certain death. Let's see what we can do about evading this salvo. Then perhaps we can locate our attacker and initiate a torpedo launch of our own. With this vessel out of the way, we can then continue undisturbed with our primary mission."

The senior lieutenant was clearly disappointed that the launch would have to be postponed. Nevertheless, he gave Chen Shou his complete support as the captain snapped into action.

"Draw up the computer-enhanced bathymetric chart of the terrain beneath us. Then interface this data with our sonar. If the gods are still with us, perhaps we can use the seamounts beneath our hull to block those approaching torpedoes. Meanwhile, I'll contact engineering and get us some steam. There's light at the end of this dark tunnel yet, Comrade!"

It took less than thirty seconds to get the *Red Dragon* underway once again. As the missile magazine was resealed, the vessel angled sharply downward on a predetermined course. This route was drawn up by the computerized charts which the senior lieutenant had just accessed. Completely at the computer's mercy now, the sub began sprinting for the cover of the underwater mountain range that lay beneath them.

Continuously monitoring the approach of three separate torpedoes, Chen Shou felt his pulse quicken as the *Red Dragon*'s turbines began whining with a vengeance. Though it was extremely doubtful that they would ever be able to outrun the trio of deadly weapons, the evasive tactic he had in mind could be just as effective.

Several months ago, a Chinese oceanographic research vessel arrived in these same waters. For three solid weeks it proceeded to chart each meter of the seabed below. This data was then used to create an exact three-dimensional model of the area's terrain. It was found to be composed of a massive subterranean mountain range, complete with dozens of lofty peaks and deep valleys, some of which extended for well over two thousand meters beneath the ocean's surface.

With a depth threshold of barely eight hundred meters, the *Red Dragon* could only hope to utilize a small portion of the surrounding terrain to its advantage. Thus they were limited to using only the tops of the various seamounts to hide the sub from any unfriendly intruders. Though Chen Shou had never considered using the terrain to counter a torpedo attack, it certainly made good sense under the present circumstances. Now, they would only need a little bit of old-fashioned luck for this novel plan to succeed.

The captain's video monitor currently displayed a detailed three-dimensional rendering of this terrain. A blinking red dot showed the present location of the *Red Dragon*, while three blue X's represented the rapidly closing torpedoes. Directly in front of the sub, some ten kilometers distant, was the summit of a particularly massive seamount. It was this serrated ridge toward which they were headed.

While the computer continually updated its calculations indicating the probability of reaching this shelter before the torpedoes struck, Chen Shou activated an adjoining sonar monitor. Even with the

376

racket created as their turbines ground away at flank speed, he was able to make out the location of the vessel which was apparently responsible for this attack. Just within range of their own torpedoes, this target was too attractive for Chen to resist. He therefore decided to gamble on attempting a high-speed launch of his own.

Two torpedoes were subsequently released from the *Red Dragon*'s stern tubes. Independently guided by a transducer that homed in on the target's sound signature, the torpedoes surged out into the sea, initially propelled by a hissing jolt of compressed air. As their engines activated, Chen silently wished them good hunting, then turned his attention once again to the *Red Dragon*'s own desperate dash for safe waters.

The computer was just indicating that they had a fifty-three per cent chance of reaching the cover of the mountains before the first of the three torpedoes arrived, when one of the blue X's abruptly disappeared.

"It must have malfunctioned, or run out of fuel!" observed the senior lieutenant.

Not ready to join his shipmate in celebration just yet, Chen watched as their survival odds improved a full nine percentage points. Yet the cover of the ridge was still several kilometers distant, and the captain knew that the only thing that could save them now was pure speed. Thus he wasted no time in contacting the head engineer on

377

the intercom.

"Chief Wu, it's imperative that you give me everything that we've got. Open those steam throttles all the way! Right now, there's no time left for caution."

"You asked for it, Captain," retorted the *Red Dragon*'s head nuc. "I'm opening them as wide as I can."

Replacing the handset, Chen turned his attention to the monitor screen. Here, one of the blue X's seemed to have jumped forward in an incredible sudden burst of speed. It was barely a kilometer away from their stern now, and the captain watched as the strike probability percentage began rapidly increasing in favor of their destruction.

Though the subterranean ridge beckoned teasingly close, the captain was just about to abandon any hope of ever reaching it, when the *Red Dragon*'s speed indicator jumped a full knot. He knew that this wasn't a mere anomaly when it jumped forward once again, indicating that the chief had indeed managed to coax some more speed out of the already overloaded turbines. It was this new velocity alone that kept the torpedo from striking them as the sub reached the seamount and disappeared around the broad ridge of rock that led to its needlelike summit.

The torpedo struck the mountain top seconds later. Even without the benefit of headphones, the crew of the *Red Dragon* could hear the resonant blast as the torpedo's contact warhead detonated. A rumbling undersea avalanche followed, as tons of broken rock tumbled downward into the black depths below.

Caught in this turbulence, the second torpedo also exploded prematurely. Only when the thundering sound of this blast reverberated into the hushed attack center, did a relieved smile turn up the corners of Chen Shou's mouth.

A quick glance at the monitor screen showed the sub to be following the meander of a wide valley now. Their pursuer was nowhere in the picture, and the captain decided to continue fleeing to open waters before once again ordering the *Red Dragon* to launch-depth to complete their mission.

"Are you certain that we didn't hit them?" quizzed Anton Valerian incredulously. "I know that the Trident is a well-designed platform, but no submarine can merely disappear!"

Absorbing the captain's shocked observation, the *Baikal*'s second-in-command looked up from his position at the fire-control station. "I know that it sounds incredible, sir, but it looks like they were somehow able to use the surrounding terrain as a shield. Our weapons appear to have exploded harmlessly into the side of an underwater mountain."

"Well, at least we stopped them from launching," countered the captain. "What is the status of their attack sub? Has it showed itself yet?"

Before the senior lieutenant could answer, the frantic voice of the head sonar operator broke in from the other end of the attack center. "Incoming torpedoes, Captain! I count two of them, approaching at maximum range, on bearing three-four-zero."

"Damn it!" cursed Valerian. "Not only has the Trident escaped us, but they were able to initiate an attack as well. Get that reactor on-line at once! If we're going to live long enough to keep them from emptying their missile magazine, we're going to need every available knot of forward speed and then some!"

Reggie Warner heard the sounds of a nuclear reactor suddenly going on-line, just as the *Copperhead* was in the process of ascending out of the thermocline, which had effectively veiled them for the last couple of minutes. This distinctive racket was emanating from a direction opposite to that of the missile-carrying vessel. This meant that it was most likely coming from the mystery sub which had attacked them initially. Hastily feeding this signature into the computer, Reggie grinned knowingly when its true identity popped up on the monitor screen.

"Well, well," reflected the senior sonar technician, who had just learned that this attacker was not a Chinese boat as they had originally presumed, but a most familiar, *Akula*-class vessel. "So much for trusting Ivan," he added, as he reached out for the intercom to share this revelation with the captain.

Samuel Fuller seemed genuinely surprised by this information. He left Reggie with strict orders to do what he could to relocate the Chinese sub, while continuing to carefully monitor the Soviets. No sooner did Reggie replace his headphones, than a distinctive, high-pitched whining sound — which was pure music to his ears — broke in the distance. Incredibly, Ivan himself was under torpedo attack!

No wonder they were so frantically starting up their reactors, thought Reggie, who listened as two separate weapons soon became audible. As the Soviets began picking up speed in an attempt to evade this attack, Reggie shifted his scan to take in that portion of the sea directly opposite. Here, he could just pick up the signature of the Chinese boomer as it steamed off for open waters.

He informed the captain of this sequence of events, then turned back to monitor the Soviets' plight. What he subsequently heard caused him to sit forward anxiously with his pulse quickening in terror. For the *Akula*-class vessel had just angled its bow downward and, in the midst of a crash dive, it was headed straight for the *Copperhead!* Even more horrifying was the fact that the two torpedoes continued homing in on their intended prey, and were thus also currently headed toward the American sub.

Feeling as if he was caught in a nightmare, Reggie notified the control room. Seconds later, he felt the deck tremble beneath him as the *Copperhead*'s propeller bit into the surrounding water in a desperate attempt to escape. The senior sonar technician closed his eyes and listened to the mad racket being conveyed into his headphones by the boat's hydrophones. Plunging downward in a violent crash dive, the Soviet sub roared away like an out of control locomotive, accompanied by the persistent high-pitched, frenzied whine of the two pursuing torpedoes.

As in the frustrating slow-motion pace of a nightmare, it seemed to take forever for the *Copperhead*'s turbines to build up a sufficient head of steam to convey them to safe waters. Yet just as Reggie began noticing a bit of additional distance between them and the spiraling enemy, the *Akula*-class vessel went abruptly silent once again. At first blaming this silence on a malfunction in the *Copperhead*'s sonar gear, Reggie realized what was occurring only after he picked up the definite signature of the two torpedoes. This could only mean that the Soviets had scrammed their reactor and buttoned up their ship in a state of ultra quiet, in the hope that the torpedoes would continue homing in on a new fleeing target, the *Copperhead!*

Cursing the Soviet skipper's ingenuity, Reggie's mouth dropped open in astonishment when this devious maneuver actually showed promise of succeeding. Though it all happened too quickly for him to get a total understanding of the situation, he remembered hearing at least one of the torpedoes definitely lock onto the *Copperhead*. He was just about to contact the captain with this terrifying news, when a deafening explosion tore at his ears. In the shock wave that followed, the chief sonar operator was tossed out of his seat and thrown headfirst into the adjoining bulkhead, where he slumped to the deck unconscious.

In the *Copperhead*'s control room, this unexpected concussion sent those members of the crew not restrained by shoulder harnesses sprawling to the floor. This included Samuel Fuller and his XO, Vincent Coria. The captain ended up pinned against the legs of the chart table, with the entire left side of his body painfully bruised. He was struggling to his feet, when the boat canted hard to starboard, and the lights blinked off. A hurtling body, which proved to belong to Chief Meinert, slammed into him, and Fuller once more found himself laid out flat on the deck. This time though, he failed to rise, for the wind had been knocked completely out of him.

As Samuel Fuller lay sprawled on the metal

deck, desperately struggling to catch his breath, the deep, firm voice of his XO boomed out authoritatively.

"Get those emergency lights on! Quartermaster, I need a damage report, all stations! Planesmen, what's the ship's status?"

A trembling voice answered, "The helm is not responding, sir! We seem to have lost all hydraulic pressure."

The emergency battle lights suddenly popped on. Illuminated in the dim red glow was a scene of utter chaos. Bodies cluttered the floor, with plenty of loose equipment spread amongst them. One of the few to have regained his footing, Vincent Coria scanned the compartment. His eyes opened wide when he spotted the prone figure of Samuel Fuller. By the time he reached the captain's side, Fuller was just finding himself able to breath once again. Ignoring the pain that coursed through his body, he caught his XO's concerned glance and somehow managed to speak.

"Jesus, Vinnie, what in the hell hit us?"

The XO knelt to hastily check Fuller's vital signs while he answered him. "It must have been one of those torpedoes, Skipper. Yet our hull seems to be intact, even though we don't seem to have any hydraulic pressure."

Groaning in pain, Fuller struggled to sit up. With his back propped up against the chart table, he watched as those who were able, attended to

384

their fallen shipmates. But a new concern tinged his voice as he once again addressed his XO.

"Don't worry about me. Just try to find out what kind of shape the rest of the boat is in."

The XO nodded, and did what he could to hurry the already requested damage reports. As the calls began coming in from the *Copperhead*'s various compartments, Coria determined that most of the damage was confined to the boat's stern. Here, the already trouble-plagued hydraulics system had partially failed, and the main propeller shaft was knocked out of alignment. Chief Kerkhoff had just scrammed the reactor for safety's sake, and for all practical purposes, the sub was dead in the water.

The XO relayed this information to Samuel Fuller, who had managed to get to his feet by this time.

"At least the hull is still in one piece," commented the captain gravely. "What's the word on injuries?"

"We've suffered plenty of bruises and even a few broken bones, but so far there's been no fatalities."

Fuller breathed a sigh of relief. "Thank the Lord for that!"

"Of course, we still have that prowling Soviet attack sub and the Chinese boomer to worry about, Skipper."

Fuller shook his head while massaging the back

of his bruised neck. "I'm afraid that without the benefits of full hydraulics pressure and our main propulsion system, the *Copperhead* doesn't have much fight left in her. In fact, I'd say that we'll be extremely fortunate just to be able to get topside once again.

"Under the circumstances, I think it's best if we blow our emergency ballast tanks and surface. Then we can only pray for that *Akula* to do its part and take out the Chinese boat before it launches its missiles."

Though he hated to admit it, Coria knew the captain was right. The *Copperhead* was no longer the effective hunter that it was before the detonating torpedo damaged its power train. They were only helpless onlookers now, with only one chance to escape with their lives. Hoping that they would have enough hydraulic pressure left to blow out the emergency ballast tanks, he followed Samuel Fuller over to the station where this process would be attempted.

In a nearby portion of the Pacific, the *Akula*-class attack sub *Baikal* also floundered helplessly, its main reactor scrammed. It was not engine damage that precipitated their current state of inaction, but a crisis of an even more dreaded nature—fire!

Anton Valerian had been in the vessel's attack center when the enemy torpedo exploded in the

386

waters directly adjoining their bow. Any lesser vessel would have been fatally damaged by this massive blast, but the *Baikal*'s unique double-hull construction limited the damage to a severe concussion. The shock wave hit the forward portion of the ship particularly hard, with the brunt of the damages being borne by the torpedo room. It was here that an electrical power surge caused the fire-control system to short out.

Fire, and the smoke which accompanied it, were among a submariner's deadliest enemies. In the contained environment of a sub, even the smallest fire could have a disastrous effect on the breathable air supply. That was why the men were trained to treat all fires with the utmost respect and swiftness.

Though it cost the life of a brave sailor, the fire was quickly brought under control and extinguished. By keeping the compartment's hatch sealed, the remaining smoke was for the most part contained. Valerian knew they were very fortunate to have survived, although the *Baikal* could no longer launch another torpedo.

With this fact in mind, the captain called together both his senior lieutenant and *zampolit* to discuss their situation. This conference took place in the boat's attack center, where a thin veil of smoke hung like a mist in the subdued red lighting.

"Well, Comrades, you know our predicament,"

commented Valerian soberly. "Are there any suggestions?"

In the distance, a distinctive blast of venting air could be heard, and Senior Lieutenant Karmanov was quick to observe, "It appears that the Yankee attack sub has successfully blown its emergency ballast tanks. It's a shame that we can't finish them off, now that they're helpless, but such is the irony of war."

"To hell with that damn attack boat!" exclaimed the red-faced political officer. "Have you forgotten about our primary objective? While we sit here licking our wounds, the Trident is most likely beginning its own ascent to launch depth. And now there's absolutely nothing that we can do to stop them!"

"Who would have ever thought that we would find ourselves with a fully operational vessel, except for one vital component—the ability to fire our torpedoes?" reflected Karmanov. "We certainly are worth nothing without our weapons, even if we are still the fastest submarine afloat."

Suddenly inspired by this matter-of-fact statement, Anton Valerian's eyes opened wide with wonder. "Why, of course! We've overlooked the most basic offensive weapon of all! We'll ram them!"

This idea drew immediate fire from the *zampolit*. "Are you insane, Captain? That would mean the death of all of us."

Ignoring this challenge, Valerian continued, "It's so simple. For what is the *Baikal* but a torpedo without a warhead? And even if it means our lives, what a glorious way to go!"

"Think of the millions of lives that would be lost if that Trident was able to empty its missile magazine," offered the senior lieutenant. "I'm certain that the crew would stand solidly behind us if they had to choose between putting their own lives on the line, or those of their loved ones back in the Motherland."

Valerian nodded thoughtfully in agreement. "Well said, Comrade Karmanov. Don't tell me that you're so selfish you don't agree, Boris Glazov?"

The *zampolit* still couldn't help but have reservations about risking his life in such a manner. "I understand your logic, Captain. But surely there must be another way."

"And what might that be, without the use of our torpedo fire-control system, Comrade?" retorted the Captain.

Quick to notice the tension building between the two men, the senior lieutenant interceded. "Who's to say that a ramming would definitely result in the loss of everyone aboard the *Baikal?* Have you both forgotten that we are outfitted with an escape pod? If we hit the Trident just as it attains its launch depth, the pod will be well within its crush threshold. Then we merely have to ride it to the surface, and eventually return home as true living heroes of the Soviet people!"

Hearing this, the *zampolit* seemed somewhat more optimistic. "I guess that there really aren't any alternatives to choose from, Comrades. I realize that the Trident must be taken out, even if it costs us the *Baikal*. Thus, I reluctantly agree with you that such a sacrifice is necessary."

Valerian was heartened by the *zampolit*'s change of mind. "Then it's agreed, Comrades! Senior Lieutenant, inform engineering to get that reactor back on-line. We're going to need every available knot of sprint speed to get to that Trident before it attains its launch depth. So put the fear of Lenin in them, and perhaps the Motherland will yet be saved from this deadly threat."

Watching as the senior lieutenant proceeded to call the engine room to convey these directives, Boris Glazov felt a troubling heaviness settle deep in his gut. This apprehension worsened as the deep rumble of the just-activated turbines sounded in the distance. Slowly now, the *Baikal* would begin picking up forward momentum, until a speed of over forty-five knots was eventually attained. At this point the *Baikal* would be spiraling up from the cold depths, with its final destination in the hands of the gods.

CHAPTER FIFTEEN

The mood inside the *Red Dragon*'s attack center was one of joy and relief. Only minutes ago, sonar reported picking up the desperate sounds of a submarine as it vented its emergency ballast tanks in a last-ditch effort to reach the relative safety of the ocean's surface. This had followed two distinct explosions, which indicated that the *Red Dragon*'s torpedo attack had been a successful one after all. Now, all that remained was for them to attain launch depth themselves and complete their mission.

Closely monitoring the vessel's depth gauge, Captain Chen Shou calculated that in approximately one more minute, the process of releasing the sixteen *Xia*-class missiles could begin. Meanwhile, his second-in-command was busy at his side, updating the ship's inertial navigation system. For their missiles to be on target, the exact position of the *Red Dragon* had to be determined. This was a complex process that was accomplished by utilizing a system of gyroscopes, accelerometers, and computers to relate their current course to that of true north. Only after this update was completed could they once again begin the actual launch sequence.

Rubbing his hands together expectantly, the captain took a deep, calming breath. He felt like an excited schoolboy once again. Though he was well aware that the mere fact of this strategic alert meant that the Republic was most likely under current attack, at least the *Red Dragon* had survived to avenge this invasion. The aggressor would soon pay a high price for his folly.

The *Red Dragon* attained launch depth seconds after the senior lieutenant completed the inertial navigation update. This means that they were free to get on with the task of releasing the missiles. Since a proper missile release code had already been entered into the computer, Chen Shou was able to proceed without having to repeat this time consuming step. Thus, his first step was to open the missile magazine's outer hatch.

While the sixteen tubes began opening one by one, Chen visualized that which would now be exposed to the open seas beyond. Inside each launch tube was a rigid dome-shaped shell enclosure which extended spherically over the end of the tube. When the missile was fired, this protective dome would be shattered by a network of linear-shaped explosive charges mounted on the underside of the shell. To protect the missile itself from this charge, an open-cell urethane-foam material was bonded to the shell's underside. This honey-combed, crushable material was shaped in the form of the missile, and would absorb the energy created by the explosion.

A split second later, a gas/steam generator system would ignite a small fixed rocket, whose exhaust was directed toward the pool of cool water that lay at the base of each launch tube. It would be the resulting steam pressure that would expel the missile itself. Only when the missile had cleared the ocean's surface would its solid-propellant booster engine ignite, and the rocket would soar into the heavens with a deafening roar.

To keep the sub from yawing violently when it suddenly lost one of these 45,000-pound missiles, the tube would be quickly backflooded with water. Since the water was actually heavier than the missile, they would have to carefully increase the *Red Dragon*'s total buoyancy by blowing off a portion of its negative ballast. Then this complex process would be repeated every fifteen seconds, until the magazine was completely empty. All in all, this would take but four short minutes to achieve. And total revenge would be theirs!

Anxiously awaiting that glorious moment when the last rocket was expelled into the Pacific, Chen Shou sat forward and faced his portion of the launch console. Two rows of eight, square clear-plastic buttons graced the central portion of this cabinet. Each button was lit with a bright red bulb, indicating that the sixteen missiles were armed and ready to fire. The captain took another deep breath and held out his right index finger, poised to touch the button marked *Tube #1*. Beside him, his senior lieutenant did likewise.

Without ceremony, Chen announced "Prepare to fire on the count of five. One . . . two . . ."

But before he could call out the next number, the frantic voice of their sonar operator erupted from the room's wall-mounted loudspeakers.

"Unidentified submerged contact, rapidly closing in from the seas beneath us, Captain! They appear to be on a direct collision course!"

Momentarily halting his countdown, Chen Shou looked up when the actual sound of this approaching vessel filled the attack center with a throbbing, pulsating roar. Sounding like an out of control freight train, this noise caused the captain's hands to tremble with fear, and his heart to pound madly away in his chest.

The firm voice of the senior lieutenant brought him back to his senses. "Sir, the launch! At the very least, let's get one missile skywards!"

Instantly restored to sanity, Chen Shou had to hold out his icy left hand to keep his right one steady as once more he began the countdown. Three . . . four . . . fire!"

There was an explosive crack above them as the

charges triggered, shattering the first missile's protective shell. Then the sound of the steam generator expulsion system could be heard igniting. Yet they had no time to shout out in celebration, for a millisecond later, the entire deck beneath them was punctured upward with a grinding, deafening blast.

As the *Red Dragon* imploded, Chen Shou's last thought was that the gods themselves had taken the vessel in hand to squeeze the life out of them. And as if in response to this thought, the very air around him exploded in a fireball of death.

The *Baikal* had hit its target amidships, squarely in its belly. As a result, the *Akula*-class vessel's teardrop-shaped bow found itself firmly embedded inside the doomed target's pressure hull. Though the missile-carrying sub was already breaking up around them, the *Baikal* was amazingly still in one piece. It's double hull reinforced by pure titanium, the Soviet ship was nevertheless fatally wounded.

As it was throughout the ship, the scene inside the *Baikal*'s attack center was one of complete devastation. Bodies and fallen equipment covered the steel-latticed deck, while thick fingers of noxious black smoke streamed in from the cracked hatchway.

Strangely enough, all three of the *Baikal*'s senior officer staff survived the collision. They were currently huddled beside what was left of the damage-control console. Here, Senior Lieutenant Karmanov had just put the last working intercom handset back on its base. Now, as he carefully dabbed at his cut chin with a handkerchief, he made his report to the captain.

"The ship is currently taking on water in both the forward torpedo room and the engine compartment. A flash fire is currently burning out of control in maneuvering, and the reactor vessel is close to meltdown. The chief reports that dead bodies are everywhere and the *Baikal* has but a few minutes of life left in her at best."

"At least we succeeded with our mission," reflected Anton Valerian, whose eyes were glazed with shock. "Are you certain that the Trident wasn't able to get a single shot off, Comrade?"

The senior lieutenant answered quickly. "The last I heard from sonar, before fire took out our hydrophones, was that the Trident was in the process of releasing its first missile when we initially collided. We hit them in just enough time to send this rocket off course, and it was last monitored sinking into the depths, completely useless."

"As the *Baikal* will soon be doing," added the dazed captain.

It was the *zampolit* who responded to this despairing statement. "Do both of you want to go down with the ship, or will you join me in the escape pod?"

Scanning the faces of the two officers as he

waited for a response, Boris Glazov watched as the captain's eyes suddenly rolled upward and he crashed to the deck unconscious.

The senior lieutenant was the first to Valerian's side, where he knelt and swiftly checked his pulse. "His heartbeat is erratic, but at least he's still alive. The captain took a wicked blow on his skull when we first struck the Trident. It's a miracle that he remained conscious as long as he did."

Looking up to meet the *zampolit*'s worried stare, Karmanov added, "Well, are you just going to stand there, or are you going to help me get him into the escape pod?"

An expression of pure relief swept over Boris Glazov's face as he bent down to help Karmanov lift their fallen comrade. The rescue pod was mounted in the attack center's ceiling. A sealed hatch led the way into the sphere-shaped device, which was positioned between the *Baikal*'s outer pressure hull and its upper exterior deck. Designed to hold up to forty individuals—for up to nine hours without fresh air if necessary—the sphere would be guided to the surface by a large buoyancy tank. Once the pod was topside, a ventilation mast could be raised or, under calm conditions, the top hatch could be opened, while an emergency radio transmitter was activated to notify Command of their dilemma.

The deck shifted hard to their right, and in the background the *Baikal*'s hull could be heard groaning as the first of the vessel's watertight bulkheads burst under the pressure of leaking seawater. Realizing that they had only a few more seconds to make good their escape, the two officers carried the still-unconscious captain to the center of the room. Without a moment's delay, Senior Lieutenant Karmanov reached up and pulled down the short ladder which led to the escape pod's hatch.

"I'll go first!" he shouted as he scrambled up the ladder, unsealed the hatch, and crawled inside. After repositioning himself, he reached out the now-open hatchway to grab the shoulders of the slumped over captain.

There was a grating, metallic crash in the background, and the deck once again shifted hard to the right. Taking a last look at the disordered attack center, the *zampolit* gratefully followed Anton Valerian into the hollowed-out interior of the escape pod.

While Boris Glazov laid the captain down on one of the pod's padded benches, the senior lieutenant positioned himself before the release mechanism. But as he reached out to activate the switch that would separate the sphere from the pressure hull, the mechanism failed to trigger.

"It's not getting any electric current!" cried the startled senior lieutenant. "We'll never get this sphere separated!"

Watching as Karmanov's face contorted in panic,

the *zampolit* shouted, "Surely there must be another way to release this pod! Think man, think!"

Tears were actually falling from the senior lieutenant's eyes. "It's useless!" he cried out in an anguished, trembling voice, "we came so close, and now we're doomed with the rest of the crew. If only one of the others were around to release the manual trigger on the attack center's ceiling, beside the pod's entrance hatch!"

Aware that the *Baikal's* second-in-command was in no condition to crawl out of the sphere and hit this switch, Boris hastily weighed his options. He could remain where he was, and die when the *Baikal's* hull finally imploded around them, or meet death in a more noble manner, alone, inside the attack center.

Either way, it was a no-win situation, and so Boris, who was not a particularly brave man, decided that if Karmanov and the captain made it to safety, his wife and children would at least have something to properly remember him by. For at long last he would be a true hero of the Motherland! A strange calmness possessed him as he cleared his throat and turned to the senior lieutenant.

"Comrade Karmanov, would you be so good as to see to the captain? I will go outside and hit the manual release button."

"But you'll be dooming yourself to certain death!" cried the distraught senior lieutenant.

Smiling and tranquil, Boris replied, "May you have a safe voyage home, Comrade. And please, if you should find the Motherland unscarred by nuclear war, be so good as to tell my family that I died so that our country will always be free."

Saluting briefly, the political officer then turned to unseal the hatch and get on with his noble sacrifice — before the fear of death made him change his mind.

Dawn was just breaking over the horizon as the *Copperhead* surged out of the black depths and broached the Pacific's surface. Even though the seas were calm, with a slight three-foot swell coming in from the northwest, the keelless submarine pitched to and fro in the gentle waves. Below deck, this lurching motion was the cause of more than one case of seasickness, but it was a minor discomfort, which the crew could easily live with.

In the captain's cabin, Samuel Fuller paid scant attention to the rolling of the boat. The one thing that mattered to him was that they had survived an ordeal that could have easily cost them their lives. As he sat at his cramped wall-mounted desk, in the midst of recording this formidable incident in his log, he realized how very close they had come to utter destruction. Yet luck had been with them, and they had been allowed to live to fight yet another day.

Thoughts of Peggy, whose photograph hung on the bulkhead before him, made this new lease on life all the sweeter. He had very nearly made her a widow, and his new child fatherless! But fate had spared him, and now he had the greatest gift of all to look forward to.

While he was thinking fondly of Peggy and the joys of impending fatherhood, a firm knock sounded on his door. Brought abruptly back to reality, Fuller responded, "Come in!"

With this, the door swung open, and in walked Petty Officer First Class Reginald Warner.

"You wanted to see me, sir?"

Taking in the thick white bandage wrapped around the senior sonar technician's upper skull, Fuller replied, "Yes I did, Mr. Warner. Please have a seat. First off, I understand that you took quite a knock on your noggin. How are you feeling?"

Reggie sat down on the wall-mounted hot seat. "I'm doing just fine, sir. Don't forget that I was a ghetto child, born and raised. We're bred to be tough, and I'll survive this little scratch."

"Little scratch?" retorted the captain. "I hear from Pills that it's more like a concussion. So you take care, and consider yourself relieved of any official duties until I say otherwise.

"Now, I called you in here to sincerely thank you for your invaluable assistance these last couple of hours. Believe me, we couldn't have made it without you."

401

Grinning shyly, Reggie responded, "I was only doing my duty, sir. But I'm glad that it was appreciated, and that I was able to help the *Copperhead* get out of this jam.

"By the way, I was down in sonar when I got the word that you wanted to see me, and the guys had just gotten the bottom-scanning sonar gear back in operation. As I was leaving, they were drawing up the first pictures of the remains of that Chinese boomer and the Soviet attack sub. From what I understand, the debris field lies spread out in a broad volcanic valley, some three thousand feet beneath us. There isn't much left but a few mangled pieces of steel, and all the way up here, I couldn't help but realize how lucky we were not to be down there ourselves."

As Samuel Fuller nodded thoughtfully in agreement, Reggie nervously added, "Not to change the subject, sir, but there's something I'd like to ask you. I realize we barely know one another, but under the circumstances, I'd like to know if you'd give some thought to being my best man at the wedding. Kim and I would be proud to have you there, Captain."

Without a second's hesitation, Fuller accepted. "I'd be honored, Mr. Warner. You two make a good-looking couple, and it will be a pleasure to take part in the ceremony."

A relieved smile turned up the corners of the sonar operator's mouth, but before he could voice his thanks, the intercom buzzed loudly. This was followed by a familiar deep voice.

"Sir, this is the XO. I'm up here on the sail, and I've just spotted something unusual that I'd like you to take a look at. It could be a part of one of those two submarines that went down around us."

His curiosity immediately aroused, Samuel Fuller picked up his intercom handset and answered, "I'm on my way up, Mr. Coria."

As the captain rose to make his way to the *Copperhead*'s exposed bridge, he remembered his guest. "Would you like to come along and see what it is that the XO has spotted, Mr. Warner?"

"I certainly would, sir," returned Reggie, who also stood, and eagerly followed Samuel Fuller out of the cabin and through the maze of narrow passageways to the bridge.

They arrived on top of the sail in time to watch the deck crew set their gaffs into a large rectangular metallic object, which was bobbing in the sea beside them. There seemed to be a sealed hatch cut into the top of this object, which the XO identified as possibly belonging to some sort of escape pod.

While their alert weapons officer stood on the deck with an M-16 in hand, Chief Greg Meinert carefully crawled on top of this mysterious minivessel, and knocked on the hatch with the side of a wrench. Soon afterwards, it popped open with a loud hiss.

A pale blond-haired man emerged. Clearly in no condition to offer any resistance, he greeted the *Copperhead*'s burly chief in broken but legible English, flavored by a definite Slavic accent. Introducing himself as Senior Lieutenant Viktor Karmanov, of the Soviet attack submarine *Baikal*, he then asked for medical assistance for the rescue sphere's only other occupant, the *Baikal*'s captain.

It was sometime after lunch when Samuel Fuller ducked into the sickbay to check on the condition of its only patient.

"He's just coming to," the boat's senior paramedic informed the captain. "Though he's still a bit dazed, he seems to know where he is, and is glad to be here."

The captain nodded. "Thanks, Pills. Do you mind if I have a couple of minutes alone with him?"

As Pills left the sickbay for a well-deserved coffee break, Samuel Fuller approached a cot on the far side of the compartment. Lying supine on its padded length was a solidly built man in his fifties, with close-cropped pepper-and-salt hair. He wore a black patch over his left eye, and there was a distinguished cast to his features. Fuller was admiring his almost theatrical appearance, when his one good eye abruptly blinked open and scanned the room for a moment before coming to rest on his host.

"Good afternoon," the captain said. "I understand from your senior lieutenant that you speak English. I am Captain Samuel Fuller, commander of the U.S. attack submarine, *Copperhead*. Welcome aboard my ship."

The patient nodded stiffly and responded in a deep hoarse voice. "Good afternoon to you, Captain Fuller. I am Anton Valerian, commander of the Soviet warship, *Baikal*."

There seemed to a cold, distrustful gleam in the Russian's eye, and Fuller replied guardedly. "I believe that you had a chance to talk with your senior lieutenant earlier. Did he tell you the identity of the other submarine that your vessel was responsible for sinking?"

"Yes he did, Captain," returned Valerian. "It is indeed ironic that what we assumed to be one of your Tridents, turned out to be an even more threatening adversary. And to think that we actually attacked your ship, all because of an inoperable radio! Why, we should have been working together to eliminate the shared Chinese threat instead of fighting each other."

"That was the initial idea," responded Fuller, who noted that a bit more sincerity had crept into the Russian's tone. "But that is water over the dam, as we say in my country. Now, I hope that my men are treating you decently. We can all rest easily knowing that a rescue ship is on its way to tow us back to Pearl Harbor. Command has also notified Petropavlovsk of your situation, and the tragic loss of your ship and its company."

"Under the circumstances, your assistance is most appreciated, Captain Fuller. After all, a couple of hours ago, we were trying to sink this ship, and your men could very well have shared the fate of my brave crew."

"Such are the fortunes of war," observed Fuller. "Before I leave, there's one more thing I'd like to know. When I first heard your name, I couldn't help but wonder if you were the same Valerian who commanded a *Victor*-class vessel in the Pacific two years ago."

The Russian shrewdly caught his host's determined stare and his mind suddenly registered what the American was referring to. "You wouldn't happen to be related to Commander Micháel Fuller of the U.S. Navy, would you?"

"He was my brother," spat Samuel, who realized with a start that he was facing the man whom he had previously sworn to wreak revenge on.

Conscious of this incredible coincidence, Anton Valerian dared to bare his soul. "Yes, Captain Fuller, I was the captain of the submarine that was responsible for your brother's unfortunate death. I know that this is long overdue, but I am sincerely sorry that he had to die because of my stubbornness. Contrary to what was admitted in the admiralty inquiry, my ship did not blunder into that towed array rig by mistake. I was under orders to trail that sonar sled as close as I dared to, and I guess that I took this directive a little too literally. For we soon became entangled in the array's tow cable, which eventually snapped and led to your brother's untimely death. And now to have us go and actually attack you as we just did. No wonder you distrust my people!"

Oddly affected by the Russian's words, Fuller found his thoughts reeling in confusion. Here was the man whom he had sworn vengeance on. But for some strange reason, he was unable to hate him. As he looked at the man lying before him, he realized that Anton Valerian wasn't any creature of pure evil who had deliberately taken his brother's life. The Russian was simply a by-product of the same Cold War mentality that had shaped Fuller himself. And the key to unlocking this fundamental misunderstanding lay within their reach all this time. It was simply called trust.

If things didn't change soon, the next time they met the world could very well go over the brink of nuclear devastation. Knowing this, Fuller decided to take the first tentative step toward a new beginning. He would do so right here, in the *Copperhead*'s cramped sickbay.

Drawing closer to the cot, he looked down at his sworn adversary and dared to smile. His unexpected display of warmth was infectious, and as the cold look of distrust faded from Anton Valerian's stare, the two warriors exchanged a sincere handshake.

"To a new tomorrow!" said Samuel Fuller, who knew at that moment that the battle was at long last over.

EPILOGUE

The day dawned hot and humid. Mei-li and Justin had left the cottage when it was still dark, and by the time they reached the ridge's summit, the sun was still less than a quarter of the way into the eastern sky. Yet both of them were completely soaked in sweat as they momentarily halted to catch their breaths.

They had traveled this same trail once before. Though that had been only a few weeks ago, it seemed to have taken place in another lifetime. So much had happened to both of them in the meantime, their very perspective on life had changed.

The natural sights, smells, and sounds that now surrounded them had a calming effect. Soothed by the magnificent pastoral scenery, the ripe scent of green growth, and the hypnotic sound of the gently gusting wind, all their past trauma was gradually forgotten. In its place rose new hope and purpose.

It was Premier Lin Shau-ping himself who had

invited them back to Guilin. This occurred not long after they arrived in Canton, physically and emotionally spent after their perilous river journey. After informing Ty Stadler of the U.S. State Department of their incredible discovery in the hills north of the Blue Swan commune, they shared this same information with the premier. Fortunately, both Stadler and the premier believed their fantastic tale, and the world had subsequently been saved from an unthinkable nuclear disaster.

Of course, both Mei-li and Justin had been sworn to keep all that they had seen and heard a secret. Doubting that any of their friends would believe them anyway, they did their best to go on with their everyday lives.

For Justin, this meant the completion of yet another full week of *West Side Story*. Fortunately for him, the cast had stayed amazingly healthy during their stay in Canton, and he only had to work two nights portraying Riff, the gang leader of the Jets.

During this time, Mei-li had returned to Beijing, where she reported to her superior at the Chinese International Travel Service. Her reception there had been remarkably cordial, and she soon discovered why. Prior to her arrival, a personal commendation had been received from the premier's office. This sincere message of praise included the invitation to return to the Blue Swan commune a week later. Justin had received a similar invitation from the premier, and both young people gratefully accepted.

They had been at the commune for three days now, and the warm outpouring of hospitality they had received on their first visit was even more apparent this time. Each night so far, a banquet had been held in their honor, and tonight there would be another one. All this would culminate in a personal visit from Lin Shau-ping himself, who would be arriving three days from now to dine with them. Needless to say, the members of the commune looked forward to this unprecedented event as the once-in-a-lifetime opportunity it was meant to be, and excitement and joy were in everyone's eyes.

Looking forward to spending some time together, Mei-li and Justin had reserved today for wandering the magnificent hills surrounding the commune. Though Mei-li's parents would be meeting them in the nearby mango grove for a picnic lunch at noon, they still had a couple of hours to reach the particular spot that had called them out of their soft beds.

A narrow goat trail led them to their destination — a dusty windswept ridge on the commune's extreme northern outskirts. Hand in hand, they looked out at the broad tree-lined valley which stretched out before them. This time, there was no detachment of sweating soldiers working amongst the blossoming acacias. All that indicated their past presence was a large stack of wooden crates that had yet to be hauled away, and several pieces of earth-moving equipment.

It was Mei-li who pointed out the distant cavern in which she and Justin had once been held captive. When her companion asked if she wanted to go down and explore this grotto, she looked up at him unbelievingly. The warmest of teasing smiles met her incredulous stare.

"Don't worry, Mei-li, I've had enough cave exploring for one lifetime. You know, with the general and his cohorts gone, this valley looks downright peaceful. Who would have ever guessed that someone would have actually planned to destroy the entire world from such a beautiful spot?"

"I guess that we were lucky to have been drawn here," Mei-li reflected. "Otherwise, who knows what might have happened."

Justin watched a large golden hawk circle overhead. "At least the planet's got a reprieve this time," he replied as his gaze followed the bird's flight. "I would like to have seen the general's face when the premier's troops closed in and informed him that his mad scheme was finished. Do you think that he knows that we were the direct cause of his downfall?"

Mei-li shook her head. "I doubt it, Justin. Although he and his kind are doomed to ultimate failure, I'm just glad that we were around to hurry up events in this case. From what I understand, his co-conspirators extend well into the senior ranks of the military. Why, one of those involved was even the admiral in charge of the Republic's entire fleet!"

"I bet that's the fellow who provided the submarine that the general spoke of," said the actor. "Someday I'd like to know exactly how that boat was stopped from launching its missiles, but I guess that's another story altogether."

Looking down as a covey of fat quail sauntered over the clearing before them, Mei-li cleared her throat and spoke out softly. "You know, I've been giving it some thought, and I think that I'm going to be leaving the Tour Service shortly. I guess this whole incident showed me how short and precious life really is. I miss my parents and this land that surrounds us. So to find myself once again, I'm going to see if I can become a full-time member of the commune."

"Why, that's wonderful news!" exclaimed Justin. "You know, I really envy you."

Looking up into the American's sparkling eyes, Mei-li responded warmly. "I'm really going to miss you, Justin Pollock. Somehow, life is just never going to be the same without you around."

Feeling a sudden fullness in his chest, Justin squeezed Mei-li's hand and whispered, "I know what you're saying, little one. You wouldn't happen to know if the folks at the Blue Swan commune would be interested in the services of a seasoned member of the Western theater? Wouldn't

413

it be something to put together our own little touring company? Why, there's plenty of talent, both young and old, back in the village. The way the folks around here are starved for decent entertainment, we could make a fortune!"

Hardly believing what she was hearing, Mei-li suddenly found herself in the American's warm embrace. Their trembling, hungry lips merged in a deep kiss and only then did she know that his loving promise was indeed a real one.

ACTION ADVENTURE

SILENT WARRIORS (1675, $3.95)
by Richard P. Henrick

The Red Star, Russia's newest, most technologically advanced submarine, outclasses anything in the U.S. fleet. But when the captain opens his sealed orders 24 hours early, he's staggered to read that he's to spearhead a massive nuclear first strike against the Americans!

THE PHOENIX ODYSSEY (1789, $3.95)
by Richard P. Henrick

All communications to the USS *Phoenix* suddenly and mysteriously vanish. Even the urgent message from the president cancelling the War Alert is not received. In six short hours the *Phoenix* will unleash its nuclear arsenal against the Russian mainland.

COUNTERFORCE (2013, $3.95)
Richard P. Henrick

In the silent deep, the chase is on to save a world from destruction. A single Russian Sub moves on a silent and sinister course for American shores. The men aboard the U.S.S. *Triton* must search for and destroy the Soviet killer Sub as an unsuspecting world races for the apocalypse.

EAGLE DOWN (1644, $3.75)
by William Mason

To western eyes, the Russian Bear appears to be in hibernation — but half a world away, a plot is unfolding that will unleash its awesome, deadly power. When the Russian Bear rises up, God help the Eagle.

DAGGER (1399, $3.50)
by William Mason

The President needs his help, but the CIA wants him dead. And for Dagger — war hero, survival expert, ladies man and mercenary extraordinaire — it will be a game played for keeps.

Available wherever paperbacks are sold, or order direct from the Publisher. Send cover price plus 50¢ per copy for mailing and handling to Zebra Books, Dept. 2423, 475 Park Avenue South, New York, N.Y. 10016. Residents of New York, New Jersey and Pennsylvania must include sales tax. DO NOT SEND CASH.

TOP-FLIGHT AERIAL ADVENTURE
FROM ZEBRA BOOKS!

WINGMAN   (2015, $3.95)
by Mack Maloney

From the radioactive ruins of a nuclear-devastated U.S. emerges a hero for the ages. A brilliant ace fighter pilot, he takes to the skies to help free his once-great homeland from the brutal heel of the evil Soviet warlords. He is the last hope of a ravaged land. He is Hawk Hunter . . . Wingman!

WINGMAN #2: THE CIRCLE WAR   (2120, $3.95)
by Mack Maloney

A second explosive showdown with the Russian overlords and their armies of destruction is in the wind. Only the deadly aerial ace Hawk Hunter can rally the forces of freedom and strike one last blow for a forgotten dream called "America"!

WINGMAN #3: THE LUCIFER CRUSADE   (2232, $3.95)
by Mack Maloney

Viktor, the depraved international terrorist who orchestrated the bloody war for America's West, has escaped. Ace pilot Hawk Hunter takes off for a deadly confrontation in the skies above the Middle East, determined to bring the maniac to justice or die in the attempt!

GHOST PILOT   (2207, $3.95)
by Anton Emmerton

Flyer Ian Lamont is driven by bizarre unseen forces to relive the last days in the life of his late father, an RAF pilot killed during World War II. But history is about to repeat itself as a sinister secret from beyond the grave transforms Lamont's worst nightmares of fiery aerial death into terrifying reality!

Available wherever paperbacks are sold, or order direct from the Publisher. Send cover price plus 50¢ per copy for mailing and handling to Zebra Books, Dept. 2423, 475 Park Avenue South, New York, N.Y. 10016. Residents of New York, New Jersey and Pennsylvania must include sales tax. DO NOT SEND CASH.